TOGETHER FOR CHRISTMAS

TOGETHER FOR CHRISTMAS

AMY J. FETZER
ELIZABETH GRAHAM
KATHRYN FOX

Zebra Books
Kensington Publishing Corp.
http://www.zebrabooks.com

ZEBRA BOOKS are published by

Kensington Publishing Corp.
850 Third Avenue
New York, NY 10022

First Printing: December, 1998
10 9 8 7 6 5 4 3 2 1

Printed in the United States of America

Contents

TWELVE NIGHTS

by

Amy J. Fetzer

To

Janet Carroll

For lunches at Ruby's
and always answering your e-mail.
For your keen insight and unfailing encouragement
and for staying my friend a thousand miles away.

PROLOGUE

On the first day . . .

He was in love with a nun.

'Twas Draegon's first thought when he'd learned his betrothed was no longer in her father's home, but here in St. Mary's Abbey.

His second thought was to pummel Sir Bryce for telling her he was dead.

His hands braced behind his back as he stood at the window, he slanted a glance at Bryce. His friend's lip was swelling and Draegon felt a small measure of regret. Very small, he thought, returning his gaze to the scenery beyond the window. 'Twas bad enough that he'd been gone three years longer than the one promised, or that he'd destroyed the trust of the one woman, the one person he prized above all others, only this morning he'd learned Julianna had been mourning him for three years. God's blood, the woman was willful enough afore, he could not imagine what years in solitude had done to her.

"Stop staring, Bryce. I swear I can feel the heat of your eyes on the back of my neck." His breath frosted the air inside the abbess's receiving chamber.

" 'Tis like looking at a ghost," Bryce said, still unable to believe Draegon stood a few feet from him.

"I assure you I am very much alive."

"My eyes fooled me on the battlefield, Drae." Bryce had seen him struck down by a Saracen. He would still swear to it. "Yet had I investigated further, you might not have spent the last years in the foulest of Moorish prisons. I regret—"

Not removing his gaze from the window, Draegon put up a hand, silencing him, then returned to his former position. "I regret, too, but 'tis naught to be done now."

"Except claim your bride."

Draegon twisted to look over his shoulder at his younger brother, his tall form leaning lazily against the stone wall. Lucan had been quiet since Draegon's return only this morn, yet now he could see only humor in his eyes. "Is there aught you should be telling me afore I greet my betrothed?" He glanced atween the two men, and although Lucan's expression was amused, Bryce flushed.

"Well, you must understand that I—we all thought you dead . . ." Bryce began.

Draegon experienced a sick premonition, much like he had each day when the Moors threatened to take his life, slice by slice. "Do go on."

"And I felt, well, honor bound to offer myself in your stead." Bryce stiffened, prepared for Draegon's rage, but his silver-gray stare was even, controlled. It felt too much like the moments afore a battle.

"Since you are not sitting at your castle with my betrothed at your side, I am to understand she denied your suit?" Draegon tried hard not to laugh at Bryce's disgruntled expression.

"She nearly took my head off with her father's sword!" Bryce hissed. "By God, Drae, you told me she was headstrong, but . . ."

"You did not believe how much," Draegon finished on a low chuckle. "Though Julianna can be sweet and tender as a lamb, when crossed, she's a bit irascible."

Bryce reared back. "A bit! She is strident and far too independent and does not know her place."

"Great days," Draegon groaned, shaking his head and staring at his boots. "I hope you did not say such to her."

"Aye, he did," Lucan said, a smile in his deep voice, and Draegon cocked a look at his brother. "Your *lamb* sent him, a knight of the Crusades, flying down the convent steps rear over noggin."

Bryce sent Lucan a silencing look, yet the man simply shrugged deeper into the fur mantle covering his shoulders.

"You have my pity and 'tis well *you* must deal with her." Bryce gave a none too false shiver.

"I need no such condolences." Draegon smiled benignly. "My Julianna will be well pleased to see me." He was certain of it, just as he was of his love for her.

Lucan snickered. "You left her when she was a *girl*, m'lord." M'lord sounded a bit like an insult to Draegon's ears, and he eyed his brother briefly. "You should remember she has not been *waiting* a'tall."

Nay. She has been mourning, he thought tenderly, his expression grim as he turned his attention to the window and the snow-covered courtyard beyond. Though touched deeply that she would commit herself to God since they could never, she had assumed, be together, he could not imagine her spending her days and nights on her knees in prayer. Not the Julianna whose last farewell was to kiss him until his lungs labored, his knees folded, and he had naught on his mind but the throbbing in his loins and how well she could ease it. Until she'd very precisely stepped back and slapped his face.

"By the gods, 'tis freezing in here," Bryce complained, poking the iron in the meager fire. "Have they no wood to burn?"

"Julianna's price alone should have kept this abbey in wood for half a decade," Lucan said, and Draegon turned. The price for a noblewoman to enter the convent was recompense to the church. And usually very high. "I paid it."

Draegon arched a black brow, unsure of what to make of the gesture.

Lucan shrugged easily. " 'Twas either that or I believe her father would have locked her away in a tower."

Draegon's lips quirked. "Julianna would have found a way out."

All three laughed softly, the sound cut short by the abbess entering the room and bringing a chilling breeze with her.

"She comes anon, my lord."

Draegon stared at the grim-faced woman, her black shroud and gloved hands wrapped around a stack of wood. Bryce leapt to assist, and though she relinquished the pile of sticks, her face was stern and without thanks. Good God, how had his lively Julianna survived in a place such as this? He'd ridden here as soon as he'd heard, demanding Julianna be brought to him, yet he had not given a thought to the cloister and its requirements. Panic suddenly swelled in him.

"Has Lady Julianna spoken her vows?"

The abbess looked up and made a sound of clear disgust.

Draegon's eyes narrowed, but the abbess straightened her spine and met his gaze.

"Lady Julianna would need another three years afore she will be ready for such a commitment."

"Is that common? So long?"

"Nay." The abbess folded her hands inside the drape of her sleeves. "But she has yet to learn the virtue of . . . restraining her tongue." Lucan and Bryce laughed under their breath. The abbess sent them both a look meant to damn them to the gates of hell afore she gestured to the window. "She comes, m'lord."

Draegon whipped around, gazing through the frosted glass at the darkly cloaked figure crossing the court. His heart pumped, fast and hard. He could see naught of her but yards of dark fabric, fur, and heavy boots, and he willed her to move faster afore he made an utter fool of himself, shattering the window and leaping into the snow to get to her.

Icy English wind whipped around her, singing up her skirts to bite into her legs and drive the chill up her spine. Her breath powdered the air in sharp gusts. *Saint Crispin, I will never be warm again,* Julianna swore, then crossed herself and asked for forgiveness. Not that God was listening to her. 'Twere far too many nuns hogging His ear with endless prayers in the chapel right now. *Least I am not numb in the knees,* she thought, thankful for the reprieve, though she could not imagine why the abbess would have need of her. 'Twas already plain she and the older woman would never be friends. The nun was too pious and lacking in feeling for aught but hours in worship. Julianna felt that since there were so many praying to God, keeping the Savior quite busy, that He would undoubtedly hear the simple prayers first, afore the long-winded ones. The abbess insisted Julianna's soul was fouled with her temperament and needed to be thoroughly cleansed in repetitive psalms. Lots of them.

Three years worth had left little marking behind, she thought honestly.

Snow crunched beneath her boots as she quickened her pace across the courtyard and into the rectory. The lack of wind did naught to ease her chill and Julianna decided the abbess was truly made of ice if she could not feel this cold. Rapping once, she swung the door open. The abbess rose from her seat behind a sparse table.

"Aye, Mother?" She stepped inside, meeting her gaze. "You summoned?"

Sister Mary David's lips tightened. Three years past and still the girl did not even bother to lower her gaze in respect. 'Twas just as well, for it appeared her days at the order were numbered. Thank the Lord, she thought, forcing down an uncharitable smile. The abbess did not think she could last another season with this tempest in her order.

"You have a visitor."

Julianna sighed, clearly irritated. "I wish I'd been forewarned." She looked down at her garments. She'd been dying wool earlier and 'twas not her best habit. "I am hardly presentable for guests." Though the prospect was intriguing, for only one other had visited her in the past years save her sisters and only then to plead with her to come home. *Home,* she thought with such longing she almost forgot she had a guest. "Allow me a moment to change, then I will attend them in the library." She made to leave.

"Julianna."

Her heart tripped at the sound of the voice, *his* voice, and slowly, afraid she'd misheard, she turned her head. "*Draegon!*" she gasped and reached for the back of a chair, staring at the man she'd missed like her breath, the man she'd mourned every moment of her days for the past three years. The man who took her very soul with him to go fight a useless war in a distant country rather than wed her. Her eyes watered and she choked on a sob, covering her mouth.

Oh, merciful God, thank you.

Her heart swept up pace, her skin warming under his close regard, and she absorbed him like a dried flower drinks the sweet rain. Instantly she noticed the slash along the sharp edge of his jaw, another crossing his forehead, and that his silver-gray eyes bore a hardness she didn't remember. She could feel his gaze roam over her and vainly wished she was prepared for his arrival.

But naught could have prepared her.

Not for the heat bursting in her cold blood.

Not for the wild dance of life running through her after feeling dead inside for so many years. *God help me,* she thought, *he is more handsome than afore.* Gone was the young man eager to follow his king into battle and afore her stood a seasoned warrior, his body proving his prowess on those foreign fields, for beneath the belted surcoat and heavy boots laced with leather thongs to his thighs, he was bigger, longer of limb, broader of chest and shoulders. And in the trappings of a lord, his blue fur-lined mantle thrown back over one shoulder, he commanded the room. Commanded her.

He made a step toward her, but she put up a hand, straightening her spine, and Sir Bryce and Lucan, Julianna finally noticed, nodded to the abbess and made to leave. At the door, Julianna caught Bryce's gaze and he burst out with, " 'Twas a shock to me as well. I swear," then crossed his heart and received a chastising glance from the abbess. Lucan offered an encouraging smile, then hastily followed the others out. Pulling her gaze from the door, she stared at Draegon, pushing her hood back and letting it pool on her shoulders.

Draegon swallowed heavily, his gaze raking her again and again. His heart waged a war in his chest the instant he'd seen her in the snow, the moment he recognized her usual brisk pace. She was such a part of him he could feel her every breath as if she were drawing it from his lungs, each movement of her eyes, sensed even her fingers rasping over the folds of her skirts gripped in her hand. Although he'd escaped prison months ago, only now did he feel truly alive. He loved her more than life, her image keeping him functioning in those dark horrible moments when he'd wanted to die. He survived to come home to her, only her.

His gaze swept her like a hungry lion examines its next meal, matching the memory with the woman herself, and he wanted to know ridiculous, inconsequential things. Things that had haunted him in the bowels of the prison, gave him aught to cling to. Was her deep red hair beneath the white wimple longer? Did she still weave it with the gold thread he'd gifted her with afore he left? Did she still abhor wearing shoes in summer, yet love the fur-lined boots he'd made her for winter? With his last thought, he lowered his gaze to her feet. The commonest of boots peeked from beneath her hem and something spilled hard in his chest. *I will change that,* he decided, his gaze climbing. *She's lost a little flesh,* he thought guiltily, meeting her gaze. Green eyes stared, unblinking, glossy.

He wanted to touch her so badly, to feel the softness of her skin again, the wild sweetness of her mouth on his and the warmth of her arms 'round him with the fierceness she always possessed. But the habit, the shapeless heavy dark robes, kept him at bay.

The sight of them was enough to drive his desire into the dirt.

This was not his betrothed, his love. This was a woman destined to be a bride of God—because he had left her naught. But he was home now and all that would change.

"I have missed you greatly, my love," he rasped, his throat burning.

Julianna's hand went to her heart and she swept around the chair, sinking into it and trying desperately not to sob for joy. "And I, you." She sniffled and fished beneath the black placket for a scrap of cloth, swiping it beneath her nose.

"Come away with me, Julianna, away from this place."

Her head tipped back, and across the distance, she met his gaze. "And do what, Draegon?" He came to her then, going down on one knee, and Julianna inhaled the scent that was Draegon—wind, leather. Home.

"And wed me, of course."

"Of course" Just like that. How like a man.

Draegon ached to cradle her hand in his, but she tucked them both beneath the robes and fur. "I have already spoken with your father . . ."

"Have you?" Her finely tapered brows rose. "Surely after all this time, you could have come to me directly."

'Twere an edge to her sweet tone, one that should have warned him, but four years apart had dulled his senses to her finer traits. "I, ah—aye 'tis true," he admitted. "But I had to discuss the situation with him, make certain you had not been promised to another."

Her chin lifted a notch. "Then you know I have not." Except to God, she thought, a commitment the sisters debated over every time she opened her mouth.

Unwed and waiting, 'twas proof of her love for him, he thought with a surge of pleasure. " 'Tis why I've come to take you home." He offered his hand, yet she did not take it, staring at his calloused palm.

Home. She'd long ago given up on such a dream. She'd spent the first year of Draegon's absence in the company of his mother and his younger brother, for her father's castle was too far from aught connected to Draegon—since the awful man had not bothered to write once. And whilst none had anticipated the death of his father and the report of his own, both women knew Draegon could have remained behind and sent his brother, Lucan, in his stead. Draegon was, after all, the older heir and the one responsible. When his mother had left this world with a defeated heart, Julianna had entered the convent and tried to find peace when she would rather have perished.

"Return to Graycliff with me, love. Now. Let me see you clothed in garments befitting my bride. I cannot tolerate seeing your beauty hidden in that thing." His gaze flicked to her robes.

She looked down at her clothing, then met his gaze, sinking for a moment into his beautiful silver eyes. "This *thing* has kept me warm for a very long time, Draegon. A companion in its bleakness, and solace whilst I grieved, believing you had died for a useless cause."

His lips thinned, yet he would not argue with her in the abbey. Once home, amongst those who loved her, he would then tell her what had kept him from her side. Yet the look in her eyes, the aged pain, made him say, "I am home and all is well."

She scoffed. "All is far from well, Draegon." She stood, forcing him to look up at her. "You have grown in your arrogance, sir. You abandoned *me*. How dare you assume I will give up the life which has offered me sustenance for more than three years, simply because you have *chosen* to return!" She swept to the door.

Draegon shot to his feet, gaping at her back. "You would send me away?" This was not going a'tall as he'd planned.

"Aye."

He blinked. "But you waited, Julianna. Tell me you were not still hoping I was alive?"

She turned, the past years of crushed hopes mirrored in her eyes. "I held no such expectation. Your dearest friend said he saw you cleaved by a Saracen sword and I, like your mother and brother, believed him and mourned."

She opened the door and found Sir Bryce and Sister Mary David, their faces pinkening guiltily. Lucan stood alone near the far wall.

"Shouldn't you be at vespers?" she delivered in an imperial tone of the abbess herself.

"Lady Julianna," the abbess said briskly. "You will give his lordship the benefit of the situation. A bit more of your time. 'Tis Christmas, after all."

"And I should be more forgiving, you say?" They eyed her, and Julianna recalled the three Christmases past she'd spent alone, forgotten, and every agonizingly lonely day atween. "Nay." She swept past, unable to look back at Draegon. "Nay, nay," she repeated over and over as she marched down the stone hall. "I have given enough."

Instantly Draegon was behind her, catching her arm, forcing her around to look at him. Their bodies collided and she inhaled sharply, her hand unwillingly going to his broad chest. Beneath her palm, his heart thumped like a warrior's drum and Julianna felt her insides shift and burn for him. *Oh, his hurt is in his eyes,* she thought and it nearly destroyed her. How she ached from her toes to the ends of her hair for him, but he had abandoned her, chose his worthless war over her without so much as a by your leave, kissed her once and left to follow King Richard. She had not forgiven him afore she learned of his death, and with his resurrection, those dormant feelings were as clear as the day he sailed away. He assumed she would fall into his arms and allow him into her life again. He assumed she would speak vows and care for his castle and bear his children without a word spoken over how he'd betrayed her for his damned war. Well, his lordship assumed wrongly.

"I demand you leave this place, Julianna. *Now.*"

She jerked free "You have long since given way the right to demand aught of me, *Lord Draegon.*" She turned, moving down the hall, her steps swift and sure.

"Julianna!" he roared, and shrouded sisters filed out of their cells.

She stalled afore her rooms, her back to him. "Go home to your castle, m'lord. I am content to remain here."

She was cold and so distant and Draegon thought he would come apart with his need of her right then. "I love you, Julianna."

Tears filled her eyes and she squeezed them tightly shut, bowing her head. Oh, he knew how to wound her still.

"You loved an innocent girl, Drae." She spoke to the floor. "And every day you were gone took a piece of me until I've naught left to give. I am an old maid, too set in her ways for the life you *demand* of me."

She stepped into her cell and turned to close the door, but his hand slapping against the wood stopped her.

"Julianna . . . ," he pleaded, his gaze rapidly searching her face.

A tear escaped her. His throat worked. A moment passed, brief and filled with the pain of being apart for so long, of lying in festering wounds with no sign of healing. Then she closed the door in his face.

Draegon jerked back, his fists clenched at his side. "Damn her stubbornness," he hissed softly. "I did not survive the torture of infidels to come home to this!"

He spun about, the heavy ring of his spurred boots muffling her heart-wrenching sobs

"She is your daughter, order her out of that place!" Draegon demanded after three days of unsuccessful pleading with his bride.

Lord Hugh paused in his frantic pacing. "You order her, she is *your* betrothed!"

"Apparently, she does not agree." That wounded the most, he thought, that she would deny what they shared.

Lord Hugh gasped, slapped his hand on the table and stared at his future, he hoped, son-in-law. He could not have his daughter leave the convent for any other reason than marriage to this man. "But you must keep her!"

Draegon blinked at Hugh's fierce tone.

"The contracts were signed, the bride price awaits, and I wash my hands of the woman." He thrust back, dusted his fingertips and straightened his embroidered surcoat.

Draegon could not believe Julianna's father would speak of her this way, and his anger showed in his dark expression, an expression that made most of his vassals run for their quarters. Yet when her father stared him down, unmoved, Draegon remembered where Julianna got her determination.

"I have no intention of forfeiting on a contract," he said softly, leaning closer.

"Good." Lord Hugh relaxed, all smiles. "Because I cannot have her back in this castle."

"And why is that?" He needed to know.

Lord Hugh crooked a finger and Draegon bent. "Look around you, man." Draegon did, briefly. The castle was filled with the happy sounds of the coming holiday, the walls decorated with greenery, Julianna's sisters gathered near the hearth wrapping gifts, three young knights attending their every whim. "Has it been that long that you forget what this place was like when she resided here?" Hugh rolled his eyes. "Her very presence causes a stir. And I cherish the day you offered for her, for you are the only one she has obeyed."

"Julianna has never obeyed a soul, m'lord, and you know it."

The jolly old man's lips curved in a tender smile. "She is a bit wild, is she not?"

'Twas only one of the reasons Draegon loved her above all else.

"My house is content, Draegon," her father said in a more serious tone. "Her sisters are amiable and prepared to be wed, all have suitors, but they've made this damned pact as children."

"Ahh, aye," Draegon murmured with a fond memory of catching the four sisters pricking their fingers and swearing none would wed until Julianna, the oldest, had Draegon for a husband. Though he had loved her long afore that moment, 'twas that night he asked his father to beg the king's favor in arranging the match. Yet even after their betrothal, Julianna would never admit to the swearing.

"My daughters are the bane of me, sir. But Julianna, she is four redheads in one. She has more of the devil in . . ."

Draegon put up a hand. "I am aware of all that is my lady, sir." The past days were proof of such.

"Then I advise you, either lock her in a tower or wed her in all haste, so at least someone has a hand over the girl."

" 'Tis why I am here. I need your assistance."

Lord Hugh grinned, calling for ale and bending over

the table, his face bright with his usual happy countenance. He would lose his rebellious daughter and gain a fine son-in-law who would undoubtedly spend his nights fighting for command of his castle. *Better he than I,* he thought, listening to his plan.

1

A Partridge In A Pear Tree

The Crusades had bred her betrothed into a pompous ass, Julianna thought as he finally set her to her feet. Hours of riding afore him, gagged and bound, then slung over his shoulder like a grain sack, made her dizzy and she stumbled, jerking her head to fling hair from her face. She glanced about, not surprised she was at Graycliff Castle, in the chambers that had once belonged to his parents. Across the separating distance, she sharpened her gaze on him.

She was done shrieking against the gag, done with wriggling whilst he carted her from the convent. And she hoped the abbess was doing a great deal of penance for aiding him. Oh, the man had a blackhearted soul to coerce a nun into his plan.

Draegon tried not to frown at the venom in her eyes. Eventually she would forgive him for this, laugh and tell the tale to their children, yet at the moment, he could not envision the day, nor dismiss his unease. An army of Saracens were no match for Julianna's sharp mind.

"I love you, Julianna." Her shoulders sagged and he took hope that he wasn't making a grave mistake. "I love you and I will fulfill the promise I made to you years past."

And my consent matters naught, she thought. Again.

Her gaze followed him as he moved to the door, leaving her bound and gagged whilst he opened it, calling out. Then he crossed to her, removing the evidence of her abduction.

"You are a despicable creature, Draegon." Her voice came in a low almost polite murmur. "And I hate you for this."

He forced his expression to remain bland. "You do not mean that. You are upset with me."

"I am more than upset with you, sir." Her gaze turned piercing, green ice on a cool lake. "And do not propose to tell me *my* needs." Since he had failed so grandly at seeing them thus far.

Draegon opened his mouth to speak, then decided against it, turning away to hide the trappings in a trunk. 'Twould not do to bring her afore a priest spitting like a captured tiger. "You have but a few moments. The priest awaits."

Afore she could respond, her sisters burst into the room, all smiles and excitement and hugging her tightly. Over their heads, she met his gaze as he paused at the door.

" 'Tis Christmas Eve, Julianna. And our king has ordered that tonight you will become my wife."

"Then if by the king's edict"—her brow arched—"how can I refuse?"

His head dropped forward, his expression infinitely sad, and she regretted the sting of her sharp tongue. He left them, her sisters gone still at the first sound of her voice.

"Julianna, do not say such things to him."

She looked down at sweet Aslain and brushed her hair back off her face. "I say as I please, child."

"But . . . is this not what you want?"

"Aye, Jule, have you forgotten so much in that *place.*" This from Laslyn with a dramatic shiver.

"That place gave me peace when I thought I would die over his death, Las."

"But he is alive and you made a promise, to honor him above all else."

Julianna had, and knew she would not break it now. Pride prevailed. She'd speak the vows, neither disgracing him afore her family or his people, nor allowing another to see how much his manipulations wounded. But Draegon, Lord of Wessex, ruler of Graycliff, would discover he could not treat his wife as mere chattel.

"You love him, do you not, Julianna?" The words came soft, from Reina, the eldest of her three sisters, yet held the impact of a blade to her breast. Her eyes immediately teared. Oh, yes, she did love him still, more deeply than she imagined possible. The years apart had done naught to weaken a shred of the bond atween her and her dearest friend. He was her true and one love.

Julianna stepped to the window and released a deep sigh, staring out onto the tilt field below. 'Twas barren, and the soulless familiarity of it swept her. Her isolation in the convent had been a choice over the agony she refused to inflict on another, yet Draegon's return had eased but a portion of that sorrow, the part which suffered the pitying glances that grew more and more frequent as the year promised came and went. After another year had approached, she could take no more and sought refuge within the stone walls, forgotten like Guinevere to Arthur.

"Julianna?"

After a moment, she looked at her sisters, the beautiful girls clustered together, their faces creased with worry.

"Aye. I love him," she said simply, then crossed to them. "Come." She drew them toward the bath and let them disrobe her. "Now tell me of these knights who believe they are each worthy of my sisters."

The girls surrounded her, and for a moment, brief and fleeting, Julianna felt needed again and loved.

Belowstairs, her bridegroom paced. What was taking her so long? he wondered, then stilled, a bitter smile gliding over his lips. He supposed it served him well to wait on her for a time, yet he did not trust Julianna not to flee. The knights posted at the only exits would be discreet for their lady's sake, though only Lord Hugh, Lucan, and the abbess knew she'd been stolen from her cloistered cell.

At the head table, her father sipped wine with the guests. Draegon's brother, Lucan, stood near the hearth, alone, his eyes ever observant, if not emotionless. The pair had yet to have a few moments in private since his return, and Draegon reminded himself to reward his brother handsomely for caring for his people and holdings whilst he was away. Afore the dais, the priest shifted with impatience. The banns had been forgone, since they had been betrothed for years, and now all they waited for was Julianna. *Ahh, love,* he thought, staring at the floor and remembering the outrage in her eyes. *Forgive me, but your wounded heart will not let you see we must begin our life together to dissolve the past.*

Then he felt it, her presence, and turned to find her standing atop the stone steps. His heart slammed against the wall of his ribs and then thundered like a stallion in full gallop. He told himself he had not forgotten how beautiful she was, that he had suffered ungodly torture and starvation with only the memory of her to guide him back home. Yet the memory did not compare. Afore, the habit had hid her vibrance, left it uncomplemented. Yet now the full power of her beauty showered him, glowed in the great hall and every pair of eyes turned toward her.

Murmurs filtered through the hall, but Draegon did not hear them. Her sisters swept around her and hurried down the steps, yet he did not see them. His eyes fixed on his bride, he came to her, mounting the stairs slowly. He swallowed hard, unable to get moisture in his mouth. *I am unworthy of such a woman.*

Her hair was left unbound, a dark red river of silk flowing beyond her hips nearly past her thighs, giving him dreams of the night to come, of burying his face in the shimmering cloud when he made her his. A narrow braid sparked here and there within the glorious mass, each shot with gold thread and ending in the tiniest of bells. Only a flawless circlet of silver banded her head, her generous body cloaked in a deep-blue gown that was dignified, yet hugged her shape enough to make men stare longer than was proper. A jeweled girdle slung low on her trim hips, delicate chains and her dagger lying warmly at the divide of her thighs. A woman's strength radiated from her like glistening dew, a mysterious lure Draegon could not touch yet experienced as if she had cupped his soul in her palm and declared it hers for the taking. And he was powerless to deny her.

She descended to him, regal and slow, and he paused a step or two below her, offering his hand. Her green gaze lowered to it, then met his. The air left his lungs in a sharp gust. He'd faced a thousand Moors on the battlefield without the slightest reservation, yet naught gave him more alarm than this tiny woman refusing him now. But she did not, taking his hand, the warmth of her touch seeping into his bones, and he nearly moaned from the pure, sweet joy of it.

"Julianna," he whispered, heat in his voice and in his gaze as it swept her, and she gripped his fingertips tightly.

"M'lord," she said, lowering her eyes briefly enough

to catch her breath. He was so fierce looking, deliciously so, his pale-gray surcoat contrasting deeply against his sun-bronzed complexion, the rich shiny black of his hair. The hue made his eyes seem brighter, more powerful, more alluring, and she felt unreasonably light of foot, as if were water beneath her slippers, and she barely felt him tuck her hand in the bend of his arm and draw her to the great hall where her family and their people gathered, where his brother waited in solemn repose to stand with him.

The priest took his position, words droning, yet Julianna was trapped in Draegon's gaze, the power of her love for him spilling as she recited her vows. The room grew silent as he spoke, his voice ringing with a strength and clarity she'd never heard in a man. Her barren heart opened, filling with the heaviness of his emotions, and her eyes burned. Her hands gripped tenderly in his, his gaze never wavered, and atween his vows, he paused to bring her hand to his lips and place a soft kiss to the back. Pronounced husband and wife, Draegon wasted not a moment and swept her into his arms. He stared at her for no more than a heartbeat, angling his head, whispering her name afore his mouth slashed across hers, kissing her like the starved creature that he was.

Julianna sank against his strength, opening wide for the hard press of his lips and the velvet sweep of tongue into her mouth. She fisted his surcoat, clinging, whimpering for more, then slapped her arms around his neck, crushing him against her mouth as if he would leave her again. He would not, never again would he be parted from her, and it showed in his possessive kiss, his claim of her granted by God. His head rolled, his lips tugging, then grinding, tender yet fierce, keeping her off guard as he pressed her lovely body firmly to his length. She gasped at the spine-shocking power he wielded and drove her fingers into his hair. Draegon moaned like a tortured beast set free.

Women sighed. Someone noisily cleared his throat and Draegon jerked back, breathing heavily and staring into her liquid green eyes.

A cheer rose.

Julianna blushed.

Draegon grinned.

And all knew that no matter what they would witness in the next twelve days, Julianna loved her husband.

The festivities hailed into the night, the teasing and ribald jests following Draegon as his knights carried him to his bride. She was already above, the women preparing her in their chambers. Draegon was never so eager, nor so nervous, and his need of her mounted during the celebration until he could scarcely walk upright. Thrust through the entrance to the antechamber, the door slammed shut, he found her near the fire, her back to him. She was clad in a sleeping gown, its thinness showing him every lush curve and hollow of her pale body. Every muscle he possessed tightened, and Julianna felt him move up behind and slide his arms around her. His hands were warm against her stomach and she leaned back into him briefly, then quickly stepped out of his embrace.

Draegon blinked at his empty arms, then his bride. "Julianna?"

"Nay."

He did not have to ask what she meant. That she would not allow his touch angered him, and he tried hard to smother it. Her life had changed drastically in the last hours and she needed time to grow accustomed. He lifted his gaze from the floor to her.

"You have brought me here against my will, yet I have wed you right and proper afore God and our people as to not shame you." She dealt him a withering look. "I abide my promises. I have honor, too." Her chin lifted, and in a quiet voice she said, "I will be your chatelaine, see to the running of this castle, and for the world out there"—she gestured to the closed door and the noise filtering through—"I will be your wife."

But not here, not in his bed. "Why do you do this, Julianna? I thought 'twas what you wanted?"

"You thought?" She folded her arms over her middle. "Ha. You consider aught but your own desires, Draegon. 'Twas your choice to go on that damned Crusade. *Your* choice to leave me to rot waiting for you."

"I had good reason, love."

She arched a brow. "Did you have it this night, to force me to wed you?"

He folded his arms over his big chest. "You were being obstinate. You do not belong in a convent," he said with disgust.

"I belong where *I* choose." She tossed her head, gold threads flickering in the firelight. "I have a mind that I can make up on my own. You disregarded my feelings yet again. You took the choice away from me *again."*

"Women do not have choices, Julianna, though you have more than most."

The instant the words were out he knew they were the wrong ones.

Poisonous eyes scanned him from head to boots and Draegon felt his desire shrink. Yet 'twas her stillness, the calm control in her body, that gave him pause. Julianna was not usually so tame in her rage. "I do not know you. You are not the man who left me years ago."

His features tightened and he unfolded his arms. "Because I am not!" he growled.

Her breath shot to her throat and she tried to ignore the agonized look in his eyes and speak her mind. If she wavered, she would fall into his arms, letting him steal her acceptance of his treatment in dark kisses and wild loving. "When the man I fell in love with comes home, 'tis then I will welcome him into my bed."

His expression was savage with his anger, hiding his disappointment in her pronouncement. He strode into their chamber and she followed, watching as he tore back the bedclothes. He withdrew the dagger from his waist and she inhaled as he jabbed it into his fingertip. He made a fist, staring into her eyes as blood dripped onto the clean white linens. Her skin fused red. The sheets would be displayed on the morrow and all would believe the marriage consummated.

Then he advanced on her, and Julianna held herself stiffly until he snapped his arm around her waist, his mouth crushing over hers. He kissed her deeply, thoroughly, until her knees softened, until her fingers raked through his hair and her tongue pressed deeply into his mouth, begging for more. Draegon absorbed the incredible intensity of it, his loins hard and thickening to be inside her. Then slowly he drew back, her breath panting against his lips as he waited for her eyes to open.

Masculine satisfaction softened his features. "You want me in your bed as much as I, Julianna."

She shoved at him, glaring. She did not need her desire thrown in her face.

He tightened his hold on her and took her mouth again, his kiss grinding, exacting a response, his strong hands molding her thinly clad body to his and proving her lies and leaving her weakened. He thrust her from him and she stumbled, catching her balance.

"I will give you this one night of vengeance on me," he growled, then stormed to the antechamber.

"One night is nay enough!" she shouted, and afore he crossed the threshold a ewer exploded against the wall near his head, shattering in a rain of crockery.

Slowly, he looked back over his shoulder, his eyes glittering like polished glass. Now *that* was the Julianna he remembered. "One night," he warned, then pulled the door shut behind him and sagged against it.

The lock bolt shot home and he closed his eyes against the finality of it. He swallowed the lump in his throat. *Julianna,* he agonized, rubbing his bloody hands over his face. *How am I to find the trust lost when you will not give me the chance?*

You have disregarded my feelings yet again.

If he was not so certain their marriage was meant to be, Draegon would have believed she did not love him. Pushing away from the door, he paced long into the night, doubting her love, the love that gave him such strength in the Holy Land that he lost fingernails scraping away at his prison walls, nearly killed his horse racing across England to get to her. And in the light of dawn, half drunk on wedding wine and self-pity, Draegon heard the sweet strains of children singing on Christmas morn, and he smiled.

At dawn, Julianna left the chamber afore he woke. It took all her will not to touch him, beckon him to her bed. Belowstairs in the hall she suffered the ribald jokes, her sister's innocent questions, to which she had no answer. The preparations for the night's festivities were underway and Julianna kept a busy distance from Draegon. Though she knew where he was, in the hall gaming with his men or reintroducing himself to his people, she often felt his gaze on her as if he'd stroked a finger down her spine. Her awareness of him was unsettling and 'twas not that she did not want him, she did, desperately, but she could not come into their marriage bed with him believing he could dismiss her needs whenever he chose. Aye, she loved him. Aye, she wanted a true marriage with him. Yet he'd made no effort to understand all she'd been through in his absence. Nor to consider it now. He stormed in and seized, conquering by right and not his need, and Julianna missed the gently spoken Draegon of her past.

Ignoring the pangs of regret, she focused on her tasks, adding spices to the roasting meats, pots of vegetables. Around her in the cook house, servants talked softly, of the new babes born on the most precious of nights, of the gifts they hoped to receive today. Julianna knew these people, she'd played with them as a child, worked with them when she'd spent nearly a year with Draegon's mother, waiting. She was at home, her home.

Suddenly the amusing chatter died and Julianna twisted, already knowing Draegon stood in the open doorway. Last night, the dismissal of her wants, his punishing kiss, and his threats flashed in her mind and she shored herself against revealing her heartache. Now was not the time to show a soul that her husband thought so little of her mind.

As if he'd read her rebellious thoughts, he regarded her thoroughly afore speaking. "Lady Julianna, might I have a word with you?"

How very pleasant, she thought, since she'd found him in the antechamber this morn with an empty flagon of wine hugged to his chest.

His gaze never left her as she crossed the crowded room, moving around servants, touching the shoulder of one and giving her approval of the dish, then asking that the serving begin once her lord was seated. Draegon felt a surge of pride. Regardless of the rift atween them, of the crockery and curses she flung at him last night, Julianna was truly the lady of their castle. She had an army of servants cleaning, polishing, sweeping, and already this morn she had seen to the menu, consulting him on his preferences. He didn't recall what he'd said, too entranced with the way her lips shaped the questions and wanting to feel them on his own again. Hot, willing kisses from his wife, not to battle through her rage to find her passion. *And I am a prisoner to both,* he thought, smiling into her suspicious eyes.

"Aye, m'lord?"

He disliked that she was so formal with him. He crooked a finger and turned out of the cook house, crossing the snow-covered yard to the great hall, aware her insatiable curiosity kept her at his heels as he veered off.

"My lord," she gritted through chattering teeth. "I am not a damned pup." He ignored her and rounded the edge of the buttery, out of sight. "Draegon? 'Tis freezing and I have work to tend!"

He turned, quick enough to startle her, and grinned. Julianna fought a smile as she pulled up her hood. He looked much the cat with cream-covered whiskers. He cast a quick look about, which made her do the same, then, from the ground behind the building, he lifted a tree, for Saint Crispin's sakes, stuffed in a basket, then a wood box. She could hear something fluttering inside.

"Happy Christmas, Julianna."

"Happy Christmas to you, my lord."

He held up the tree and the box. " 'Tis a partridge in a pear tree."

Hugging herself against the cold, she looked at the shrub, then peered atween the box slats afore coolly meeting his gaze. "I have not grown stupid in the past years, Draegon. 'Tis but an English sparrow and an elderberry bush." To be certain, she viewed it once more and added, "Aye. 'Tis." She looked at him, her expression bland, her irritation visible. After last night, did he think her so easily won with mere gifts? "Was there aught else you needed, m'lord?"

You, he thought, *without your bloody contentiousness.*

"Nay . . . aye . . . nay," he grumbled, dumping the tree in the dirt. How could she be so remote when he was dying for her?

Julianna nodded once, feeling he at least understood what 'twas like to be taken lightly, even if for a brief moment. "Then please take your seat at the table, so that I may begin feeding our guests."

He snorted nastily and she swept past him, leaving her scent in her wake and her husband bereft. Draegon kicked the tree and released the bird, wondering how the years in a house of God had made his woman cold and heartless.

Draegon's despair lingered through the day, his smile forced and his mind trying to understand that of his bride's. She ignored him unless another was about, and for hours he felt he was losing her. Until the evening meal.

Whilst musicians filled the air with sweet melodies, Julianna sipped mulled wine, trying to decipher his odd smile. Considering the situation, a pleased Draegon made her cautious.

He cut a piece of meat, speared it with his eating knife and held it out to her.

She closed her lips over the morsel and chewed, offering a bite to him. Though she ate, she did not taste it, her concentration dissolving under his tight regard. The man touched too deeply with just his eyes, saying little but speaking volumes. The message made her insides sing.

"You have grown more beautiful, my love."

His husky tone warmed her skin and she lowered her gaze briefly. "My thanks, m'lord."

He touched her hair, brushing the long bloodred tresses off her shoulder, his fingertip lingering to trace the edge of her gown. A blush stole up to her cheeks, yet she made no comment.

"Your father tells me that once word reached that I was dead, Prince John bid you wed one of his barons." He'd only discovered this by accident, and the result gave him hope.

She looked away, the memory of hearing of his death slicing through her as if it happened this night. He caught her chin, forcing her to meet his gaze. "Aye," she finally said.

"Yet you did not." His fingers lovingly feathered her jaw.

She arched a brow, fighting the piercing energy of his touch. "Your point, m'lord?"

He bit the inside of his mouth. She did not like being cornered. "The prince bid you several times." His thumb rasped over the seam of her lips, his gaze intent on the task. She caught the tip atween her teeth and his eyes flared. He met her gaze. "Yet you defied him, refusing to wed and entering the convent instead."

She leaned back a bit, blinking. "Is m'lord suggesting I blatantly challenged the Crown? Me? A mere woman?"

Such sass, he thought happily. "So you are saying your father is lying?" His hand lowered, the back of his knuckles brushing under her jaw, along her collarbone nearer to her breast. Her breathing increased noticeably. "And your sisters, too?"

An exquisite tingling skipped down her body, drawing her nipples tight against her shift with an exquisite friction. She licked her lips, trying to force her desire behind her annoyance, unwilling to admit a bloody thing, especially when he was wallowing in his power over her. Yet in her heart she knew even when the king's brother paraded his lords afore her, she could never marry another. Princely order or nay.

"You know 'tis not so" came on a soft whisper.

His lips twitched with satisfaction, her response to his touch doing more to him than her defiance of John. Both showed him she fought her feelings. "Why did you not wed, Julianna?" He leaned close, brushing his cheek across her hair, scenting spice and flowers and murmuring his pleasure over it. Around them people dined, troubadours sang, servants moved. "Certainly there were suitors."

Benumbed with sweet sensations, she gripped his forearm. "Several. Your brother for one." He tensed and she felt it.

"Oh?"

"Like Sir Bryce, he felt naught but pity for my position, Draegon."

Possession roared through him and he ground his mouth to the spot afore her ear, teething her lobe. She inhaled and he felt the sweep of air as if he owned it, wanted to hear it again, coming faster, lusher, when he was pleasuring her body.

"Why did you not accept?" whispered into her mind, intoxicating her. "Why?"

She closed her eyes, lost to his touch, tipping her head for his nibbling lips. " 'Tis only you I love, Drae. Only you and no other."

In the next heartbeat, his mouth covered hers, his tongue sinking deeply into her wet mouth. And Julianna received and gave. The guests in the hall roared with laughter and good cheer. She gave some more, telling herself they were watched and she must not shame him, but by the saints, Draegon was a master at kissing. Beneath the table his hand covered her thigh and she jolted, yet he stole the advantage, his touch moving upward, squeezing gently, shaping her leg, strong fingers dipping deeply atween.

Julianna felt a rush of moisture there and kissed him harder, inching closer.

He broke the kiss and in the curve of her ear, he whispered, "I long to feel your legs wrapped round me." She gasped, her hands gripping his embroidered surcoat, and he added mercilessly, "Pulling me into you, Julianna. Deep inside you." He stroked through the fabric. "Here." She whimpered and he pressed his mouth over hers once more, hard and wet, afore leaning back in his carved chair.

Julianna blinked, reeling with desire.

His eyes glittered like a lazy cat inspecting his next prey.

"One night," he reminded.

2

Two Turtle Doves

Draegon stood and offered her his hand. She hesitated and his eyes let loose a challenge. Elegantly, Julianna placed her hand in his and rose. Though her smile reeked of sweetness, he knew 'twas for sake of the eyes watching them. And her desire, the swift passion that drove him to madness moments afore, was extinguished.

"Do not threaten, m'lord," she whispered through a loving smile. "I have faced down Prince John." She proceeded him, leaving him to admire the tight sway of her rump as they headed to their chamber. She spoke not a word as he crossed the room and added wood to the fire. Without so much as a glance, she wiggled out of her gown and, wearing a thin shift, slid into bed. She met his gaze, jerked up the coverlet and turned her back on him.

Draegon never felt so powerless in his life. He commanded legions of men, could cleave a horse's head with one swipe of his broadsword, had a castle full of people prepared to please him, but this woman made him feel ineffectual and dismissed. And he felt the fool, standing here burning in his braes for her whilst she was sleeping! Great days, would he ever understand her. One moment she was breathless from his touch and the next—he smiled suddenly—and the next she was declaring her love, sharing a heated kiss. If he knew one thing about Julianna, her passion was as insatiable as her curiosity. He decided to stir both.

Removing his tunic and sitting on a stool, he unlaced the thong securing his leather boots, and although his gaze focused on his task, he heard her turn in the bed under the guise of restless sleep. Smothering a smile, he stood and stripped down to his loincloth. Her indrawn breath echoed in the quiet chamber. Pouring water into a bowl, he washed away the day's grime, then slowly toweled himself dry. Afore he tossed the cloth aside, he looked up and found her staring.

"You do this a'purpose, Draegon." She flicked a hand at his powerful body.

His brows rose with innocent question. "I bathe to be clean." Methodically, he folded, then dropped the cloth on the table.

She sniffed indelicately. "Do you seek to seduce me?"

"You are my wife," he said simply. "I need not play such games."

That he would not even bother spilled resentment through her. He assumed, as afore, that he could order her to spread herself and she would comply. Hah!

But then he moved toward her in naked glory and Julianna could not keep her gaze from his arousal tenting his cloth. It seemed to enlarge with every step. Her gaze roamed freely over his body. Not an inch of him jiggled. A giant of a man with a soft tread. War had honed him like this, she thought, gave him powerfully wide shoulders and arms as big as her thighs, roped with muscle and curving smoothly into his chest. And war gave him the heavy scar marring his skin from shoulder to his flat brown nipple. She wanted to ask about it, but his masculine show of nakedness distracted. The ridges in his stomach were like steps to his hips, to the dark hair marking toward his groin. He bulged beneath the loincloth, the length of him defined. *He will rip me in two,* she thought, yet knew beyond doubt that Draegon would not take her by force.

She raised her eyes to his and expected mockery, yet found his expression blank and strangely tight.

His thigh flexed as he pressed one knee to the bed. "Move aside, wife."

She wanted to tell her husband to go straight to the devil, yet she loved this man, crack-brained sot that he was about most things. She wanted to be near him, reasoning that if he were outside in the antechamber, they would have no chance to repair the damage atween them. She scooted to the far end of the mattress and he climbed in.

Bracing his hands behind his head, Draegon stared at the tapestry bellying from the ceiling. He was not the least bit embarrassed that he was aroused and ready for her. He wanted her to know he was suffering. But he would not take her, for with Julianna, ignoring her brought only a passing curiosity, ordering brought outright rebellion, and he recalled the first day he'd seen her, riding alone without escort. He'd told her to go home afore she got hurt and she promptly knocked him from his saddle and left on her own power. Julianna's will was a delicate and powerful thing. If he wanted her, which was without question, she had to come to him. Patience. He'd learned that in prison and she would discover he could not be bested in this. He would have his wife, in every way and not just beneath him.

Suddenly, he shifted to his side to face her, propping his head in his palm.

"Cover yourself," she said with a nervous glance down his body.

He didn't and leaned over, brushing his mouth over

hers. She did not move, holding herself stiffly for his assault. Then he cupped the back of her skull, lightly imprisoning her for the deepest of kisses, his tongue sliding atween her lips and tasting her all over. Without a sound, her body gravitated toward him. The fierce need to touch her, to slide his hand beneath her shift and feel that dampness atween her thighs, nearly drove him to push her on her back and ravish her right then. But he didn't and deepened his kiss, putting his emotions as well as his expertise into coaxing Julianna.

Yet naught was simple about her, and seconds later, Draegon called himself a fool for even touching her but once. Her mouth was hot and wet and molding, the tips of her breasts hard and grazing his skin like cinders. 'Twas a fire burning in her and he was losing control.

Julianna ached, so deeply, so wonderfully, her body throbbing and pulsing for more of his touch, more than his lips on hers. Atween her thighs flushed with warm liquid and she'd almost forgotten how strong the passion was atween them. She missed being a woman, missed feminine lure and being sought after for more than her handsome dowry. She craved Draegon, and that he was aroused, prepared to pleasure her, drove unspent desire through her most intimate places. Her breasts ached and swelled, calling out for his hands, his lips upon them with such a fierceness that she thought she would launch herself at him and demand he taste her.

Inside you, he had said at dinner. *Deep inside you.*

The rush of heat came again, hotter, stronger. *Oh, aye, my love, say the words. Ask me. Give me the choice this time.* Her hand slipped to his bare shoulder and he drew back. She almost cried out. Then he whispered good night against her lips and promptly gave her his back. Julianna sank into the bedding, blinking at the ceiling.

Apparently he'd no true desire to take his husbandly rights as he'd threatened. One night meant only *sleeping* to Draegon, and though Julianna told herself 'twas a victory, she could not calm her body nor forget the sight of his, baked by the Saracen sun to a warm bronze. Bare. Oh, Lord, gloriously bare but for that one secret part she ached to explore. She wanted to touch it, feel it grow beneath her fingertips and, unwillingly, she moaned aloud.

"Julianna, are you ill?"

She squeezed her eyes shut. "Nay."

Facing away, he grinned. The single word was breathy and hot. "A bit of bad beef mayhap? Soured wine?"

Her lips thinned. "There is no bad beef nor soured wine in this castle, Lord Draegon."

Was the insult to her larder worse than insulting her passions? he wondered. "Then, pray tell, what has you moaning?"

She eyed his broad back. Was that a smile she heard in his voice? "Naught, naught, go to sleep."

He felt the covers jerk with agitated moves and Draegon grinned, utterly pleased. Yet 'twas a long while afore he could consider sleeping, and her scent, mixed with her desire, followed him into his dreams.

In the morning he woke to find her body curled around his, her face buried in the bend of his shoulder, her hand on his chest. He smiled to himself. Was sleep the only place she could not resist her heart? His hand rested familiarly on her buttocks and slowly he felt the softness of her skin beneath his palm. She was dead to the world, her shift hiked to her hips, her leg thrown over his thigh. He knew 'twas not kind what he planned, yet she was irresistible lying there, lush and ripe. Mayhap winning back Julianna started here and not beyond the walls. Or both. Lightly, as to not wake her, he touched the soft down atween her thighs, watching her expression. His fingers probed and pried the warm flesh, then, with great care, he slid a finger atween the dewy lips, his touch tender as if stirring water, light as a kitten's brushing. Moisture, hot and slick, drenched him and her thighs shifted. He stroked her slowly and her hips moved, meeting his touch.

Draegon grit his teeth and found himself caught in his own trap. He wanted to touch deeper, taste her there, drink in her sweet musk. Angry, she was unchangeable. Aroused, she was the fiery tempest all men dreamed about. Draegon wanted to give her something to think about when she was in her tower of righteousness. She flexed on the bed, against him and moaned. Afore she would waken, he slowly he drew his hand away and slipped from the bed. He dressed quickly and left her to her dreams.

Julianna stirred stretching, her body humming with a hunger she could not devour. She squeezed her thighs tightly together and moaned, burying her face in the pillows. She had dreamt of him making love to her and it seemed her body could not tell the difference atween the real and the mist of dreams. The throbbing lingered through her toilette, whilst breaking her fast, and halfway through the morn.

It left her mood sour. Something Draegon did not consider.

Draegon heard her snap at everyone, then apologize. The process was ongoing through the day, and when she stormed across the hall, scowling enough to scare the servants, he left the conversation with his men-at-arms and caught her close. She pushed at his shoulders.

"Leave off, Dragon. There's work to be done."

"Can you not spare a moment for your beloved?"

The words met their mark and she sagged, the fight leaving her.

"Forgive me." She rubbed her temple, a pain brewing. "I do not know what is wrong with me."

He did and swept her up in his arms.

"Cease this nonsense." She squirmed. "Put me down, I say."

"You are unwell and need rest."

She wiggled to be free as he mounted the stairs to their chamber. The last place she wanted to be was alone with him. "I have a pain in my head, not the ague. And I have been resting for *years*."

Ignoring the jibe and her protests, he ordered watered wine for her as he carried her to their chamber and set her gently in a chair near the hearth.

She stood.

He pushed her back down, and when the servant entered his gaze threatened. She shifted away, rubbing her head and gazing at the fierce blaze warming the room. When they were alone, she sipped wine whilst Draegon went to the antechamber. Julianna glanced at the doorway, hearing him move about, then leaned out for a look. As he returned, she jerked back into the dull position he'd left her in. He was not fooled and schooled his features, crossing to her. She lifted her gaze, looking bored. He presented her with a small gilded cage. Inside on a swing were two turtle doves.

"Happy Christmas, my sweet."

Warmth speared through her, but her foul mood and wounded pride won. "I need no pets," she said, offering it back.

Sighing heavily, Draegon rested the cage on the chest next to her. The birds chirped and the corners of her mouth curved. She peered at them, poking her finger in the cage.

"Where did you find them?" Her expression softened and she sipped more wine.

"The cage came from Jerusalem, the birds, here."

"Have they been fighting?" She gestured to the lack of feathers on their backs.

Draegon frowned at the birds, just noticing the pink skin peeking through. "No more than we, I suppose."

Her gaze flew to his. He smiled, and she could not resist returning it.

"My thanks, Drae." Setting the cup aside, she lifted the cage to her lap. The birds swung happily and she grinned. He went down on one knee afore her and she looked up, reaching out to brush an inky lock of hair from his forehead. Her gaze searched his features, rugged from war, scarred yet so beautiful. Without thought, she leaned forward and brushed her mouth over his. "Happy Christmas."

It took all his will not to drag her into his arms and ravish her sweet mouth, yet he held himself back, letting her kiss him, letting her decide when to end it, and he nearly moaned when she did.

He stood. "Rest a bit, love. 'Tis difficult going from a convent to a castle so quickly."

"Are you saying I am incapable?"

"Nay. I did not mean to imply . . ."

She put up a hand. "Get you from my sight, Draegon. And do not insult me again." He took heart in that she was smiling when she said that.

He left her alone. Julianna played with the birds, watching them peck at the gilded cage, then returning to their chamber twice to check on them. The third time she began to worry, for they were plopped on the bottom of the cage, unmoving, their tiny black eyes staring up at her. Refreshing their water and grain, she left.

* * *

Later that eventide, Draegon found her in the solar, the bird cage on her lap. She was bent over the tiny home, sobbing helplessly, quietly. Dread raced through him, and when he called to her, she looked up, swiping furiously at her eyes.

"They are dead."

Julianna knew it was silly to mourn birds, but finding them on their backs reopened an old wound, stirring the memory of losing her own mother, Draegon's parents, then the only man she would ever love. She'd never forgotten the horrible despair, only learned to live with it, and the death of the birds brought home how stubborn she was being and her inflexibility to consummate their marriage, for starting anew, ate at her. She stood abruptly and, without pause, headed down the stairs and out of the castle, the cage in hand. Castle folk paused in their work to stare at lord and lady. Cold wind blasted her as she passed through the bailey, striding to her private garden in the courtyard.

Draegon was right behind her.

Dropping to her knees, she dug in the snow, and dug and dug until, to Draegon, she looked more like a dog hiding a bone than a noblewoman burying tiny birds. His heart ached for her and he glimpsed the girl Julianna, not the termagant he loved, but the innocent who'd scolded him for hunting a beautiful pheasant, insisting they were too pretty to eat. He knew without asking what she was feeling: innocent life stolen without reason. For years she'd thought his life taken—and to Julianna, Draegon knew, she'd thought it for a useless cause. He could not imagine the pain she must have experienced when told he had died.

A pounding drew his focus. Dusted in white, she smashed the snow over the cage with clenched fists and he went to her, grabbing her wrists and pulling her from the ground. Then she pounded him.

"Damn you," she hissed, and he let her beat his chest like a drum. She sobbed and he held her. She gripped his shoulders until he felt the tormenting dig of her nails, the fabric tear through the clasp of his cloak and he let her, blowing on her frozen fingers, telling her he was sorry, that he only wanted to give her something sweet and gentle of her own. He did not know whether she was angry over the doves' deaths or at him for not dying in the Holy Land. Fate was being cruel to them again, their happiness short-lived.

As he held her in the crystal-white beauty of her private garden, Draegon wondered if he would ever cease causing this woman pain.

3

Three French Hens

He'd never known her to be so quiet, Draegon thought with concern. And her influence stretched beyond him, he realized with a glance around at the folk who should be celebrating the third day of Christmas with vigor. A musician played softly in the corner near the entrance, his music scarcely muffling the noise whilst the servants cleared and stored the tables. Julianna sat across from his padded chair, her gaze on the fire. He stood, pulling her to her feet. She did not protest, preceding him to their chamber. Despondently, she disrobed and slid into bed. Draegon joined her, wearing his braes, and immediately she slid into his arms. He held her warmly beneath the furs and he closed his eyes.

'Twas a long moment afore she said, " 'Tis not your fault they were ill, Drae."

He inhaled and let it out slowly. "I know."

" 'Twas the gold in the cage. They pecked at it."

He tipped her head to look her in the eye.

"I found flecks in their beaks and in the bottom of the cage."

His face was creased as he caught her chin atween thumb and forefinger, rubbing there. "At least you do not think 'twas intentional."

Her brow knitted softly. "I would not believe that of you."

"But you believe I would cruelly dismiss you and go off to war."

"You did."

"Julianna." He sighed.

"Nay, you did, Draegon." She rose up on her elbow, her hair a dark curtain over one eye. "You could have remained. 'Twas your *duty* to remain."

He scowled, his eyes warning her she trod too far. "Do not speak of my duty, woman. I know it well."

His tone sent hurt stinging through her. "You are my husband. This is our bed. If I cannot speak freely here, where can I?"

His lips tightened. "Have I a choice in this?"

She scoffed as if he were asking for the moon and she sat back on her heels, hands folded on her lap. "You are the elder, the heir. Did you consider, for one moment beyond this disgusting need to conquer a people who have survived longer than the English, of what you have done to Lucan?"

A dark brow quirked in surprise. He'd thought she would be addressing their relationship. "My brother has suffered naught because I joined the Crusades."

"Ah! Then you are as blind as you were four years ago." She scrambled from the bed.

He frowned. "Explain yourself, Julianna, and quickly."

She snatched up a fur, wrapping in its warmth. "He is the second brother. He has naught to take to a marriage but what he has won in tournaments or with a bride, yet he has foregone all, caring for your lands, your people, your castle," then added in a softer tone, "your betrothed."

Draegon's expression darkened and for a instant his trust in Lucan wavered. "Julianna."

She put up a hand, aware of the vein of his thoughts. "Nay, do not debase him by asking. You were thought dead, he was liege lord. He offered for my hand only out of duty, like Bryce. I love Lucan like a brother I never had. He protected me, sheltered me, and we shared our grief over your parents," pain flickered over Draegon's handsome features, "and you. He was the only person who came to the convent save my sisters."

Mollified, Draegon nodded, folding his arms over his chest and watching her move about the room, gathering her thoughts. Her naked legs lured his imagination down dangerous paths, especially when he could feel the fight in her from across the room.

She stopped afore the fire, staring as she said, "Did you once comment on how well this castle has been cared for? The improvements he has made? The people's fondness of him?" She looked at him. "He has naught of his own, yet you selfishly sailed away expecting him to take your place, denying him the chance to find a fortune of his own. He wanted to follow Richard and, by right, he should have."

He unfolded his arms, sitting up. " 'Twas my right."

She adjusted the pelt like a queen in her robes. "Nay, 'twas your privilege. What has he to expect now?"

"I am a bit concerned over your adoration of my younger brother." He started to leave the bed, swinging his legs over the side.

She made a face. "Do not be an ass, Draegon. By God, can you not see beyond yourself? Your return has taken all he thought his, and in ignoring his fine hand at his duty, you have smashed his pride." A moment stretched, stares clashing and her voice grown soft as she said, "He has turned bitter, Draegon. And I fear 'tis directed to you."

"I concede he has become a bit too quiet, but I have seen naught of what you claim."

Spreading her draped arms like wings, she said, "Have you bothered to look beyond? To speak to him, to ask after his desires or award him for his faithful service?"

He had not, not for a moment, so concerned with winning back Julianna, Draegon had ignored the only relative he had. His neglect shamed him. Afore he left Graycliff, Draegon was an innocent, too young, eager, and unseasoned, yet the need to earn his spurs at the side of his king and not because title and land were his right by lineage, overpowered all else. For Lucan had earned his knighthood honestly, in battle and tournaments.

Julianna was right, he groused silently. He had denied Lucan the opportunity to join the king, and what did a second brother have but only the chance of winning his lands, vassals, and mayhap a castle or keep?

His brother had naught to possess except what came with a bride or what was awarded him by the king.

Or by you, a voice said.

And if behavior was a constant for ruling, Draegon thought with self-reproach, Lucan should be lord of Graycliff.

Draegon mashed a hand over his face, staring at the floor. He would not wish the experience of the Crusades on any man, the waste of human life abominable, and for an instant, the dismembered limbs and children hacked by knights caught too deep in the vigor of battle for restraint splintered through his mind. He squeezed his eyes shut, trying to block it out. Lucan was lucky, yet he doubted his brother would share his opinion.

"I will speak with him on the morrow, Julianna, and once again you are right."

There was no victory in her smile, only sympathy.

Across the room he held her gaze in his, his smoothing brow creasing again with concern. She was fidgeting, and Julianna FitzWarren did not fidget.

"Speak of it, love, I would have some rest this night."

After a few false started she burst with, "What appeal did the Crusades have . . . that I did not?"

He chuckled softly and her eyes narrowed. "I often wonder at that, sweet." He'd three years of regret in prison, he did not want it more. "For 'tis none that I find now."

"But you promised me one year and took four."

Bracing his elbows on his knees, he clasped his hands. "I was a prisoner."

Castle gossip had told her thus already, yet she'd waited to hear it from him. "So was I."

His brows rose and he straightened on the edge of the bed. " 'Twas your choice to join a convent, not mine."

She gawked at him. "Would you rather have come home to find me well wed and fat with another man's child?"

He jumped to his feet, pointing a finger at her. "Ah ha! So you did hope I was alive."

She slapped his hand away. "Do not twist what I am saying, Draegon." The man was far too certain of his appeal.

"Admit it, you hoped."

"Nay! I did not." One hand on her hip spread the fur, exposing her to his gaze. "I mourned, I had my very soul ripped from my chest and for three years I bled."

His sympathy was tempered by her lush breasts visible through the transparent shift. "Why?"

She let out a little shriek of indignation, and with every word, gave him a shove back toward the bed. "If you are too stupid to know that, then you are too stupid to be my husband."

He grinned in the face of her insult, plopping onto

the mattress. Her fire was magnificent and he loved it. "I am stupid. You are not. Now, enough of this prattle. Come, sleep." His eyes glowing, he patted the space beside him.

Her gaze slipped to it, then to him. "I cannot sleep now." He was too tempting, to be sure.

"Then let me just hold you."

She eyed him warily, her gaze lingering warmly over his disheveled hair, his bare chest, bronze and carved. Her mouth went dry. But Draegon had not yet admitted the errors of his choices and giving him intimacy would give him her last coin to the conqueror. She was asking so little, she reasoned, whilst he wanted total acquiescence.

He threw back the covers. "I promise to keep my braes secured."

" 'Tis not you I am worried about," she muttered, then crossed the room, crawling across him, dropping into the mattress. He snuggled her close and she went with only a little protest.

"Tell me about prison, Drae."

He pressed his lips to the top of her head. 'Twas the first time she'd asked about the Crusades.

In a mild tone, he related from the last moment they'd seen each other, to the instant he was injured, to his time in prison and in his arms. In his arms she sobbed for him. But Draegon could not tell her that 'twas she alone who truly kept him alive. For after the past days, he knew that Julianna held more power over him than he imagined. If he did not discover the solution to her objections to making love with him, for giving all to him, he feared he would be lost.

Julianna frowned at the maid holding out the sack. Something was moving inside it and the girl looked as if 'twould bite her. Was this another of her husband's strange gifts?

"M'lord bid me give you these."

Ahh, we begin again. "And they are?"

"French hens, 'e says to tell ye."

Julianna took the sack and peered inside.

Just then he came around the edge of the west wall, his stride long and lopping, and Julianna was struck by the handsome figure that was her husband, her knight. He wore a leather tunic with a wide belt circling his waist and had donned only a breast plate and chain mail hauberk for protection. Yet she could see the blood on the side of his neck. Dismissing the maid, she rushed to him, dropping the sack and stopping him where he stood to examine the wound.

"Have the Crusades taught you naught about protecting yourself?" she hissed, blotting the cut with the edge of her cloak. He made no comment, his gaze on her bowed head, his mouth curving with tender humor. "You have people to safeguard. Villeins depended on you for their very lives."

"I know, Julianna."

Her gaze flashed to his. "Then do you wish to see your holdings squandered to John's Norman barons?" She could not repeat such a loss again and survive.

"Nay, I do not and will be more cautious if 'twill please you."

"Good, then use that head of yours for aught other than a target."

She tries so hard to hide her love, he thought. "I see you have my gift." He gestured to the rough bag.

"Aye." Gathering it up, she held out the wiggling sack. "And you are wrong."

She liked telling him that too much, he thought. "How so?"

"They are naught but underfed pullets, Draegon. And have no French breeding about them."

The point of his sword in the dirt, he braced his palms on the hilt. "You are familiar with French livestock?"

"Nay, but . . ."

"Then I say they are French hens," he challenged. *"Three French hens."*

"You are mistaken."

He tipped his head slightly. "You would defy your lord?"

"My Lord is my God." Her chin lifted. "You are my husband."

Merely, was missing from that statement, he thought, fighting a smile. "They are French hens, Julianna."

"Hah."

He arched a brow, a black wing taking flight. " 'Tis all you have to say?"

"Nay, m'lord, but people are watching. But I will. Later."

He moved mere inches afore her, forcing her to lose the sack afore he stabbed his sword in the ground and gathered her in his arms. "Later? In our bed?"

"In our chamber," she corrected, suffering his embrace though she wanted to melt into it. He'd kissed her awake this morn and she stared at his mouth, wanting to feel its softness moving over more than her lips. *My abstinence in the convent has made me brazen,* she thought.

"Where is the woman who wept for tiny birds?" he asked, searching her face.

Her features tightened a fraction. "She grew old and grew up when she did not want to do either."

"Age has its advantages, wife." His hand slid slowly down her spine to her buttocks. Gently he squeezed and shaped. Her eyes widened and she glanced at the people moving about them.

"Cease!"

He did not, pressing her to his arousal.

"You would shame me?" she said on a gasp.

"I would soften that tongue, woman. In my mouth."

He kissed her. And kissed her, deeply, thickly, fisting his hands in her cloak and grinding her to him. Her arms slapped around his neck, then her hands drove into his hair and she held him, begging for more, taking more and dueling with his tongue. His moan was a savage sound, an untamed growl, and he was aware of the snickers and giggles passing around them, aware they were displaying their passion for the world, but Julianna was coming undone all over him and he wanted more.

Abruptly she pried him from her mouth and stepped back.

"Soft enough?" she said with an arched brow. When he simply stood there, gasping for air, his codpiece threatening to rip free of his braes, Julianna's lips curved. She swept up the sack and headed into the castle, her step light.

Lucan came up beside him, staring at his lady, then his brother. " 'Tis dangerous, toying with her."

"Aye," Draegon managed atween breaths, then grinned. "The Crusades do not compare to that."

"I would not know."

Draegon looked at his brother, yet saw only his retreating back.

At dinner that eventide, when Draegon was sure he was making progress with his bride, a clarion sounded and three servants entered the hall bearing silver trays. Perched upon them were the "French" hens, plucked, butchered, and roasted. His gaze shifted to her and she smiled innocently, then took up a knife and stabbed the crispy skin of a bird, cutting off a slice. She diced it, speared it, and held a chunk out to him.

"Pullet, m'lord?"

"Hen," he said, taking the meat in his teeth.

"A bit like eating crow, aye?"

He savored the flavor. "Your knowledge of birds is astounding, wife."

"You will find that I know much and see all, husband."

Her gaze swept down his body to his codpiece, and beneath the table she brushed her fingers over the embroidered fabric, drawing the shape of him there. Draegon choked, grabbing his goblet and gulping back some wine. She settled back into her chair, toying with her knife, her smile satisfied and eyes glittering with power.

Draegon recognized the fire of retribution brewing in her.

It made him nervous.

4

Four Calling Birds

Draegon woke with a desire-laced groan, his arousal hard and throbbing. Instantly, he reached for his wife and found his bed empty. His gaze searched their chamber. The fire was high, water warming for him, yet Julianna was nowhere in sight. Sinking into the pillows, he could still smell her scent on him and he wondered how long he would last afore he took what he wanted. He could seduce her, he thought. Her passion he possessed, 'twas her heart, her loyalty to the future of their marriage he was still uncertain about. And that devious look she had last eve made his sleep restless. He kept waiting for her to play some trick on him, so occupied with his mistrust, he'd forgotten to speak with Lucan. Yet she came to bed and fell asleep quickly. He was awake half the night, suspicious.

He heard the splash of water and left the bed, wrapping a pelt about his shoulders and padding to the door. Opening it, he found her in a tub, and the scene afore him drew the air from his lungs. Firelight sheened her bare wet skin in deep gold, only the tips of her breasts hidden beneath the water. Her hair pooled in the water and draped over her arms as she dragged the cloth down her throat. Her head tipped back, her maid poured water over her hair, wringing it out foot by foot, then laying the mass over the lip of the tub. Julianna rose and Draegon's groin tightened to near bursting. She was exquisite, her breasts plump and full, her waist nipping to flare into gently rounded hips. The deep red patch atween her thighs glistened with droplets, and in the warmth of the darkened room, he scented her like a stag scents a doe.

Oh, God, I will come apart with my want of my wife, he thought, his fingers gripping the pelt as he sagged bonelessly against the door's frame. Slowly, her gaze lifted, and in the shadows he saw her blush. Yet she made no move to cover herself, her posture proud. The maid glanced benignly at him as she wrapped her mistress in a drying cloth, helping her from the bath. Draegon moved toward his bride, his gaze lingering over her bare shoulders, the roundness of her breasts and her dark pink nipples pressing against the wet fabric.

"The water is still warm," she offered, the maid silent with drying her hair. Softly, Julianna dismissed the girl and she gathered her basket and left.

Draegon seized the moment and dropped the pelt, then peeled his braes down. He stared at her, naked and erect, his silver eyes begging for her touch.

Julianna spared the unsettling length of velvet steel a glance, not giving in to the desire peaking through her and moved to the fire. She heard him step into the bath. He thought to shock her, but she'd touched him this morn, toying with him as she'd recently realized he'd done with her the morning afore. 'Twas a living thing, she'd discovered, his manhood. Flexing to her touch, elongating for her and weeping a smooth liquid like a drop of dew. She wanted to experience the hard slide of him into her body, his moisture melting with hers. Her breath shuddered and she held his gaze, his silver eyes smoldering over her with a silent message of sexual hunger. She moved closer to the fire, letting the drying cloth drop to the floor and felt his gaze on her back like the heavy stroke of his hand. She let him look, aching for him, then slipped into a heavy robe and combed out her hair. 'Twas torture not to run into his arms.

They spoke not a word, yet watched the other intently. Neither made a move to take what they desired, and Draegon thought he should be knighted again for his restraint. Loving Julianna would be wild and rich, but she had to come to him. Or there would be no living with the woman.

He soaped his hair and she took up a pitcher, waiting in silent question. Draegon cast her a suspicious glance, then nodded, enjoying the sluice of warmth liquid, her fingers massaging in his hair. She picked up the square of cloth, soaping it afore stroking it over his back. Her touch was slow and filled with intent, and Draegon leaned forward and prayed for patience. Her hand moved slowly across his skin, low on his spine, then she shifted to the side of the tub to wash his chest. He leaned back, his gaze lingering over her profile, and he resisted the urge of sliding his hand inside her gaping robe and feeling the satiny weight of her breast in his palm. She dipped the cloth beneath the water, over his stomach, and the back of her wrist brushed his manhood. He flinched, his gaze flashing to her bowed head. Yet she seemed not to notice, completing the task, then rinsing him without meeting his gaze. Done, she moved toward the chamber door. Pausing on the threshold, she glanced back, the heavy robe gathered at her breasts, her flawless shoulders exposed.

Draegon never wanted to make love to her more than in this moment.

"Good morn, my love."

Her smile was elegant and light. "Good morn, m'lord," she said in a husky voice. "Sleep well?"

Draegon eyed her. 'Twas a strange mischief in her green eyes. He was not certain he wanted it clarified. She gave him her back, letting the robe slide luxuriously down her spine as she swept into the chamber. Draegon hurried though his bath, yet by the time he'd scraped his beard and managed to find a drying cloth, she was clothed and on her way out the door, leaving him dripping wet, aroused and alone.

"Draegon!"

Draegon was in the tilt yard when he heard it—his name screamed in terror. He dropped his shield and with sword in hand, he ran, busting into the castle and taking the stairs two at a time. Outside the antechamber Julianna's maid wrung her hands, her face cloaked in fear. Numbly, the girl pointed, and just as he reached for the latch, the shriek of his name trembled the walls. He thrust open the door and froze.

Four squawking birds were making a nest in her hair.

"I swear by all that is sacred I will roast you like your kin," Julianna muttered, then winced. "Draegon!"

"Aye."

She spun about, her eyes sharp with anger.

His lips quivered. 'Twas painful not to laugh. Each bird had found a spot on her mass of red waves and was swiftly drawing it into knots.

"Help me, you fool! Or I will have to shear myself like a Norman!"

Instantly, he crossed the room and unlatched the window. The birds immediately perked to the cool air and fled. Julianna sank to the floor, rubbing her scalp.

"Are you harmed?"

"Other than my pride? Nay." She cocked a look to where he was leaning against the casement.

"Seal that afore the bloody things come home to roost."

He did, chuckling faintly, yet not soft enough to suit her mood.

"What possessed you to leave those awful things uncaged?"

"The vender swore they were tame and would sing," he said, collecting her comb from the chest and crossing to where she sat on the rug afore the fire.

"Well, they shrieked worse than the wind, stunk like the privy, and your coin was wasted."

He settled to the carpet, taking up a lock and working the tangles as if he'd done so for years. She eyed him. "Four calling birds. Honestly, Draegon."

"I apologize, love." He met her gaze and smiled, chagrined. "You were a most amusing sight."

"I am delighted to entertain you." Yet again it proved the man still did not think beyond the moment. How he had even survived battle and prison was a mystery. Yet he had. He'd survived and was home, so near, so eager to take her as his true wife. And she wanted to be in his arms. His head bent on his task, she stared at it, touching the soft black waves falling to his shoulders.

" 'Tis you who are in need of a shearing," she said softly. And she remembered this morn, his carved body stone-hard lying against hers, his warm arousal in her hand whilst he slept, seeing it at his bath. Her skin flushed hot and she licked her lips, trying to control her quickening breaths.

"You can do it this eve tide, if you've the notion."

"Trust me with aught so sharp?"

Only his gaze shifted. "I trust you with my life, Julianna, and my heart."

She felt dragged into his silver eyes, her heart pounding faster. "Trust you my judgment?"

His forehead knitted briefly.

"Have you spoken to Lucan?"

His features tightened guiltily.

"Why does this not surprise me?" she muttered dryly.

"There has not been a proper moment."

"You summon him to the solar and speak. What moment need you?"

"Julianna," he sighed.

"I do not understand you, Draegon." She snatched the comb from him and, lifting her hair, worked furiously at the knots. "You have all any man could want and 'twould have fallen to ruin without Lucan, yet you cannot thank him?" She shook her bowed head. "Is your pride so great?"

"Nay, for you have humbled me enough these past days."

She looked up, and he was surprised to find her eyes misted with unshed tears. "Apparently nay enough."

He scowled. "Do not press me on this, woman. I forbid the discussion."

Abruptly, she stood, and he rose, holding her gaze. That she brushed at tears cut him to the core and he reached for her, murmuring her name. She batted his hands away, stepping back.

"Had I not chosen the convent I would be wed to Lucan now." His features yanked taut. "To me, you were dead. To him, you were dead. He did not offer for my lands and dowry, he offered for your memory. For his love for you alone, Draegon. His duty to you!" A tear rolled down her cheek. "You shame me by not acknowledging it. And you shame this marriage in front of his very eyes and those of the people. Think you they do not talk of it?"

His spine stiffened. "None would dare say such—"

"Make no excuses for the truth, Draegon."

He folded his arms over his chest. "And that is?"

"Your delay in righting the wrong leaves your honor tarnished."

They were deadly words and she knew it.

He lowered his arms slowly, his posture punishingly straight, his expression so black with anger she thought he'd explode.

Yet she met and matched it with a withering glare of her own. "And do not think to forbid me aught, husband."

She plopped on the bed, dragging the comb through her hair, then braiding it swiftly.

"I am your husband. I forbid you to speak of it and you have no choice."

She met his gaze as she stood, her voice grown soft. "We all have choices, Draegon." She smeared a tear from her check with the back of her hand. " 'Tis the decision of honor or self that makes us each worthy in God's eyes. He is the judge, not I."

She brushed past him, ignoring his demands that she return immediately. Draegon ground his teeth with impotent rage. The woman tried and judged, whether she chose to admit it or nay. Raking his hand through his hair, his gaze fell to the bed, and the gold threads she had woven into her hair so often they were frayed and in spots tied together to make one. He gathered them, fingering the twine, closing his eyes and dropping his head forward. His negligence pummeled him like a lash and he did not like the picture she'd painted of him. How fortunate he was that he'd come home to find her in the convent. Had he found her sharing his brother's bed, round with children that should be his, he would have turned about and gone back to Cypress. His world meant naught without Julianna. His return was no victory, but a challenge to reenter the lives he'd altered by his choices. By God, he thought vehemently, he would sooner fall on a sword point than lose her.

And in the encroaching darkness of eventide, Draegon admitted he was fearful that his brother would never forgive him for taking his right to join King Richard, and if God chose, his right to die on the battlefield.

5

Five Golden Rings

"Lady Julianna," Lucan called softly, and she looked up from her meal, then blotted her lips, leaning close. She could feel Draegon's gaze focusing on her back, as she had since their argument last eventide.

"Aye, Lucan. Is something amiss with your meal?"

"Nay, but with my sister-in-law."

She frowned softly.

"Do not give him grief over me, sister, I beg you."

"He has not righted a wrong, Lucan."

Lucan's broad shoulders moved restlessly. "I am no longer the boy, Julianna. I can take care of myself and need not to have the lady of Graycliff defend me."

She covered his hand with her own. "This I know, but be aware, 'tis not simply his negligence to you that he must rectify."

"So you hold yourself from him till he meets your demands?" Her skin pinkened and he leaned closer, his voice softer. "I am a man, I can see it. My brother is mad for you, Julianna. He speaks of you so often I am, frankly, ill from it. You confound him and he is miserable."

Her lips twitched and he noticed.

"You are vicious, woman," he chastised with a half-grin.

Her chin lifted. "I am not. I am just." Her principles were all she had right now.

"To what cost?" He squeezed her fingers, his silver-blue eyes demanding she hear him in more than words. "Know you that Draegon has not truly returned until he is returned to you. Completely."

Julianna twisted a look at her husband, and though he was addressing a servant, his gaze remained on her. His lips twisted wryly, his silvery gaze sweeping her heavily. 'Twas determination in that look, and Julianna, despite her unease, the desire pricking her body since he'd returned, increased to a deep gnawing hunger that left little room for coherent thought. Daily her reflections were interrupted by the image of him standing naked and proud afore his bath, the sound of his groans when she held him vulnerable in her hand and silently she admitted her mind was agog with ways to pleasure him.

"You hold a power, m'lady."

She dragged her gaze from Draegon to Lucan. "Giving of the flesh is nay all a marriage entails, Lucan."

"Oh, Julianna, this I know." He chuckled, low and masculine. "You have been an example of it. I pray when I find a woman, she is much like you, sister. Should I find such a prize, I am certain the marriage will never be a wearisome chore."

She patted his hand, smiling. "I will think on your words, Lucan of Graycliff—" The corner of her mouth quirked. "And since I am so adept at prayer, I will pray for a fiery love that will burn you for eternity and keep you from considering a journey to Cypress."

His grin crinkled the corners of his eyes and he drew her hand to his lips, placing a soft kiss to the back.

"Should I be jealous?" Draegon's voice came close to her ear and she jolted, turning in her chair to look at him. His face was so near she could see the flecks of black rimming the silver of his eyes, smell the exotic scent of him.

"If you are, 'tis your own foolishness."

Draegon's gaze shifted to his brother, and behind Julianna's back, the man grinned, winking. A kindred sensation connected the brothers, and though he'd caught only snatches of the conversation, he knew Lucan was true to him.

He met her gaze. "I *am* jealous, my love. I want only your attention, and you to give it only to me."

Though a warmth of love spread through her, she blinked innocently. " 'Tis folly. I am chatelaine." Her time was demanded, she was saying. "Mayhap his lordship should learn to fend for himself at times."

He refused to rise to her bait and caught her about the waist, pulling her close to whisper in her ear, "What I have in mind, only you can see to, my sweet." His teeth raked the shell of her ear, his lips tugging at her lobe, nipping her throat, briefly, hungrily, afore he drew back a fraction. Her breathing quickened and his hand at her waist shifted, the back of it rubbing beneath her breast, tucking under its plush weight. Julianna swallowed visibly, inching into his touch, impatient and aching for the feel of his palm covering her.

"Lucan, a word with you in the solar." His gaze never wavered from hers, yet her brows rose.

"Aye, Drae. If you can pull yourself away from your wife."

His eyes were filled with tender humor and made a brief, meaningful sweep down to his groin. " 'Twill be painful, but I will manage." She smiled, smug. He straightened and stood.

Julianna held his gaze, her hand lingering on his afore he nodded to Lucan. The two men left her and she struck up a conversation with Bryce whilst she waited for their return. 'Twas an hour past afore the brothers returned, smiling as they took their seats. Neither spoke of their meeting and Julianna, ever curious, simply looked at Draegon and said, "Well?"

" 'Twas a private conversation, Julianna."

She socked his shoulder. He laughed deeply, feigning an injury, and she realized she struck his old wound. Immediately contrite, she apologized, rubbing the spot. "Forgive me?"

"Always, my love." Her lashes swept up. He would, and 'twas the only reason she kept to her beliefs. "If you wish to know all, ask Lucan."

She glanced at his brother, his frown noticeable.

"Lucan?"

"With Richard's approval, I am in possession of a castle, lands, and people to care for."

She smiled brightly, glancing at her husband, then back to Lucan. Her expression fell into concern. "Yet you do not look happy over this."

"How can I go to the Crusades then?"

Battle, she thought, always battle. "Appoint a trusted steward and go. You have no bride to leave behind."

He lifted his gaze from where he was toying with his eating knife. "Is it wrong to wish for someone to miss me, to want me to return alive?"

"Nay, but I do not have to tell you the unfairness of it."

She felt her husband stiffen beside her. 'Tis another battle she still waged, she thought.

"In truth, the quest has lost its appeal."

Draegon let a breath out and Julianna knew without asking that he'd hoped to keep his brother in England and alive. She commended him for giving Lucan the choice, yet all was his decision. None could know a man's heart.

"You've plenty of time, Lucan. And must train your men," Draegon said.

Lucan simply nodded, deep in thought. Julianna turned to Draegon, her gaze slipping and sliding over him as he sat in the padded chair. Her eyes teared a bit and she reached out, cupping the side of his strong jaw. He covered her hand, turning his face into the palm and kissing the center.

Only his gaze shifted. "You are pleased?"

"You know I am."

"I would like to see you do more than smile, Julianna," he said with purpose in his tone. Understanding made her skin prick with anxiousness.

Her fingers caught in his, Draegon gestured to a servant. A yellow-haired page arrived at his side, a carved box in his hands. Draegon released his wife to push the chair back a touch, then opened the case. She inhaled at the sight of the bands of gold on blue velvet.

He removed the silver one around her head and replaced it with a delicately etched circle of gold. She touched the band at her forehead, yet quickly he captured her hand, opening yet another ring of gold and clasping it over her wrist, repeating the measure with her unadorned hand.

Sliding to one knee, he grasped her foot and drew it to his lap, brushing up her skirts and circling her ankles with the finest strands of gold she had ever seen. The entire hall had gone silent to watch, and with each circlet of gold, Julianna gasped and cried his name in a breathy rush. Tears wet her eyes.

She admired the pieces, then put her feet to the floor. He leaned forward and gazed deeply into her green eyes.

"Five golden rings, my love," he said, as if she would challenge him again.

"Oh, Draegon." She wept his name, then gave him five very long and lush kisses that brought a roaring cheer from the witnesses.

As the sound died, Lucan asked, "Why five, Drae?"
Julianna stared at her husband and the couple burst into laughter, neither answering the question.

6

Six Geese a'Laying

Snow swirled in great gusts outside the dovecote and within the confines of the woodshed, Julianna huddled in her fur robe, staring at the cart full of geese. Six geese. Where he had found them in this weather, uncooked, she did not know, but it bred an excitement over how her husband would find the means to portray the Christmas song in living creatures. She could not wait for ten lords a'leaping.

Only the geese were not a'laying a thing.

She'd checked them several times during the day, having had them presented to her like chained dogs for the hunt whilst she was breaking her fast this morn.

Last night in their bed, Draegon had once again kissed her good eventide and fell asleep. And 'twas her turn to lie awake with her body singing like a choir. It made her temper quick, and she knew if she did not do something, she would find herself unsociable company for anyone, let alone six barren geese.

Venturing closer, she made to touch a goose, but it balked at her invasion, flapping its wings. "Cease or you will be served for my lord's supper on the morrow."

The birds settled and Julianna reached, grasping a pair of webbed feet and upending the bird. She hurrumphed, then inspected each in turn, yet afore she examined the last, she heard Draegon call to her.

"Great days, woman, 'tis freezing out here. Get you inside afore you become ill."

She looked at him, holding the last goose upside down. " 'Tis a male, Draegon. In fact"—she waved to the squawking group plopped in the mound of timothy—"they are all males."

He blinked, looking at the birds, then her. "You are certain?"

She shoved the bird at his chest, forcing him to take the wing-flapping creature. "The accouterment is . . ." she eyed him with a sensual smile, "unmistakable."

"You count yourself an expert?"

Her hand slid inside his cloak, palming his groin with open desire. He choked, nearly snapping the bird in half. "Only on you, my love."

Draegon tossed the bird into the cart and grabbed his wife, backing her up against the nearest wall and crushing her mouth beneath his, lips rolling, his head angling to take more of her mouth. She responded without hesitation, her hands seeking inside his robes as his swept over the swells of her breasts, fondling them with heavy caresses. She moaned darkly, gripping his waist and arching into his hardness and, galvanized, Draegon kissed her and kissed her, hurriedly drawing up her kirtle, seeking warm flesh in the cold breeze. He unearthed it, scooping his hands beneath her bare bottom and grinding her to him. She lifted her knee to fit him closer and his hand slipped atween her thighs. He found her hot and wet and swiftly parted her flesh, pushing two fingers inside her. She shrieked against his lips and drove her tongue deeply into his mouth.

He thrust and withdrew, wanting her naked so he could taste her nipples, her warm skin, and the liquid essence drenching his fingers. Yet Draegon wanted to feel her climax more than his own needs. His probing quickened and she whimpered over and over, fingers digging into his back. He tasted her hot, quick breaths, and against her lips, he chanted her name, how he wanted to replace his fingers with his mouth and taste all she was, all she had. He whispered what he wanted to experience with her, how he ached to be joined as one. He brushed his thumb over the bed of her sex and felt her clench down on his touch. He pushed deeper, kissed her harder, thrust his hips to hers and experienced her feminine muscles flexing and grabbing, the sudden hot gush of her desire.

He cupped the back of her head, gazing to her eyes to watch her shudder with rapture. He felt the ripple of it to his boot heels.

And still he stroked her.

She climaxed again, sobbing with the flood of passion.

Voices reached them, and Draegon finally ceased his intimate torture, aware he'd brought her to another lush peak, yet refused to have the castle folk find their lord and lady rutting in the dovecote like animals. Though that's exactly what he wanted to do.

His mouth softened on hers, tugging at her lower lip whilst she caught her breath. 'Twas incredible, seeing her pleasure, feeling it so deeply. Her lashes swept up and she stared into his eyes.

"Oh, Drae, 'twould be so with you inside me?"

The innocence in her tone unmanned him. "Better, I swear it." He stroked the nub of her desire and she inhaled on a hiss, her lids fluttering, her hands on him tightening.

He did not have to tell her the choice was hers. She knew it. Just as she knew her husband's patience could stretch only so far. Julianna wanted him to bed her, badly. So badly she would have taken the floor of the dovecote as a mattress. And when he brought his fingers to his lips, tasting her essence, Julianna nearly begged him to open his braes and mount her now. Pride was an ugly thing, she thought, yet her need to touch him overwhelmed, and through the fabric of his garments, she cupped his erection. He closed his eyes and groaned, pressing her hand tighter to his arousal.

"Ahh, Julianna. Why do you torture me so?"

" 'Tis a pain for me, too, Draegon."

He looked at her. "Then why do you not come to my bed?"

Her brows rose. "Why do you not ask to come to *mine?*"

"Julianna," he growled, thrusting into her hand.

"Ahhh, I see the truth. You wish me to come a'begging."

The quick shift of his features gave her the truth. She pushed him back, adjusting her garment.

Draegon thought he'd snap in half. "Have I not given you what you wish? Lucan has lands and a fortress finer than this and coin enough to see to its running for at least three years if he chooses to leave. What else must I do?"

She was plain about her want on their wedding day, yet the man still could not see beyond the moment. He had to discover that she wanted only to be *asked* of her choices, that she wanted to be his partner, not his chattel. There was no malice in her voice when she said, "Look deeply into yourself, Draegon."

She moved around him, running into the keep, and Draegon felt the uncontrollable need to smash something. He rubbed his aching manhood and wished he would get a sign from God as to how to deal with this female. He longed for a sedentary life, peace and quiet and children at his feet and to never pick up his sword again, save to teach a squire or two.

But his wife was tormenting him to the ends of his will.

7

Seven Swans a'Swimming

Draegon lost his tolerance for the temptation of her body next to his in the bed that night and slept afore the fire, leaving his bride to stare at his back. He did not doubt that she did. He could feel it. Deep into the night he racked his brain for the solution eluding him. At dawn, he discovered naught except that he was swiftly losing a battle he wasn't certain he needed to fight.

And it made him angry.

Whilst in the tilt yard the next morn, discussing strategy with Lucan, he heard his wife shriek. He saw castle folk scatter, yet continued with his conversation.

"Draegon," Lucan said with impatience. "Do you not hear that?"

"Aye."

"You chose to ignore the calls of a lady." 'Twas a knightly offense to do so.

"I ignore the rantings of my stubborn wife."

Lucan reared back, his brows high. "Surely the rift is not that great?"

"I do not know, for she will not tell me where it begins and ends," he groused, and winced as her voice carried to him. Then he saw her, a trail of swans, swans he had put in the frozen moat, following her like hungry children. She lurched forward when one nipped at her behind and she twisted, swatting at the creature with a broom, then rubbing her abused behind. Draegon bit the inside of his mouth in effort not to laugh. Another pecked at her braid, dragging her head back and she gathered the rope of hair, shoving it down inside her cloak.

"You trained them," she accused, stopping afore him. "You have taught them to be mean to me."

"Julianna, be serious."

"Why else do they peck only at me?" The swans surrounded her, so close she nearly fell. Draegon took pity and grabbed her afore she did. A swan beaked her cloak and tugged. She rounded, shrieking like a Scots warrior and brandishing her broom. The swans simply stared blankly at her, and Julianna did not have the heart to beat them into submission.

"There will be stuffed swan for dinner tonight," she warned with a wagging finger. As if they understood, the swans parted and she marched toward the castle proper, the broom at her shoulder, ever the ready. Control slipped and Draegon burst with laughter. She froze, looking back over her shoulder. He ceased instantly, smothering a smile.

Lucan looked at his boots. Bryce turned his back, his shoulders shaking suspiciously.

She glared at her husband, embarrassment at being made the fool heightening her color. "Do not forget that I sleep with you, Draegon of Graycliff, and you have to close those eyes sometime."

Draegon blinked. She dared much, he thought, striding to her, liking that her eyes widened with a touch of uncertainty. Swiftly, he gathered her in his arms and kissed her soundly, so hard he bent her back over his arm. Amidst the cheers of knights and pages, Julianna paid him in kind, losing the broom and gripping his hair by the fistfuls and ravishing his mouth like a crusader in full charge.

Suddenly he straightened, winded. It took him a few seconds to collect himself. Good God, the woman had an incredible mouth. "Remember the same liberty is mine, wife." He spun her about, patted her behind and gave her a shove toward the hall.

Julianna glared back at him, looking like a great red cat about to attack. 'Twas the devil in the woman, he thought warily, and 'twas time to clip her claws.

8

Eight Maids a'Milking

Draegon refused to sleep on the floor that night.

So Julianna did.

She could not share his bed when he would not see that 'twas to her he needed to make amends. To her, he needed to admit he'd been wrong. 'Twas a battle of wills, a test of their love. And she knew they both wished to be the victor. The next morning, when Draegon strode into the antechamber, interrupting her bath and followed by three maids, Julianna's mind raced through the stanzas of the song.

"What do you now, Draegon?" she asked in a bored tone.

She scrubbed her hair, then propped her foot on the rim of the bath and proceeded to take great care in cleansing her calf and thigh.

Draegon clenched his fists at the lush display for his benefit. He would not, could not yield, he thought.

"I see only three maids," she said.

The maids deposited the buckets and left in a run.

"Ahh, but eight buckets of milk."

Julianna spared the buckets a glance, hiding her smile. Clever, she thought. "You have overworked the goats needlessly, husband. They will not bear milk for some time now." That was not entirely accurate, but she needed something to throw at that smug expression. "What do you plan to do with them? Drink them?"

"Nay." She was staring at her delicate foot when Draegon dumped the first over her head. She screamed at the icy douse of liquid and struggled to rise from the tub. But he pushed her down and dumped another and another, until he held the last above her head.

Through the milky mass of hair, she spat out a mouthful and stared up at him.

"Do you call a cease to this ridiculous battle, wife?"

And give in to defeat? "Nay."

He splashed some milk into her upturned mouth. Julianna choked, waving her hands for him to cease, then shoving her hair from her eyes.

"Do you?"

"Am I only a pair of thighs to spread for you, Draegon?" The hurt in her tone was evident, yet he dumped the remaining bucketful, then shoved her under the surface. Watery milk spilled over the side onto the floor. She popped up, coughing hard.

"If you believe thus, then you are not the same woman I left four years ago."

By the time she had her hair out of her eyes, he was gone. Julianna looked around at the intolerable mess. Oh, the stink of soured milk will be hard to clean, she thought, then chastised herself for her own temperament. Silently, she insisted abstinence was worth it, would be worth it, for Draegon had to see he could not rule her. Not even her father could. Nor Prince John. Only Richard and his cause had ruled her life.

If she ever met the king again, she swore she would knock him silly for giving her so much grief.

A day later, she had more than a few misgivings about her marriage.

She wanted no more than an apology and the simple act of asking for her hand in marriage, instead of taking away the choice. She wanted to be treated as if she had more in her head than the roots of her hair. Yet the incident with the milk, which took hours to clean and even longer to rinse from her body, was the last link in the restraint of his temper. She knew Draegon too well. His patience had snapped. He'd barely spared her a glance last evening and was gone afore she stirred in the morn. The dunking created a line atween them. He spoke to her only if necessary, was cordial but cool, and he'd not kissed her once since the swans had bruised her bum.

Sighing heavily, she reasoned that it could have been worse.

He could have tossed her over his lap and beat her. But he would not.

He could have taken her body without thought to her pleasure. His temperance proved he would not. Pleasure shared was too great a prospect to ignore.

He could have sent her away. Away from her family, away from him, but she knew he needed her, knew he loved her. Yet without contact, without the gentle talk and his seductive smiles, Julianna felt alone in a castle teeming with people.

Bent over a shank of spitted meat, she sampled the sauce, then asked it be ladled over the mutton as it roasted. Was she being aught but a waspish fish wife? she thought, returning the ladle to the crock. Yet when she thought of how demanding he was, how he barged back into her life, made it his, molded the world to suit his wants and needs, she half admired him for his assertion of power. Half. Men were such bullying sorts, and King Richard the worst of them. Julianna had a power to wield, yet her body was nay a weapon and she would not use it. Regardless of how, the mere prospect sent a soft tingling down to her thighs. There were other ways bring him 'round, if only she could find them.

Her mind diverted by necessary chores, she checked the preparation of the remaining dishes, then headed to the hall to make certain the musicians were ready to perform, the hall swept, and the rushes replaced afore she went searching out her husband.

"Seen you Draegon, Cullen?" she asked the smithy. The beefy, armed man looked up from his work, then straightened and rushed to her side.

"Nay, m'lady, I think I saw him in the stable. I will fetch him, if you wish."

"Oh, nay, Cullen, you've work to do." She patted his arm affectionately. "I will find him." He nodded and, smiling to himself, went back to work. Julianna walked to the stable, yet found it nearly deserted and nay, none had seen their lord. 'Twas irritating, she thought. She'd inquired after him four times, and on each occasion, she was one step behind him. Then she found him in the armory, inspecting his hauberk. There were several pages and squires busy hammering dents from armor, grinding away spots of rust. She called to him, yet he did not look up from his chore, the young page aside him intent on his instruction.

He spoke to the boy afore turning to her. Julianna's heart leapt the instant her eyes met his, the air pushing from her lungs. How could she miss him when she could see him so clearly?

Draegon schooled his features into an impenetrable mask, when all he wanted was to go to her and kiss her daft. "Need you something, m'lady?"

"Aye, to speak with you."

He shook his head, crossing to the squire standing near a neat stack of arms. "I have to practice with Lucan." He started donning the body shields.

Her expression fell, the effect like a blade to his gullet. Would this woman forever have the power to move his emotions so brutally? "Mayhap later," he conceded in a cool tone. "At noon."

She nodded and, bowing her head, left. Draegon stared after her, his gaze lingering on her drooped shoulders, her brisk step. Yet her somber face hung in his mind. Grinding back the urge to follow her, he turned toward the squire and bid him attend his armor.

Beyond the practice field, Julianna watched her husband wield his sword at his brother, and Lucan struck back, blow after punishing blow ringing in the crisp winter day and making her wince. They were smiling at each other, she realized, having fun. Around them small groups of knights and squires sparred in mock battle, the youths with wooden swords and shields, yet no less vicious than Draegon and his brother. Tapping her foot, she folded her arms over her middle and waited for him to notice her. She did not want to call out, for although the squires used wood swords, Draegon did not, and she feared startling him might leave him vulnerable. When the battle was over, 'twas Lucan who gestured to her. Draegon spared her a glance, spoke to Lucan and another knight, then, with sword and shield in hand came to her.

"Julianna." He nodded cordially, then removed his helm, tucking it under his arm. He was winded, his hair matted to his skull, his practice armor dented and smudged with mud where he apparently had fallen. It gave her a start to think a man so big could be brought down without suffering a wound.

" 'Tis well past noonday."

He glanced at the sky. "Aye."

"You are not prepared to speak with me, are you?"

She tried to keep the irritation from her voice, but, thus far, she'd arrived at the appointed time only to be turned away when he sighted that more important matters needed his attention.

"Nay. I have practice to tend and then the quintain."

She glanced beyond him, catching Lucan's eye as he bent to position a sword in a young lad's hands. He waved and she returned it, then brought her gaze to Draegon's.

"Cannot Lucan do this?"

His spine stiffened. "Nay."

"Not even for a moment?"

" 'Tis my field, Julianna."

She nodded sagely, staring somewhere in the distance. "And like all of Graycliff, only you rule it."

" 'Tis the way of things, woman."

She lifted her gaze to his, her lips pulled tight. "So it is."

Draegon inhaled sharply. The defeat in her eyes wounded him and he struggled against the urge to take her in his arms and soothe her.

"Mayhap later, when you can spare a bit of time," she muttered, then turned away.

With a burdened heart, Draegon watched her go, aching for her, longing to discard the heavy armor and a millstone of a day to spend the afternoon in the privacy of their chamber. He missed simply talking with her, the comfort of watching her go about her day, having her close to feel her delicate presence. For the past two days, he had not come close enough to even scent her fragrance, and his soul ached for the simple lack, his imagination keeping him in a painful state of readiness around her. So he avoided her.

He was finished with her contentiousness and rebellion. He had tried patience and seduction, attempted to lure and cajole and tease. Naught was successful and he was well done with sleeping alone and always wondering if his words would provoke her. If Julianna wanted this marriage, she had to come to him.

"I have only seen her look like that once afore, Drae."

Draegon glanced to the side, arching a brow at his brother. "Oh, when?"

"After she learned you had been killed."

Draegon's features tightened.

"I do not think this plan of yours will work."

Draegon slid him a tight glance.

"To avoid her to make her want you more. 'Twas your intention, aye? And then mayhap she will do aught you bid?" The truth of his words unfolded in his brother's expression and Lucan shook his head. "Prison addled your brain, brother. Did you forget that Julianna was content with her own company for three years?"

Not liking that he'd been found out so easily made his voice harsh. "She could have left. The convent was her choice."

"Nay, not really. 'Twas the only place she could grieve for you."

Draegon scowled. "Did she not have privacy here or in her father's home?" That she had grieved at all tore at Draegon. Ahh, that he could have kept that from her, he thought regretfully.

Lucan shook his head, laughing mirthlessly to himself. "Not when she was slaughtered with men begging for her hand. *After* turning away me and Bryce."

"Julianna had a large dowry," he said matter-of-factly, ignoring the image of men slobbering at the feet of his wife. " 'Tis understandable that every landless knight for leagues would pursue her."

Lucan looked at him with complete disgust. "Good God, ofttimes you can be a complete ass." Julianna was [illegible] exciting creature, beauty undefinable, wild in the heart, and Lucan was envious. He actually ached for the heartache loving entailed. Aught would satisfy this emptiness he was constantly fighting.

Draegon faced him, his expression grim. "Need I thrash you on the field again, little brother?"

Lucan studied him. "Is it me you wish to fight or her, Drae? And what if you estrange her completely?"

" 'Tis a risk I must take. I need all of her. Not just bits and pieces."

"And what has she of you? What have you given without demanding? What have you asked of her, brother, and not taken because 'tis your right? Because of a contract signed four years ago?"

The pair stared each other down, Draegon's voice gone deadly. "You go too far, Lucan. My marriage is mine to deal with."

Lucan looked to the sky and shook his head. When he returned his gaze to his brother, he wanted naught but to beat the stuffing out of him. "I have known the woman as long as you—nay, in fact, longer, and we both know Julianna is just stubborn enough to flee to a keep in one of her holdings and do battle when you try to take her back."

"And I would." He could not live without her, yet he could not live with this wild ride of belligerence. He needed total compliance. He was, after all, her lord. If his bride did not obey, how would his people, his knights? He had humiliated himself enough for her.

"I know now I am not suited for battle in the Holy Land," Lucan said. "I cannot stomach conquering simply because I can." With that, he strode from the practice field.

His brother's words rang through his mind and he gazed across the field, catching a glimpse of her near the dovecote and remembering kissing her in there, feeling her slick warmth beneath his touch, her gasps when she found rapture in his arms. He swallowed and briefly closed his eyes, more confused than afore. Warring with going to her side or nay, Draegon finally turned toward the field and the men awaiting his command. Yet throughout the remains of the day, he wondered how had he ever thought his life here would be easier than in the belly of a prison.

9

Nine Ladies Dancing

Music floated on the warm air of the hall, men begging the favor of festively attired ladies. Tables glinted with pewter goblets and garnished platters laden with roasted mutton, crisp brown-skinned starlings, and capons stuffed with cinnamon pears. Around Julianna people laughed and drank, stole kisses, and danced to lively music. Above her, boughs of greenery hung from the rafters above the dais, ribbons of blue, green, and winter white entwined and draped, brushing her cheek. She batted at the silken strands and plucked a crust of bread from the trencher atween her and her husband. She did not eat it, her appetite gone. She offered a smile to the castle folk wishing her well for the new year and hid the fact that her husband had not so much as spoken to her this eventide.

Not even to ask her to dance.

She toyed with the crust of bread and admitted to her confusion. The distance atween them had grown more poignant in the last day and Julianna conceded that mayhap she'd been a bit harsh in her demands. The only way to reach him was to show him she loved him enough to make the effort to change. Was she not the wife he wanted, curbing her tongue and obedient to him? One would think he'd be preening with satisfaction, yet his remote look spoke of displeasure. She wanted to shout at him that she'd changed for him, that she was the bride *he* demanded, yet she kept her lips tightly clenched, the simple act scraping the very fabric of who she was. Silence was never her finest virtue.

He must reciprocate in this marriage, too, she thought. He could not expect her to concede all that she was whilst he offered naught. Telling herself that his dismissal of her feelings did not sting was a lie and she prayed they would find their way back, yet wondered just how far the divide could reach afore they could no longer touch.

She swallowed the sudden stone in her throat at her last thought and as she had done for years, kept her wounds bandaged under a polite smile and paid her attention to the gentler brother. Until Lucan excused himself to join the dancing. She felt unreasonably abandoned and chanced a look at her husband. He regarded her through suspicious eyes.

"Your meal not to your liking?" she inquired cordially.

" 'Tis fine."

"Would you care for more wine?"

He nodded and she poured, holding out the goblet. Their fingers brushed innocently, and for the briefest of moments, they remained poised, both holding the cup. She searched his handsome face, his silver eyes, for a smattering of emotion, but he broke contact, draining the goblet. Julianna cut slices of meat and pushed the trencher closer to him, then speared a dice of mutton.

" 'Tis exceptionally tender."

He leaned forward, the move quick and startling her. 'Twas ridiculous. She was not afraid of him and tipped her chin, holding out the morsel. His teeth snapped it off the tip of the blade and chewed, his gaze intense, and she wondered what was going on in his codfish of a brain.

"You wanted to speak to me. Now is the time." His caustic tone left her little prospect for harmony this night and her throat closed.

She feared for her marriage and the very notion made her heart clench in her breast. "I have naught to say any longer."

His brow arched, a single wing of inquiry.

She shrugged elegantly clad shoulders. For days she'd been plain about her disappointment in him and his unfair demands on her. He chose not to acknowledge her feelings. " 'Twas useless, m'lord. I see that now."

His heart lurched. She sounded dull, even a bit forlorn, and he watched her wipe her fingers on a cloth, then solicitously offer him the best cuts, order the finest of wines uncorked for his pleasure. This was not the Julianna he craved. This woman felt distant and meek. And alone. Remorse filled him and he scooted close, inviting casual conversation.

For a time he felt as if she were tolerating him, giving him one-word responses, neither voicing her opinion nor smiling. When she brought the chunk of meat to her mouth, he stopped her, taking it, holding it out to feed her himself. She regarded him skeptically and he arched a brow, his challenge clear. Her chin tipped a fraction and she opened her mouth, taking the meat from him, her tongue sliding across his fingers. His eyes flared, and for the first time in hours, he glimpsed the woman he loved. He offered her more, spooning a bit of seasoned peas.

"I can feed myself, m'lord." She stared at her trencher.

" 'Tis my choice."

Her gaze lowered. "As you wish, m'lord."

His brow furrowed a bit, but afore he could question her, she obediently tasted the dish, then prepared portions for him. Shaking his head, he offered her hot, spiced wine, then called for a platter of cheese. He watched her, entranced as her lovely lips pulled at the soft cubes with a sensuality that made Draegon's throat tighten. Yet she did not speak unless spoken to, did not touch him nor look his way, and he felt unease ripple through him. 'Twas as if her body was poised aside him, yet with pieces missing, tucked away from only him. His gaze on her, he gestured again for a servant, and with great flourish, a young maid with garland wreathing her hair, presented a platter stacked with orange balls.

Julianna gaped at the pile, then him. "What are these, husband?"

She'd not called him by name all evening and Draegon longed to hear it on her lips. "Oranges."

"I see that."

His lips quirked and he plucked one from the mound, slicing and paring it for her. She hung close, scenting the fruit.

" 'Tis a divine smell," she said, inhaling deeply, and his gaze flicked to the rise and fall of her bosom pillowing against his arm. Gowned to perfection, she would make any man proud to call her wife, the gold-trimmed, deep green velvet brightening the shade of her hair, the rosy hue of her skin. *She wears the five rings,* he realized suddenly, and considered what else he'd missed in the past days. He offered her a portion of the fruit, showing her different ways to eat it, and when she peeled back the fruit, juice squirted him in the cheek.

Julianna pinkened, her eyes wide. "Oh, dear." Hurriedly, she blotted the drip, juice glistening her full lips. He wanted to lick them. He wanted to lick her everywhere. As if she understood his thoughts, she quickly focused on her fruit. " 'Tis from the west?" she asked.

He eyed her briefly afore nodding. "They have some magnificent foods and spices, though I did not have the luxury in the prison, but afore that, 'twas incredible, the riches of that land," he said with a longing he did not notice.

"Do you wish to return, m'lord?"

His heart slammed to a halt and he looked at her, intense and probing. "Why do you ask this?"

She shrugged, unwanted hurt swelling in her throat. "You do not seem happy here, with me." She pushed the platter back and wondered why she invited this heartache.

"I do not wish to return."

"But you miss it."

He shrugged casually. "Battle has its own appeal."

She closed her eyes briefly. "I see naught but blood and dying, m'lord."

"Aye, so do I," he said after a small silence and she looked at him. "I want naught but to remain here, Julianna." Her gaze searched his, as if prying after a lie. "I want naught but you."

Her green eyes watered with sudden tears and Draegon groaned, tossing aside the half-peeled orange. *Ahh, God. How easily I have crushed her spirit,* he thought, bending close and pressing his lips to her forehead. He felt like the lowest form of life for allowing even one moment of doubt to give her such heartache.

"I love thee, Julianna." She choked on a sob, covering her mouth with her hand, the other gripping his sleeve. He tipped her chin and her lashes swept up. "I always will."

Her lips quivered against a sob, her eyes filled with uncertainty. "But we are coming apart, Draegon."

"Nay," he insisted fiercely. "Nay. I will not allow it."

Unmindful of the eyes watching, Draegon cupped her jaw in his palms and laid his mouth over hers. She whimpered against his lips, her own trembling with tears. His throat felt raw, his Adam's apple shifting as he tenderly kissed her, his lips whispering back and forth over hers. That he'd perpetrated her mistrust by ignoring her severed his heart and his chest tightened. He deepened his kiss, softly coaxing her to respond, then tasted the salt of her tears afore drawing back, his silver eyes smoldering with desire and an apology.

They released a shuddering breath together and he sat back, clutching her hand in his. But Draegon's discomfort did not abate, for she wore no smile, her eyes on his thumb making slow circles over the back of her hand.

She looked utterly lost and he did know how to find her.

With a nod from him, the music changed and Julianna looked up to see her ladies leave their chairs and move afore the dais. They dipped a curtsey, then swept in a colorful swirl across the floor, their eyes seeking the approval of their lord. But Draegon saw only his wife.

The shadow in her eyes gave him pause, and he wanted to hold her, comfort her. He counted himself an imbecile for giving her a moment's doubt of his love, his desire to make a home with her. He'd dreamed of a sedentary life with her and he thought again of how fortunate he was that he'd come home to find her without a husband and children. He wanted children with her, fiery little red-haired females to drive him insane. He needed that wild madness. And he was desperate for her to come to his bed and share hers with him.

He squeezed her hand and Julianna met his gaze, her breath catching at the smoldering look in his silver eyes. It swept her, her awareness of him suddenly keen, sharp with want and sparking through her blood. The sensation intensified when he leaned closer, his broad shoulders blocking the light, hemming her against the back of her chair. The air grew heavy with the scent of him as he brought her hand to his lips, kissing her palm, the inside of her wrist.

Her breath shuddered softly and Julianna licked her dry lips. "I count only eight ladies dancing."

His gaze shifted to hers. "Do you?"

She nodded, entranced by his mouth moving over her skin.

"Mayhap we should make it nine?"

Slowly, he drew back and stood, gently pulling her to her feet, and without hesitation, Julianna accepted his hand. Leading her to the open space, he took her through the intricate steps, his gaze holding her prisoner, his touch, a touch she had not felt in days, bewitching her. To the music, she turned, and his hand lingered at her spine, sliding over the velvet waist of her gown with warm familiarity afore he stepped away. They came together and his gaze raked her with undeniable hunger, a clear invitation of carnal pleasure, and Julianna thought her knees would melt.

She wanted him, beyond all the trouble, she wanted him.

Why do I hold myself from him, when he has my heart? she wondered. *Am I seeking what is not in him to give? How long can I bend a man of such strength afore I break all we have?*

Around them the stone floor stood empty, the folk circling to watch. He was graceful for a man his size, and Julianna could not recall a time when he had looked so handsome. His surcoat of black velvet shot with silver magnified the power he exuded and she wanted to feel this strength around her. 'Twas as if the years apart had not yet been bridged with a single touch, a fiery kiss, and she were looking at her resurrected love for the first time in so many years.

And she wanted to be held and touched and tasted by him.

"Julianna," he growled as he spun her afore him like a child's top. " 'Tis a danger in looking at me like that."

She glanced back over her right shoulder. "A danger to whom?"

"Your virtue."

" 'Tis yours, m'lord," she said simply.

His brows shot up and he stumbled to a halt.

Her gaze on his chest, she took a breath and spoke softly. " 'Tis the only gift I can give you that no one else can."

Grasping her upper arms, he pulled her close. "You do so willingly?" Draegon swallowed, gazing down at her.

He did not breathe until she nodded shakily.

The music played and people stared.

And Draegon realized she'd been pleasing him all evening and wondered if now was included. "I care not for submission in my bed," he murmured. "Do not come to me only to reconcile, Julianna." His grip on her arms flexed and his voice went husky. "I could not bear it."

Her head tipped back, she searched his gaze. "I come for my need of you, Draegon. For this hunger you build in me." Laying a palm to his broad chest, she softly rubbed the black velvet, and the simple touch jolted him to his boot heels. "I give to you not out of your right as my husband, but of mine as your wife. My choice. My gift. For you and no other."

Something solid shattered inside him, breaking loose the passion he'd capped for days.

"Draegon, you ruin the dance!" Lucan shouted over the music. "If you wish to converse with your wife, do it elsewhere."

Staring at her, he said, "We bid you all good night,"

then caught her hand and fairly dragged her along to meet his long, eager strides. Julianna blushed, for all knew his intent, and the very thought of losing herself in his arms sent a tingling heat skating over her warm skin. As she mounted the steps, her thoughts swelled with the moments in the dovecote, the rocking thrust of his fingers inside her body and the glorious explosion that followed. She quickened after him, atween her thighs warming with anticipation of more.

'Twas not until he had passed through the antechamber, dismissed the maid attending there and closed the door behind them, that he turned to her.

They stared, breathing heavily, bodies alive and pulsing.

Julianna felt perched on the edge of the tower ledge, waiting for the stone to crumble and hurl her into the unknown.

Draegon was afraid he'd break her in half if he so much as touched her. His body bore years' worth of expectancy, so tight and throbbing he thought he would climax with a simple kiss. His fingers curled into fists at his side. *Please, Lord, don't let me hurt her.*

Then she reached, her fingertips brushing over his nipple hidden beneath the velvet surcoat. He inhaled, racked with the sweetest of sensations.

"Julianna."

Her hand slid lower and the muscles of his stomach clenched. She took a single telling step. "I want you, Draegon. Come to me."

With a growl of sheer masculine hunger, he gathered her in his arms, crushing her mouth beneath his. She sank into him, her arms wrapping around his neck, her body lain to his like plush fur. His tongue raked her lips, her teeth, then pushed atween, and Julianna moaned with pleasure, a sound Draegon coveted. He fell back against the door, pulling her atween his spread thighs, ridiculously anticipating the feel of her fingers in his hair, and when it came, he shuddered with the familiar feel of it, deepening his kiss. He did not question the why of her acquiescence, not clearly, almost afraid he was dreaming. His hunger to claim his wife, to bind her to him, roared through in his dark possession, in his broad hands roughly mapping the contours of her spine, her buttocks, and pressing her to his arousal.

Julianna arched into it, his excitement giving her a power she was impatient to explore. The need to touch him, to give him the pleasure he'd given her in the seclusion of the dovecote overwhelmed her, and she tore at his belt, flinging it aside, then seeking skin beneath the surcoat. He tugged at the laces of her gown.

She worked the surcoat upward, and he stopped kissing her long enough to yank it off over his head and come into her arms.

"Draegon," she cried softly. "I need to touch you." It wasn't enough and she pulled his lawn shirt off over his head. Her hands raked over his bare skin, her nails teasing as he tugged frantically at the laces of her gown. Impatient, he withdrew his dagger and cut them. Sleeves fell, the bodice gave, and he helped it down, tasting every lush inch exposed. Then he wrapped his lips around her nipple, drawing it deeply into his mouth. Julianna gasped, then dropped her head back, offering him a feast for the starving.

"Oh, God above," he murmured, wildly laving at her breasts and pushing the gown lower, revealing her waist and trim hips. He lifted her high in his arms, his mouth on her breast as he stepped over the pile of clothing and advanced toward the bed. He never made it there, sliding her down his length and taking her mouth again afore her feet touched the floor. His kiss was never ending, even as she kicked off her slippers, even as his palms filled with her breasts.

Even as she tore at his braes and dipped her hand inside.

Draegon threw his head back and Julianna watched his expression, the pain and pleasure blending in his features. She stroked him, smoothed her fingers over the tip of him, and with a quick snap he caught her hand, bringing it to his chest.

"Do not," he managed on a hot breath. "I will ruin this for us."

"Only once," she said, and his expression darkened, his smile full of sensual promise. He bent to strip off his boots, but never made it, her touch branding him, the wild ride of her hands over his muscled body leaving him weak and barely hanging on to his control. He caught her against him, showering her throat, her shoulders, with hot restless kisses and loving her whispery breaths, the way her head rolled, her hair sweeping lazily over his back. Draegon tortured her, his hands and mouth creating a tingling moist path over her skin. Again and again he came back to her breasts, as if not to neglect a single portion of creamy flesh. He turned her and devoured the flesh tightly drawn on her spine, the cushioning swell of her buttocks. He feasted as he was wont to do for years. On his knees, he tasted the lean line of hip to thigh, his fingers dipping into her moist softness, taunting her passion until Julianna was panting and groping for him.

The dense patch of femininity lured, and he covered her softness with his mouth.

"Drae!" she cried out, and his tongue probed. "Oh, sweet heaven!" She twisted and he cradled her hips, imprisoning her for his assault, laving the sweet musk of woman. Her fingers plowed his hair, her body undulating with the coming explosion. He took her to the brink and then receded until she shrieked in frustration, beating his shoulders. His chuckle hummed against her flesh and he drove deeper, peeled her wider.

"Draegon, cease. I will perish!"

Suddenly, he pulled her to his lap, fitting her thighs over his hips and thrusting two fingers inside her. She arched sharply, gripping his shoulders.

"I want you there."

" 'Twill hurt, love."

"No worse than now," she panted and looked down. He was thick and erect and her fingers closed over his arousal. He groaned and worked for air, and Julianna stroked the tip of him back and forth over her slick flesh, guiding him inside her. He quaked, his hands on her thighs flexing with his restraint. She rubbed her breasts across the carved marble of his chest, inching higher on his lap and her body stretched to accommodate him, his fullness wild in coming.

Her breath came in short gasps and he let her control the moment.

She stared into the eyes of the man she loved. "I want no restraint from you, Draegon."

He brushed loose strands from her face and kissed her, her own glorious essence on his lips, his hips gently rocking into her when he was wont to push her to her back and pound to completion.

"My gift awaits," she whispered.

And Draegon took it, grasping her hips and thrusting upward, impaling her. She gasped at the sudden burst of pain, shuddering in his arms as he smothered a groan and held her tightly.

"Would that I could have spared you," he said, raining kisses over her face, her throat. He slipped his hand atween their bodies, delicately stroking the bead of her sex.

Julianna shivered with pleasure. "Oh, sweet mercy."

" 'Twill be none for you this night," he promised, and he moved a fraction, giving her hips motion and showing her she commanded, that he was at her mercy. The pain of her virtue vanished with the essence of slick heat and escalating passion. Julianna moved, leaving his body, then sinking onto him again and again, each thrust, each returning plunge blossoming with new discovery, every inch of her sensitive to his touch, to his strong thighs atween hers, his thumbs circling her nipples. Her skin glistened with dew and he licked it. She gripped his shoulders, gazes locked, his features tightening as she shoved harder and harder against him in intense quick pulses.

He was coming apart and Draegon prayed for control. Naught was more erotic than watching her ride him, feeling her soft, slick skin yield to his hard staff, rhythmic friction shooting her body closer to the summit. Sensations came harder, her body moving faster, wilder.

"Oh, Draegon." Her fingers raked through his hair, her head angling back and forth in a thick, liquid kiss and he felt her impatience. "Draegon!"

"Aye, aye, take, my love, take your pleasure," he whispered in her ear, meeting her every thrust, understanding her hunger. "Let me feel you find it."

He shoved and feminine muscles flexed and jerked, squeezing him, and Julianna slammed back, a fountain of exquisite pleasure propelling her into a new bright world of carnal indulgence.

Hot liquid drenched him and Draegon threw back his head and growled, jamming her down onto him, arching, pushing and pushing, spilling his seed into her. They strained against each other, silver eyes staring into green, their breaths mingling as they sought to prolong the rapture of becoming one.

Eyes remained locked, long after the passion faded,

and when she sagged bonelessly against him, Draegon stood, her legs wrapping his hips, his body still heavy inside hers as he moved to their bed. There he knelt, carefully lowering her to her back. He made love to her again, slowly this time, discovering her secrets and letting her discover his.

And for one glorious night, the lord and lady of Graycliff found peace.

10

Ten Lords a'Leaping

He'd never been this happy, Draegon thought, his eyes on his slumbering bride as he fastened his belt. Last night burned through his memory again, her abandon, her wildness. Once introduced into the play of love, Julianna was insatiable, her lack of inhibition taking him to places he'd never dreamed existed. When she stirred softly, arching like a graceful cat, Draegon felt his body call to her with a swiftness that was almost embarrassing. She twisted to her side, the sheets falling away from her breasts to pool at her waist.

"Good morn, husband."

His smile was full and genuine, his gaze raking her lush bosom. "Good morn, my wife," he said, moving toward the bed and pressing a knee to it. Immediately she rose up, reaching for him and pulling him atop her. Draegon covered her mouth with his own, warm hands enveloping her breasts, thumbs softly circling her nipples.

"Do not toy with the lock if you do not wish to take the prize," she moaned against his mouth, spreading her thighs for him.

His chuckle was more of a growl, his breathing as rapid as his growing need of her. "I took it last night."

Julianna wedged her hand atween them, seeking and

finding his engorged manhood. Excitement sped through her. "Ah, 'tis more there for you, my lord husband."

With frantic moves, he tore at his clothing, releasing himself and pushing into her soft depths, filling her completely. She purred for him, wrapping her legs around his hips and dragging him deeper. He smoothed her hair back from her face, pushing slowly, purposely, withdrawing and watching her pleasure unfold with each measured stroke.

"Find the prize, Julianna."

"Only with you," she said, her feminine muscles gripping him. He pulsed inside her, growing tighter, harder, and she urged him on, begging to bring them to fulfillment now, quickly, for she could not suspend her desire. Draegon lost himself in her, pounding her across the bed and she laughed, welcoming him, her hips rising to greet the sudden insistent push of him.

Tremors slaughtered them, trapping them in a place only they could find, and she strained, cupping his buttocks, grinding him to her. Draegon threw his head back and moaned her name as they quaked with spasm after spasm. They sank into the ticking, breathing hard, and 'twas several long moments afore either could move.

He kissed her leisurely and loved the disappointment on her face when he left her body, the look tempting him to stay.

Julianna rose from the bed, walking to the pitcher and bowl. He crossed to the fire and lifted a pot of warming water and brought it to her. She looked up at him, smiling tenderly and he could not resist stealing another kiss.

"Dress in something," he pleaded. "Or I will never leave you in peace."

Her eyes glowed with her new found power. "If I do not wish to be left in peace?"

"I cannot. I have to go." He dropped a kiss to her forehead and turned away to wash and finish dressing.

"What takes you from me so early?"

He laughed shortly. " 'Tis nigh past noon." Her eyes widened. "Aye, and the hunting party awaits."

Excitement lit her features and she hurried through her toilette. "Oh, 'tis been years since I've had the chance—"

"You cannot attend, Julianna."

She stopped pulling on her kirtle and stared. "Why not?"

" 'Tis for men."

"Ridiculous. You know I can hunt as well as any of your men."

"As my squire, mayhap."

Her eyes narrowed, her expression tight. "Draegon."

She *could* hunt, but he would not risk an accident. "We hunt boar and 'tis too dangerous. I forbid it."

Her expression fell into sadness. "You have not changed, Draegon. You have not even made an effort."

He scowled at her. Had he not righted the past four years and wed her? Had he not given Lucan holdings to please her? Was he not acting the fool with his gifts, hoping one would put a smile on her face? "I have done more than my share."

"Yet you do not cease to rule me."

"I am your husband. I know what is best."

Julianna jerked her kirtle about her hips, adjusting the fit afore she sat to put on her slippers. "*You* know, *your* way," she muttered. "Saint Crispin, I should have realized." Could he not see she wanted only to be considered in decisions? That aught he did affected her life? Under her breath she said, "And how the bloody hell could he know what was best for her, he'd been gone for four years!"

"Do not mutter."

She stood, her eyes filled with green fire and hurt. "I *will* mutter. I shall scream and throw crockery, if I feel the need. And I will *hunt* if *I* so choose. I decide what is best for me!"

He stared down at her, clenching his fists and wanting to shake her. "You will remain behind!"

"I have remained behind for years, Draegon. If you cannot do the courtesy of asking after my wants instead of being blind to any but your own—"

"I saw to your wants last evening," he interrupted with a rascally look down her body.

She inhaled. "Beast! You crass . . . insufferable brute! I regret that your touch made me addlepated." His expression darkened, his eyes flickering with something akin to hurt. "Last eventide you said you no longer wanted submission and I believed you had accepted me as I am, that you loved me enough to want more from me than to be chattel and whore."

His eyes flared. "Do not speak such."

She opened her mouth, then snapped it shut. "As you wish, m'lord."

He arched a brow. Her sudden acquiescence disturbed him, and he realized he preferred her fire to this silence. "My sweet." He came to her, gripping her upper arms. She lifted her gaze to his and Draegon could not read her emotions deeply cloaked in a bland expression. "You argue over inconsequential things."

Her lips tightened, yet she did not comment.

"I only wish to see you safe."

"Do not speak to me of safe, my lord." She jerked out of his grasp and, still plaiting her hair, marched to the door. "I am not the one who got himself wounded and thrown into prison."

Draegon stared after her, then raked his fingers through his hair. Last eve he had a wild, loving woman in his arms. He could not have been more blessed than the moment she had come to him. He wondered through the day and the hunt how he had managed to make a mess of such a peaceful night. Apparently, taking Julianna to his bed did not mean he had won her heart.

Julianna did not go on the hunt, yet 'twas her choice. She did not want to be near her husband for fear he would kiss her till her body melted and her will vanished. Her head bowed, she moved aimlessly through the bailey, unaware of the odd looks tossed her way. She sighed, her shoulders drooping inside the heavy cloak. How could he not see she asked so little? The man had never asked for her hand in marriage, he took it. He never asked of her wants; he forbade, demanded, or ordered. Julianna had never liked being ordered about and strove for years to always take a person's feelings into consideration. Resentment brewed too easily with cold demands and orders. The servants of the castle worked harder and faster at their jobs when she asked them to perform a task. Though none would dare defy her, the consideration was worth the friendships and respect she had with her people.

And somewhere atween England and the Holy Land, Julianna had lost her best friend. And she wondered how to make him see *his* friend was still here.

Deep in her thoughts and walking without direction, Julianna did not hear the thundering hooves until too late. She swung around, her eyes widening as a stallion sped past her, close enough to brush her cloak and send her stumbling back. She spun away only to dart from the path of another knight astride a horse. Horses and riders jumped over logs and barrels and even carts. Over the din, she heard Draegon call out to his men as he raced across the yard to her She stood perfectly still, her heart pounding as she waited for the riders to give her space.

Gasping for air, she flinched when Draegon touched her shoulder, and she rounded on him.

"Are you hurt?"

When she simply blinked at him, his hands raced over her, searching for wounds. "Julianna!"

"Nay. I am fine."

He clutched her to him, but she fought his embrace. " 'Twas your damned lords a'leaping!"

He stumbled through an explanation. "Aye, but I thought you would stop when they began, yet—"

The fight died swiftly and her body relaxed in his strong sheltering arms. "My mind was not on my feet," she muttered.

"Then on me, mayhap?"

She met his gaze, and Draegon watched her expression close to him.

"Indulge yourself with the fantasy, m'lord." His indifference to her wants was no longer tolerable. "For 'twill be the only place you can."

Scowling, he released her and stepped back. "Why do you this, Julianna? Over a bloody hunt?"

"A hunt!?" She blinked. "You think my anger is for—ahh, never mind." She waved him off. "Mayhap you have sustained too many blows to the head to see me clearly."

His look turned thunderous.

It had no effect on her whatsoever. Brushing past him, she walked across the field leaving Draegon to contemplate every word she had said to him in the past eleven days.

* * *

"Speak to me."

In the antechamber, she looked at him, yet said nothing.

"Woman, I swear I will beat the words from you."

Her expression said his threat held no value and he knew 'twas so. He could no more strike her than allow this silence and submission to go on. Without a word, she'd tended his every need, serving him, helping him with his clothing, bathing him, and when she went to dry him, he'd had enough.

"Cease!" He snatched the drying cloth and finished the task himself. "Get you to bed."

She bowed her head and obediently swept into their chamber, promptly slipping beneath the mound of furs. Through the open door, Draegon watched and disliked the silence, the compliance. Yet her disregard for his orders was intolerable. She was his wife, for God's sake. He demanded her respect and obedience.

Robed, he moved into the chamber, yet did not climb into bed. Dropping into a cushioned chair, he stretched his legs out to warm his feet. *Aye,* he thought, *I have her obedience. Now.* Yet gone was the warm conversation and sensual teasing. Gone was the fire and quick wit and verbal sparring he enjoyed with her. Gone was his friend, leaving him with naught but a mere shadow of the woman he loved.

11

Eleven Pipers Piping

Yet the shadow of a woman he saw was only in his presence, Draegon realized as he glanced up from the instructions he was offering a page. He watched her move about the bailey, her voice carrying on the wind.

"Mind you take this to the hall, Ester?"

The maid smiled and curtsied, taking the basket of bread so fresh it steamed the air with its warmth. Julianna thanked the girl and walked toward the smithy. Leaving the boy, Draegon discreetly followed.

"How goes the gift, Cullen?"

The big armed man moved quickly toward her, showing her something wrapped in a tanned hide, but at this distance Draegon could not see clearly. Yet he saw delight spread across her features, her bright smile directed at the smithy's handiwork. And she rewarded him with a kiss on the cheek. The burly man blushed, folded the hide, and with a few whispered words, went back to work.

Draegon ducked out of sight, watching as she moved from spot to spot in the bailey, making several trips from the cook house to bring hot wine to the guards, a bit of bread and cold meat for Cullen and the cooper. And on each occasion, Draegon noticed the smiles and willing service they gave her, the way she joked with them, how she stopped to throw balls of snow with several children. He stepped out of hiding and one hit him in the chest. The children gasped and scattered, even with her assurances 'twas only an accident.

He stared at her.

She lowered her eyes to the ground.

The subservience irritated him and he stepped closer. Even at this distance, he ached for her. Draegon realized that Julianna was more lord here than he. That Julianna was more considerate than he. She asked for help, did not demand it. He'd seen her do such since his return, yet he ignored it and the full value of its meaning. Julianna did not like to be told what she could and could not do. He had always known this. Had he not reminded himself that her will was powerful, that patience was his only route?

And why had he wanted a different woman than the one he'd loved for years, the one he'd fought Saracens to hold again?

"Is there aught I may do for you, my lord?"

Draegon ground his teeth in frustration. "Will you look at me, Julianna?"

She did, her eyes green cool and distant.

Draegon felt as if he were floundering in a river. "Where is the woman who knocked me from my horse when she was but ten summers old?"

Her features softened a fraction. "She is here, m'lord."

"She would not allow herself to hide beneath rules."

Her chin tipped a notch. "I have little choice, as you have seen to."

The truth stung. "And what have you given me but a fight?"

" 'Tis a battle you have wrought, Draegon." Her voice wavered. "And only you can end it."

With that she spun away and rushed to an old woman struggling under the weight of a bundle of sticks.

Julianna sat in the solar, ruining the stitches of a tapestry she had begun four years ago. Irritated that she could not concentrate, she dismissed the ladies gathered with her and plucked the threads from the cloth. Her eyes watered and she paused, her head bowed as she fought fresh tears.

Again, she asked herself if she could have explained her point more plainly, yet she knew Draegon was not stupid. If he wanted to see it, he would.

The sudden high-pitched melody shattered her solitude and she frowned, leaving her stool and following the noise to the window. Struggling under the frozen latch, she opened the wood door and peered over the casement. Below in the courtyard were, she counted to be certain, eleven pipers. Most playing off key. Behind them, leaning against the west wall of the castle, Draegon stood, his arms folded over his middle, his shoulders swathed in snow-dusted furs. Wind ruffled her hair and Julianna snatched up a coverlet, wrapping warmly and staring back. She tried to look at the pipers shivering in the cold, but her eyes strayed to her husband. How could he continue with this silliness when 'twas more at stake atween them than twelve gifts? She would much rather have twelve nights in his bed. Twelve decades of loving him.

When the melody finished, she applauded, shouting down for the minstrels to come inside and warm themselves, that she would see them well fed and with a place to sleep the night.

Draegon's features tightened at that and he knew more and more that he was hearing Julianna without her speaking the words. When he followed the players inside, he found her serving them herself until servants scurried to do the job. She finished pouring spiced wine for a flutist afore handing the ewer over to a servant.

If you cannot have the courtesy of asking after my wants . . .

Yet Julianna saw to the smallest need of a lowly musician. Draegon had not thought to even offer the players such accommodations. 'Twas her position to see to these things, he thought righteously. Nay, he realized, it was *their* position. And Draegon was addressing only to his own. He moved toward her, not liking how her posture stiffened, nor the fraudulent smile plastered across her lips. He caught her hand and pulled her from earshot.

"I need to speak with you, privately. Will you meet me in the solar?"

"Why?"

He cast a discreet glance about and felt every pair of eyes upon them. "Care you to have our problems aired for the entire castle?"

She leaned closer. "The problem lies in you, Draegon. I have changed. I have become the wife you desired."

"Nay, you have not."

Her brows rose. "Have I not seen to your needs and those of our people?" Her tone was even. "Have I not *asked* after your desires? Have I not accepted your wishes and obeyed you?"

"Aye, aye, aye!"

People looked up and stared.

Julianna did not spare them a glance. "Are you not pleased?"

"Nay."

She reared back with false shock. "Me thinks my lord does not know his true wants."

'Twas true, damn her, but admitting he was confused out of his mind would not be done in the hall. He inched closer, his voice low. "Your lord would like privacy to discuss those wants with you."

"Have I a choice?"

A growl rumbled in his chest. He would get her to listen to him, talk with him. But by God, if he had to humble himself, he would not do it in public. *That* he was done with.

"Aye, Julianna. I await your summons." He stepped back and bowed slightly, then moved to the hearth, quickly joining the conversation with his knights.

Julianna stared at him for several moments, hope pulling at her heart, and would have remained there half the night, simply staring at him, yet she was called away.

She did not summon him, yet he did not come to their room that night. Impatient, she peeked around the curving stone wall of the staircase and she saw him, deep in his cups, he and his brother tipping back goblet after goblet of wine. For a time she perched on the cold stone steps and watched him, then returned to their chamber, pacing. She waited and waited to speak with him as he had asked, yet he did not come. Hours later, when blue-magenta colored the night sky and still he did not come, she crawled into their bed. Inhaling the scent of him on the sheets, Julianna curled into a ball and gave in to her fear. The fear that they would never find peace if they did not find it afore the twelfth night.

12

Twelve Drummers Drumming

At first 'twas amusing, the boys trailing her through the morn, yet now the incessant drone of drums made from crates and pots and whate'er the boys or Draegon could find was slowly driving her to the brink of losing her temper. She refused to give it fruition, though the boys did try their best, remaining outside her chamber when she was wont for a bit of silence. Snickers and sympathetic smiles chased her as she went from chore to chore. Julianna smiled sweetly and continued. The boys were running out of stamina around noon day, and on her way to the smokehouse, she caught a glimpse of Draegon on the practice field. She waved, noticing his bleary eyes even at this distance. Poor man. But then, he would not be feeling the effects of a drunk had he come to their room last evening. Mayhap he did not, in truth, wish to speak with her?

Hesitantly Draegon waved back, frowning. The noise was agitating the bloody life out of him, why not her? She did not drink herself into a stupor, he thought, wincing at the rhythmic thump in his head when the boys started up again, trudging after her toward the smoke house. 'Twas near eventide when he noticed the sound had blessedly ceased and he went searching for her.

Draegon froze at the entrance to the hall, eyeing the twelve boys sitting at a trestle, their mouths full of food. Julianna stood at the far end of the table, arms folded and chin high, her very stance daring him to deny the boys a meal and warmth.

Draegon gallantly saluted her effort to silence his "gift."

She curtsied elegantly, her demeanor feeling more remote than ever, and Draegon wanted to shake her, needed to talk with her, but in his present state, with his head pounding like the lad's drums, he knew they would only make a grander mess of his marriage. He was not willing to risk it. Rubbing his temples, he turned away, not seeing her frown of concern nor take a step toward him.

Draegon was in the stable, currying his horse, recounting his failings, when a maid cleared her throat. He turned, scowling, and the cloaked girl retreated a step. He forced his features into calm and offered a smile.

"Ester, what brings you here?" She wore Julianna's cloak, he noticed.

"M'lady asked if I would bring this for you." She held out a steaming cup. "She said 'twas for your aching head." The girl tilted her own. "Does it hurt greatly, m'lord?"

He crossed to her, smiling gently and accepting the thick stone cup. "Aye. Too much wine, I fear."

The girl nodded thoughtfully. "Well, you drink that." She gestured to the cup as he blew on the hot liquid. "M'lady's cures always work quickly. 'Ad one meself this morn."

"Did you?"

"Oh, aye, m'lord. M'lady said she didn't want the last day of feastin' to be ruined 'cause none had sense enough to use a little . . ." Her brow puckered as she searched for the correct word.

"Restraint?" Draegon offered with feeling.

She laughed softly. "Aye. You should see 'em in there." She tossed a thumb over her shoulder toward the hall. "M'lady 'as knights lined up like children, each drinkin' one o' them." She nodded to his cup.

How like his wife to see to the welfare of others so well, he thought, smiling. The girl blushed, waiting as he tipped the cup back and drained it. She took it, curtsied, and with a wish for his pain to leave him enough to enjoy the night, she left him alone.

Draegon stared after her, noticing her jaunty step and that she struggled to keep her mistress's cloak out of the mud. With a heavy sigh, he turned back to his mount, gently smoothing his black coat.

He could not credit himself for the happiness of his people. Not of his brother and certainly not of his wife. Julianna was the reason the folk were happy, and his own stupidity was the reason he was miserable. He'd none to blame but himself. How often had he thanked God he'd returned to find her unwed, and yet he'd repaid her loyalty with kidnapping her from the safety of a convent and forcing her to wed him or be shamed. He'd been an idiot for storming in and taking. Winning Julianna totally did not come in commanding her, but in accepting her. He did not like the woman who recently addressed him like a servant, without feeling, without opinion. She was a shell now, and he'd forced her to this. He'd demanded too much from her and now, he had so little.

He raked his fingers through his hair, then mashed a hand over his face, so filled with regret and rage at himself he could scarcely stand. His mind burst with sudden disjointed images: her bland expression when he'd given her the partridge and pear tree, her grief spent for dead doves, her contrariness over the "French hens," and her refusal to concede to him. His lip curved as he envisioned the swans nipping her rear and his body hardened as he thought of the moments in the dovecote and the one night in their bed.

I give to you not out of your right as my husband, but of mine as your wife. My choice. My gift.

She wanted only the choice. Yet he had denied her a simple want of a hunt and, in return, his wife had become the woman he had told her he wanted. Compliant, obedient. Dull. Had he not sat at the table drinking till dawn, itching to fight with her, to feel the rush of desire their battles spawned?

What have you given without demanding? Lucan had said. *What have you asked of her and not taken because 'tis your right?*

Silly representations of a rhyme and heartache, he thought.

Have I not become the wife you desire?

Nay, he thought. She had become the wife he *thought* he desired.

Have I not accepted your wishes and obeyed?

Aye, dammit. *Aye!*

She had. She did.

Years afore he'd fallen in love with her spirit, her fiery passion, her amusing defiance. Yet 'twas a youth's love, a young man still wet behind the ears with his own arrogance. His love of her was born in those qualities, yet grew with her compassion and patience, with the indomitable strength she wore like a cloak. And for making him see his own truth without destroying them. He loved her for who she had become, not the girl she was.

He wanted the fire back, and Draegon was an ass for snuffing out the flame.

The emir should have beat him more, he thought with a self-deprecating smirk. For 'twas truth he had not grown a brain in the past four years. And he needed it now to repair the damage his demands had done.

Hours later, when the festivities were high with chatter and song, when the wine flowed fast and plentiful on this twelfth night, Julianna caught sight of Draegon, at the moment unguarded, his expression so defeated and solemn, her heart cracked. He was staring out the lower window, a glass his mother had shipped from Italy, and in the evening light the colors cast blue and red and green over his features. His finger stroked the frosted glass, his head braced on the heavy frame. Tears filled her eyes and Julianna slipped back behind the throngs of people, donning her fur-lined cloak and slipping out of the castle.

Draegon flinched when someone tapped the glass, and he squinted to see through the colors. His lips curved when Julianna pressed her nose to the glass and crooked a finger. Immediately he pushed away from the frame and strode quickly to the door, snatching his mantle and heading outside. Brisk night air bit into him and he shivered, drawing the cloak around his neck as his gaze searched the bailey. She was nowhere in sight.

"Julianna." Did she seek to taunt him?

He heard geese squawk and strode toward the barn. A soft light glowed from the shed of wood and thatch, and as he stepped inside, his gaze sought the source. He took several steps and froze on the edge of light. She sat on a small milking stool, a lamb on her lap.

Draegon watched her unawares, her fingers sliding through the animal's lush coat, her profile cast in delicate shadows and light from the branch of candles on a small table near her. All at once he imagined her holding their child, singing the babe sweetly into dreams and his heart gave out, sinking to his stomach.

"Julianna."

She looked up, neither a smile nor a frown on her face. She let the lamb slide from her lap, and as it trotted away, she pushed her hood back. Ermine-lined velvet pooled on her shoulders. His gaze swept her with unsuppressed hunger. God above, she was so beautiful and he felt undeserving.

"You'd wish to speak with me, m'lord?" she said in an efficient tone.

Her coldness wounded, making his voice harsh. "Great days, woman, can you not even call me by name?"

"When you have acted the mighty lord and not my husband? Nay," she snapped, then pressed her lips together and looked at her lap.

"Do not hide from me, Julianna."

Her gaze flashed to his. "You have not wanted to see what I am, Draegon. What matters now?"

His feature tightened, the corner of his mouth quirking in self-deprecation. "Ahh, how you can sting me with your truths, woman."

Julianna gazed at her husband, afraid they would never recapture the love slipping atween her fingers. "I know only one truth, Drae, that we cannot keep this battle waging afore one of us is so deeply wounded we never heal."

"How do we end it? Surrender?" He took a step closer, his gaze intent, his heart impatient for the ease of hurt. "I—I . . ."

Her brow knitted softly. "Speak your heart, Draegon, I will accept no less."

"You wanted me to feel wretched about leaving you, even more for allowing you to suffer with believing I'd died." His words came in a rush. "I do, yet I will not spend my life apologizing for it."

She folded her hands neatly. "You have not apologized once."

He scoffed, raking his fingers through his hair. "I regret leaving you, Julianna, but I am not sorry."

Hurt scored her features. "I see."

"Nay, you do not. I was a spoiled youth, for want of naught when I left to follow Richard, and I returned never wanting to crush the will of another again."

"Yet you crush mine." She leapt to her feet, righteous anger sparking her tone. "You came back with the notions that because you are male, you know best for me. Well, you do not. And until you can grow a child in your belly and feed one from your breast, you will never know! You understand naught of what needs I hold nor those of our people. Nor did you bother to even ask!"

"I know!"

She blinked.

"I know," he said more softly. "God save me, I will never understand women," he said with a rueful look. "Least of all you. But know that I did not mean to hurt you, for I did not think I was inflicting a wound. I wanted only to protect you."

She shook her head. "You wanted everything here as you left it, without change. Forbidding me the choice of my own will not make me the girl you loved years past, Draegon. She no longer exists."

"I know this. Great God, do you think me stupid!?"

She folded her arms over her middle and cocked her head. "Of late, aye."

He made a low, growling sound and took a step closer. "I did not have *all* the sense beat out of me in Cypress, woman. I know you are changed!"

Her hands jerked to her side, fists clenched. "Then why do you not say it! Accept it!"

"Because I was afraid!"

Her eyes went round as coins and she reared back.

Draegon plowed his fingers through his hair, let them bleed down over his face. "I was afraid if I did not make you mine, I would finally meet the death I fought for three years." He stared at the hay-strewn floor. "I had only one thought in that hell, Julianna." He tipped his head back and met her gaze. "You. 'Twas the memory of your fire that kept me alive, that I knew life with you would never grow boring, that loving you would be exciting enough for one man and I would never want to leave." His eyes filled with memory, his voice a rasp of need locked away in a dank cell. "Oh, how I looked forward to holding you," he said on a dark groan. "To talking with you deep into the night. I was so certain you would wait for me. 'Twas all I had to cling to then. And when I found you in the convent, it only assured me that I was not forgotten, that you still wanted my suit. Even after you sent me away." Silver eyes flooded with his emotions. "I had so much stolen from me in that prison that I held no thought save never allowing another to rule me, defy me again." He swallowed. "Not even you."

Julianna absorbed him, his words, staring across the small expanse, close enough to reach out and touch. She could feel his heartache and despair as if she wore it, fragile and poignant. She never thought to hear him confess himself like this.

"I sought to put you in that prison, so you would never escape me. I was a fool to believe that a wedding and mere concessions to Lucan would be enough to please you." He inhaled shakily and let the breath leave his body in a slow frosty breeze. " 'Twas foolish of me to believe that I could take from you, Julianna, without asking."

In the recesses of the barn, sheep baahed. A litter of kittens cried for mother's milk. Livestock stomped and shifted. Their warm breath powdered the cold air like a kiss of fairy dust. A goose honked.

She did not speak and Draegon's shoulders sagged. He moved away, each step feeling as if it would snap him into two.

Julianna inhaled, afraid, yet he stopped on the edge of the darkness, his back to her. She approached slowly, and Draegon turned and looked down at her, his eyes suspiciously glassy.

She held out a loosely knotted ribbon made of polished silver and fashioned into a clasp.

"What is this, Julianna, another manner in which to torment me?"

"Nay, my love." She moved closer, her fragrance enveloping him in a cool mist of desire. " 'Tis a gift."

"Of what?" he said, clearly not in the mood for games.

"My love, my heart. There are no ends to it, you cannot capture it." She fastened the clasp to his mantle. "You cannot hold it and say 'tis here or there. For 'tis in me." She met his gaze pointedly. "Nor can you give me yours—in gifts."

He said naught, his gaze moving over her features with an intensity that left her breathless.

She reached, brushing a black lock from his forehead and, briefly, he closed his eyes, savoring her touch. "Am I worthy of your love, Drae? Have I pummeled it with my combativeness until there is naught left to nurture?"

Julianna waited for him to speak, her heart teetering on the edge of happiness.

He cupped her jaw in his calloused palms, regret in his eyes. "Tis I who must ask that of you, my sweet. 'Tis you I beg forgiveness."

"Ohh, Draegon. You have it."

He smiled with relief, then suddenly went down on one knee. With almost a reverence, Julianna touched his hair, his cheek. He grasped her hand and brought it to his lips for a warm kiss and her breath escaped in a soft puff.

"Marry me, Julianna." Her eyes flared with surprise. "Be my lady, my true wife. I beg you. Speak a vow with me this night of your own choice, your own words."

He waited, the air locked in his lungs, his face tilted up, eyes pleading.

She choked on a sob and sank to her knees, holding his palm to her cheek. "I take thee, Draegon. I take thee as my husband, my partner, as I did twelve nights past, for you are my strength, my purpose for breathing. I cherish the frailty you've shown me and the power you wield over me. This night, I give my heart, my body, my soul to your keeping." She paused to swallow and felt his gaze score her like the heat of his touch. "I vow this, for I love you. You and no other."

Draegon's eyes burned, and briefly he turned his face into her palm, kissing the center. "I accept thee, Julianna. My wife, my love, my friend. I swear no power will part us, for I cannot draw a breath without you. I accept the gentleness you try to hide, the strength you show the world—" His voice dropped to a husky whisper. "And the passion you give only to me." He brought her hand to his chest and her fingers unfurled, feeling the rapid thunder of his heart. "I lay myself bare to the blade of your will and offer myself and all I have to you.

I have no heart without you. No soul to live inside. I am alive because you love me." His fingers slid into her hair and he tipped her head back, his lips a whisper away from hers, his words fierce and rasping. "I *am* because I love you, Julianna. I always have."

"Draegon," she gasped. "Seal this now. I beg you."

His mouth covered hers, his wide hands—hands rough from battle—held her with exquisite tenderness. His lips moved slowly, tasting the nectar of her, his tongue sliding erotically over the line of her lips. Her breath tumbled into his mouth and he drank deeply of her, and Julianna clung to him, her cries muffled against his warm assault. He swallowed her in his strong arms, burying his face in the curve of her throat. For long moments they simple held each other in the center of the manger, feeling the match and melt of heartbeats. The pair were almost asleep on their knees, nestled in each other's arms, when a lamb cried out. Reluctantly, Draegon stood, taking her with him. He brushed a kiss to her lips and swept his arm about her waist, hugging her to his side. She laid her head in the crook of his shoulder as he guided them out of the barn. A flurry of snow covered the castle grounds like diamonds against a lake of black.

As they strolled, the strains of the "Twelve Days of Christmas" floated to them from the hall.

"Appropriate," he said with an arched look.

Julianna tipped her head, her thoughtful expression dancing with mischief. "You know . . . I have always disliked that song, Draegon."

How like her, he thought, with a slow smile. "And now?" he murmured, his lips pressed to her forehead.

" 'Twill remind me of the fool you made of yourself for me."

He jerked back and blinked. "A fool?"

"Aye." Stepping away, she walked briskly into the hall.

Draegon dogged her heels. "How can you say such a thing?"

" 'Tis true. Would you like me to find witnesses?" She gestured to the folk well into their cups.

Draegon threw his hands up. "I swear, my darkest days in the prison were never this difficult. Must you joust with me at every turn?"

At the base of the stairs, Julianna glanced over her shoulder, her expression full of seductive promise. "Aye, my love." She beckoned him toward their chamber. "For to the victor, go the spoils." She dashed up the staircase, ignoring the reverie teeming in the castle.

Draegon grinned, chasing after her. At the door, his steps slowed, and as he tossed aside his mantle, he entered their chamber. He found her reclined on their bed of furs, her cloak and gown nearly shredded in her haste. Her skin was flushed, the furs and a river of red hair hiding and revealing her luxurious figure.

His body responded to the glorious sight. She patted the space aside her and Draegon advanced, tearing at his clothes.

"Draegon." She laughed at his boyish eagerness. "We have more than this night."

"Ahh, but the siege was long and hard, Julianna." He dropped the last of his garments to the floor and climbed into their bed, pulling her into his arms.

"I see that."

His chuckle was a velvet growl as he rolled her beneath him, covering her lovely mouth with his in a kiss filled so deeply with his love that it stripped the soul from her body and carried it into him. And he cradled it gently, promising to protect their love beyond this life and into the next. Long into the twelfth night, they gave of their love and for thousands of more after, Draegon, Lord of Wessex, reaped the rewards of winning his lady, Julianna.

EPILOGUE

My True Love Gave To Me . . .

Draegon paced afore the great hearth in the solar, his spurs chinking with every step. His young son and two daughters were lined up like soldiers, his son Reese looking straight ahead, his daughters, as usual, their tilted chins hinting at defiance. Draegon yanked off his gauntlets and slapped them on a nearby table.

Not one of them flinched. He'd credit their mother for that and swore she encouraged their behavior.

"Ofttimes I've warned you not to venture into the tilt yard, Arianna."

"Aye, Father. You have."

"Then why did you go there?"

"It looked as if it might be fun."

He rounded on her. "*Fun!* Great days, child! You could have been killed. Your uncle will need a year to recover from nearly lopping off your head!" He flicked at the lock of hair cut short from her close encounter with a broadsword.

" 'Tis but a piece of hair," she said with a shrug. "And I was not injured. Reese was there."

Draegon shot a cold look at his son, and like his sisters, the lad did not flinch. "Reese is a learned squire," he said with a measure of pride. He was glad he'd fostered him to Lucan, for Draegon could not bear to be parted from his son for long. "And he will be a knight." His gaze shifted to his daughter. "A position you can never aspire to."

Her lips tightened and he knew she was holding back her temper. Yet when Arianna spoke, her voice was soft as a nightingale. 'Twas deceiving, he knew.

"If you would not forbid me to be there, I would then understand the workings of the yard and therefore decrease the opportunity of becoming injured."

His silver gaze knifed her. "Absolutely out of the question!"

She stared him down, utterly fearless, and he had to admire her for it. She was the image of her mother: fiery red hair, green eyes, and a face that could halt a war. But she was as defiant and headstrong as Julianna had ever been and he feared he would lose her to her wild adventures.

"But, Papa, I *can* wield a sword."

Oh, the little vixen used that cajoling voice sparingly enough that it hit Draegon with the impact of a mace blow. It took him a moment to regain his defenses. "Nay, you cannot."

"Aye, Papa, she can," Raeda said, and Arianna shot her a deadly look. It did not ruffle the child a whit. "I have seen her. Reese teaches—"

"Sweet Jesu, Raeda," Reese muttered, shaking his dark head.

"You taught her!" Draegon roared, glaring down at his son, appalled.

"Aye. I did." He gazed back, his hands clasped and braced at his spine. "Actually . . ." He tilted his head thoughtfully. "She is quite good, Father. Very strong for a girl."

Arianna blushed. "My thanks, Brother."

Draegon shook his head, then looked to the heavens, praying for a smattering of patience.

"Uncle Lucan made her a shield," Raeda added.

It snapped. "Julianna!" Draegon shouted and the children flinched.

"You bellowed, my lord?"

The children snickered and he glared them into silence, then watched his wife approach with a brisk, efficient step. His heart slammed against the wall of his chest, his love renewing every time he saw her. She still held her lush figure after three children, and though her rebelliousness was tempered with their love and understanding of the other, she kept his life more exciting than he had thought possible.

"Saint Crispin, my love. I can hear you all the way in the cook house." She moved afore him, her hand going to his cheek, and he bent to kiss her softly.

"She was in the tilt yard again," he complained. "I swear I am reliving your defiance all over again." A nunnery was looking rather pleasant right now.

"Perhaps if you teach her yourself, you will not have this heartache."

His eyes flared. "Julianna," he warned.

She leaned closer, her voice low, her hands going to the leather straps securing his breast plate. "She adores you, Drae." She tugged at the buckles. "She will obey if you give her the respect she tries to gain from you." Self-admonishment flickered in his features. "To deny her will only serve to make her want it more. Give her an honest taste of the field, the weight of armor, and I assure you she will come running back to the solar and take up her tapestries."

He snorted with disbelief.

She arched a brow, setting the breast plate aside. "Reese is just home and he feels he should protect his sisters. And if 'tis to oversee her sword play, when he knows she will do it without aid, then so be it." She paused for effect. "Or would you rather she took up weapons alone?"

Draegon's expression chased with fear. "Damn me, I cannot stomach the thought of even one hair harmed on my daughters."

"I know," she said. "And they know you would die for them."

"Did you not see the hank of hair missing from Arianna's head?" He nodded toward his stoic daughter, then worked at the silver plate covering his forearms.

"Nay, my love. I will speak with her," she promised, touching the contrasting spots of silver hair at his temples. "Mayhap if she braided it when she worked with the sword, she—" Her words died at his harsh glance. "Mayhap I will simply have a chat with her," she conceded quickly.

"Aye, do so. Afore I lock her in a tower."

" 'Tis just begun, Husband. Wait until the knights come a'calling."

A look of absolute horror shaped his handsome face and Julianna laughed, coaxing him toward the table with a warm meal and wine. Behind her back, she waved, shooing the children. They bolted, Reese looking rather undignified for such a large lad.

Instantly, Draegon called out to his children, but Julianna pressed her fingers to his lips, silencing him.

"You four conspire against me," he said against her fingertips, then bit the tip of one.

Her lovely eyes flared and she replaced her touch with her mouth. Instantly his arms swept 'round her, crushing her to him. His lips toyed and seduced and she gave, sinking her fingers into his hair, eliciting a primal groan of pleasure from him.

"Admit it, you conspire," he murmured.

"Aye. I do," she said atween kisses. "I interfere just so I can soothe you."

His dark brow quirked. "I am still angry, Wife."

"Oh? Then we must adjourn." She caught his hand, tugging. "Make haste, m'lord. This, I fear, will take all night."

From the alcove near the stairs, the siblings watched their father follow their mother up the steps with the eagerness of a child on Christmas morn. Raeda giggled. Arianna sighed, her heart, only ten and four summers old, aching for a love like her parents'. Behind her, Reese smiled gently, ushering his sisters out, all three resigned to the extra duties for disobeying their father.

Abovestairs, Julianna pulled at Draegon's clothes, her body singing for his touch. And he did touch, his hands already beneath her gown and stroking her secret places into moist heat and need. Oh, the magic this man could wield, she thought with a hungry look.

"Arianna must be punished."

"Aye, but later," she panted, yanking off his surcoat, then attacking his braes. "I will make her work in the cook house."

"Taste the food first." He loosened the laces of her kirtle. "She does not have your talent for seasonings."

Julianna grinned, yanking off his boots. He did not cease touching and kissing, his mouth playing heavily over her warm flesh. Her gown dropped to the floor and she fell back on the bed, pulling him atop her. Bare as a babe, he entered her in one swift stroke.

"Sweet mercy, Julianna. 'Tis heaven to be inside you."

"Oh, Draegon, how I love you."

With both hands, he brushed her hair back off her face and pushed deeper. " 'Tis the reason I still breathe, my love." He withdrew and adored the way her body rose to greet him. She soothed and tempered, loved with every inch of her soul, and taught him that a fine mind was not always housed in a male body.

Loving her so deeply he ached, Draegon thanked

God he'd had the intelligence to accept his wife for the magnificent woman she was. Had he not, he thought with a tender smile, oh, what he would have missed.

CHRISTMAS HOMECOMING

by

Elizabeth Graham

PROLOGUE

. . . Christmas Eve and twelve of the clock . . .
—Thomas Hardy
The Oxen

Brightwater, Pennsylvania—1878

Dane Kendall couldn't keep his eyes off Tess Bayley. Her golden-brown hair gleamed warmly in the lamplight. The lamp also struck fire from the gold-and-rose locket around her slender throat. Her gray eyes were luminous. Her green velvet dress seemed to him the most beautiful gown for the most beautiful woman he'd ever seen.

He shook his head, trying to clear it of these strange, disturbing thoughts.

This was Tess. The girl he'd grown up with—who'd been his best friend until her father took her to Philadelphia three years ago.

She moved her arm and the diamond in the ring on her left hand also caught a gleam of light.

Tess was no longer a girl, but a young woman.

A woman engaged to be married to a man she'd met in Philadelphia.

Dane's heart gave a painful lurch. His feelings of strangeness deepened.

Tess suddenly looked up. Her gaze met his and held.

Her eyes widened, her hand went to the locket and stroked it. A ripple moved down her throat as she swallowed.

The roomful of people gathered for Tess's grandmother Edith's annual Christmas Eve party faded from Dane's awareness.

He and Tess seemed to be alone together somewhere.

Somewhere outside of ordinary space and time . . .

Tess abruptly rose from the brocade settee. Marianne Walters, an old school friend, chattering beside her, gave her a startled glance. Tess murmured something, then quickly left the room, heading for the stone terrace that led to the elaborate maze of gardens that were Edith's pride . . .

And his and Tess's hideaway during their childhood when they were evading the grownups. They'd discovered one place, deep inside the rose garden, where no one had ever found them.

With a sureness beyond logic, leaving no room for doubt, Dane knew that was where Tess was going. He excused himself to Hallie Andrews, who'd scarcely left his side for the last hour, and followed Tess.

The evening was unseasonably warm for Christmas Eve, and the French doors to the terrace were open.

Dane saw with no surprise that the terrace was empty. Tess wasn't leaning against the stone railing, but he caught a glimpse of moonlight on golden-brown hair and a flash of deep-green velvet disappearing into the gardens.

The moon went behind a cloud, but Dane's footsteps were confident as he headed for the innermost part of the shadowy gardens. The moon came out again as he reached their old retreat, showing Tess sitting on a low stone seat.

She glanced up and, just as a few minutes ago, their

gazes met and locked. His heart leapt. He moved forward.

"Tess . . . !"

Dane's voice shivered through Tess like dark, smooth velvet.

She felt her heart jump, then begin racing. The intense attraction to Dane that had swept over her in her grandmother's drawing room, causing her to flee here in confused alarm, sharpened. She couldn't seem to take her eyes away from him.

He looked so . . . wonderful! The fitful moonlight made his dark hair shine, deepened his brown eyes to almost black. His brown suit fit him to perfection, making her acutely aware of the muscled body beneath.

Was this the same boy she'd known all through childhood? The boy who'd been her best friend?

No, this wasn't a boy at all.

A virile man stood before her, staring as if he'd never be able to look away.

Just as she couldn't move her gaze away from him.

What was happening to them? Panic swept over her. She was engaged to Hugh Landon! She was to be married in less than a month!

But those facts changed nothing in her feelings now. Tess jerked her head around, breaking the connection of their eyes, got up and looked wildly about.

Then Dane was so close she could feel his body heat, smell his clean scent. Her heart beat ever more wildly.

She had to get out of here! Before . . . before something happened between them that could never be undone. She took a step forward, and felt Dane's hand on her sleeve.

"Tess, don't go. You can't go . . . now."

She drew in her breath at his words, the meaning implicit in them. She couldn't seem to take another step no matter how she urged her feet forward.

Dane's hand burned its way through the fabric of her sleeve, making her long for more than just that touch. She turned slowly toward him.

Again, the moon hid itself, plunging them into blackness. Dane's hand slid upward to her shoulder, to her neck, caressing her bare skin.

The touch inflamed Tess with sudden intense need. She reached for him, finding the slightly hair-roughened skin of his lower face. Her hands curved around the remembered squareness of his jaw. She heard his gasp, felt the sudden stiffening of his body.

"God, how I want you!" His voice sounded strangled as if he desperately tried to hold the words back, but couldn't.

Now, *now,* she had to pull away, tell him they mustn't do this . . .

But she didn't. She couldn't. Instead, she moved her hand until her fingers found his mouth, then slowly and gently traced the outline of his lips.

Dane groaned and pulled her to him. Tess gasped as his hard body molded itself to her softer one. Frantically, they pressed their lips together, their bodies together.

The small, round coolness of the family locket she'd been presented with just tonight, on her eighteenth birthday, pushed into her chest.

Despite the balmy evening, she felt herself shivering at the contact, her skin tingling where the locket touched.

They sank to the grass of the small clearing, holding each other as if afraid the other would disappear. Tess no longer even tried to stop what was happening. The feeling of relentless inevitability had completely taken her over.

This moment had been waiting for them all their lives. There was no avoiding it. Something stronger than themselves was involved here. A shiver again went over Tess at this incredible thought.

Then Dane kissed her so sweetly and hotly all thought left her. She ardently kissed him back, responded to his ever more intimate touches.

Frantically, they unfastened buttons, pushed aside the clothes separating their bodies from each other.

Hot bare flesh met and clung, lips pulsed and clung . . . their feelings spiraled out of control, urgency increasing until both found their completion.

Still held tight in Dane's grasp, Tess's breathing and heartbeat slowly returned to normal. The moon came out again, bathing them in its weak gleam.

Reality hit her with the impact of a crushing blow.

Tess jerked out of Dane's embrace, stumbled to her feet, shakily adjusted her clothing.

"Oh my God, what have we done?" she whispered, her voice faltering. "I'm *engaged!* I'm to be married in less than a month! How could I have betrayed Hugh like this?"

Dane stared at her for long moments, his face mirroring the shock she felt, with something else added . . . something she couldn't read.

He turned away, adjusted his own clothing, got to his feet. Finally, he turned to her again.

"Forgive me, Tess, I'm very sorry," he said, his voice remote, now sounding cool. "I had no intention of letting this happen."

Cold swept over Tess, dissolving the remnants of the warmth and closeness she still felt for Dane.

Sorry? He was sorry? He hadn't intended for this to happen? Well, of course not. Neither had she! But it had.

She realized that, despite her appalled shock at what they'd done, she'd wanted, *expected,* Dane to reassure her. Make her believe what had just happened between them was right and good. Inevitable, beyond their control . . .

What a fool she was! How could it possibly be right for her to make love with Dane when she'd promised herself to Hugh?

But just the same, she'd thought, *expected,* Dane to say he loved her. And always had. That, like her, he just hadn't recognized that love until tonight.

Until the moment their glances had met in her grandmother's drawing room.

Double fool!

Fierce pain shot through her. Whatever strange force had taken possession of them, caused their out-of-control behavior, Dane had just told her it meant nothing to him now.

She meant nothing to him now.

Force? Possession? *Don't keep on being a fool,* she told her hurting heart and body. They'd simply given in to sudden, unexplainable lust for each other.

She lifted her chin a bit. "Neither did I want it, of course," she answered, forcing her voice to sound as measured and cool as his had been. "We'll have to forget this ever happened."

Choking down the tears that threatened to engulf her, Tess, head held high, turned and walked out of the rose garden, not looking back.

Dane started after her, then, his hands clenching into fists at his sides to keep down the pain inside, he forced himself to stop.

He had to let her go. She'd just made it bitterly clear she wanted that. Wanted no more of *him.*

When, afterward, she'd reacted with such shock to their lovemaking, he'd tried to calm her down, telling her he hadn't planned to seduce her. That he hadn't set out to make her betray her fiancé.

He'd been unable to stop what had happened between them, just as she had seemed equally overcome by her feelings, their mutual need for each other.

He'd thought she'd tell him that no matter how wrong it seemed, they belonged together forever. But she hadn't. Instead, she'd coolly said neither had she wanted nor planned this . . . that they had to forget it had ever happened.

His mouth twisted. He'd never tell her now that no matter what promises she'd made, she had to break them. Or that she had to marry him, because he loved her with everything inside him.

He should feel relieved she'd kept him from making a fool of himself by declaring his unreturned love.

He didn't, though. He felt as if his heart had broken into pieces inside him.

Dazed, he saw something gold and shiny on the path by his feet.

It was the locket Tess had been wearing. Its rose-embossed face glittered up at him.

It seemed to be trying to tell him something.

Something very important.

Dane's jaw tightened at this crazy fancy. Hadn't he been enough of an idiot tonight?

He scowled at the piece of jewelry, started to walk on by. Something stopped him.

He scooped the locket up, dropped it in a pocket, then headed away from the direction Tess had gone, away from Edith Bayley's house toward home.

1

Brightwater, Pennsylvania—December, 1884

Tess stopped outside the familiar brick building, memories sweeping over her. The big front window was as sparkling clean as she recalled it, the crimson lettering just as brilliant.

The Brightwater Gazette. Her grandparents' weekly newspaper, run by her grandmother since her grandfather's death twenty years ago.

And now her grandmother was selling it.

Tess felt the same clutch at her heart as when she'd read her grandmother's letter last week.

"It's time for me to step down, Tess," she'd written. "Time to hand over the reins to someone younger. I've had a good offer, but I haven't decided yet to accept it . . ."

"Mama, when are we going in?" Anne asked impatiently from beside her. "I want to see Gramma Edith!"

Tess smiled at her five-year-old daughter. "Right now, punkin!" She followed her words with action, walking to the front door and opening it.

A merry jingle of bells filled the air. A gray-haired, sturdily built woman glanced up from a walnut rolltop desk against the right-hand wall. Papers spilled out of its cubbyholes, and were stacked all over the desk.

Despite the chaos, Tess was sure her grandmother could unerringly put her hands on anything she wanted to find.

The woman's eyes widened. She pushed back her chair and got to her feet. "Teresa Bayley!" she exclaimed. "What on earth are you doing here?"

Tess moved toward her, smiling. She wished her name still were Bayley, she thought, then quickly denied that. No, she couldn't wish the last six years never to have happened. One good thing had come from them—Anne.

"We got in on the morning train, left our luggage at the house and walked here. Margaret was as surprised as you."

Edith enveloped Tess in a warm hug, then Anne. "This child has grown six inches since I saw her last. I was beginning to think you'd never set foot in Brightwater again. Why, you haven't been home since you and Hugh married."

No, not since that disastrous Christmas six years ago.

Tess quickly buried the bittersweet memories rising at that thought, which was followed quickly by another one she'd wrestled with since she got this idea.

If she moved back here, she'd be bound to run into Dane on a regular basis. But she could learn to deal with that. She'd have to.

"You are staying on for Christmas?" Edith asked.

Tess firmly met her grandmother's gaze. *Get it over with,* her mind urged. "Yes, and maybe for good. Grandmother, I want to buy the *Gazette.*"

Edith raised her brows. "What are you talking about?"

"You want to retire—and I don't want to let the paper go out of the family. Father's never had any interest in it. That leaves me. I've never liked living in Philadelphia and now, with Hugh gone, all his family gone, there's nothing to keep me there."

No, not even the small, shabby house they'd lived in these last four years. Her landlord's recent message that he'd sold the house and she and Anne would have to move by New Year's had given her the final push into this decision. She'd have a hard time finding another house for what she could afford to pay.

The other woman's expression changed. She bit her lip, frowning. "I don't know what to say. You never showed any interest before, and as I said, I've had a good offer."

"But you haven't accepted it yet, have you?" Tess quickly asked, surprised and dismayed. She'd expected her grandmother to be thrilled.

Edith shook her head. "No-o, not formally. We haven't signed any papers yet."

Tess let out her held breath in relief. "Thank God! I was so afraid I'd be too late!"

Her grandmother's frown hadn't left. She glanced down at Anne, now leaning tiredly against Tess's garnet cloak.

"Why don't you come over to the table and I'll give you some scissors and a magazine to cut pictures out of," she suggested to the child.

Anne's small face brightened. "Can I cut out a-l-l the pictures I want?" she asked.

"Of course." Edith smiled, took Anne's hand and settled her at the worktable next to the big desk.

Edith motioned to several chairs along the opposite wall. "Let's sit down and talk about this."

"All right," Tess agreed, tension rising at her grandmother's words and tone. Convincing her grandmother to sell the *Gazette* to her wasn't going to be as easy as she'd thought.

When they were settled, Edith patted Tess's knee. "Now, dear, are you sure about this? It isn't just an impulsive idea? Like you and Dane used to get when you were growing up?"

Tess's tension increased. She didn't want to talk or think about Dane.

She gave her grandmother a wry smile. "It's been quite a while since I've done anything impulsive. I know what I'm doing. I have enough of Hugh's insurance left to make a down payment on the business, and I could pay the rest in monthly installments."

Then Tess realized she didn't even know how large an offer Edith had received. Her tension increased. "That is, unless your asking price is too much, or you don't like that kind of plan," she amended.

The older woman waved her hand in dismissal. "The financial arrangements don't matter to me. You know I haven't run the paper all these years to make a lot of money. Your grandfather left me an ample amount to live on."

She paused and gave Tess a significant look. "And for you and Anne to live on, too, as I've told you a hundred times. If you weren't so stubborn—"

"Let's not get involved in that," Tess broke in. "We couldn't live with you. You wouldn't want us around all the time."

Pride hadn't let her take money from her father. Pride hadn't let her admit Hugh had gambled away his inheritance, was unfaithful and abusive. Never trained to earn a living, he'd gone from one poorly paid job to another, also gambling away most of his meager wages.

Tess had done sewing to help them survive. When Hugh was killed in a drunken brawl a year ago, profound relief was Tess's strongest emotion.

She'd eked out an existence since then with a small

insurance policy Hugh had left and her sewing, finding it harder and harder to make ends meet each month.

Edith gave her an incredulous look. "I'd like nothing better than for you both to live with me. I've missed you so much since you left. And I haven't seen nearly as much of Anne as I'd like."

Tess firmed her mouth. She wasn't going to weaken now. "I'm a grown woman with a child. I don't want anyone to support me. I want to be independent. Owning the *Gazette* would give me that!"

Edith sighed, her frown deepening. "Stubborn as a rock, just like your father and grandfather. Well, you see, dear, the problem is the person who made the offer wants the *Gazette* for the same reasons as you."

Tess swallowed, again surprised at her grandmother's attitude. She didn't want to do this, but it looked like she'd have to.

"But I'm your *granddaughter,* doesn't that mean anything to you? Don't you mind the paper being sold to someone outside the family?"

Edith sighed again. "Well, yes, of course, but you see, he doesn't really *seem* like an outsider." She suddenly got up. "Come on, let me show you my new printing press. If you're interested in the business, you need to see what you'd be getting."

Tess followed her to the other room, frustration building. This wasn't going at all as she'd thought it would. And who was this mysterious man who'd made the offer—who Edith was so close to?

A sudden thought struck her. Could her grandmother be interested romantically in another man—at her age?

"Isn't it a beauty?" Edith said, gesturing at the gleaming printing press, beaming with the pride of a mother showing off her firstborn infant. "I've only had it for six months. It's one of the small Potter cylinder models. George and I can do all the work ourselves."

"Yes, it is," Tess said, smiling at her grandmother's enthusiasm, despite her worries. Edith was still a very attractive woman. It was completely possible she could want to marry again.

But in that case, why would she *sell* the *Gazette* to this man? There would be no need of that . . . and besides, now that she thought about it, a prospective husband of her grandmother's would also be of an age to want to retire, not start running a business . . .

Tess shook her head and looked around the neat premises. With the one exception of her desk, Edith would tolerate no sloppiness in her establishment. Tess remembered George Wilcox, her grandmother's typesetter and general handyman, grumbling about having to clean up all the time. But he'd stayed on all these years. No doubt because Edith, although a stern taskmaster, was fair and paid excellent wages.

A new worry hit Tess. Could she afford to keep George on if she bought the place? Would he stay on if she offered him less than Edith had paid?

She dismissed the thought. That wouldn't matter if Edith didn't sell to her. She had to convince her grandmother to do that.

"Are we going to stay here for always?" Anne's eager voice was so unexpected, Tess jumped, glancing into the other room. Anne, holding the scissors, looked expectantly toward her and Edith.

Tess's heart sank. She'd told Anne nothing more than that they were coming for a visit.

"Maybe, sweetie. We'll have to wait and see." Tess's glance met Edith's. The older woman looked uncomfortable again.

"Oh, goody! I love it here. I could play in the gardens all the time."

Although they'd only stayed at Edith's big estate for a little while this morning, Anne had at once been captivated by the gardens. Tess's heart twisted. Just as she'd been, all through her growing-up years here. She and Dane . . .

With an effort, Tess kept her smile in place. "Well, not all the time. We wouldn't be living in Grandmother's house."

"Why not?" Anne demanded. "It's so-o-o big and Gramma rattles around in it all by herself."

That was a direct quote from Edith's last visit a few months ago, and the older woman gave a bark of laughter.

"Right you are, Annie. I don't see why you and your Mama can't stay there and cut down on some of the rattling."

Behind Tess, the bell over the door, embellished with red and green Christmas ribbons, jingled again.

Edith glanced over and her smile widened, while at the same time another expression appeared in her eyes . . . an anxious look? "Hello, Dane."

"Good morning, Edith."

Tess stiffened, a chaotic mixture of feelings sweeping over her. His voice had deepened, but its timbre still rang familiarly in her ears.

His footsteps creaked the wood floor as he crossed the room. Tess fixed a smile on her face as she turned toward him.

"Hello, Dane," she said, relieved her voice sounded casual.

He'd changed. There were fine lines around his dark eyes even if he was only in his late twenties. And a tense look to his face.

Could that be due to this sudden encounter? She dismissed that idea at once. Why should she think that would bother him?

Just because it bothered her.

He took his time answering her greeting. His gaze moved from her hair, pulled back into a chignon, down her traveling suit of green twill, to her feet in black, laced shoes.

"Hello, Tess. It's been a long time."

"Yes, it has," she replied. But to her it seemed only yesterday she'd last seen him. Did her green suit remind him of the velvet gown she'd worn that last night . . . make him remember those stolen minutes when they'd lain in each other's arms?

Stop it! she chided herself, dismayed that her resentment was being overcome by these other, unwanted feelings. *If you're going to live in this town, you'll have to get over this nonsense.*

What if she couldn't? And what if the wild emotions that had so suddenly and shockingly erupted in them that night still lingered in Dane? As they did inside her heart and body . . . no matter how many times over the years she'd tried to deny them.

She drew in her breath at that notion and firmly pushed it deep into her mind.

Of course, Dane felt nothing for her.

He'd proved that the night they'd made love.

Tess heard the clump of Anne's feet as she got down from the chair. A few moments later, she stood beside Tess, beaming up at Dane as if they were old friends.

Dane looked down at her and gave her an easy return smile.

An ache hit Tess's heart as she watched her daughter, and the familiar guilt hit her. Why had she gone ahead and married Hugh? When she'd realized she didn't love him, could never love him?

"Maybe Mama and I are going to live here for always," Anne said, beaming at him.

Tess saw a muscle in Dane's jaw tighten. He raised his head, glanced at Tess.

"Is that right? Now that is a surprise."

"Mama's going to buy the *G'zette,"* Anne added, still beaming.

Oh, Lord! Tess inwardly fumed. Why had she thought Anne was paying her and Edith's conversation no attention? Obviously she'd been wrong.

Dane's face tightened more. He glanced at Edith, a question in his eyes.

Edith cleared her throat. "Oh, my, I don't want you two fighting over this."

Puzzled, Tess looked at her. "Fighting over what?"

Her grandmother lifted her shoulders. "Well, Tess . . . Dane is the person who made me the offer."

Shock swept over Tess. "What?"

"And a very good offer," Dane said, his voice cool.

"Yes, that's true," Edith said. She cleared her throat again. "That's very true " she repeated.

Everything suddenly fell into place for Tess. Her grandmother's evasiveness, her saying that the person wanting the paper was almost like family.

Dane *had* been almost like part of her family when they were growing up. As she'd felt like a part of his.

And why should she have thought all that had changed because of what had happened between her and Dane? Edith knew nothing of that . . . incident. Neither did Dane's family.

Slowly, Tess turned toward Dane again. His dark-brown gaze steadily met her own, a challenge in its depths. Tess knew her eyes held an answering challenge.

"I'm sorry, Dane," Edith finally said. "Until a few minutes ago, I had no idea Tess was interested in buying the paper, too."

"I believe you, Edith," Dane answered. "The question is, which one of us are you going to sell to?"

2

Edith drew in a deep breath and let it out. She looked from Tess to Dane, then threw up her hands. "I don't know! How can I choose? You both have very good reasons for wanting to buy the *Gazette*. I need time to think about this. I care about both of you. Dane, you're like a grandson to me."

She glanced at Tess. "I love you very much, Tess, but this isn't an easy decision to make."

How could her grandmother be doing this to her? Tess glanced up and met Dane's dark glance.

Without warning, a frisson of memory shivered through her. He'd looked at her like this that night . . . and she'd looked at him. And then she'd run to the gardens and he'd followed . . .

She gave herself a mental shake. No, no! What was wrong with her? He wasn't looking at her like that at all.

And what difference did it make anyway?

"I'm going to do my best to get Edith to accept my offer," Dane said, his voice even and cool. "I want to make a living at this."

Tess swallowed, his words and tone dissolving the disturbing memory. She drew herself up a little straighter. "That is my plan, too."

Her peripheral vision showed her Anne's small, worried face. Tess's face softened as she smiled down at the child, who stood between her mother and Dane.

Protectiveness for her daughter filled Tess. She wouldn't argue with Dane here in front of Anne. Her daughter had witnessed enough unpleasantness between Tess and Hugh during her short life. She'd be spared any more if Tess could do anything about it.

Dane had followed her glance and his frown smoothed out. He, too, smiled down at Anne. "I hope you and your mother decide to stay here," he told her.

Instantly, Anne's face lightened. "Me, too," she said happily.

He glanced over at Tess, and that challenging look she remembered so well from their childhood again shone out from his eyes.

I won't say anything more in front of your daughter, the look told her. *But this isn't finished. And I meant what I said. I'll fight for the paper.*

Confused, she returned his look with a similar one. *And so will I.* Why had he told Anne he hoped they'd stay and then given her that look that said just the opposite?

"I guess you're here to put in the restaurant advertisement," Edith hastily stated, obviously trying to smooth things over.

It was a little late for that.

Dane's expression softened again. He smiled at the older woman and nodded. "Yes. The Christmas specials did so well last year, we're going to start them early."

"Guess you have the advertisement written as usual? If you didn't want to buy the paper, I'd hire you to write advertisements," Edith said lightly.

Tess saw the muscle in Dane's jaw move as he handed Edith a sheet of paper filled with neat writing. "Yes, here it is," he said, not commenting on her last words.

Dane turned back to Tess. "Good-bye," he said. "I'm sure we'll be seeing more of each other."

"Of course you will! Now that she's here, I'm sure Tess will be helping me with the orphanage party, and you'll be playing Santa as usual."

"Good-bye, Mrs. Bayley, Tess." Dane bent his knees until he was on Anne's level. "It was very nice meeting you, Miss Anne," he said.

The child's eyes widened. "How did you know my name?" she asked. "I didn't tell you!"

"I've heard lots of nice things about you from your great-grandmother," he answered, his smile now warm and genuine.

Alarm went through Tess. She couldn't bear for Anne to ease her hunger for a father by latching on to Dane! What a tangled mess that would be!

"You have?" Anne's smile was so huge it broke Tess's heart. "I've never heard anything about *you,*" she answered.

Dane stood, his glance once again finding Tess, holding for a moment.

Tess hoped her mix of roiling emotions didn't show on her face. After what he'd done to her, she couldn't bear for him to know how much he still affected her.

Frowning, Dane walked down the street toward *Kendall's,* the family restaurant.

This was a pretty mess! He'd been so sure Edith was about ready to accept his offer for the *Gazette.* She had been, too. His face tightened.

Edith hadn't expected Tess to also want the paper. Hell, Edith hadn't even expected Tess to visit! She'd have been sure to mention it, as she always passed along tidbits of information about her family.

Encountering Tess like that, after all these years, had profoundly shaken him.

God, she'd looked so good! In that wine-colored cloak, her hair shining like burnished gold, it was clear the years had treated her well. Why was she back here with this sudden notion to buy the paper? Bored with her life in Philadelphia? Wanting to play at being a newspaper owner?

Resentment toward her flared up in him.

That wasn't a good enough reason! His was better, stronger. Why couldn't Edith see that?

Hell, don't be a fool, he told himself. Tess was Edith's granddaughter, and no matter how close Edith and he were, blood was always thicker than water, as they said.

In a moment, despite his anger and resentment, his thoughts softened toward Tess.

When he'd seen her, the memories of that long-ago Christmas Eve had come flooding back into his mind. Not that they were buried very deep.

He'd burned to take her into his arms right there in the newspaper office. Right in front of Edith and the little girl.

Anne. Tess's daughter. The child Edith had often talked to him about. A child whose dark curls and brown eyes reminded him strongly of his niece, his brother Roger's daughter.

Even Anne's smile had seemed hauntingly familiar.

Halfway down the second block, Dane halted so suddenly a passing woman gave him a curious look before walking on by.

The idea that had struck him with the force of a blow was one that had tortured him for weeks after his few minutes of bliss with Tess that night six years ago.

What if their time together had gotten her with child?

When she went ahead and married her fiancé only weeks later, he'd regretfully dismissed that idea. Despite the way that night had ended, despite his bitter knowledge she'd preferred Hugh Landon to him, if Tess were carrying his babe, she wouldn't marry someone else. She couldn't do that to him . . . and to herself.

When Edith had told him of Anne's birth, he hadn't let himself dwell on the thought he might be the father.

Although the time was right, or close enough. Although Tess had never returned to Brightwater until now. Although now that he'd seen her, he realized Anne didn't resemble Tess or anyone in her family.

Sudden pain pierced him. Could the girl, woman, he'd discovered he loved with blinding intensity six years ago be capable of such deceit? Could she have cheated him out of seeing his baby grow into this enchanting little girl?

Cheated them both out of their own happiness with each other?

"Kendall, you're being an idiot," Dane muttered, resuming his walk, his steps slowing as he neared the fieldstone building on the corner of Main and Chestnut.

How he hated this place! Hated the smell of cooking permeating it, hated the endless planning, the bookwork. Hated the wrangles with his father because Dane wouldn't put his heart into the business that had been in the family for three generations.

No, not wouldn't. *Couldn't.* Something his father and brother felt was lacking in him. Always had been. Running a very successful restaurant that served the best food in the county didn't excite him or fill him with pride. Didn't make his blood race.

The thought of running the *Brightwater Gazette* did.

And now the possibility that he might be able to live the dream he'd had since he was fifteen had been dashed a few minutes ago.

By Tess. His childhood pal. His one-time love. The woman he'd never been able to forget. Not even when he was engaged to someone else, had almost married her. Thank God he'd realized in time he'd never be able to make Joan a good husband. To love her.

As he still loved Tess. If he'd had any doubts about that, they'd been shattered a few minutes ago when he'd seen her again.

His mouth twisted. Obviously, she didn't love him. Had never loved him except for her childhood fondness for him. She'd only been caught up in whatever had happened to them that extraordinary, magical night.

His mouth twisted. The memory of her dazed, horrified expression after their lovemaking was still etched into his mind. Her only words to him were ones of regret for what had been the most wonderful experience of his life.

She'd only been concerned that she'd betrayed her fiancé. He'd been so stunned, so heartbroken, by her reaction, all he could do was pretend he felt as she did. That they'd been carried away by lust, done a terrible thing.

Lies, all lies. He hadn't felt that way at all. He'd been carried away by love, exulting in what he thought they'd shared. Wanting to be with Tess forever. Sure she'd felt just the same. And that they would be together.

Hurt pride played a part in what you said and did, too, something inside him said. *So what if it had?* A man had to have some pride.

"Stop being a fool and get in there and get to work," he told himself grimly. "You'd better learn to like it, too, because it looks as if you're stuck with it. Edith isn't going to sell the paper to you if her granddaughter wants it."

A recurring thought entered his mind. He could leave here, go somewhere else and buy a newspaper. He'd saved his money over the years. But he didn't want to leave. His love for this town he'd been born in equaled his father's and brother's love for the restaurant.

Looks like you're stuck between a rock and a hard place, Kendall. You love the town and the Gazette *and the woman you still love more than either of these things is going to take that dream away from you.*

Tess's vibrant image swam into his mind's eye, causing his body to harden and a pain to shoot through his chest. Anne's pert little face followed close behind that first image.

She could have been his daughter . . . if only Tess had married him instead of rejecting him and running away that night.

Anne could have been his daughter and maybe she was.

Cursing silently, Dane forced the crazy thought deep into his mind and opened the restaurant's side door, leading to the office.

His father looked up from the desk and the ledger he pored over, frowning. "Took you long enough," he grumped.

"I was only gone half an hour," Dane said, his own voice short, his temper not far behind. "Go on back to the dining room. I'll finish up here. I know you hate this bookwork."

"You bet I do!" Oren Kendall glared at his son. "When are you going to get over that foolish idea of buying the paper?"

A day ago—hell, an *hour* ago—Dane would have shot back that he'd never get over the idea. That Edith Bayley had accepted his offer. That Roger would have to take over the paperwork. Or they could hire someone. He didn't care.

So, you're just going to give up your dream?

Stubborn determination rose in Dane at that thought. He'd lost Tess years ago.

All he had left was this dream he'd carried inside so long. He set his jaw.

He'd make Edith see he, not her granddaughter, was the right person to continue her life's work.

As he'd told Tess a few minutes ago, he'd fight for the *Gazette.*

3

Tess's steps slowed as she approached the door of Hosham's, Brightwater's finest men's haberdashery. She straightened her shoulders, raised her chin, and fixed a bright smile on her face.

She felt her heart racing and took a couple of deep breaths. How she *hated* to do this! How she hated to beg. But it was part of the life she wanted so desperately.

The life that she hadn't even dreamed of a week ago and now was working single-mindedly toward acquiring.

Asking for help with the annual Christmas baskets wasn't really begging, because it wasn't for herself or her family.

It was for Brightwater's less fortunate citizens, another of the things Edith did for the town, under the auspices of the *Gazette.* It mostly benefited the older people who could no longer work and had no families to care for them. A basket of food for Christmas would go a long way toward brightening that holiday for them.

Like the Christmas Eve party for the orphanage, Edith had been doing this for years. *She* could certainly do it, too, Tess told herself. She took another deep breath and let it out, firmed her smile, then walked briskly to the door.

Just as she reached for the knob, the door opened

and a tall, broad-shouldered man, dressed in a well-fitting short coat over tweed trousers, stood framed in the opening.

Tess fell back a step, feeling her smile falter, her heart begin to race in a different rhythm. She was suddenly glad she wore her most becoming garnet velvet cloak, that she'd taken pains with dressing her hair.

"Hello, Tess," Dane finally said, stepping back himself so she could enter. His polite smile looked strained, as if he found this unexpected encounter disturbing.

"Good morning," Tess returned, striving for a brisk tone. Obviously, Dane wasn't glad to see her. And she wasn't glad to see him, either. "Lovely day, isn't it?"

"Yes, indeed," Dane returned, then touched his bowler. "I'd best be getting on."

Tess nodded and swept inside, finding her bright smile again as she spied the store manager and walked over to him.

"Mr. Hosham! How nice to see you." Tess inwardly winced at her overly vivacious tone. *You'll get used to doing this,* she reassured herself. *It's just part of the job.*

The elderly man facing her smiled. "Good day, Mrs. Landon. May I help you?"

Tess swallowed. Now came the hard part. "I certainly hope you can, Mr. Hosham. I'm here on behalf of the *Gazette.* We're counting on your usual generous donation for our Christmas basket fund."

A puzzled look came over Mr. Hosham's genial face. "I already pledged Dane Kendall my support. Only a few minutes ago."

Embarrassment swept over Tess. So that's what Dane was doing here! Surely he knew why she'd come, yet he'd said nothing and let her make a fool of herself. Anger joined the embarrassment.

With a supreme effort, she kept her smile in place.

"I'm so sorry, Mr. Hosham. I guess Dane and I forgot to double-check our lists with each other."

He nodded. "That's all right, Mrs. Landon. Might I say I'm glad to see you back in Brightwater? And looks like you're planning to stay, since you're helping Edith at the paper. Need more young people here."

"I'm giving serious consideration to staying," Tess answered sweetly, although inside she fumed. "I'm sorry for the mix-up. It won't happen again."

She forced herself to walk with ladylike steps to the door, feeling her cheeks flaming.

No, it wouldn't happen again! She'd march right over to the restaurant and tell Dane to mind his own business. That her grandmother had assigned this job to *her!*

Opening the door with more force than required, she saw that wouldn't be necessary.

Dane stood on the sidewalk, as if waiting for her.

She glared at him. "I'd like to talk to you," she said frostily.

He nodded, his face serious. "I figured you would. You look like you could bite a few nails in half. Do you want to tell me off here on the street or would you rather do it somewhere private?"

She stared at him, her mouth hanging open, her righteous indignation fading at his words, replaced by other emotions. *Somewhere private?* What did he have in mind?

Unbidden, the never-forgotten memories of that night in the deep privacy of the rose garden crept into her consciousness.

"We could go to the restaurant," he said after a moment. "It won't be crowded this time of day."

Tess couldn't think of an alternative. "All right."

Stiffly, she fell into step with him to walk the well-remembered two blocks, careful not to let their clothes brush together. They walked in silence for several moments.

"If it does any good," Dane finally said, "I didn't know Edith had given you this job. I've been doing it for the last four years."

"So you didn't bother to check, you just went ahead?" Tess demanded, trying to regain the momentum she'd lost.

Trying not to think about being so close to Dane she could touch him. If she wanted to. Which she didn't, of course.

"Yes, that's exactly what I did. I haven't seen you out and about town this last week. Didn't figure you'd be doing this kind of thing."

Neither did I, Tess thought. *I wouldn't have, either, if Grandmother hadn't pushed me into it.*

A sudden thought hit her. How could Edith have forgotten Dane had done this job for the last four years? She might be getting older, but her mind was still sharp as a young woman's.

Was her grandmother stirring the pot? Did she want Tess and Dane to clash? If so, why?

Tess felt even more of her anger seeping away. Dane's words had the ring of truth. She realized she believed he hadn't deliberately set out to humiliate her.

Now that she thought about it, she also realized he wouldn't do something like this, because it would reflect badly on the *Gazette.*

He wanted the paper too much to do anything to tarnish its reputation.

She forced a smile. "All right, I believe you. It was just a mix-up. We'll have to talk these things over . . ."

Her voice trailed off. What was the matter with her? They wouldn't talk anything over!

Then why was she going with him to his family's restaurant?

Tess stopped walking and looked over at Dane.

"There's not much use in going to the restaurant. There's nothing else we need to say."

Dane gazed down at her from his superior height. His dark eyes hid his feelings as well as they always had when he wanted them to. "Come along and say hello to Pop and Roger," he suggested. "They've been asking about you."

Tess started to refuse, then couldn't think of a good reason. She looked up at him. "All right, and I guess we do need to discuss this after all. Hosham's was the first business on my list. Have you gone anywhere else?"

He nodded. "Johnson's Mercantile on State Street."

The mercantile was down at the bottom of Tess's list. Her dark suspicions of her grandmother's motives grew. "Is this the order you always do the visits in?"

Dane nodded again. "Yep. Got so used to it now, I don't even need to write down the list."

They'd reached the restaurant. Its sturdy fieldstone facade looked just the same as it had nine years ago, when she'd moved to Philadelphia with her father and his new bride. She'd spent her childhood living with her grandmother since her mother's death when she was a baby. Her father's only occasional visits had made him seem almost a stranger.

How she'd hated to leave! Warm memories flooded her mind as Dane opened the door and stood aside for her to enter.

She inhaled deeply. It smelled just the same, too. That mixture of simmering soups and stews and spicy baked goods which always made her mouth water.

As it was doing now. She'd come here with Dane after school for delicious snacks they'd shared in the kitchen. Dane's mother had died when Roger was born, so both boys had grown up in the restaurant.

The memories tumbled thick and fast through her mind. His father had presided over the big stove and the immaculate worktables, pretending to be so fierce, his handlebar mustache trembling at her. He'd never been able to conceal a grin, though.

Tess's mouth curved into a smile. "Does your father still do a lot of the cooking?" she asked before she knew she was going to say it. She glanced at him as he led the way through the almost empty dining room toward the kitchen.

Their glances met. Gray melding into brown. The moment drew out. Finally, Dane smiled back.

"Yep. Still thinks no one can do it like he can.

"I doubt if anyone can," Tess said.

Dane pushed the swinging door open and held it for her.

Oren Kendall glanced sharply up from a huge pot of soup he stirred at the stove. His eyes softened as he saw Tess.

"Come on in, Tess!" he bellowed, putting down his spoon and hurrying toward her. "Took you long enough to come see us."

"I've been busy," she answered, smiling back. She glanced around. "Where's Roger?"

"Had to go get some supplies at the train depot," Oren said.

It was the strangest thing, Tess thought. For the first time since she'd come back to Brightwater, she felt as if she had truly come home.

Instantly, she tried to deny that. No, she didn't feel that way. She *couldn't* feel that way! Not about this place.

Oren hugged her as if she were still the eighteen-year-old he'd last seen. Tess hugged him back, carefully keeping her glance from Dane.

Oren gestured at the table along a wall where the family ate. "Go ahead and sit down. You still like sticky buns as much as you used to?"

Her mouth watered at the thought. "Of course." She sat down at the table, adjusting her heavy cloak.

"You might as well take that thing off and stay a while," Oren said, hurrying to a big covered pan on the back of the stove. He glanced up at Dane, who was standing in the middle of the floor.

"Go ahead and keep Tess company," he said gruffly. "I don't need your help. Especially since you've been gone all morning."

Dane gave his father an even look, but Tess saw that muscle in his jaw twitch. "I worked in the office late last night. I told you I'd be gone this morning."

Oren waved an impatient hand. He glanced over at Tess. "Glad you're back in more ways than one. Word around town is you're thinking about taking the paper over. Hard to think of Edith retiring, but at least now maybe Dane'll get those crazy notions out of his head."

Tess froze. She couldn't look at Dane, still standing in the middle of the floor, but was aware of his stiffening, fearing an outburst. She'd had no idea Dane's father was so bitterly opposed to Dane's buying the paper.

She couldn't tell Oren her grandmother hadn't chosen between them yet. She wanted, *needed,* the *Gazette,* but she wouldn't add to this friction between father and son. "I'm not sure I'm staying," she finally said, keeping her gaze on Oren.

Oren's fleshy face fell. "Is that so? Brightwater too dull after living in Philadelphia all these years?"

Thinking of the small, mean houses she'd lived in, the anxious counting of pennies, Tess's mouth twisted. She shook her head. "No. I—I'm just not sure yet," she repeated.

She was sure. When would her grandmother choose between Tess and Dane? What was she waiting for? And what would Tess and Anne do if she chose Dane?

Dane still stood in the middle of the floor. It was clear

he wouldn't sit down now that they couldn't discuss anything here.

Tess got up, her smile turning apologetic. "I really can't stay, Mr. Kendall. I'll have to take a rain check on the sticky buns. I have some more errands to do for my grandmother."

Oren tilted his head and gave her a shrewd look. "No need to get upset about Dane and me having a few words. Got to keep after him so he doesn't go off and do something foolish."

His father treated Dane as if he were still a boy, Tess thought, biting her tongue to keep from telling the older man so. It was none of her business, and obviously Dane was holding himself back to keep from starting an argument in front of her.

Besides, his father's opposition might cause Dane to withdraw his bid for the *Gazette.*

At once Tess felt ashamed of herself for those petty thoughts. But Edith did have to choose between them. They couldn't both buy the paper.

And she needed it far worse than Dane. He didn't face a life of poverty otherwise.

You don't, either, her mind said. *You know your father and your grandmother will be glad to help you.*

Yes, she knew that—but at what cost? Her father wanted to dominate her life more than Oren did Dane's. If she accepted help from him, he would do just that.

Edith wouldn't. She never had. She'd be delighted to welcome Tess and Anne into her big house permanently. She'd like nothing better than to take care of them.

But something inside Tess rebelled at that choice, too. Not only was Edith getting too old for that, but Tess was a grown woman with a child to raise. She wanted to be able to do that job herself.

She'd made a bad choice of a husband. And she'd

paid for it. Dearly. She could afford to make no more mistakes. And she was beginning to suspect that Edith dragging her feet deciding who'd get the *Gazette* was at least partly a guise to keep Tess and Anne here in Brightwater. Keep them safely ensconced in Edith's big, comfortable house.

Otherwise, why was she acting so strangely?

Unless she wanted to try to get Dane and Tess together.

That was ridiculous, wasn't it? But once there, the thought wouldn't be dislodged.

"I'll walk you outside," Dane said, his voice tight.

"All right. Good-bye, Mr. Kendall. I'm sure I'll see you soon."

"See that you do," Oren said, going back to his soup tending.

"We need to plan the Christmas donation requests," Tess reminded Dane as he opened the front door and walked outside with her.

His mouth tightened. "You don't have to say it. We couldn't do it in there. I'm a fool! I should get the hell out of this town and make my own life."

He glanced over at Tess. "Sorry," he muttered, "but Pop really riles me. He can't understand why I don't want to spend my life helping run Kendall's. Thanks for not mentioning Edith's trying to make up her mind between the two of us."

Tess bit her lip. If she had any sense, she'd encourage Dane to leave town. She'd get her chance with the paper and a new life. And it would also probably be the best thing for Dane.

But she didn't want to. The thought of living here the rest of her life with Dane gone pierced her heart with a pain she couldn't deny.

"I don't want you to leave," she said.

4

Dane stared at Tess. He couldn't believe what she'd just said.

The expression on her face made his heart leap. Her lips were pressed together as if she'd like to bite her tongue out for blurting out the words—but her eyes said something different.

For a moment he caught a glimpse of the woman he'd loved that night in the gardens—and the girl who'd been his childhood friend.

Then a veil came down over her eyes, and she shrugged and smiled. "It's none of my business, of course. You need to do what you feel you must."

His heart settled down, but hope still filled him. There was another woman behind the poised facade Tess presented to the world.

Could that woman still care for him? Although she was trying hard not to admit it—even to herself? He remembered how stubborn she'd been as a child. Just like him. Pushing her would do no good.

If he was guessing right, he had to try a different tack, throw her off, not let her realize he'd seen that crack in her shell.

"What I *want* to do is stay here—and buy the *Gazette*

and run it," he told her, a challenge in his voice. "You already know that."

To his relief, Tess gave him a wry grin. "Yes. You're just as determined as you were ten years ago, Dane Kendall. As tenacious as a bulldog."

Good. They were back on a surface level again. Back to arguing about the paper. His best hope now was to maneuver to be with her as much as possible, wear down those hidden resistances, whatever their origin, without her realizing what he was doing.

"As I remember, Tess Bayley, you were never very far behind when *you* wanted something."

"I had to be tougher and smarter than you or you'd never have bothered with me."

Dane felt a grin stretch his own mouth, a warm feeling spread through him. Somehow, these last few minutes, they'd rediscovered their old friendship, buried beneath the layers of time and events since they'd last seen each other.

That thought sobered him. And it was exactly that final night they'd had together that was the big thing between them now. Somehow, he had to get behind that barrier.

"All right, I'll give you a challenge," he said. "I bet I can get larger donations for the Christmas fund than you."

Tess's eyes widened, then she frowned. "That's not fair! You've been doing this for several years. Of course, you'll have better luck than me."

"Not necessarily," he countered. "Most of the merchants are the same ones you knew. They'll have a soft spot for Edith's granddaughter."

Tess's eyes flashed. "Do you think I'd take advantage of anything like that?"

Dane shrugged. "Sure. Why not? All's fair in love and war, they say. So is this . . . war?" He held his breath.

He hadn't meant to say that after the lecture he'd just given himself.

But Tess only narrowed her beautiful gray eyes. "Of course it is! And may the best . . . person win!"

"Fair enough," Dane managed to say easily. A passerby gave them curious stares. "Uh, maybe we should divide the list and each take half. But somewhere else besides the sidewalk."

Tess seemed to become conscious of their surroundings for the first time. Her cheeks pinkened, making her look even more beautiful, and he had to clench his fists at his side to keep from taking her in his arms right here in front of a good portion of the town.

"Let's go back to the *Gazette* offices," she said. "I've left Anne with my grandmother long enough anyway. I should be checking on her."

Anne. Dane felt that odd feeling he had yesterday. He wanted to see the little girl again. "All right."

At the *Gazette* offices, Dane opened the door to a scene of controlled frenzy. Edith, a billed cap holding her hair back, a big apron covering her gown, fed sheets of paper into the printing press.

George, his back now bent with age, operated the levers that worked the machine.

In the other room, Anne sat on a wooden chair at a worktable, wielding a small pair of scissors on a magazine. She looked around as the bell jingled their entrance and her face lit up. She jumped down and ran toward them.

"Mama! I'm so glad to see you." Anne reached up for a hug and Dane's heart contracted as Tess, her face softened, bent down to the child.

"Mr. Dane!" Anne demanded. "Look around. Can you see what I did to help Gramma Edith?"

Dane gave Tess a quick, startled glance for help.

She smiled demurely at him, then tilted her head toward the rolltop desk.

Dane saw nothing different about the ancient fixture. Papers still were stuffed in every cubbyhole, still covered the desktop.

He frowned at Tess, who shrugged and rolled her eyes, as if he were too dense for words.

"I give up," he finally said, smiling at Anne. "What did you do?"

Anne ran to the worktable and picked up a feather duster and waved it at him. "I dusted the furniture," she said. "Can't you see it looks all cleaned up now?"

Her brown eyes sparkled at him. Again, Dane felt that frisson of not quite recognition, but something . . .

He shook his head, trying to fight off the feeling. He wasn't going to start that nonsense again. "Of course I can, now that I'm looking at it closely. You did a very good job."

Anne nodded, her dark curls bobbing. "I *always* do good jobs," she said firmly. "Mama taught me to so Papa wouldn't get mad and yell at us."

Beside him, Dane heard Tess's quick, indrawn breath. His sideways vision showed her widened eyes.

"You did a splendid job, sweetie," Tess said quickly. "Now why don't you finish cutting out your pictures? Mr. Dane and I have some business to discuss."

"All right." Anne climbed back on her chair and picked up her scissors again.

"Grandmother is too busy to deal with this," Tess told Dane. She reached into her cloak pocket and brought out a folded sheet of paper. "Here, just take half of these names and I'll take what's left."

Her smooth mask was in place again, her cool smile, the kind reserved for casual friends.

But deep in her eyes something else lurked, Dane

saw. Something that made him think of a small, hurt woods creature.

He took the proffered sheet. Tess was still the warm, loving girl he remembered. He was sure of that.

But someone had badly damaged those emotions. After Anne's remarks of a moment ago, and Tess's reaction to them, Hugh Landon, her dead husband, seemed to be the logical choice.

Dane's face tightened. Maybe Tess and Anne had also been hurt physically. His hands curled into fists. *The bastard!*

"Dane? Is something wrong?"

Tess's anxious voice brought him back to himself. *Yes,* he wanted to say, *a lot of things are wrong. But I'm going to do my damndest to fix them.*

But he couldn't. Not yet. That would only send her into full retreat. Maybe even all the way back to Philadelphia.

"No, but I've got to be going." Dane counted down and tore the sheet in half, handing Tess the top part.

Forcing a half-amused challenge into his voice, he said, "I expect I'll be finished with my list by tomorrow evening."

To his relief, Tess tilted her chin up. Good, she still had plenty of spunk left, whatever had happened to her.

"And I expect that I will, too!"

The urge to kiss her was so strong, he could feel the texture of her soft lips under his own, feel her opening to him, her body pressing against his . . . as it had that night . . .

Too soon, too soon, he reminded himself, forcing the feelings back. "Maybe Edith could use a hand," he said, nodding to the inner room, where the two people still labored.

Tess shook her head. "No, Grandmother told me she

and George could manage by themselves quite well today. She'd rather I did the solicitations."

"I've taken George's place a lot the last year or two. And Edith and I figured out this new press together."

Tess's chin went up another notch. "In other words, you're way ahead of me in knowing how to put out this paper. I'm aware of that. But I'm a fast learner. And I love this place."

Dane gave her a tilted grin, although, inside, his emotions were a mass of raging contradictions. "So do I, Tess," he said. "So do I."

He turned and headed for the door, forcing himself not to look back. He twisted the knob and opened it.

"Mr. Dane! You didn't tell me good-bye!"

He heard Anne's chair scrape on the floor, then the pattering sounds her feet made as she ran across the room.

Dane slowly turned, keeping his glance on Anne's small form now standing in front of him. "I'm sorry. Good-bye, Anne."

Her wide smile revealed a dimple he hadn't noticed before. "Good-bye. Will you come back again tomorrow?" she asked hopefully.

"Mr. Kendall is a very busy man, Anne," Tess said, her voice still cool and even. "He and his father and brother run a restaurant."

He'd just taken a swipe at Tess's newspapering abilities, so Dane knew he deserved that dig. The reminder that he didn't need this paper to earn himself a living.

Anne's eyes widened. "Can Mama and I eat at your rest'rant?"

Her question took Dane aback. He hadn't expected this. He nodded. "Of course. Any time your mama wants to bring you."

"Will you be there? Can we sit with you?"

"If your mama wants me to." Dane raised his head, looking at Tess.

Her mask had slipped a little. Her eyes had an uncertain look, her mouth was half open. Dane felt ashamed of himself for even the small amount of needling he'd given her. The girl and woman he loved was still there, still full of life and spunk. But hidden beneath layers of something else. And she needed help to become that woman again.

His help? How could he do that and try to win her back, while still continuing to try to best her in this battle for the *Gazette?*

A new thought slipped into his mind. *If you marry her you could share the paper.* Another one followed close behind. *Of course, it might be hard to convince Tess you love her for herself—and not just as a way to gain the* Gazette.

Damn it! His life had been complicated enough before, when all he'd had to do was talk Edith into selling to him, and try to extricate himself from the restaurant without completely alienating his father and his whole family.

Now things were in a tangle he didn't know how to sort out. But sort them out he would, he vowed.

"Mama?" Anne turned to her mother, her eyes alight. "Did you hear what Mr. Dane said? Will you take me to his rest'rant?"

Dane saw Tess's chest rise in a visible breath. "We'll see, punkin," she said.

Anne turned back to Dane, her lower lip poked out. "She always says that when she really means no," she told him. "Can you change her mind?

"Anne! That's enough," Tess said sharply.

Too sharply. Tears formed in Anne's dark eyes. "You don't have to yell at me," she said, her voice trembly.

Tess was at the child's side before Dane knew she'd

moved. She knelt before Anne, pulled her close. "I'm sorry, honey."

A tear rolled down Anne's face. She put her arms around her mother's neck and squeezed.

The picture the two of them made caused something to squeeze around Dane's heart. He swallowed.

"I've got to go," he said quietly, and this time made his escape with no further interruptions.

He couldn't resist one last glance back, though, as he closed the door behind him.

Mother and daughter still hugged each other. That tug at Dane's heart came again. He wished, how he wished, he was part of that scene.

That *he,* not Hugh Landon, was Anne's father.

Maybe you are, that shadowy voice in his mind said, and this time it was harder to push it away.

5

"Thank you, Mrs. Miller, for bringing your column in. Your news of the local doings in your community is always so interesting."

Tess smiled at the elderly woman in front of the counter, feeling a twinge of surprise at her last words.

She wasn't trying to flatter the woman. Agnes Miller's weekly column *was* interesting, despite its limited content. Agnes had a flair for colorful turns of phrase. The column had been a fixture in the *Gazette* since Tess could remember.

The Brightwater Gazette was a truly good paper, she was discovering. Edith's editorials were lively and thought-provoking. Several other contributing columnists provided helpful or entertaining reading.

"Thank you, Tess," Agnes said, beaming at her. "I'm so glad you're back here to stay. I knew Edith was thinking about retiring, but I didn't realize you'd be taking over."

The bell over the door jingled as Agnes began her last sentence. Dane entered, brushing a dusting of snow from his overcoat.

Just the sight of him made a ripple go down Tess's spine.

Tension gripped her. She didn't want to see Dane

today. Not here, not now, not alone. Maybe she could continue talking to Agnes to keep the woman here.

No, of course she couldn't. What was the matter with her? She could deal with Dane.

It had been a week since they'd divided up the merchant's list. She'd seen him in passing a couple of times, but that was all. They'd come out almost even on their lists, both managing to get nearly everyone to pledge a donation.

Dane glanced over at Tess, his face unsmiling. Had he heard Agnes's last words? Did he think Tess had told Agnes that Edith had finally made her decision?

And in Tess's favor?

Tess felt her cheeks warm. Didn't he know she wouldn't do something like that? *Why would he?* her mind asked. *Didn't he say anything's fair in love and war?* She instantly pushed away the first part of that statement. He'd also said that this was war.

Dane crossed the floor toward the counter.

Agnes was staring at Tess, her mouth open, and Tess realized she hadn't responded to the woman's last remark.

"It's very nice to be back," Tess said evasively. "Now, you have a wonderful Christmas!"

Agnes looked at Tess in surprise. "Oh, I'll be in again before then."

"Of course you will." Tess felt her face grow warmer.

Dane had reached the counter, still with that serious expression on his face.

"Why, hello, Dane," Agnes said, almost simpering. "I swear you get better looking every time I see you!"

Dane's face softened into a smile. "So do you, Mrs. Miller," he said gallantly.

The older woman blushed. "You always were a polite boy. Well, good-bye to you both." She headed for the door, her heavy body waddling a little, and let herself out.

The smile on Dane's face faded. He gave Tess a straight look. "So Edith has decided you're the one to have the *Gazette?*"

He had heard Agnes's last remark. Tess gave him an equally straight look. "No. If she had, do you really think she'd spread it all over town before telling you?"

His face softened again, into another smile. "Of course not." He reached inside his coat and brought out a folded sheet of paper. "Here's the restaurant ad with the specials."

Tess reached for the sheet and missed. It fluttered to the battered countertop. She reached for it again, just as Dane did.

Their fingers touched. A jolt of electricity flowed up her wrist into her arm. Tess gasped and drew her hand back, clutching the paper, not looking at him.

She hoped Dane hadn't noticed her reaction. It was the first time they'd touched since that long-ago Christmas Eve. She'd felt the same way that night . . . when Dane touched her . . . in much more intimate ways . . .

Tess took a deep breath and fought for control, glancing down at the paper. "This seems in order," she said briskly. "All ready to be typeset."

She glanced up, forcing a bright smile. The look in Dane's dark eyes was so intent, so disturbing, she almost gasped again.

Then it faded and he smiled casually back at her.

"It should be. I've been doing it for enough weeks and months and years."

His voice wasn't as casual as the smile. It held a challenge. Another reminder that he was far more qualified to own and run the *Gazette* than she.

Tess's emotions began to roil inside her again with all the complex feelings she had in his presence.

Strong attraction, and a strong desire to push him away. Sympathy for his wish to acquire the *Gazette* and an almost as strong resentment because he was trying to keep her from having it.

Dane moved his head, glancing around the room. "Where's Anne?" he asked.

Something in his voice disturbed her even more. Was she only imagining it, or had he managed to imbue those two short words with too much concern for a child he'd only met a few times?

Like Anne was part of his family. Almost like . . . he was her father.

Don't be such an idiot, she advised herself, putting the advertisement in the tray where it belonged. "Grandmother took her downtown to see the Christmas decorations in the stores," she said, forcing lightness into her tone.

"Oh. I was hoping to see her. She's a . . . wonderful child. You've done a good job with her."

His eyes seemed to be trying to probe beneath her calm surface, to all those rioting emotions underneath. "Thank you," she said, hearing the shakiness in her voice.

Dane's glance roamed over her face, as if to memorize it. When it reached her mouth, she drew in her breath. She could feel his glance like a warm touch . . . she remembered that night when she'd outlined his lips with her fingertips . . . before he pulled her to him and crushed her mouth beneath his own . . .

Somehow, Dane had pushed through the opening in the counter; somehow, she was in his arms and he was kissing her just like he had in her dreams . . .

And she was kissing him back, pressing herself ardently against his hardening body, never wanting this moment to end . . .

A burst of laughter came from the street outside,

breaking the spell. Tess jumped back, away from Dane, her eyes widening in shock.

"Tess, I'm sorry . . ." Dane took a step toward her, frowning. "I didn't intend for that to happen."

Pain shot through her at his words. *He was sorry . . . he hadn't planned that.*

The same things he'd said that other time.

"Mama! We had so much fun!"

Anne burst into the room, Edith behind her. Desperately, Tess collected herself, managing a smile for her daughter.

"Did you, honey? That's good."

Anne pushed through the counter opening. "Mr. Dane! I'm *so* glad you're here! I haven't seen you in a lo-o-ng time." She smiled up at him.

Without looking at Tess, Dane stooped down to the child's level. "I'm glad to see you, too, Miss Anne. Tell me what you did."

Tess's heart squeezed painfully at the tender note in his voice. Oh, everything was so wrong!

Anne's dark eyes shone with excitement. "We saw lots of pretty decorations and candles in the store windows. And there was this bi-i-g window that was full of toys!"

Dane nodded gravely. "I know the one you mean."

"You do? Do you know that a-l-l those toys are going to be given away? To the children who don't have Mamas and Papas? At Gramma Edith's party on Christmas Eve?"

"The orphans." Dane nodded again. "Yes, I do."

Anne's big eyes grew dreamy. "I saw the most prettiest doll in the world there. She had on a white dress with lace and . . . and ruffleys."

Edith had also let herself through the railing. She glanced at Tess and nodded slightly. Tess knew that Anne was going to find a doll exactly like the one she'd described under the tree on Christmas morning.

Edith's shrewd eyes went from Dane to Tess. Tess felt her face warming again and wondered if her lips still looked as kiss-swollen as they felt. Was she disheveled? She kept herself from patting her hair, glancing down at her gown to check.

"I'm hungry! Real, real hungry!" Anne announced, rubbing her stomach. She looked at Dane again, who'd risen. "Mr. Dane, could I eat at your rest'rant now?"

Dane smiled at her. "Of course you can—if your mama wants to." He looked at Tess, his face showing only genial friendliness.

Was that all he felt?

Tess fumed. He'd put her on the spot. She turned to Edith. "What about you, Grandmother? Would you like to eat at the restaurant?"

Edith waved a weary hand. "No, not tonight. That child has worn me out. I'm going home and have Estelle fix me some soup, then I'm going to bed. You two go on ahead."

Tess gave her a concerned glance. "Are you feeling ill? I'd better stay with you."

"No, no," Edith said hastily. "I'm fine. Just tired. Now you run along. I'll just close up here and go on home."

Her glance didn't quite meet Tess's. Tess pressed her lips together, then quickly released them when their still-tender surfaces touched.

Her grandmother had put her on the spot, too.

"All right, honey. We'll go to the restaurant."

Anne clapped her hands together. "Goody!" She turned to Dane. "Will you sit and eat with us, Mr. Dane?"

Dane glanced over at Tess again. She met his look with a cool stare, his words after their kiss still burning in her mind.

He hadn't planned to kiss her today any more than

he had that other night. He hadn't *wanted* to kiss her. So why had he?

"Yes, I would be pleased to sit with you," Dane finally said, smiling at Anne again.

The child reached for Tess's hand. "Come on, Mama. I'm st-ar-ving!"

Tess allowed herself to be tugged into the outer room, to get her cloak, to pretend that inside she wasn't seething with anger. And burning with the kiss just past.

Glancing back over her shoulder as she left the offices, she caught a glimpse of Edith. The older woman had a small, satisfied smile on her mouth.

All that business about being so tired was just an act.

Tess frowned at her, then closed the door. She walked beside Anne, who was chattering away happily, one hand clasped by Tess, the other by Dane.

Tess realized she'd never seen Anne so animated, so . . . much like a normal, happy child should be as right now.

Talking to Dane. Enjoying his company. As she'd never been able to enjoy Hugh's. Even when Hugh had been in a good mood, there was never any assurance it would last. Anne had learned early a wariness that no child should have to learn.

From the moment she'd first met Dane, Anne had trusted him.

Quick tears came to Tess's eyes. Her conflicting feelings twisted inside her.

Dane had kissed her. Then at once apologized for it. Just as he had that night years ago. She'd kissed Dane and felt her whole being consumed in his.

Just as she had those years ago.

If she had any sense at all, she'd pack and she and Anne would leave here tomorrow.

But she knew she wouldn't.

6

Anne's small hand rested trustingly in Dane's as they walked down the cobblestone walk in the gathering dusk of the wintry evening. Emotions he'd never before felt surged through him. Warm, protective feelings. He'd give up his life for this little girl.

He was astonished at the depth of his feelings, but couldn't deny them.

Neither could he deny other deep emotions the kiss he'd just exchanged with Tess had reawakened in him.

But even while he'd gone to her, while she'd moved into his arms and their lips and bodies had met, he'd known he shouldn't be doing this.

Too soon! Too soon! Something inside him had warned. But he hadn't listened. That other voice of the body, of passion, had been stronger.

When he'd tried to tell Tess he regretted pushing her into this, it had only made things worse. She'd looked affronted, as if he'd insulted her.

He gave her a quick sideways glance. Her garnet cloak brought out highlights in her hair, made gold glints appear in her gray eyes. Her chin was tilted, she looked straight ahead. Her mood hadn't changed.

Damn it! How could he straighten out this mess? He couldn't talk to her now, or at dinner with Anne there.

Or maybe never. If he had any sense he'd leave, make a new life for himself somewhere else.

But he knew he wouldn't.

Dogged determination was his way, not running. He didn't want to run. His dream had expanded. He still wanted to buy the *Gazette*, but he also wanted to marry Tess and raise the little girl skipping beside him as his own.

Maybe she was.

He cursed himself for starting up those fruitless thoughts again. Even if that were true, even if Tess had done such a thing, would she ever admit it to him?

Even if he did persuade her to marry him? And he knew that was going to be no easy task. And it was complicated by the fact that if they married, he'd get control of the *Gazette* no matter what Edith decided.

Anne tugged at his hand. "Mr. Dane—are we almost there?"

He forced all these thoughts inside. "Yes, almost. See that big building on the corner? That's it!"

"Oh! Gramma Edith and me went past that today. It was full of people eating."

Dane smiled down at her. It was easy to find a smile for this child. "Just like we're going to be eating in a few minutes."

Anne nodded. "Can I have anything I want?"

Dane gave Tess another glance. She'd turned her head their way. He kept the smile on his face, hoping to coax one from Tess. "You'll have to ask your mama about that."

Tess's full mouth softened into a smile. God, how he wanted to pull her into his arms, kiss her until all doubts and problems between them were gone, washed away by the strength of their passion.

Their love. Did Tess also feel that? Or only the desires of the body?

"We'll see," she said. When Anne's lower lip started to poke out, she added, "I don't mean you can't have at least one thing you choose."

"Thank you, Mama!" Anne gave her mother a brighter smile.

Tess returned it. Then her rising glance collided with Dane's. For an instant there was a rapport between them, like that between parents enjoying a beloved child.

Inside, the restaurant was still almost empty. It was too early for the dinner crowd. Dane led them to a secluded table by a side window. A festive red cloth was spread over the white damask beneath. Tall white candles with greenery at their bases stood in the middle.

"Tess! How good to see you again." Oren bustled over, smiling widely. "And this is your daughter? Ah, she's pretty, just like her mama!" He beamed at Anne, who smiled happily back.

Oren glanced from Anne to Tess. "Pretty, yes, but she doesn't look like her mama. With those big brown eyes and dark curls, she could be one of my granddaughters."

Dane's heart lurched. His glance darted to his father. Oren met his gaze with wide, guileless eyes. Oren meant nothing by that remark. He could have no suspicion of what had happened that Christmas Eve six years ago.

"Anne resembles her father's family," Tess finally said. Her voice sounded oddly stiff, Dane thought, as if she had to force the words out.

Why? What she'd said was a harmless remark. Unless it hid a double meaning only his ears detected.

Oren nodded. "I was sorry when Edith told us of your husband's death last year."

His gaze moved from Tess to his son, taking on a speculative gleam.

Dane inwardly groaned. Oh, Lord. Things were in a

big enough jumble without his dad getting ideas about him and Tess. It was a wonder Oren hadn't started this last week when Dane had brought Tess to the restaurant kitchen.

In addition to their arguments about the *Gazette,* Oren frequently complained about thirty-year-old Dane's unmarried state.

"Tess! Good to see you." Dane's younger brother, Roger, appeared at the edge of their group. He waved at the table. "Sit down. Sit down."

He pulled out a chair for Tess with a flourish, then one for Anne. "You need a cushion, young lady. I'll go get you one." His eyes rested on Anne for a moment.

Dane tensed, sure Roger would also comment on the child's dark coloring. But he bustled off to get the promised cushion without saying anything else.

Dane still stood behind Tess's chair. He wasn't needed in the restaurant this evening, but he half expected his father to make some remark if he seated himself like a paying guest.

Oren surprised him. "Sit down and eat with Tess and her daughter," he told Dane expansively.

Dane did, although something in his father's glance told him he had an ulterior motive. Dane swore inwardly.

"Chicken pot pie is our special tonight," Oren said.

"That sounds wonderful," Tess answered. "I haven't had it for ages. And *never* like yours, Oren."

The older man gave her a gratified smile, somehow managing to include Dane in it, ending with a significant look at his son.

Dane ignored all the byplay, wondering why he'd thought he'd managed such a coup when Tess had agreed to come here.

"I want that, too, Mama," Anne put in. "And some ice cream for dessert?"

"We'll see," Tess replied. "And this time I *do* mean it. It all depends on whether you finish your meal."

Dane was relieved when a new waitress served the meal instead of Lila, Roger's wife. She'd have been sure to comment on Anne's looks. He'd had enough of that for one day.

"You know, I think we could increase the *Gazette*'s advertisement revenue a lot if we gave better discounts for multiple ads and for several issues," Tess said into the silence that had fallen.

Dane, his fork halfway to his mouth, gave her a surprised look. Her glance met his squarely. But something lurked in the depths of her eyes. Wariness. Distrust.

An unexpected thought hit him. Could she believe he'd had a hidden motive for kissing her?

Such as trying to acquire ownership of the *Gazette* by marrying her?

Could *that* be the real reason she'd given him that stunned look afterward? Another unexpected thought entered his mind. What if he'd also been wrong about Tess's financial situation and that was why she was trying to think of ideas to increase the paper's profits?

Maybe her husband hadn't provided well for her and Anne, and she truly needed the income from the paper.

"Even if this is war, I'll play fair," he told her. "I think you're right about the ads. That's a good idea. A very good one."

Tess couldn't keep the surprise from showing on her face, and he hoped she'd picked up on his intentional double meaning.

She'd expected him to disagree. Even to help his own cause, he couldn't. Because it *was* a good idea. One he'd thought of himself. But he wouldn't tell Tess that now.

"You do?" she asked. "Grandmother doesn't. She

doesn't think anything at the *Gazette* needs to be changed."

Some of the wariness had left Tess's eyes. Her tone was a trifle warmer. Dane felt encouraged to probe further.

"Edith doesn't need any more income from the paper," he said. "I would."

He'd give Tess this opening to talk about her own financial situation, see if his suppositions were right.

Tess's face stiffened a little, her cheeks pinkened. In a moment, she nodded. "No, she doesn't. But if I take it over, I'll also need more income than it's generating now."

Anxiety and tension came through clearly in her tone.

So Hugh Landon hadn't left Tess and Anne well provided for. Tess's motives for wanting the *Gazette* were as important as his own. Maybe more so.

Wait a minute, his mind cautioned him. *You don't know if any of this is true. You've built this up from a couple of glances, a few words, a tone of voice.*

He glanced at Anne. She was engrossed in her meal, not paying them any attention.

"You weren't happy in Philadelphia, were you?" he asked in a low voice. "You don't want to go back."

Tess's blush deepened, her face tightened. "It's none of your business," she finally said.

He shook his head. "I've thought all this time you were fighting me for the *Gazette* mostly because you were bored and wanted something to play around with. You'd hate to see it go out of the family, but that's not the big reason you want it."

She looked at him for several more moments. Finally, she nodded. "No. I—need the paper so that Anne and I can be independent."

Tess's pride was keeping her from admitting any

more than she had to, but he'd bet her financial situation was bleak—also her prior life in Philadelphia. But that didn't mean she had no other choices.

"Edith's told me a hundred times this last year how happy she'd be if you'd live with her."

Tess tilted her chin up. "I don't want anyone taking care of me and Anne."

Not even me? he burned to ask, but didn't.

If he stayed on at the restaurant, he might not be happy, but he'd be earning his own way. Hell, yes, he would! No slackers in the Kendall family.

If Edith decided to sell him the *Gazette,* Tess didn't have another good choice. Not in a small town like Brightwater. She'd have to go back to Philadelphia or let her grandmother support her and Anne. He knew a lot of women who'd be happy to live that kind of life and who'd think Tess a fool for not accepting and welcoming that choice.

But, damn it, he understood! That was one of the reasons he wanted the paper. He'd never feel independent working at his family's restaurant—even if he and his brother and father *were* equal partners.

No matter how he looked at it, Tess's reasons for wanting the paper were more urgent than his own. Being a man, he had other choices, such as leaving and making his way in some other city. She didn't.

What if he told her she could have the *Gazette?* That he wouldn't fight her for it any longer.

He thought about that idea a moment, then dismissed it.

She wouldn't believe he'd suddenly changed his mind, lost his interest in acquiring the *Gazette.* It might make her even more suspicious of his motives.

Or the undeniable fact that if they married, he would own the paper anyway. There was no getting around that.

Given that, how was he ever going to convince her he wanted her for herself alone?

"Mama, I finished a-a-ll my chicken pie. Can I have ice cream?"

Anne's light voice brought him out of his dark thoughts. His heart softened as he smiled at her and got a radiant return smile.

No, Tess wasn't all he wanted. He also wanted this little girl in his life.

This child who might be his own flesh and blood.

As much as he burned to, he couldn't ask Tess if Anne was his child. No matter how hard it was, he had to wait until she was ready to tell him the truth.

This situation was a mess, no doubt about it. But somehow, he was going to convince Tess to marry him.

He had to plan his campaign as carefully as any general. But hadn't he reminded Tess that all was fair in love and war?

She desired him already. She couldn't have kissed him so passionately an hour ago if she didn't.

Wasn't that half the battle won?

7

Dane clapped the pages of his hymn book together and smiled at the group standing around the piano in his living room. "That's it, folks. Tonight's the night. If we don't know these carols now, it's too late to learn them this year."

Some groans arose. "I say we skip the third verses," Marianne Walters said. "No one can ever learn them, since we only do this once a year."

"I second that motion," Roger Kendall fervently added, followed by general sounds of agreement.

Tess kept silent, wondering why she'd let herself get involved with this. The *how* was simple enough. Dane had caught her by surprise and she hadn't had a ready excuse, except that she was out of practice.

He'd assured her it was strictly an amateur group, not many of the people even members of a church choir. But now, after several years, it had become a town tradition.

So she now found herself two days before Christmas, on the coldest night so far this winter, bundled up in her warmest clothes, ready to traipse around the town—hopefully to entertain people, who'd come out on their porches to listen to the old songs of love and peace and goodwill.

She gave a wistful thought to her grandmother and Anne, before a crackling fire in Edith's sitting room, and trudged out with the others.

The gold locket around her neck, with its embossed rose, felt oddly warm against her gown.

She hadn't worn it for years. Not since she and Dane had made love in the garden six years ago.

The locket seemed to grow warmer with that thought.

Don't be such an idiot, she told herself. *It's only a piece of jewelry.* She'd lost it that night in the gardens and Dane had found it and given it to her grandmother. For the first time, she wondered how Dane had explained that so Edith didn't think it odd. Her grandmother had given it back to her a few days ago. Edith had seemed very pleased to see her wearing it tonight.

Somehow, she found herself walking beside Dane. Tess was sure he'd managed that, but so adroitly she hadn't noticed.

In the week and a half since they'd shared that restaurant meal—that sweet and passionate kiss—Dane seemed to be everywhere she looked, everywhere she went.

George's cold had gotten worse, turned into grippe. Today was his first back at work. Although Tess had tried to help Edith all she could, her lack of experience had made her grandmother eagerly accept Dane's help with the paper whenever he offered it. Which was often.

At first, Tess had fumed, sure Dane's eagerness to help was primarily to show her up, make Edith see how much better he could run the paper than Tess.

But after a couple of days, she'd changed her mind. Puzzled, she'd watched Dane expertly handle all the myriad details of the business, but not once had she detected any triumphant glances directed her way, any indication her suppositions were correct.

"Warm enough?" Dane suddenly asked, so close she

jumped, so close she felt his warm breath in the frigid air surrounding her.

"Yes," she answered, not turning toward him, edging a little farther away as they reached the first house. The town streets were almost empty tonight, everyone with sense home in front of fires.

"All right, let's give it all we've got!"

Dane was a natural leader, she thought as the dozen shivering people obediently formed a compact group and began to sing.

"Silent night, holy night . . ." floated into the still, cold air, puffed out by the singers' frosty breaths.

Dane had moved closer. The nubby tweed of his overcoat brushed against Tess's velvet cloak, reminding her of another time . . . another touch. She shivered again, and not from the cold.

She tried to concentrate on the sweetness of the carols, and Dane's dilemma. Why this had suddenly become so important to her, she couldn't say.

But it had. Dane shouldn't spend his life working in the family restaurant, dominated by Oren, who was also a natural leader. He and Dane would constantly butt heads. Roger, on the other hand, she remembered from childhood days, had always been willing to follow others. As he followed his brother's lead now.

Oren was strong and healthy. It would probably be years before he'd retire from the business. Years of misery for Dane . . . unless he bought the newspaper. Or went away from Brightwater to find a paper somewhere else.

And left her here, contentedly running the *Gazette*, just as Edith had done for years.

Contentedly? Without Dane? The bleakness that filled Tess at that thought terrified her, made her finally accept her true feelings. How had she let herself fall in love with Dane all over again? How could she ever be content or happy without him now?

How could you be happy with *him?* her mind asked. *If you married, he'd have control of the* Gazette, *not you. He'd have control of your life—and Anne's. You'd have no security, just as you had none with Hugh.*

Dane isn't like Hugh! she protested.

How can you forget he betrayed you once—how can you trust him not to do it again? You've already made two big mistakes in your life. You don't want to make another.

Numbly, her feet, even in her fur-lined boots, growing as cold as her heart, she opened her mouth and kept on singing with the group.

She smiled at the families crowding their front porches, offering welcome hot drinks, cookies, and candy. But it all seemed unreal to her. The only real thing was Dane's nearness, the occasional brush of his sleeve against her cloak. The flash of his smile.

At last it was over. They'd made their proscribed circle and were back in front of Dane's small house. "Come in for hot cider," Dane offered.

"Sounds good to me," Roger said. "I need to thaw out."

Tess's frozen heart woke up. "So do I," she heard herself saying. "My feet are numb."

That was true, but Tess knew it wasn't why she was staying. Edith's house was only a twenty-minute walk away.

She tried not to think about why she was staying.

Everyone else shook their heads, murmuring their thanks, saying it was getting late. Tomorrow morning would come early.

Marianne Walters gave Tess a knowing smile as she turned to go. Tess ignored it.

She caught the gleam in Dane's eyes as she and Roger followed him inside. Of course since she'd stayed, even with Roger there, too, Dane would be sure to think she wanted to be with him.

And of course he'd be right, her mind told her. *You're being a fool.*

She ignored that, too.

Dane quickly built up the still-smoldering blaze in the fireplace. He turned to Tess, patting the settee close to the fire. "Come on and sit down—take off your boots and warm your feet."

"Don't even care that your only brother probably has frostbite!" Roger chided, a grin belying his words.

"You're big enough and old enough to take care of yourself," Dane returned, grinning back.

Roger's grin included Tess. "So's Tess. Old enough, anyway. Still not very big, though. Remember when all the kids teased her about being so short?"

Tess felt a pang of disappointment when Roger settled beside her, and didn't even try to deny what caused it. Dane sat down on a chair half facing them.

"Yep, and she used to get so mad she wanted to black some eyes," he said.

Tess's peripheral vision caught his glance on her, too intent for the casual words he'd just said.

"Will you two stop talking about me as if I'm not in the room?" Tess asked crossly. She reached down and unlaced her boots and took them off, then wiggled her numb toes.

"You can't deny we speak the truth," Dane teased.

Tess glanced up, meeting his dark gaze. The look in his eyes didn't match his light banter. Its warmth sent heat spiraling through her.

"I'm all grown up now," she returned, not lowering her gaze.

"Yes, you are," Dane answered, and this time his words matched the expression in his eyes.

The silence drew out. Tess couldn't seem to take her eyes away from Dane's.

Roger suddenly rose, breaking the spell. Tess gave him a startled glance.

"Guess I'd better be getting home. Lila will be wondering what happened to me. And Mikie will probably still be awake, since I promised I'd bring him a cookie."

He fumbled in his pocket and brought out a molasses sugar cookie, one of the treats they'd been offered during their caroling stint. He sighed in relief. "Thought I'd dropped it."

Pain pierced Tess's heart at Roger's words, his loving tone as he talked about his small son. They were ordinary, everyday words.

But ones Anne had never heard from Hugh. Not once.

They all exchanged good-byes and Roger left. Tess finally realized the abruptness of his departure was probably caused by the way she and Dane had been looking at each other.

As if they were alone together.

Which now they were, in truth.

Tess didn't know what had come over her these last few minutes, but she didn't care what Roger thought. What the other members of the caroling group thought.

More fool, you, her mind said.

Again she ignored that voice of reason, pushing it back. All she cared about was the fact she and Dane were alone. Together. For the first time since that day in the newspaper office when they'd kissed.

For the second time since that magical, wonderful, devastating night in the gardens six years ago. When they'd also kissed . . . and done much more than that.

"Are you getting warm?" Dane asked into the silence.

Tess nodded. "Yes." Again their words had double

meanings, and again she was sure it was no accident. And that Dane was as aware of that as she.

She should put her boots on, and leave now. While she still could. But she knew she wasn't going to. Her thoughts sounded strangely familiar, and then she realized they were almost the same ones she'd had that other night in the gardens.

The difference was, tonight she didn't feel that panicky fear mixed with her love and desire for Dane.

Tonight, she wasn't promised to another man.

No, but there are other reasons for you to stop this! You can't trust Dane any more than Hugh! Remember how he made love to you once, then rejected you . . . The voice in her mind was weaker, fading away . . .

"Tess . . ."

Dane was suddenly beside her, kneeling on the rug before the fire. Her heart leapt in her chest, and she found it hard to breathe.

His arms came around her, tugging her gently onto the warm soft rug beside him.

They came together eagerly, bodies clinging. Warmth suffused Tess. She tingled all over with exquisite awareness of every touch Dane gave her.

She pressed herself against his hard body, feeling the imprint of him, feeling the small, round heat of the locket around her neck pulsing, pushing into the hollow between her breasts.

Dane's lips found hers, covered hers, filled her with sweetness and passion. The warmth of his fingers pushing her cloak back, off her shoulders, unbuttoning her gown, added to her own warmth. She fumbled for his shirt buttons and drew in her breath when at last their bare, heated flesh touched and clung.

Dane groaned, deep in his chest, his mouth finding her breasts, suckling them, then returning to her lips again with her own scent on his mouth . . .

"Love me," Tess urged Dane in a breathy whisper. "Love me forever!"

He'd do his utmost to grant her wish, Dane thought as their trembling bodies, their yearning hearts, sought and found fulfillment in each other.

They lay nestled together afterward. Sweet contentment filled Dane. This was so different from that other time when Tess had jerked away from him, guilt and horror filling her eyes, in every line of her body.

Everything was right with them this time.

They were so close he could feel her heart beating with his own. "I love you," he whispered. "I'll always love you."

Tess stirred . . . then moved away a tiny bit . . . then a bit more. Dane glanced down at her, smiling, ready to give her more of the words of love that had been in his heart for so long.

Her expression made the smile freeze on his mouth, the warmth leave his body.

The dazed, horrified look of that other time was on her face again.

Evading his eyes, Tess quickly got to her feet, quickly adjusted her clothing, scooped something up from the floor, something that gleamed in the lamplight.

Her locket. The same one she'd worn that night.

She jerked her cloak around herself, stuck the locket in its pocket, then headed for the door, not looking back.

Dane's stunned gaze found Tess's boots still in front of the settee. He broke through the coldness surrounding him and got to his feet, adjusted his own clothing, feeling a horrible sense of déjà vu.

"Tess! What's the matter—where are you going?"

Her hand was already on the doorknob. Her back stiffened, and she didn't turn around. "I—I have to go. It's late. Anne will be worrying about me."

Her wooden voice added to the wrongness filling the room. Anger and determination suddenly surged through Dane.

"No! This isn't going to end like that other time," he said, his voice hard and determined. "This time there's no reason for it to!"

He lunged across the room, caught Tess's hand on the knob before she could turn it.

Her small hand was icy cold beneath his, as if those moments in his arms when their warmth had enveloped each other had never happened.

"What is wrong with you?" he demanded.

"Nothing's wrong," Tess said, her voice stiff. But it also trembled. She shrank away from him, tugging at her hand still imprisoned under his.

He stared at Tess's rigid figure, her glance not quite meeting his. Coldness swept over him again.

Maybe there was still a reason for things to be wrong between them. For guilt to fill Tess's gray eyes. An important reason.

Such as who Anne's true father was.

You know the answer to that, his mind said. *You can't keep on denying it to yourself.*

Anne's your child.

He took a deep breath and let it out. He lifted her boots. "Come back to the fire and put these on and then I'll walk you home," he said evenly.

8

"Hosham's have been so wonderful this Christmas. Not only giving us a generous donation, but volunteering to deliver all the baskets, too." Edith's voice was full of satisfaction.

Tess gave her grandmother a weary smile. This had been a long, tiring day, helping Edith with the last-minute details of the Christmas baskets and the party tonight.

The mention of Hosham's reminded her of Dane.

Pain shot through her, feeling as if it pierced her heart.

Today, almost everything reminded her of Dane.

No wonder after what had happened between them last night—and its aftermath. Thinking of that silent walk home beside him, she winced.

She felt heat flooding her face, another frequent occurrence today.

What had gotten into her last night? Why had she made such a fool of herself? Brazenly staying there alone with Dane after Roger left. Practically flinging herself into his arms. Acting like an idiot afterwards.

She'd known he wanted her—had known that since they'd kissed each other right here in the office. And she'd wanted him.

Just like the first time, their lovemaking had been wonderful. Afterward, drowsily content, she'd lain there in the circle of Dane's arms.

Then he'd said the words she'd wanted to hear, longed to hear, for six long years.

He'd told her he loved her. That he wanted to be with her forever.

And instead of delight and happiness, doubt and fear had shot through her. Making her draw away from Dane, get up . . . leave.

As she'd done six years ago.

Now there was no fiancé. No broken promises.

But there were other reasons she couldn't let herself love Dane—couldn't marry him.

She couldn't put herself and Anne at the mercy of any man—not ever again.

Why had she forgotten that?

Forgotten that before they married Hugh had also told her with every evidence of sincerity that he loved her.

And hadn't meant a word of it. He'd laughed at her for being a gullible, foolish young girl. She winced with pain at these memories.

"You look flushed, Tess." Edith's concerned voice broke through her reverie, brought her back to the present.

"I'm fine. It's just a little warm in here." Tess forced another smile for her grandmother, and for Anne, who'd heard Edith's words and now came over, anxiously glancing up at Tess.

"Are you sick, Mama?"

"No, honey," Tess reassured her. "I'm fine."

The bell over the door jingled. Tess's head jerked around. It was only George, his arms filled with a basket of toys. What were these? Carmichael's had already sent a carriage over to the house with the bulk of the orphans' toys to be given away at the party tonight.

He set them down, puffing from exertion. "They overlooked a few," he said.

Edith gave him a distracted wave. "Just leave the basket there. I'll take it home with me when I close up here."

She glanced at the big clock on the wall, and let out a relieved sigh. "And, thank God, it's nearly time for that."

"Well, if that's all, I'll be going along." George hurried to the door before Edith could think of anything else for him to do.

"Are you coming to the party?" Edith called after him. "We're expecting you!"

"Don't think I'll be able to make it," George mumbled over his shoulder, then quickly closed the door behind him.

Edith gave Tess a tired grin. "I ask him to the party every year and every year he says that same thing. Dyed-in-the-wool old bachelor, that one. Set in his ways as a rock."

Anne left her seat and her ever-present scissors and joined them. "*When* is going to be time for the party?" she asked, for undoubtedly the twentieth time today. "I want to put on my red vevlet dress."

"Velvet," Tess corrected, then summoned up a warm smile for her small daughter. "Soon, honey. Soon now."

Too soon for herself, Tess thought, putting the last stack of paper in the basket on the counter to deal with after the holidays.

Much too soon to have to face Dane again. What would she say to him? What *could* she, after the stupid way she'd behaved last night? Making love with him, then running away.

She'd made him so angry he hadn't said a word to

her all the way home. So maybe she wouldn't have to worry about tonight. He probably didn't want to see her any more than she did him.

But she *did* want to see him again. She pushed that errant thought down.

At least that initial meeting tonight would be easier, because Dane would be dressed as Santa Claus, distributing gifts to the children.

"I'm looking forward to seeing Tess and that pretty little girl of hers," Oren told Dane.

Dane, seated at the office desk, finished the column he was adding, then glanced up at his father.

The older man's face was bland. As if butter wouldn't melt in his mouth, Dane thought. As if all the hints and sly remarks the last couple of weeks hadn't meant a thing.

Dane stared down at the ledger. He'd worked here all day to get caught up on end-of-the-year records. He wasn't quite finished, but he could do it later.

He slammed the ledger closed with a loud clap and pushed his chair back. He was so sick of staring at columns of numbers he couldn't stand another second of it.

He also couldn't stand another minute of this stupid game-playing his father was doing. Or going back and forth over what he was going to do about the paper. And about Tess.

"Finished already?" Oren asked in surprise.

Dane shook his head. "Nope. Don't care, either. It can wait."

"No, it can't," Oren protested. "You know we always get the end-of-the-year paperwork done on Christmas Eve."

Dane felt all the emotions he'd repressed all day boiling just under the surface, ready to erupt.

"Pop, I don't care if we've been doing it like this for the last thousand years! This year it's going to be different."

Oren stared at him, moving back a step. "What's gotten into you today?"

"Life, Pop, that's what!" He felt excitement suddenly gain headway inside him, pushing the other feelings down.

Suddenly, everything became clear in his mind. He knew what he had to do. What he *would* do.

"You can stop dropping all these hints as to why Tess would make a good wife. I know all that. I'm going to ask her to marry me tonight. And I'm not going to take no for an answer!"

Amazed pleasure took over Oren's features. He moved forward, clapped his son on the back. "Now that's the smartest plan you've had in a long time!"

Dane smiled back at his father, feeling excitement rise in him. He couldn't wait to get to Edith's house, get the gift-giving over with and take Tess off to a quiet room where they could be alone.

She already knew he loved her. But he'd tell her again—and again.

But that wasn't all he'd tell her.

He clapped Oren on the back.

"Come on, Pop. We've got a party to get ready for!"

9

Anne, preening in her red velvet dress in Tess's bedroom, watched her mother get ready for the party. Edith, wearing a creamy ivory gown, also supervised Tess's toilette.

Anne picked up the gold locket from the dresser where Tess had left it yesterday evening. "It's so-o-o pretty, Mama. Are you going to wear it?"

"No," Tess quickly answered. It would remind her of last night. She didn't need or want any reminders.

Anne's face fell. "Why not?"

"Yes, why not?" Edith put in. "It will look nice with that dress."

Tess, not able to think of a reasonable-sounding refusal, gave in. "All right."

With one small finger, Anne traced the embossed red rose on the locket's face. "Does it come open?"

"Yes." Edith leaned over and pushed the catch. The locket sprang apart, revealing Tess's likeness on one side.

"Oh! It's you, Mama!" Anne exclaimed. "Why isn't there anyone on the other side?

Tess winced inwardly. Hugh's portrait should be on that other side. But it wasn't. It never had been.

Thankfully, Anne didn't ask her that question.

Edith closed the locket with a snap. "Maybe it's not time yet, little one," she said.

Tess, startled at that unexpected remark, the odd tone in her grandmother's voice, glanced over. The older woman gave her a serene smile and got up from her chair, holding the piece of jewelry.

"I'll help you with the clasp. It's a tricky one. I remember losing it a couple of times."

Just as she'd lost it, Tess thought.

"*You* used to wear this locket, Gramma?"

Edith nodded. "Yes," she said, her voice turning soft and dreamy. "I got it on my eighteenth birthday, just as my mother and your mother did. Someday it will be your turn. I was wearing it when I met your great-grandfather. It's a very special, magical locket."

A wry smile curved Tess's lips at her grandmother's fancies. There was certainly nothing magical or special about the locket. Both times she'd worn it, everything had gone terribly wrong.

The locket settled into place against Tess's throat, revealed by the low neckline of her moss-green velvet gown. As it had last night, it felt warm and strangely tingly against her skin.

No wonder, after what her grandmother had just said. Tess grimaced at her reflection in the mirror.

She gave her hair, pulled back into an elaborate chignon, a last poke.

Behind her in the mirror she saw Anne's reflection.

Anne's dark eyes were wide. "Oh, I can't wait till it's *my* turn! That will be so 'citing! Won't it be 'citing, Mama?"

Tess's heart softened with love for her child. The last few days, with all the Christmas preparations going on, Anne had discovered the word exciting and had been using it at every opportunity. "I'm sure it will."

She gave herself a last look. Her hair had turned out

presentably, but her face was pale and strained, making her gray eyes seem huge and dark. No hope for it. She didn't feel festive tonight. But she'd have to pretend for Anne's sake.

Tess got up, shaking the folds of her wide-skirted gown into place. "Ready?"

"I've been ready, girl." Edith's glance met Tess's, an odd, knowing look in the depths of her gray eyes, so like Tess's own.

As if her grandmother knew all about what had happened between Tess and Dane last night. Knew how confused she felt, how much she hurt.

Tess swallowed. Was she that transparent? "Then let's go downstairs."

"It's snowing, Mama!" Anne exclaimed as they reached the drawing room. She ran to the French doors leading to the terrace and stuck her nose against the panes. "Look at it snow! Can I go sledding tomorrow?"

"If the snow lasts," Tess promised, coming up beside her daughter, watching the thickly falling flakes.

"No danger of *this* snow melting," Edith declared from beside her. "Just look at it coming down. Be plenty of sleighs on the road tonight!"

Why was there such magic in the first heavy snowfall? Tess wondered, feeling some of the excitement Anne was exhibiting. She didn't know, but there it was.

The next half hour was a blur. Tess helped Edith with greeting the guests, settling the wide-eyed orphan children in the comfortable area they'd arranged for them in the big drawing room, which was decorated with fresh greenery and red and green bows and smelled pleasantly of pine and fir.

Finally, Tess settled herself and Anne beside Edith on a sofa.

An air of tension permeated the room.

"Anne, dear, please stop kicking the sofa," Tess said, hoping her smile didn't reveal her nervousness.

Dane was due to make his grand entrance any second, dressed as Santa Claus, with his big bag of gifts.

"Mama, I'm so 'cited I can't be still," Anne answered. "I'm trying, but my legs just won't stay quiet."

"Well, try harder," Tess said, still smiling. Idly, she stroked her fingers over the rose-and-gold locket, wishing she hadn't worn it. It still felt strangely warm and tingly against her skin.

It still reminded her of last night's wonder and delight.

And the painful aftermath. Magical, indeed! If so, it was a bad kind of magic. Maybe she should take it off right now . . .

A small commotion at the double doors leading into the room made most of the people occupying it turn that way.

A rotund, white-bearded figure, dressed in a red-and-white suit, stooping under the weight of a huge burlap bag, stood just inside the room.

A chorus of oohs and ahhs sighed around the room.

"There he is, Mama!" Anne squeaked. "There is Sanda Claus!"

Tess's heart beat faster as she, too, looked at the figure. No one would guess it was Dane, she thought. He made his way to the cleared-off space around the tall fir tree, gaily decorated with strings of popcorn and cranberries, delicate glass balls, and glowing candles in one corner.

No one but herself. She would recognize his direct, dark look, his steady walk, anywhere. Anytime.

Dane added the contents of his sack to the wrapped packages already under the tree, making another chorus of oohs and ahhs arise from the gathered children.

Anne's hand slipped inside her mother's. "Mama, is Sanda going to give *me* a present, too?"

"I'm sure he will, dear," Tess answered, glancing at her grandmother.

Edith's face had a look of pleased anticipation, not unlike the children's. She'd told Tess not to worry, she'd provide Anne's gift. Tess was sure she knew what it would be, too.

A stack of candy canes were the first things to be given out. Then Dane began reading names from the packages, and, while the children sucked blissfully on the sweets, the gift-giving began in earnest.

Iron fire engines and horse-drawn trolleys, cap pistols, and marble shooters made their way into small hands around the room.

And dolls for the girls, of course. Tess watched Anne's awe-struck face as little girls clutched beautifully dressed china dolls, some fitting the description of the one Anne had fallen in love with in the store window.

"Anne—Landon," Dane boomed.

Anne stiffened beside Tess. She looked at her mother, all her usual animation gone.

"Go ahead," Tess urged, smiling encouragingly. "It's your turn."

Biting her lip, Anne slowly made her way to the tree, where Dane stood, holding out a box.

"Have you been a good girl this year, Anne?" Dane asked, mock sternly.

Tess could see Anne swallow. "Yes," she said in a small voice. "I—I b'lieve so."

"I believe so, too," Dane said, his voice softened. "Here you are." He carefully placed the box across Anne's outstretched arms.

"Thank you, sir," Anne said, still in that small voice. She turned and headed back toward where Tess and Edith sat, a smile beginning to turn up her mouth.

"Can I open it now or do I have to wait until tomorrow morning?"

"Of course you can open it now, child," Edith said. "Don't you see all these other children doing that?"

Anne nodded. "Yes, but they don't live here. They have to go back to the orph'nage. I'm so glad I live here!" she said fervently. "I won't ever have to be an orphan girl, will I?"

Tess's heart squeezed. Did Anne miss Hugh? Miss the semblance of the normal family life she'd had?

"Of course you won't," Edith said, her voice firm and decisive. "Now open your gift and let's see what it is."

Tess pushed down her gloomy thoughts, smiling at her grandmother, who looked as if she'd open the box herself if Anne didn't get a move on.

"All right." With Tess's help, Anne unwrapped the box and took off the lid. Inside, a nest of tissue covered the contents. Anne carefully moved it away, then her eyes widened, her mouth hung open.

"Oh, it's the most beaut'ful doll in the world! The one I saw in the store window!" Reverently, she lifted the splendidly attired doll out and put it in her lap and just looked at it.

"Isn't that a big surprise?" Tess asked, giving her grandmother a smiling glance. It wasn't the doll from the window, of course. That one was being admired by some other little girl in the room. But Edith had managed to find a remarkably similar doll.

Soon, all the gifts had been distributed. Dane picked up his now-empty sack, waved at the roomful of people, and left the way he'd arrived.

He turned as he reached the door, and his gaze once more scanned the roomful of people until it found her. And lingered.

Warmth went down Tess's spine. The locket around her neck tingled.

Once changed from his costume, was Dane coming back to the party? She'd greeted his father and Roger and his family earlier. So surely he would.

What if he didn't? she asked herself. *Wouldn't that be best—at least as far as you're concerned? After all, you've decided you can never trust another man, not even Dane.*

Was that true? How could it be? Even if he had rejected her those years ago, sent her on to marry Hugh and live with him those six long, miserable years.

She'd run away from Dane, too, that night. Maybe she shouldn't have . . . maybe if she'd stayed and they'd talked . . .

It was far too late for that!

Wasn't it?

Not if he loved her, as he'd said last night. Not if she loved him. Did she truly know what love was? Did anyone?

Tess huffed out a sigh, trying to shut out her chaotic thoughts. No matter what happened between them, she had to talk to him.

She had to tell him that she would no longer fight him for the *Gazette.* She couldn't have any kind of a happy life here, knowing how Dane yearned for the paper.

Why was she trying to fool herself? She couldn't have any kind of a happy life, here or anywhere else, without Dane.

Somehow, now, her doubts and fears seemed as unsubstantial as the delicate snowflakes coming down outside.

But hundreds of snowflakes piled on each other aren't delicate or fragile, her mind told her. *They're heavy enough to cave a roof in, destroy it. Just like trusting in another man's professed love could destroy my life and Anne's.*

"Let's go see to the refreshments," Edith said, rising. "Margaret always needs a bit of prodding."

The next hour was another blur of excited talk and laughter. Anne was still in a state of bemused wonder over her doll, like many of the children over their gifts.

Tess's spirits rose despite her anxiety. Outside, the snow still fell thickly, covering everything with a gleaming, perfect garment of white. Inside, all was laughter and warmth and good food.

But Dane didn't return.

Tess's spirits began to fall again. He wasn't going to come back. *And wouldn't that be best for both of you?* the voice of reason asked.

Firmly, she closed it out. She wouldn't listen to it tonight. She was going to trust to something deeper than reason inside her.

If she had the chance.

Finally, the crowd began to thin. The sleighs arrived to take the orphans back to their home. Most of the other guests with small children also left with their yawning, still-excited charges.

Anne drooped on a sofa, small feet dangling, her doll still clutched firmly in her arms. "Come on, honey, time for bed," Tess said briskly.

"Do I have to go to bed now?" Anne's pleas were halfhearted, interrupted by a huge yawn.

"Yes, you do. You can barely stay awake. Come along now."

A half hour later, Tess same out of Anne's room. As tired as she was, Anne still couldn't settle down. Twice she'd called Tess on one pretext or another. Now she seemed to be firmly asleep.

Tess walked halfway down the wide staircase overlooking the foyer and the open doors into the drawing room. Only a few people still remained, she saw.

Was Dane among them?

She walked down the rest of the stairs and to the drawing-room doors and looked into the big room. A few knots of people still lingered in chattering groups. The punch bowl was nearly empty.

Edith was talking to Oren.

Dane was not in the room.

Disappointment swept over her, so deep it made her feel ill. She made herself face the truth.

Of course he wasn't. If he'd intended to return to the party, he'd have done so long before.

Oren looked up and saw her. His face lit up. "Tess!" he called. "Come over here. I want to talk to you."

"And so do I," a deep voice said from behind, close to her ear. "Which of us would you rather have a conversation with?"

Tess shivered, a thrill going through her. She quickly turned. Dane stood behind her, snow coating his tweed overcoat. "You," she said simply.

"Good." Dane's dark gaze probed her own.

Tess kept her gaze firmly on Dane. Resolution suddenly filled her. *No more evasion,* she told herself. *No more waiting.*

"You two come on over here," Edith commanded.

Tess looked from her grandmother back to Dane. "It looks like we're stuck."

Dane let out an exasperated breath. "Not for long," he vowed. His gaze settled on her mouth.

Tess felt warmth sweep over her. "No, not for long."

10

Together, they walked across the big room to where Oren and Edith stood before the fire.

Dane inwardly fumed. He didn't intend to get tied up with his father and Edith now. He'd deliberately waited until he thought almost everyone would be gone before returning.

So he'd have a chance of finding Tess alone. Be able to talk to her. Finally tell her what was in his heart. And maybe she'd finally tell him what was in her own.

Edith moved over, made room for Tess and himself in their circle. She looked at both of them. "Oren and I have some things to say to you two."

He caught Tess's glance. She looked as frustrated as he felt.

"Can't it wait, Grandmother?"

"No," Edith said. "I don't think so."

"Don't pussyfoot around, Edith," Oren said. He fixed Dane with his gaze. "I won't stand in your way any longer if you still want to buy the dang paper. You're a grown man now. Have been for a long time. You need to make up your own mind about what you want to do for your living. Took me too long to see that, and I'm sorry."

His father's words stunned Dane. He'd never have guessed he would back down on his stand like this.

"I also have something to say," Edith announced. "I've given this matter of the paper a lot of thought. I've watched the two of you these last weeks. You're both smart and capable and can do a good job of running the *Gazette*. Both of you want it."

Beside him, Dane heard Tess's sharp intake of breath.

"So," Edith continued, "there's only one fair solution to this problem. You'll have to share *The Brightwater Gazette*. You'll have to be partners."

Silence followed her last words, settling heavily on the big room. Dane stared at Edith. His peripheral vision showed him Tess was also gaping at her grandmother.

Dane recovered first. He turned to Tess and raised his brows. She gave him a small nod, a stunned expression still on her face, then looked at Edith again.

"We have to talk this over," she said. "Dane and I."

Edith nodded affably. "Of course you do. Why don't you two go to the front sitting room where it will be nice and quiet."

"That sounds fine to me," Dane quickly said.

"To me, too," Tess answered just as fast.

Hope rose in him. Tess's mood seemed completely different from last night, after their lovemaking. Her voice was steady, so was her gaze. Although she was pale, that wild look, full of doubts and fears, was gone from her lovely face.

"You two young people go right ahead," Oren said expansively. He beamed at them both, as if giving his blessing.

Tess and Dane walked together out of the room and into the study across the foyer. A warm fire blazed in the small stone fireplace. Snow whispered against the windowpanes, accentuating the cozy feel of the room.

"Shall we sit here?" Dane gestured toward the settee before the fire.

"Yes." Tess seated herself and Dane settled beside her.

Silence followed. Dane frowned. It had seemed so simple to tell her how he felt when he was thinking about it. Now it didn't.

Tess was looking down at her velvet skirt, picking at a thread. She suddenly glanced up, her expression determined.

"Tess . . ."

"Dane . . ."

"Go ahead," he said, wanting to reach for her hand, enfold it within his own. But he didn't. If they touched each other, nothing would be resolved.

"What are we going to do about Grandmother's proposed solution?"

It looked like they'd have to work up to the important things gradually. "It seems feasible to me," he said.

"To me, too." She paused, then bit her lip. "That wasn't all I wanted to talk to you about. I wanted to . . . explain . . . about last night. To tell you . . ."

Her words died away. Pain glistened in her eyes.

"Tess," Dane said urgently, jumping at the opening she offered. "You don't have to explain. I understand why you did what you did. I'm sure at the time you felt it was the only thing to do, because of the circumstances."

He moved closer and turned more fully toward her. He couldn't stand being this near and not touching her. He reached over and took her hand. "I know how hard it would be to tell me after all these years. Don't torture yourself with guilt any longer. I already think of Anne as my own. No one but the two of us will ever have to know that she is truly my daughter."

Tess's face whitened and she stared at him. "What on earth are you talking about?"

Dane patted her hand, wishing he hadn't been so blunt. But he couldn't back down now. "It's all right, Tess. I understand. I forgive you."

She pulled her hand out from under his and jerkily got to her feet. *"Understand? Forgive me?* Are you crazy?" she demanded. "Anne isn't your child! She's Hugh's."

Dane rose, too. He tried to stay calm, told himself she'd denied this so long, probably even to herself at times, it would take a while for her to admit the truth. He forced a smile.

"I suspected the first moment I saw her. Those brown eyes, those dark curls are just like mine—like my family's."

"They are also like *Hugh's!"* she said, her voice rising.

He was taken aback, but only for a moment. He thought he heard a noise and glanced at the door. He saw it wasn't fully closed.

Turning back to Tess, he saw her standing with her chin tilted, her nostrils flaring, fists clenched at her sides. He had to calm her down, before the whole house heard them.

"Let's not talk about it any more now," he said, his voice soothing.

"Will you stop acting as if I'm a child or feebleminded?" she said loudly. "Listen to me. I didn't dream you had such mistaken ideas! Why didn't you tell me this a long time ago?"

Shocked, Dane stared at her. *Why, she'd never have told him on her own.* Never. She might have married him, still keeping this secret.

He felt heat rising to his neck, his face. "I love you, Tess. I was going to ask you to marry me tonight. But not with this between us. You have to tell me the truth."

Swift anger came to Tess's face. "I *am* telling you the

truth, you pompous ass! Did you think all you had to do was ask and I'd fall into your arms? So grateful for your 'understanding,' your 'forgiveness'?"

Her angry words deepened his shock. "No, I didn't think that. I thought you loved me, too—but you were afraid to tell me about Anne."

"Tell you *what?* There's nothing to tell you! But since you refuse to believe me, then just get out of here!"

Dane rose, deeply angry, deeply shocked and hurt.

But it was better to learn what a fool he'd been now, rather than later, he tried to convince himself as he turned and left the room and the house.

11

. . . O! Stay and hear; your true love's coming
. . . Journeys end in lovers meeting . . .
—William Shakespeare
Twelfth Night

The door closed behind Dane. Tess picked up a book lying on a table and threw it at the wood panels.

It hit with a heavy thud, then fell to the carpet.

She let out her breath in disgust at not keeping her temper. Now she'd probably have her grandmother or Oren popping in here, demanding to know what was wrong.

Everything was wrong! She sat down on a chair, taking deep breaths to calm herself. After a few moments she felt a little better. She closed her eyes and took a few more.

Slowly, the anger drained from her, surprise replacing it.

Why, that had been like one of the rousing fights she and Dane had as children. Tempers rising, both stubborn and determined, neither willing to give in. Even when one or both knew they were wrong.

But this wasn't the same. This wasn't a mere difference of opinion. Dane actually believed that Anne was his daughter!

It still took her breath away that he'd interpreted her fears and doubts to mean that.

The doubts and fears that, inexplicably, seemed to have left for good.

How she wished Dane *were* Anne's father! If he were, she'd never have gone ahead with her marriage to Hugh . . . would she?

She swallowed. Would she have had the courage to come back here, pregnant, to confront a man she thought didn't love her and demand he marry her?

Maybe not. Maybe this awful snarl could be even worse.

If she *had* done what Dane accused her of, she would be a truly despicable person.

How could he even have been civil to her, let alone tell her he loved her, if he believed she'd kept his child from him all these years?

Still, he *had* said he loved her. Both last night and again a few minutes ago. Surely, when he calmed down, he'd believe she'd told him the truth about Anne.

Both of them had said rash things a few minutes ago, things they didn't mean. A smile tugged at her mouth. Well, he *had* been a pompous ass! She didn't know if she could apologize for calling him that.

Tess took another deep breath and got up. She'd go to bed. And tomorrow she'd go to Dane if he didn't come to her first.

She walked to the door and opened it. No one was in the foyer. A clatter of dishes came from the drawing room. The last guest must have left and Margaret and Estelle were cleaning up.

Tess walked quietly up the carpeted stairs, into her bedroom, where Margaret or someone had left a lamp burning low. She turned up the lamp and opened the connecting door into Anne's smaller chamber.

The light from her room showed her Anne's bed was empty, the covers thrown back. Tess shook her head.

"Anne—where are you? Don't hide from me now." Tess walked into the room and glanced around, even under the bed.

But no grinning little face yelled boo! No small form lunged out at her from some hiding place.

Where could Anne be? Although she'd been wakeful tonight, it wasn't like her to get up and wander about the house. Tess hurried out of the room, searched the two unoccupied bedrooms, then quietly eased Edith's door open.

It, too, was empty. Her grandmother must still be downstairs. Relief filled Tess. No doubt Anne was with her. She hurried back down the steps, and into the drawing room.

Edith was helping Margaret clean up. They were the only ones in the room. Edith glanced up at Tess's approach.

"Have you seen Anne?" Tess asked, trying to keep the fear that had started to gnaw at her from her voice.

Surprise came over Edith's face. "No. I thought she was asleep."

"She was, but now her room's empty."

"She must be around somewhere. All this excitement tonight was too much for her." Edith gave Tess a significant glance.

Tess ignored it. Splitting up, the three of them thoroughly searched the big house, but found no trace of the child.

"Oh my God, the little thing must be out in this storm!" Margaret said, as they met again in the foyer.

Tess had been fighting this fear. Now she faced it. Her glance flew to the coat rack in the corner of the foyer. Anne's cloak was gone. So were her boots.

A memory tugged at Tess's mind. Something . . .

when she and Dane wore fighting . . . the door hadn't been closed. There had been a noise at it . . .

Had Anne listened outside the door, heard their angry voices? Run outside in fright? But where would she go?

Tess ran to the coat rack, grabbed her cloak and donned both it and her boots, then jerked open the front door.

"Wait!" Edith said. "Let's get the sleigh."

Tess shook her head. "There's no time to waste. If Anne is out in this . . ."

She didn't finish, but plunged outside. The snow had stopped, she saw with relief. But it was very cold now and several inches of snow covered the ground.

Margaret appeared at her side, her sturdy body well covered with her heavy cloak and high boots covering her feet and ankles. "I'm going with you," she said.

"All right," Tess agreed. "Let's go."

"I'm going, too," Edith called from behind them.

Tess turned to see her grandmother shivering in the doorway. "No, you stay here, in case Anne comes back before we find her."

Edith huffed, but finally said, "All right, I guess you're right."

The snow was crisscrossed with many footsteps from the guests who'd been here tonight. At the street, they found the long marks of sleigh-runners and several sets of footprints leading away from the house.

Tess waved to the left. "Look that way for Anne's footprints," she told Margaret, knowing that was a well-nigh impossible task. "I'll look this way."

All the prints Tess followed were too large to be Anne's, she saw in a few moments.

"Miss Tess!" Margaret called, excitement in her voice. "Come here."

Tess's heart leapt. She hurried to where Margaret

stood. A single set of small footprints, inside a much larger set, led toward the west.

"Where in the world is that baby going and why?" Margaret asked.

Tess was already following the prints, which led in a straight line toward the west.

Toward Dane's house.

That sound at the sitting room door must have been Anne. She must have awakened, come downstairs looking for Tess, heard her mother and Dane fighting, saw Dane leaving. She'd followed Dane, put her small booted feet inside his prints to find her way.

But why?

Tess brushed the question aside. That didn't matter now. All that mattered was finding her daughter. What if Anne lost Dane's prints, wandered off . . . got lost . . .

Tess firmly pushed down a vision of Anne's small body, covered with snow, freezing to death . . .

Margaret huffed behind her. "I hope these are her tracks," she said, a tremble in her voice revealing her own fear.

"They have to be," Tess said firmly. "We found no more small ones. But just in case, they aren't, you . . ." She swallowed, her heart lurching at the thought, then went on, "Look in the ditches, I'll follow the prints."

They hurried through the snow-covered, deserted streets, Tess, with her head bent, following the two sets of prints, one within the other, Margaret doing as bid.

Thankfully, the snow made the night light. They saw no trace of Anne. Tess's fear began to ease as she pictured Anne safe at Dane's house.

Tess stopped, abruptly. Ahead, the large prints continued on.

But the small prints no longer were within them.

Her fear rose again, smotheringly. She battled it down.

"Margaret!" she called frantically.

The older woman hurried over and they both stared down at the prints.

Tess lifted her head. Ahead, Dane's house waited at the end of the block. "Come on! Maybe Dane turned and saw her, then carried her the rest of the way."

If not . . . No, she wouldn't even think about that possibility. Their assumptions had to be right. She struggled on, Margaret beside her, her snow-filled boots numbing her feet, shivering in the raw wind that had sprung up to swirl the snow about them.

Finally, they were there. The yard was deserted, but a lamp burned in a front window.

Tess hurried up on the porch and pounded on the door, Margaret behind her. She heard movement inside and the door swung open. Dane's big body filled the opening.

"Is Anne here?" Tess gasped, stumbling on her numb feet.

"Yes, she's here. She's safe."

"Praise be to God!" Margaret cried.

Tess's numb feet and legs sagged. Dane caught her before she fell, supporting her until she was steady, then moving back a bit to let both her and Margaret enter.

Anne sat before the fire, wrapped in a quilt, a cup in her hand.

Sweet relief swept over Tess, making her weak. "I looked in your bed . . . you were gone!" she cried.

Anne's face puckered up. "I'm sorry, Mama. I didn't mean to scare you."

"But you did! You did! Don't *ever* do anything like that again!"

"I won't," Anne promised, nodding. "I promise I won't."

"Come in here and get those wet boots and cloak

off," Dane commanded, leading Tess toward the fire. "You, too, Margaret."

"I'm not even wet," Margaret said. "I'm going back and tell Mrs. Bayley everything's all right."

"Wait and I'll take you," Dane protested.

She shook her head. "No, let me go. I'm fine."

"All right, Margaret," Tess said. "But be careful."

Margaret snorted. "I been careful for a lot more years than you been on this earth, Miss Tess."

With that she was gone, closing the door firmly behind her.

Tess broke away from Dane, enfolded her daughter in a fierce hug which Anne returned.

Clumps of snow fell from Tess's cloak, landing on Anne and the carpet. "You're getting me wet, Mama," Anne said, then smiled. "But that's all right. I'm so-o-oo glad to see you!"

Tess moved back a little, fought for control. "I'm glad to see you," she finally said, her voice uneven, but no longer frantic. "Why did you do this?"

Anne bit her lip, looked from Dane to her mother. "I woke up and came downstairs, and . . . and you weren't with Gramma Edith in the big room, and then I heard you and Mr. Dane talking loud, and . . . I heard you tell him to go away."

Anne's eyes filled with tears, her lower lip trembled. "I went back to the stairs and then Mr. Dane came out, looking real mad and went away . . . I just wanted to ask him to come back."

Tess drew in her breath. She stared at Anne, not knowing what to say. One thing for sure, the little girl didn't need any more scolding tonight.

"Get those wet things off," Dane again commanded, and this time Tess did as he said, then sat close to the fire.

"Why didn't you bring her back?" Tess asked. "Didn't you know we'd be frantic with worry?"

"Because she was shivering with cold and her feet and hands were half frozen," he said evenly. "I planned to take her home in the sleigh as soon as I got her dry and warm."

"Oh. Of course." Tess felt chastened.

She glanced over at him, standing before the fire, saw he still wore his damp clothes and boots. "I'm sorry," she said. "I—I'm not thinking straight yet."

"That's all right. Neither did I at first. Scared me more than a little."

"Mama, I'm so—oo sleepy," Anne mumbled. "Can I go to sleep now?"

Tess glanced at her daughter, whose lashes were trembling closed over her eyes: her brown eyes, that were a lot like Dane's.

A sudden thought hit her. Had she been drawn to Hugh originally because he resembled Dane? Had she thought he was like Dane inside, too?

Tess glanced over at Dane. He looked back at her steadily, the anger she'd seen on his face earlier this evening completely gone.

"We need to talk," she said in a low voice.

He nodded wearily. "Yes, we do."

Tess examined Anne's toes, which were warm and pink again. So were her hands. Tess smiled at her. "Just lie down here on the sofa, and I'll cover you up nice and snug."

Anne slid down, something gold and shiny falling out of the pocket of the robe she wore over her nightdress.

Tess picked it up and saw with surprise that it was the gold-and-rose locket.

Anne saw it, too, and reached for it. "Can I keep this for a while?"

Tess nodded, "Where did you find it? I didn't even know it had fallen off."

"On the stairs . . ." Anne mumbled again, her eyes closing.

She was asleep before Tess had the quilt pulled up over her, still clutching the locket.

Tess took a deep breath and raised her head.

Dane was looking at her. He rose. "I'll get you a cup of cocoa."

"All right."

He brought it to her, along with one for himself. Then he sat down on the chair he'd occupied last night, unlaced his boots and removed them and his socks, then rubbed his feet with a nearby towel.

His bare feet were bright red with cold. His hands, too. He'd made sure Anne was taken care of before he even thought of himself.

Of course he had. Dane was a loving, caring man. He always would be. He was nothing like Hugh. He'd never treat her as Hugh had. Why had it taken her so long to see that?

But he rejected you that night, six years ago. How can you explain that?

She couldn't, but she was certain there was an explanation for it. One she was finally ready to listen to and accept.

"I'm sorry," she plunged in, keeping her voice low, so as not to wake Anne. "I shouldn't have got so mad at you like I did. But you took me so by surprise—"

Tess's voice broke off.

She sighed. "Do you still think Anne is your daughter? Because if you do, there's nothing more for me to say."

Dane let out a sighing breath. "No, I don't. I—guess I just *wanted* to believe it so much, I convinced myself it was true."

She gave him a tremulous smile. "I wish it were." She paused, bit her lip, then went on. "That wasn't what was bothering me. What I couldn't talk to you about."

His gaze was deep and probing. "Can you talk about it now?"

Tess nodded. "Yes. You see, Hugh was . . . he wasn't a good husband. He should never have married me. Or anyone else. He didn't like children."

Tess threw a quick glance toward Anne. The girl was still fast asleep. She turned back to Dane. "He didn't like Anne."

He was scowling, his hands clenched into fists. "I should never have let you go that night. I should have barged into your bedroom and dragged you out and got the preacher and married you!"

Their glances met and held. Tess smiled. "Yes, you probably should have. I . . . was so shocked by what we'd done I wasn't thinking straight. I believed you didn't love me. Only . . . wanted me that once . . ."

She held her breath. For the first time since all this started six years ago, she'd been completely honest with Dane.

Dane was staring at her, a muscle moving in his jaw. "And I thought the same thing about you. God, what fools we've been! How much time we've wasted!"

He surged from his chair, almost knocking it over, then remembered Anne and stopped. "It looks like you'll have to come here," he growled.

Tess went quietly. Dane's big arms enfolded her, pulling her cold body to his equally cold chest and holding her there.

His heart was beating next to hers. It felt so good, so completely right. She felt herself warming. She felt Dane warming.

She lifted her face to his and he kissed her, long and

deep. "I didn't think I could ever be a good wife. That I could trust a man again. Even you."

He searched her face. "Are you sure now?" he finally asked.

"Yes," she answered quickly, without hesitation. "Tonight, all those doubts and fears left me. At the party, I saw you with all those children. Saw how good you were with them, remembered how you were with Anne."

"So all you want is a father for Anne?" His voice was stern.

She gave him a startled glance. "No! Of course not . . . I want—"

Tess's lips slowly curved up in a smile as she saw his own lips twitch.

"I know what you want," he told her in a slow, low rumble. "The same things I do. This . . ."

He kissed her, again long and deep. "And this . . ." He pulled her close against him and held her there. "And being together always," he whispered.

Tess felt safe and protected. And loved. So deeply loved. She moved back a little and looked up at him. "You told me you loved me last night . . . and I ran away like a scared schoolgirl."

"Are you going to run away now?"

She shook her head. "No. Never again. And . . . I love you, Dane Kendall. More than I can ever tell you."

"We've got a lifetime for you to try," he said. "I love *you,* Tess."

They kissed again for good measure.

"Mama . . . Mr. Dane," Anne's sleepy voice said into the silence. "Why are you kissing each other?"

Startled, they broke apart. Tess turned around, smiled at her daughter. "Because we—"

"Because we love each other," Dane finished, his

arms going around Tess's waist to draw her up against him.

"Oh, good!" Anne said, beaming. "Will we all live together in Gramma Edith's house?"

"I don't think so," he said after a moment. "How would you like to live in this house?"

Anne tilted her head, considering. "I guess I'd like it. I'd miss the gardens, but we can go visit Gramma Edith, can't we?"

"Of course," Tess reassured her.

Anne reached down beside her, fumbling. When she raised her hand, it held the locket. "When I'm all grown up, I get to wear this, just like Mama does now and Gramma Edith did," she told Dane.

Somehow, the catch had opened and the locket was spread apart, revealing the inside.

Anne lovingly touched it, then stared. "Mama! You're not alone in here anymore."

Tess smiled, ready to indulge Anne's precocious imagination a little on this special Christmas Eve night. "That's nice, dear," she said, giving the locket a cursory glance.

Then she stiffened, her gaze fixing. She wriggled out of Dane's grasp, walked over to Anne.

Tess saw her familiar likeness in its accustomed place on the locket's right-hand side.

But on the left was now another image.

Dane's.

Tess swallowed, a ripple going down her spine.

Anne still stared at the locket, awe on her face. Finally, she looked up at Tess.

"Remember when Gramma Edith said tonight that she guessed it wasn't time for another picture to be in the locket?"

Tess nodded.

Anne's face wreathed itself in a happy smile.

"It must be time now, then, isn't it, Mama? You don't have to be alone in there anymore!"

Tess turned, glanced at Dane, who looked merely puzzled. Of course he hadn't put the likeness of himself in the locket. Neither could her grandmother have done it.

"No, darling, I . . . we don't have to be alone anymore."

"Good," Anne said, her voice satisfied. She gave a huge yawn and slid down on the sofa again. "I'm sleepy again. Re-eal-ly sleepy this time."

Her hand dropped to her side. The locket fell out.

It lay there, light from the fire glinting on the two smiling faces within.

THE MAN IN RED

by
Kathryn Fox

1

Fort McLeod, Alberta, Canada
Fall of 1877

Anna Snow landed on her back with a thud. Air from her lungs rushed out and everything dimmed. She struggled against the weight on her chest, gasping for breath.

Susie's face hovered over her, an aspen leaf hanging off one ear. "Are you all right, Miss Anna?"

Had she had any air left in her lungs, Anna would have laughed. She nodded and Susie tumbled off her.

"Tommy! Miss Anna's hurt!" Susie cried as she rolled to her feet.

The ground beneath her rumbled and two more worried faces appeared, blocking the sun out of her eyes.

"I'm fine, children." She struggled up on her elbows, pasting a smile on her face that she didn't feel.

Tommy pursed his lips and frowned, doing his fourteen-year-old best to imitate an adult expression. "Perhaps we should go."

"Nonsense. I'm fine. I just had the wind knocked out of me." Anna removed the leaf from over Susie's ear and placed it over her own. "Go and play while you can. We have to go in soon."

"Mrs. Snow?"

Anna jerked around. Mrs. Stanton stood with her arms crossed over her ample bosom, a disagreeable expression on her face. Mrs. Fitzgerald stood at her side, a yellow tabby cat cradled in her arms. The cream of society, as far as that went at Fort McLeod.

They *would* come calling today.

"Tommy, take the children home, please, and get them started on their chores," Anna said, narrowing her eyes at his unspoken argument.

Rising, she brushed the dirt and leaves from her faded calico skirt, painfully aware of the patched holes and rips, as the children filed down the hill, back toward the stockaded settlement.

"Yes, Mrs. Stanton. Mrs. Fitzgerald." She dipped her head at the pair in acknowledgment.

"I was hoping to have found you at home working on my Christmas ball gown, Mrs. Snow. Instead, I find you here, wallowing on the ground like a . . . an animal."

Anna fought down a laugh and wanted to clap a hand over her irreverent mouth. "It's a wonderful fall day, Mrs. Stanton. Beautiful weather for the children to enjoy the last of the warm days. And these lovely leaves. They're just begging to be rolled around in." She retrieved the aspen leaf and held it out. Mrs. Stanton regarded it down her long nose, then directed her attention to the other two women.

"I might as well come out with it, Mrs. Snow. We," she nodded at her companions, "don't believe that you are an appropriate guardian for these children."

Anna's anger flared. "And what would make you believe that?"

"You are a widow, Mrs. Snow, and subject to certain rules of behavior, which you flaunt, I might add. You certainly wouldn't see Mrs. Fitzgerald out here rolling around on the ground with the children. The children should have their minds on more important things. School, for example."

Anna brushed at a bit of moss clinging to her blouse. "The children finished today's lessons this morning. In fact, they did their sums in record time and with exemplary results in anticipation of this outing."

"They should be in school with the rest of the children of the settlement. You and I have had this conversation before. Back East, I taught in a girls' school and we never—"

"Yes, Mrs. Stanton, I believe that you have mentioned that before. I realize the children's educational needs. As *I* have mentioned before, I, too, was a teacher before my marriage."

Mrs. Stanton threw a glance to her companions and Anna could have cut her tongue out. Why did she bring up the subject of her marriage?

"We're here to let you know that we intend to lodge a formal complaint with the authorities in Ottawa about the placement of these children. A woman such as you—"

"Such as me?" Anna stepped forward, staring nose-to-nose with Mrs. Stanton. "What do you know about me? Nothing. None of you have ever cared to find out about *me.*"

"Your husband was a notorious whiskey trader, one of the scourges that the Northwest Mounted Police were sent here to quell. He was killed over a load of . . . of rotgut whiskey." Mrs. Stanton's face reddened, and Mrs. Fitzgerald, cat in her arms, moved back a step.

"Yes, he was. What does that have to do with my life now?"

Mrs. Fitzgerald smiled tentatively and stepped forward. "My dear, what Mrs. Stanton is saying is that you have chosen to conduct your widowhood in a most . . . unusual way. You have raised some eyebrows, dear."

"You have no visible means of support, save your seamstress work, which I might say leaves something to be desired." Mrs. Stanton tugged on the lacy neck of a blouse Anna recognized as one she'd had to remake three times.

"My support is of no concern to you, ladies. My seamstress work is very good, except for picky, hard to please *old biddies.*" She leaned toward Mrs. Stanton. Some voice in the back of her mind whispered discretion while another voice screamed rebellion.

"I won't stand here and listen to any more of this abuse." Mrs. Stanton's neck reddened all the way to her generous ears. "I intend to file a complaint," she threw back over her shoulder as she hurried away, the other two women on her heels. "You'll see that you can't conduct yourself in such a loose manner and not face the consequences. I'll have the Mounties look into this. They are the government's representative out here. They'll take those children away from you." The rest of her words were lost in gasps for breath and distance as the pair struggled down the hill.

Anna flopped down onto the mossy ground. Why couldn't she learn to curb her tongue? What little devil goaded her into verbal fencing with the two curmudgeons of Fort McLeod society? Now, she'd have to apologize to the old witch and offer to make her a new gown for the Northwest Mounted Policemen's Christmas Eve ball.

She lay back against the warm ground, soaking up the last rays of sun. But the threat of the police lingered with her. Mrs. Stanton could bluster and sputter all she wanted, but the Mounties were the law in the Alberta territory and could sweep in and take everything that was dear to her. Just as they had killed her husband five years ago.

Jasper was better off dead. She could think those words now without guilt. He was a drunk, a mean, abusive drunk, and he had become deeply involved in the whiskey trade. He smuggled wagons of whiskey across the United States border, which were immediately sold to the Blackfoot Indians.

With a sigh, she sat up and wrapped her arms around her legs. She had loved Jasper once, but his greater desire for money and whiskey had killed that love long ago. That and his abuse.

Anna threw back her head and let the sun shine down on her closed eyes. But her enjoyment of the day was gone. She opened her eyes and squinted toward the settlement. Mrs. Stanton's ample figure was hurrying through the front gate of the fort.

"Do you reckon he's dead?"

"Naw, he ain't dead. See that lump on the side of his head?"

Ben's thoughts rattled past in a kaleidoscope of confusion. Whose voice was this? A whiskey trader, come to finish him off? He struggled to open his eyes, but failed.

"It's Santa Claus!" the childish voice piped, high and melodic. "We gotta take him home and make him better, Tommy."

"He ain't Santa, Susie. He's just a damned old Mountie." The older voice spoke again, cynical and hard.

"You swore! I'm tellin' Miss Anna and she'll whup you good. He is too Santa. He's got on a red coat. Don't you remember that story Miss Anna read us?"

"Santa Claus is fat and he's got a white beard. I've

seen pictures. Wonder what this Mountie was doin' back here?"

"We gotta take him home with us. Please, Tommy. I'm sure he's Santa, and if we don't make him well, there won't be any Christmas."

The ground beneath him was cold and hard and one leg was bent at an odd angle, its pain just now reaching his confused thoughts. If he could just straighten his leg or sit up, maybe he could stave off the black numbness threatening his fragile consciousness.

"All right, Susie. Help me get him up and I'll see if I can carry him." The hard voice had softened, gentled.

Someone yanked on his arm, sending shards of pain through his whole body. He raised a hand to swing at his attacker. A groan vibrated through him, and he heard the scramble of feet. He struggled to rise, his right hand fumbling for his weapon. For a brief second, the streets of Fort McLeod came into hazy focus along with a crowd of tiny, dirty children, then darkness tunneled in and his head struck the packed dirt of the street.

Strange dreams interrupted his sleep. He raised a sluggish arm to brush away the images that crowded his mind like spider webs. He was walking his patrol along a dirty back street, when something struck the back of his head. He pitched forward, seeing the ground rush up to meet him in a blur of brown and black. He had to catch himself, break his fall. He raised an arm, but something caught his hand and held it.

Welcome coolness spread across his face and down his arm, like tiny feet marching across his skin. Like swimming up from the depths of a lake, he rose above the buzzing in his head and opened his eyes.

Overhead were stout, dusty beams. Reason returned slowly as he shifted his gaze to the side. The biggest, darkest eyes he'd ever seen stared back at him. Long, dark lashes swept down and up like the wings of a butterfly and tiny fingers tightened on his hand.

"I told you he was alive." The voice came from the haziness beyond his vision. Ben tried to focus his thoughts. He'd heard that voice before. It was the voice from the street.

"Mister, are you all right?" This voice was his angel of mercy. The one who'd wanted to bring him home and thought he was Santa Claus. But, where was home?

Ben opened his mouth to speak, but a stab of pain shot through his jaw.

"I told you, Susie, you can't kill Santa Claus. Some of them no-gooders just knocked him in the head for his loot, that's all." Again the voice with no face. It was a boy's voice, a boy bordering on manhood. He was afraid and covering it with false bravado. Yet the words were gentle, reassuring. Brother and sister, maybe? Had they brought him to their home?

He closed his aching eyes and relied on his hearing.

There was more than one person in the room, several in fact. And all of them were standing close to him. He was lying on some sort of bed where he could smell the soft, welcome scent of newly laundered clothes mingling with the lingering odors of the previous day's baking.

He opened his eyes, and stared into worried faces. He'd bet money the face at the end of the bed belonged to the cynical voice of reason.

"See? He ain't dead. Now let's get him out of here before Miss Anna comes home. You know how she feels about the Mounties." Some unspoken message passed between the children, something he felt rather than heard.

"No, Tommy," the face with the large, dark eyes chirped. "We can't let him go until we know he's well.

He's Santa Claus. It's our duty to make sure he's not hurt."

Tommy rolled his eyes to the ceiling. "He ain't Santa, Susie. There ain't no Santa. I've already told you that. He's just some nosy Mountie we were stupid enough to drag home. Now Miss Anna's gonna be hopping mad."

"He is too Santa." Susie dropped his hand and sprang to her feet. "He is too. He's wearing a red coat and he had that bag with him. Miss Anna told me there was a Santa. She told me all about him and how he's coming here on Christmas Eve. And he ain't gonna leave you nothin', Tommy Weathers, if you don't take back what you said." Fists balled, she advanced on the young man until he backed away looking sheepish.

"All right. I'm sorry." His voice mellowed again, softened to a gentle tone Ben somehow knew he saved just for her. One hand reached out, then rested possessively on Susie's shoulder.

"Mister Santa? Are you all right? Do I need to send somebody to see to your reindeer?" A different voice whispered softly next to Ben's left ear. Ears peeped out from underneath unruly red hair, framing a pinched face covered with freckles. Fighting down the urge to laugh, Ben slowly shook his aching head. He felt like Gulliver in Lilliput.

"What was you doing out there, anyway? Ain't you supposed to be making toys?" Brilliant blue eyes sparkled despite a frown that wrinkled a turned-up nose. "Don't you know it ain't safe to be out after dark? Miss Anna says so all the time, and when she comes back, she'll give you the scolding she always gives us when we ain't home on time."

"What on earth have you children done?" a feminine voice asked. Ben turned his head in the direction of the words, but found that a quilt, hung on a rope, blocked his vision.

The fresh scent of new snow swept in on a blast of cold air. The children scurried around the quilt and out of sight. There were hurried whispers and soft, urgent questions and answers he couldn't quite make out.

He closed his eyes as another wave of pain swept across him. Cold, soft hands swiped across his forehead and down his cheeks, leaving a trail of gooseflesh and the faint aroma of lavender. Her weight made the bed mattress dip as she sat down beside him.

"Oh, dear. What happened?" Two soft palms cupped his face and moved his head to the side. "Somebody caught you not looking, didn't they?"

Errant wisps of golden hair framed a small, delicate face, too small for the huge, blue eyes gazing down at him.

"Back of my head," Ben managed to croak out, wondering just what the damage was.

Her gentle hands turned his head to the side and she ran a finger over a fiery lump. "Ooh, that's a nasty bump. Just lie still and I'll get some snow to put on it."

Her skirts made a gentle rustling noise, then he heard the door open and felt the cold draft again. From somewhere beyond, the odor of cooking food increased and his stomach churned.

She rolled him onto his side and seated a bag of snow against the lump on his head. As the aching began to subside, more reason returned.

"I'm Anna Snow and you're here in my home, Constable." She placed a cool cloth on his forehead and again sat down at his side. There was a warning in her words, unspoken, yet perfectly clear.

"How did I get here?" Ben asked.

She shook her head and more strands of hair escaped and curled around her face. "I guess my babies must have brought you home."

Babies? What kind of husband would have a wife and children living in this section of the settlement? A brothel and back-street saloons dominated this street along with run-down shacks for wanderers that occasionally passed through town.

"I should get back to my post." He tried to rise up on his elbows, but overwhelming nausea and dizziness set the world a-tilt.

"Lie still before you throw up. I wouldn't want the children to see Santa lose his lunch." She removed the cloth from his forehead, dipped it into a basin and replaced it, newly cold and icy.

"Why do they think I'm Santa Claus?"

She smiled, tiny crinkles furrowing the corners of her eyes, and something within him leapt to respond. He wondered if he'd been whacked on the head a little too hard.

"I suppose I'm to blame for that," she was saying. "I read them a Christmas story last night and I guess I set their imaginations racing. Your red uniform is very striking, you know." She lowered her eyes and adjusted the quilt covering him. He noticed for the first time that his jacket, shirt, lanyard, and gun belt lay over the back of a chair at the bedside. He could see his blue uniform pants draped over the chair's seat. Dipping his head, he saw his suit of winter underwear was, thankfully, still on him.

She slanted a glance to the chair as if in response to his thoughts. "I'm to blame for the state of your undress, too. Not directly, of course," she corrected with a faint blush. "I don't allow them in bed with their clothes on. Under any circumstances." She turned her gaze back to him. "What is your name, Constable?"

"Ben Parker."

"Well, Ben Parker, since my children think you're Santa Claus, I'd like to ask you not to tell them any different while you're here." Her expression turned from pleasant to serious.

"Of course. That's the least I can do, I suppose." He frowned slightly as relief passed across her face. Had she been so afraid he would say no?

"These children have precious little magic in their lives. For some of them, this is their first real Christmas, and I can at least give them this. Please don't do anything to ruin the illusion for them."

"These are not your children?"

Worry replaced her sternness and she looked away from him. "No, not by birth. But they are my babies until I find them a permanent home."

"They're orphans?" He glanced over her shoulder, his vision clearing with the lessening of his pain. Three children clustered in the kitchen, remnants of the preparations for dinner falling on the floor and table while they watched him. One of the children with dark eyes and dark skin was Blackfoot. He'd bet next months' pay on it. These must be the children Mrs. Stanton had blustered and stormed about several months ago. She'd insisted that the Mounted Police look into having the children removed from their home. At the time, Ben was tied up chasing Red Ferguson, the whiskey trader, across half of Alberta Territory and he'd handed the whole affair over to Constable McGuire.

The tiny red-haired child who had stood at his bedside smiled and cradled a withered left arm. Tommy, apparently the older voice, wore the expression of hard-won experience. Only Susie appeared to be a child easily placed in a home. The problem was not unknown to Ben. As more settlers moved into the area, children were sometimes orphaned from either death or sickness. And often that situation fell into his lap. Foreboding added to his headache.

He glanced back to Anna. She watched him intensely, distrust written across her face.

"I can see they're well taken care of," he said slowly.

She plumped the pillow beneath his head and gently exchanged the cool cloth again. "They are, Mr. Parker. Rest assured that I will love them as if they were mine until I find someone who will love them as much." She fixed him with a gaze stern enough to rival that of his commanding officer. "And no one, not even Santa Claus, is going to interfere with that."

Ben slept fitfully throughout the evening, awakened when Anna came to change the ice on the back of his head. Once or twice, he opened his eyes to find her bending over him, brow furrowed in concern, aware she had intentionally roused him to see if he was all right.

Morning was a faint pink promise spilling through the window above his head. Anna was removing another bag of snow from behind his head. When he attempted to roll onto his back, he found a quilt had been rolled up and lodged behind him to keep him on his side.

"Lie still, Constable," she whispered, "else you'll lay on this lump on your head and it will hurt mightily." She smoothed his hair as she removed the ice, then her fingers felt the lump again. "The swelling is going down. You'll be fine in a day or two."

She moved around the bed into his sight. Her hair fell in tangled wisps about her shoulders. An old quilt lay over one shoulder and wrapped around her faded gown. She disappeared around the corner and he heard the door open and the scrape of a metal pan against the snow. She returned to his bedside, filled the cloth bag with fresh snow, and leaned across him to place it behind his head.

"How are you feeling?" she asked, her fingers resting briefly on his forehead, checking for fever as if he were another of her orphans.

"Better."

"Would you like a drink of water?"

Ben nodded.

She filled a tin cup from a metal pitcher on the table and pressed the cold metal to his lips. The cool water slid down his throat and he reached for more.

"That's enough." She removed the cup. "Too much water might make you sick."

"I should get back to my patrol." He wondered if the words sounded as unconvincing to her as they did to him. The last thing he wanted was to leave this bed and her presence. A senseless thought, he acknowledged. Silly, even. There was no place for a woman in his life, yet he missed the gentleness, the compassion, a woman's presence brought.

"I'll send one of the children to your headquarters this morning to let them know you are being cared for. Do you know what happened?"

Ben moved his head slightly, the dull ache beginning again. "Somebody bashed me on the head from behind."

"Why would someone want to do that?"

"I make a lot of enemies." Especially one whiskey trader. He'd been after Red Ferguson for months now. The man was operating a whiskey ring right within the walls of the fort, yet he had neatly alluded capture. Just when Ben was closing in, Red had slipped through his fingers again.

"I'm sure you do, Constable." She pulled the quilt

closer over him and tucked it in at the sides. "Try and get some rest."

She rose with a last lingering touch and moved away into the predawn light and sleep claimed him again.

The clatter of dishes awoke him to full morning. The sugary aroma of flapjacks filled the house along with cheerful children's voices. A dropped plate rang sharply, followed by firm admonishment. Her voice again. With his eyes closed, he conjured up her image of last night. Soft, gentle, beautiful. Intoxicating to a man long denied the company of a woman.

He drifted in and out of sleep, seeing and hearing bits and snatches of their lives. They ate their meal at a rickety table that rocked back and forth with a comforting creak, neatly set with cracked and mismatched dishes. But before the food was served, she quietly gave a prayer of thanks and asked for the children's continued good health. He had the feeling that prayer was repeated often and that God always heard Anne Snow's prayers.

Assigned chores were accomplished while his periods of consciousness narrowed into deep, restful sleep.

When he next awoke, it was late and dark. The fire popped quietly, burning down to coals. The house was still, save for soft snoring coming from the loft above. A quilt had been carefully tucked in around him and his damp pillow had been exchanged for a dry, clean one. He raised himself up on one elbow, then stopped, waiting for the world to stop spinning. When his vision cleared, he looked around the room. It was neat and clean, but sparse. The howling wind flung snow and ice against the window, erasing any clues of who had clouted him on the head.

A makeshift bath screen stood between him and the fireplace. The wooden frame, draped with a sturdy cloth, curved modestly. But a sudden puff down the chimney set the fireplace crackling and the flames climbing. Firelight silhouetted a bathtub and one long, slim leg. The rest of the image was lost in the form of the tub and the edge of the screen. Soft humming accompanied the gentle slosh of water. The silhouette raised its leg, toe pointed, and an arm smoothed down the length and back up until the motion was lost in shadow.

Ben swung his legs over the edge of the bed and sat up, gripping the edge of the mattress as the room heaved and bucked. Despite the pain raging through his head, his thoughts suddenly took an extreme turn, and long-forgotten wants sprang urgently to life. The innocence of her actions was more seductive than any whore's whispered promises.

Her soft voice represented qualities he had neither seen nor enjoyed for a very long time, unremembered until now. He had to find his pants and get out of here. Now, before his addled thoughts got him into trouble.

The figure behind the scene suddenly stood, and the huddled form turned into the seductive curves of a woman. Softly rounded breasts led into a small waist and gently flaring hips. She dragged a cloth down each arm, smoothing it over her breasts, her waist, and down each hip and leg.

His blue uniform pants lay over a chair across the room. With only a step or two, he could reach them and be on his way. Ben tried to stand, wobbled, and grabbed for the bedpost. His knees collapsed beneath him, leaving him clinging to the bedpost like a limp puppet.

"Constable? Is that you?" she asked, urgency in her voice. Her shadowed figure grabbed for a wrapper.

"I'm fine," he lied, struggling to get his feet beneath him.

"What possessed you to try and get out of bed at this hour?" Her hands, still damp and warm from the bath, gripped his forearms to steady him. The flannel wrapper clung to her body, quickly absorbing the remaining droplets of her bath.

"I . . . have to go . . ." He pointed toward the door, across a distance that seemed a mile, a long mile.

She stared at him as if he were crazy, a notion he was entertaining himself. "I'm afraid, Constable, we shall have to make other arrangements tonight." Her tone warned no nonsense, a well-practiced routine, he was sure.

Wishing with all his soul he'd stayed in bed, Ben meekly nodded and let her help him sit back down among the soft quilts. She reached beneath the bed and brought out a chamber pot. "This is what civilized people use on a night like tonight, Constable. Although I'm sure *you'd* prefer a foray out into the icy woods."

He stared down at the vessel, feeling both chided and angry. What was that tone in her voice? Sarcasm? Teasing? Or did she think him an uncivilized ogre?

She left him and moved back behind the screen. "I assure you I am used to such requests with the children. I don't have a squeamish bone in my body. I promise I won't hear a thing." With that, she began to splash heartily as she dipped water and threw it out the window.

A prisoner of his own body, he had two alternatives. He could do as she instructed or, come morning, the children would awake to find that Santa had wet his bed.

2

A shaft of sunlight crept across the green-and-red bear's claw quilt, sprinkling Ben's brown hair with dancing red highlights. Anna reached out a hand, but stopped short of touching him.

A heavy beard shadowed his cheeks and dark-blue circles rimmed his eyes. One hand cradled his cheek in a gesture of innocence she felt sure he never exhibited. After all, it took cold, hard men to serve in the Mounted Police, men who left their hearts in Ontario or London or from wherever they hailed. And Ben Parker was a hard man. She was sure of it. Perhaps Ottawa had sent him at Mrs. Stanton's insistence. Perhaps he had been coming here to take them away when some drunkard bashed him on the head.

She glanced over at his coat, wondering if his pocket contained the papers that would break her heart; orders that would take her children away and send them to far-flung homes across the territories, out of her sight and reach.

Anna shook her head and scolded herself for being silly. He'd been caught in the wrong part of town at the wrong time. And the children, excited about Christmas, a real Christmas, had seen his red uniform and assumed he was Santa Claus, thanks to her overzealous storytelling abilities. Now, she had to figure some way to get him out of her bed and her house and still keep the children's belief intact.

And her heart.

Especially when he smiled in his sleep like that.

She leaned closer, scolding herself for foolish, romantic thoughts. His eyelids twitched and his lips curled at the corners. Perhaps he wasn't so cruel a man. Perhaps he was just devoted to his job. Perhaps he was different from the other men who left their lives and families behind to answer the call of the Northwest territories. *No,* a stubborn little voice demanded. *Be careful.*

"If that's my breakfast, you're going to spill it on me, Miss Anna." He opened his eyes and she stared straight into the little flecks of green mingled with tiny flashes of gold.

He smiled, sat up and took the tray from her hands.

"You're better," Anna stammered, hating the breathlessness in her voice.

"Much. Thank you . . . to you and the children. Where are they? I wanted to thank them and say goodbye."

"You really should sit back and not try to balance that tray on the edge of the bed." She lifted the food and waited while he leaned back against the headboard. Then, she returned the tray, embarrassed by the dark hair curling over the unbuttoned top of his suit of underwear. "The children are all out and won't be back until later."

He took a spoonful of the broth and closed his eyes as he swallowed. "This is wonderful." Then, he stared at her intently. "Are the children in school?"

His pulse jumped in the little hollow just below his neck. Alarm bells sounded in Anna's head and her suspicions returned. "No, I school them myself. I taught school back East."

"Working then?" He watched her with his calm, green eyes, and she began to sweat beneath her clothes despite the cold draft coming through the cracked windowpanes. Little shivers darted up her spine.

"Yes. Tommy, the older boy, works in the general store in the mornings. The others do odd jobs where they can. Susie is spending the morning helping Tommy restack blankets at the store. Satisfied?"

He shot her a quizzical glance. "I didn't mean to be nosy. I was just wondering. They seem happy children. How do you find them homes?"

Anna bristled, resentment washing over her stronger than desire had a few moments ago. "I contact the church, some of the ladies' sewing circles. I post announcements inside the store. I am very careful with whom I trust my children, Constable."

He swallowed another spoonful and cocked an eyebrow at her. "I'm sure you are, Miss Snow." Finished, he set the tray down on the bed and stood. His one-piece suit of knitted underwear defined masculine curves.

"What are you doing?" Anna followed his height up until he towered over her. Funny, he hadn't looked that tall lying in her bed.

"I appreciate your help and that of the children, but I have to get back to my duties. No one knows where I am and they are probably already searching the streets for me."

"Tommy went yesterday morning and told your commander about your misfortune. We told him you should be recovered in a day or two." Anna's thoughts flew, guiltily trying to think of some reason to keep him here just a moment longer. Then caution gratefully returned. He should go. As soon as possible.

"Yes, you must get back to your work. Let me see your

wound." She leaned around him and reached up to touch the purplish knot on the back of his head. "I'd have the surgeon look at that as soon as you get back." She let her fingers drift across the goose egg and down to the nape of his neck. Shocked at her actions, she drew her fingers away as if from a flame.

His crooked smile told her he'd noticed. "If I could have a moment, please." He nodded toward the clothes on the chair.

"Oh, of course." She left and yanked closed the quilt that curtained her bedroom off from the rest of the house. Setting the tray on the table, she quickly washed the few dishes. Resisting the urge to glance in his direction, she turned her back and began to set the kitchen to rights for the midday meal. The children would be home soon and they'd be hungry.

"Again, Miss Snow, I appreciate your help."

She turned at the jingle of coins and could see how the children might be enchanted by his appearance. He was a wall of scarlet from his chiseled jaw to his slim hips. Immaculately brushed, except for a thin bloodstain she'd been unable to get out, his uniform would certainly draw attention.

He held out a handful of coins.

"No, no. I can't accept." She shook her head, quick tears smarting her eyes. Somehow, offering her money seemed so . . . impersonal. And moments ago, her thoughts of him had been very personal.

"For the children."

"No, the children and I do quite well." Then a plan formed. "But I will ask you a favor."

He pocketed the coins. "Ask."

Dangerous excitement welled up within her, like hanging from a tree branch with one hand or standing on the edge of a cliff. She stared up at him, wondering if he felt the same rush of recklessness. No, of course he didn't. She scolded herself for doing what she was about to do for the wrong reason. "Will you came back Christmas Eve night and give out the children's gifts? Play Santa? It would mean so much to them."

His eyes sparkled, and he smiled again that I-know-a-secret smile of his.

As if he knew her thoughts.

"I'd be glad to." He turned and retrieved the chamber pot from beneath the bed. "I'll be right back."

He had to duck to get through the door. Anna stepped back and gripped the edge of the table. When was the last time her knees had gone weak? When had her heart hammered against her ribs like this? When had she ever allowed herself to look past the day at hand, to dream of tomorrow?

But, her little voice reminded, *he could crush your dreams with one action, one legal maneuver.*

He returned the vessel beneath her bed and moved toward her, a rush of cold, sweet air sweeping with him. "Please tell the children good-bye for me. Tell them if they're good, Santa will see them Christmas Eve and that he is watching."

His last words should have alerted her, made her take pause, but she couldn't think when he stood this close, his chest, his fingers, inches away.

He leaned closer, his breath soft and warm against her ear. "Santa's watching you, too, Miss Anna."

"Miss Anna! Miss Anna!" Susie burst through the door, sweeping in a shower of snowflakes. "Something's terrible wrong with Tommy!" Her face was gray, her eyes huge and tear-rimmed.

Ben leapt toward the door, Anna close on his heels. Tommy slumped on the porch, his eyes closed, stains down the front of his clothes. Anna clamped a hand over her mouth at the foul, sour odor that came up from him.

"Mr. Stanton said Tommy didn't show up for work this morning when I went in to help him," Susie said with a yank to Anna's skirt. "He was awful mad. So, I went around back of the store and found Tommy there. He had throwed up all over himself. I tried to wash it off." Tears spilled over her cheeks and a sob jerked her small chest.

"Tommy's all right." Ben picked up Susie and held her close. "He's just a little sick right now."

She shook her head until her black curls bounced. "There was a bottle next to him with some awful-smelling stuff in it. Maybe somebody poisoned him." The thought brought new tears, and she clamped her arms around Ben's neck and buried her face in his shoulder.

Ben looked at Anna, and her heart dropped into her toes. Bootleg whiskey. She'd know that smell anywhere. The side alleys reeked of it sometimes when men slipped back into their section of town to drink and gamble. This would be all the excuse he needed to take away the children.

He turned his attention back to the child in his arms. "Don't you remember that Santa is magic and he can do anything?"

Susie nodded cautiously.

"Well, I'm Santa and I can fix him. Right?"

She turned her head and eyed him suspiciously. "Tommy says you're just a damned Mountie."

Ben's lips twitched as he glanced at Anna again. She could almost feel the children slipping away.

"Well, Tommy shouldn't be saying things like that. I'll have to have a talk with him when he's better, but still and all, I am Santa Claus. You see, it's so far from the North Pole, sometimes I get a job close by so I can really see who's good and who's bad. This way, on Christmas Eve, I can just fly up there, pick up the toys, and come back here."

Susie's eyes widened and she smiled. "And you can fix Tommy, too. Please, Mr. Santa. I love him a lot. He's my brother."

Ben's wide hat hid his face as he hugged the little girl and set her down. "Go inside and fix Tommy a bed by the fireplace."

Susie scampered inside, and Ben threw Anna a stern glance. "Has he been involved in anything like this before?"

"No," she said with a shake of her head. "Never. They're all good children, Constable."

He scooped Tommy into his arms and took him inside. Susie had stripped the bed of its covers and was just spreading the last one when Ben knelt and laid Tommy down. He took off his uniform jacket and tossed it over a chair.

"Make a pot of coffee and bring me a bucket of cold water," Ben said over his shoulder.

Tommy moaned and moved on the quilts.

"Susie, would you please run down to the general store and buy me some peppermint candy? I think Tommy might like some when he's feeling better." Ben placed the coins in Susie's hand. She stared down at the money and back up at Ben. "And get yourself two sticks, too." He winked at her, and she grinned and ran out the door.

"Bring me that chamber pot quick." He shoved it under Tommy's head just as the boy emptied what was left in his stomach.

"Judging by the smell, it's a wonder he isn't dead off that rotgut." Gently, Ben cleaned the boy's face and lowered his head to the pillow. Anna knelt on the other side and smoothed the curls away from Tommy's forehead. Tears streamed down her face, but she didn't care.

He'd come to her dirty and hungry. A family had found him wandering out on the prairie three years ago. No one ever knew how long he'd been out there or what had happened to his parents, but he'd been on his own for several days. Blisters had formed and burst, bloodying the bottoms of his feet. But he never cried. Not even when she washed away the filth, and most of the soles of his feet with it.

He became her first charge.

A young, idealistic teacher, accustomed to the safety and convenience of eastern life, she had longed for adventure and, against her parents' advice, had come west to seek her future. But instead of adventure, she'd found a husband, then a life of hell.

Widowed and heartsick, she'd found the poor, needy children, and they her. Her path was forever altered.

"Is that coffee ready?" His voice broke into her thoughts. He stared at her, reading her.

"Almost." She glanced over her shoulder to where the pot boiled on the stove. "My children do not engage in this sort of thing, Constable. There has to be some explanation here."

He met her eyes across Tommy. "I'm sure they don't, Miss Snow. I'm not here to take your children away from you, if that's what you think."

Somehow, he had tapped into her deepest fears.

The anger in his eyes sent a bolt of fear all the way to her toes.

"The Mounted Police don't arrest children and they don't take them out of their homes because of an irresponsible act. But, if I can find whoever gave him this, I will arrest them, and pour what's left of it down their throats."

"Feeling better?"

Tommy moaned and curled up in the bed to wrap his arms around his stomach.

"Where'd you get it?" Ben leaned down from his seat in the chair and wiped the young man's head with a cool cloth. His own head throbbed as much as he knew Tommy's did. He and Anna had taken turns all day sitting at Tommy's bedside while he sobered up. Now, twilight crept in through the windows.

He glanced to the fireplace. Anna slept in one of the chairs, her head lolled to the side and resting on her shoulder. Golden wisps of hair had come loose from her bun to tickle cheeks etched with lines of worry and tear stains.

"What happened?" Tommy asked, cracking open one eye.

"Seems you decided to celebrate Christmas early." Ben stood and stretched.

Tommy looked toward the darkening windows. "What time is it?"

"Almost dark."

Tommy rolled over onto his back and rubbed his stomach. "What happened to me?"

"Where'd you get the whiskey?" Ben sat back down and leaned closer. Maybe he could get the boy to tell him before Anna awoke. Something told him she'd take the questions as interference.

Tommy stared at him, determined stubbornness on his face.

"I found the money in your pocket, son, and I suspect it didn't come from Miss Anna. What are you involved in?"

Tommy turned his face away. "I don't know what you're talking about."

Ben placed a hand on Tommy's shoulder. "Listen to me. You're almost a man and soon you'll have a man's responsibilities. Miss Anna and the others are going to need you. What they don't need is the trouble these friends of yours are going to bring to this house. I can help you if you'll let me."

"I can look after my family by myself. I don't need you coming in here with your red uniform and your orders to help." Tommy turned back, his face filled with distrust and hate.

"I've been your age, son. I know how it can be to find friends who see you as a man and not a child. But these people mean you no good. They're using you to accomplish their own purposes and they have no consideration for your well-being."

"I pick my own friends, Mountie. Been doing it for years. I don't need any help from you." Tommy closed his eyes and grimaced against another stomach cramp.

Ben rose stiffly and picked up his jacket. "If you decide you want to talk, you can come by headquarters."

"I won't. Oh, and Mountie."

Ben shrugged into his jacket and turned around.

"I don't believe you're Santa Claus, either."

Tommy's face was a sad mixture of stubbornness and lost innocence.

Ben moved to Anna's side. She looked so peaceful and at the same time powerfully arousing.

"I'm going, Anna," he whispered, tracing a finger down her cheek.

She moved beneath his touch, then sat up, as if suddenly aware of where she was.

"Will you report this?" she whispered.

"No. But I am going to find out who gave him the liquor." At the panic that crossed her face, he quickly added, "I won't jeopardize you or the children. I promise." He wanted to touch her again, but, instead, he moved away.

He paused at the door and glanced back at Tommy, small and white amidst the quilts, and saw the changeling that every man is for a brief time in his life. His jaw set, his face stern, he would never tell where he got the whiskey or the money. Ben would have to find that out on his own.

"Do you reckon ol' Red Ferguson's got himself a bunch of delivery boys?" Stuart McGuire balanced the straight-backed chair on two legs and picked his teeth with a whittled-down willow branch.

Ben watched him, waiting for the chair to skitter out from beneath him and dump Stuart's generous girth onto the wooden floor. "Could be. Enlisting children would be just his style."

"How's he gettin' it inside the fort, do you suppose?" Stuart sat forward and the front two chair legs hit the floor with a thump.

Despite the disheveled appearance that kept him in constant contention with his superiors, Stuart had a nose like a bloodhound when it came to illegal whiskey. "It could be coming in a hundred different ways. You know that. How he's getting in enough quantity to be profitable puzzles me. And why sell it a bottle at a time, if that's what he's doing?"

Stuart shrugged and hurriedly stuffed his shirt into his pants at the sound of scuffling feet outside the door. "Maybe he figures to build up a list of customers, get 'em hooked like, then offer 'em more in larger quantities. But I'll bet you money he's got a whole bunch of boys sellin' for him." Stuart leaned across the desk. "Think about it. Nobody thinks anything of a whole gaggle of young'uns running through the streets. Who's to say they ain't got a bottle or two tucked into their pockets? And soon's they deliver it, they'll have coins to jingle together. At least until they get to the general store with it." Stuart picked up an ink quill and waved it toward Ben, splattering fine droplets of ink over everything on the desk. "Now take a boy like Tommy. If he hustled, he could bring in a respectable amount of money in a week's time. And it sounds like the household could use it. He feels responsible to the woman for taking him in and he'll do anything to help out. Ain't that how you figure it, Ben?"

Ben stared out at the still, early-morning streets. Yes, he figured Tommy would do just about anything for Anna and the children, and they for him. Just how involved in this was she? Could she be cooperating with some whiskey trader to get money for the children? Perhaps she decided that providing a home for the children justified the steps she had taken to achieve that. After all, she didn't seem to have any means of income. Where did the money come from?

"Maybe I should look into this further." Ben watched dawn creep up the gray side of a building, a nibble of guilt already gnawing at his conscience.

"And a good opportunity to see more of the widow Snow."

He turned from the windows to meet Stuart's mischievous grin. "Widow?"

"You didn't know? She was married to old man Snow. You remember. He was a merchant, followed James McLeod out here in '74. Set up shop right outside the gates and made a fortune until McLeod found out his store was a front for whiskey traders."

Feeling the floor fall out from beneath him, Ben ran over in his mind everything he'd heard about Jasper Snow. Indeed, his downfall had made quite a stir.

"I don't remember anything about him having a wife."

"Well, she weren't his wife for long. He was shot right though the bars on that there window." Stuart pointed to the jail occupying the corner of the room and the small, barred window. "Some folks said Jasper left her a mint of money, buried someplace out on the prairie. But she didn't leave and she didn't build herself no fine house. Some say she lost her mind. That's why she lives on the back streets and takes in all those stray kids."

"So, she could be living off money left by her husband." Ben paced across the floor.

Stuart rapped pudgy fingers on a stack of papers on his desk. "What have you gone and got yourself mixed up in, Ben?"

"I'm not mixed up in anything. I just don't want to see the children hurt."

"I know you, Ben boy, and it ain't the children you're worried about." Stuart leaned forward. "Gossip has it she's had a long list of lovers." He dropped his voice to a whisper. "And that she knows . . . things. You know, she does things to make a man not think straight."

The image of her silhouette through the bath screen shoved its way to the front of Ben's thoughts. Had she been trying to seduce him? To buy his silence? "Don't you know not to listen to gossip? She was very proper."

"That's the way they say it starts out. That she's as proper as any schoolmarm, and then . . . Well, I know this one man that said she . . ."

Ben held up a hand and Stuart stopped in midsentence. "I don't think I want to hear this. I'll find out for myself."

A wide grin split Stuart's face. "I'll bet you do, lad. You'll tell ol' Stuart what you find out, won't you?"

Ben chuckled. Stuart was messy and disorganized, but a good constable and a better friend. But how he did love gossip.

"What's the snow forecast for today?" Ben asked, lifting his heavy coat from a peg by the door.

Stuart shook his head. "Won't snow for a day or two. There's already enough on the ground. This old tooth says so. Where are you going?"

Ben buttoned up his overcoat. "Looks like a good day for greenery gathering."

"Why didn't you bring your reindeer?" Susie asked, leaning over the sleigh seat, her elbows digging into Ben's back. She'd been delighted when he showed up at the door, complete with sleigh and horse, with the suggestion that they help him collect greenery. Anna was another matter. She'd politely accepted the offer on behalf of the children, but obviously she thought he had some other purpose in mind. It was written all over her face.

And maybe he did.

He turned to look back at Susie. The wind had polished her cheeks to the rosiness of ripe apples and her eyes sparkled with excitement. The other children's squeals rang out across the snow-covered prairie, their laughter tinkling like bells.

"Well, I can't be flying around in the broad daylight, else everybody would know who I am."

"Oh," she breathed, her eyes wide with amazement. "Nobody but us knows?"

Ben smiled. "It's our secret. Okay?"

Susie bobbed her head, setting her curls dancing. "Don't you miss the reindeer? Ain't you had 'em for a long time?" She squirmed forward and locked her arms around his neck.

"Sure I miss them. But they're safe at home in their barn. Besides, horses are much less noticeable."

Susie frowned and chewed on the tip of a tiny finger. "How do you keep 'em from flying around all the time when they're in the barn?"

Threads of Christmas-morning stories told by some of the married officers entered his thoughts, stories of precious confusion and giggling children.

"Well, now. That's a job, I tell you. I just tie rocks around their feet to keep them on the ground."

"Don't that hurt their ankles?"

Ben glanced at Anna and she stifled a smile. He was drowning in his own yarn.

When she didn't come to his rescue, Ben plunged on. "It doesn't hurt them because I put special socks on their feet."

Susie dissolved in giggles and fell back into her place between Tommy and Pat. Ben glanced over the seat. Sinopa, the little Blackfoot girl, huddled in a corner, watching the others laugh with a mix of envy and anger.

"Sinopa."

She glanced toward Ben, a spark of interest in her eyes.

He asked her a question in the Blackfoot tongue and she answered him in the same melodic language.

"She spoke to you," Anna exclaimed, amazed. A family of settlers had appeared at her door one afternoon, this tiny child wrapped in a tattered blanket. They'd found her sitting alongside the body of her dead mother. When they tried to bring her along, she'd protested loudly. So, they bodily picked her up and hauled her to the fort. Since then, she'd barely spoken, eaten little, and haunted the corners of the rooms like a lonely little ghost.

"Of course." Ben turned toward Anna. "Hasn't she spoken to you before?"

"No, just a few grunts. I just assumed she couldn't talk."

He asked Sinopa another question and her face lit up. She chattered back, then smiled as she finished.

Ben answered and she giggled and covered her mouth with one hand.

"What did you say?"

"I asked her if she enjoyed your story about Santa Claus. She said yes and wanted to know why I wasn't fat anymore."

"She understood what I said?"

"I suspect that she understands English very well, she just doesn't choose to speak it."

"And what did you tell her?" Anna whispered. "About not being fat anymore?"

"I told her I had gotten too big for my pants and that I had to lose weight."

Anna laughed and glanced back at Sinopa, who intently listened to the conversation of the other children. "Where did you learn to speak their language?"

"When I first came to Fort McLeod, my patrol area included a Blackfoot village. I learned out of necessity."

Ben asked Sinopa another question and she scooted forward in her seat.

"San-ta says to tell you my name means like a fox."

Anna stared at the child, both delighted and angered. Many hours she'd coerced and begged, anything to get Sinopa to speak.

"Ask her why she hasn't spoken to me before."

Ben asked and Sinopa replied, then shrugged and made a helpless gesture with her hands.

Ben turned toward Anna, his eyes sad. "She says that the Blackfoot are taught not to speak when they are captives."

"Oh, dear God." Anna glanced toward Sinopa, who shrank back against the seat. "Does she really think I am holding her prisoner?"

"All she knows is that she was waiting for her mother to wake up and some white people came along and took her away. They left her with you, and she thought you were the spirit woman who takes away disobedient children."

Hot tears sprang to Anna's eyes as she imagined the child's despair. All this while she had thought the child simply didn't understand her, when she'd been living in her own torment.

Ben's fingers crept around Anna's hand and squeezed. "It was all she knew, Anna. She had no reason to believe otherwise and that's no fault of yours."

"Yes, but, I didn't think . . ." Her throat tightened. "I always thought she'd somehow sense I meant her no harm." Anna glanced over her shoulder and met Sinopa's dark eyes.

"I think she did in some way, but she couldn't understand that her mother was dead, so she explained the situation to herself as best she could. I'm sure she sensed nothing but kindness from you, Anna." His grip on her hand tightened and his fingers laced intimately with hers.

"Look!" Tommy shouted from the back and pointed to a stand of evergreens ahead.

Ben veered the sleigh toward the patch of dark green and brought it to a halt at the edge of the forest. The children filed out of the sleigh and immediately began a game of tag. Tommy watched them, hands shoved deep into his pockets.

"Go ahead, Tommy. I'll help Miss Anna get the greenery," Ben suggested.

Tommy shot them both a glance from underneath lowered brows and sauntered toward the game. In a few minutes, he ran and dipped and dodged with the rest.

"Did he ever say where he got the whiskey?" Ben asked as they began the climb up the incline toward the pines.

"No. He hasn't said another word about it. Did you find out anything?"

He wanted to confide in her, share with her what he had learned, but something cautioned him. Her first loyalty would be to the children, and he still didn't know what part she played in this. "No, nothing yet."

He reached a level place and waited for Anna, a step or two behind because of the steep incline. He looked out over the children, absorbed in their game. Little Pat, withered arm and all, was dodging and weaving as adeptly as the rest. "I know about the other children, but what about Pat."

Anna paused at his side and a tenderness filled her expression. "He's mine."

"Yours." Ben hated the shock that echoed in his words.

"Yes. I'm a widow." She turned and met his gaze squarely, challenging him to pass judgment on her.

"I didn't know."

"Of course you did, or else you're not doing your job very well." She glanced up at him, her eyes taunting beneath thick lashes.

Touché. "Okay, I knew, but I thought you might not want to talk about it."

"Don't think I don't know what the rumors are. That my husband left me a small fortune buried out on the prairie someplace. That I'm crazy because I don't belong to any sewing circles or haven't remarried. That I'm insane for taking in other people's children. That I have a sullied reputation for living how and where I do. Does that about cover what you've found out about me?"

Her frankness was both jarring and refreshing. "Just because I hear things, doesn't necessarily mean I believe them. And the fact you don't belong to a sewing circle confirms you're *not* crazy."

Anna smiled, but continued to watch the children.

"I know for a fact that your husband didn't leave you a fortune, because most of his money was confiscated. As far as being insane for taking in the children, definitely not. And as for having not remarried . . . well, maybe the right man just hasn't come along."

Her cheeks colored, but she didn't look away from the children's game.

Ben started up the hill again. The snow deepened as they reached the evergreens and Anna faltered as her skirts tangled around her ankles. Ben reached back and took her hand. Her fingers curled around his, warm and soft in his grasp.

The sharp scent of fresh pine rosin was strong on the cold air. Here and there brown needles poked up out of the snow like candles on a birthday cake. Overhead, the branches murmured on a brisk, sudden breeze.

"Nothing can whisper like a pine in the wind, can it?" Anna asked, breathing deeply.

"No. That's true." Ben produced a small saw from the inside of his coat. "My mother used to string boughs like this all through the house," he said as he began to saw off small branches. "Now, whenever I smell pine, I think of her."

"Where is your home? Besides here, I mean." Anna held out a large basket.

"Ottawa."

Anna touched a finger to the oozing rosin. "What made you want to be in the Mounted Police?"

Ben snapped off another piece of greenery and fingered the delicate silver-green needles. "Adventure, I guess. I'd always dreamed about seeing the territories."

"Don't you get lonely?"

His hand stopped and he turned to look at her.

"For your family, I mean," she finished.

"Yes, I miss them, but there's something about this land, something that calls to a man, binds him to it."

"You make the territories sound like a woman."

Sharp squeals echoed against the mountain and Anna turned. Susie rolled over and over in the snow. "Look, Miss Anna. I'm a snowman." She scrambled up and waved her arms, producing a shower of snowflakes.

"You love the children very much."

Anna turned to find Ben staring at her, his hazel eyes dark and serious.

"Yes," she answered, meeting his gaze. "I do love them. As much as if they were all my own."

"But you take them in with the idea of eventually letting them go."

"Yes, I hope that I will someday have to let them go to families and homes of their own."

"Why would you put yourself through that pain?"

"Because the children need me. They need someone."

"You know there are governmental agencies for that."

She visibly stiffened. "Yes, I do, but I feel that no agency can give them the love and attention that I can. I hope you will include that in your report, Constable Parker."

Her whole body was alert, ready to do battle. He had to bite back a smile. Her maternal instinct was powerfully seductive.

"I'm not here to file any report, Anna. I am here as Santa, gathering greenery for Christmas."

She eyed him, unmasked suspicions in her expression. Then, he spied mistletoe clinging to the lower branch of a leafless aspen tree.

"Look." He reached up and plucked off a bunch. She looked up at him, her cheeks red from the cold.

Wisps of hair curled against her face. Slowly, he raised the mistletoe over her head, knowing he would regret the next few minutes for a long time.

Fear flickered through her eyes, then doubt, and finally desire as her eyes drifted closed. Her lips were soft and warm, igniting in him a want so strong that he shivered. He wanted to yank her close, mold her body to his, brand her with his touch, but the quivering of her body reminded him of a frightened deer on the edge of flight. He dropped the mistletoe and put another arm around her.

She moved deeper into his embrace, leaning against him, and suddenly he was overcome with an overwhelming feeling of belonging, of being loved and wanted. Her arms slipped around his waist, her hands gently pressing against his back—so gentle, yet so powerful. Beneath her outward appearance of tranquility, there burned a fire within, barely tamed and controlled, waiting to be fanned into flame. Stuart's warnings drifted briefly through his mind.

"Mrs. Santa is gonna be mad with you." Without a sound, Susie had come to stand beside them and now looked up, lips pursed, hands on hips.

Anna colored and moved a step away, suspicion in her eyes. Had he kissed her to discredit her?

"Well, Susie." Ben bent down and picked up the child. "You see, there really isn't any Mrs. Santa Claus." He brushed a smudge of mud off her cheek and leaned closer to her. "It's just a story. Really, it's just the reindeer, the elves, and me."

"Why would somebody make up a story about you like that?" Her eyes were wide and blue, and he felt himself falling under her spell . . . just as Anna had.

"You know what I think?" he whispered conspiratorially.

She solemnly shook her head.

"I think somebody just made that up so people wouldn't think Santa was lonely."

"Don't you get lonely not having a Mrs. Claus?"

His traitorous eyes were drawn to Anna, standing a few feet away, intent on his answers to Susie.

"Yes, Susie. I do."

"Well, then," she proclaimed in a grown-up voice. "We'll have to find you a wife before Christmas." She poked the center of his scarlet uniform jacket with a plump finger. "That will be *your* Christmas present."

3

The sleigh skimmed across the snow, racing the setting sun that teetered on the horizon, huge and orange. Anna glanced into the rear seat. All three children were asleep, Pat and Sinopa's heads resting on Tommy's shoulders. Susie had snuggled in between her and Ben, her head leaning against his side. A buffalo robe covered their laps and Ben stared straight ahead.

They hadn't spoken of what had passed between them. Susie had broken the spell, and her absence from the game had brought the other children clambering to help cut greenery.

Anna closed her eyes and remembered again the feel of his arms around her, his lips moving against hers, gently asking for more. But lurking on the edge of her memory was the reality that she had let him kiss her, willingly went into his arms in full view of the children. Scandalous behavior for a woman of her age. She should be ashamed of herself. That act, coupled with the rumors that circulated about her, could cost her the children.

What had prompted him to kiss her? Had he believed the rumors, despite what he said? Did he wonder if she was a lonely, desperate widow? Was he testing her morals, deciding if she was fit to mother the children? She shook her head to dispel the questions tumbling about. But the fact remained she had enjoyed it. More than she should have.

"Cold?" Ben tugged the robe tighter around her without taking his eyes off the road ahead. Sunset had taken on the mantle of night, the reds and oranges deepening into lavender, then deep purple. Reflected light from the snow made the world seem like the fairyland she had once imagined it to be.

"No, not at all," she replied.

"I owe you an apology for this afternoon. I was forward and I'm sorry."

"No offense taken." Her heart plummeted. So, he *had* been toying with her. The rumor mill ground away in fine working order. "I'm afraid I got a little carried away with the season, too." So what had she expected? That a man such as Ben would be interested in a woman like her? A penniless widow with four children to support . . .

Admonishing herself for girlish dreams, Anna tried to turn her thoughts to other things, but his closeness, his hands inches away, the reins gently entwined through his long, strong fingers, kept interfering.

The streets of the fort were quiet and still. Yellow light spilled out windows, making a quilt pattern on the sparkling snow. The sleigh slid to a stop in front of Anna's house, and Ben jumped down.

"I'll help you get them inside." He lifted Susie into his arms and Anna woke the other children. They filed sleepily into the house and went straight to their beds.

"She sleeps in here with me," Anna said over her shoulder as she hurried to her curtained bedroom and pulled the makeshift trundle bed out from underneath her own. Ben knelt on one knee and gently placed the child in her bed. He untied her bonnet and quickly removed her coat, then pulled a quilt up to her chin.

"You look like you've had experience doing that," Anna said as he paused over the sleeping child to touch a chubby cheek.

The edges of his ears colored. "I've put many a sub-constable to bed after too much whiskey." He slid the curtain closed along its wooden rod and turned to Anna. "I should be going."

"Can I offer you a cup of coffee?" Anna glanced at the stove, hoping there was some in her pantry.

"No. Thank you."

"You can leave the greenery on the porch. I'll have the children string it together tomorrow."

He nodded and walked out the door. She heard the rustle of evergreens, then he strode back inside. An awkwardness filled the space between them.

"Don't forget Christmas Eve," she reminded.

"I won't."

"Thank you for the use of the sleigh. The children had a wonderful time."

"You're welcome."

He moved forward a step, then pressed something cool into her palm. "Save this for me. Good night."

Anna waited until the door closed behind him before she opened her hand. The sprig of mistletoe lay nestled in her palm.

Ben shuffled through the ankle-deep snow, following the stained and furrowed path from the stable, wishing he'd had the cobbler fix the hole in the bottom of his boot. High, thin clouds flirted with a full moon, animating the shadows of buildings and fences.

He stopped in the center of the parade ground and stared over his head, silently finding and identifying the constellations. A brilliant star in the east reminded him of the Christmas star, and the stillness of the night brought to mind childhood memories of other Christmases spent surrounded by the love of family and friends. As he gazed into the star-filled sky, Anna's face replaced his long-ago memories. Her warmth, her touch, the love she spun around the children like a golden cocoon, all filled him with the same contentment as those distant memories. His thoughts returned to Anna and her children. If not for her, what Christmas memories would they have?

A sudden, chill breeze brought him back from his thoughts, urging him toward patrol headquarters. Pushing away a jarring thought, he stuffed his hands into the pockets of his buffalo coat and resumed his path toward headquarters.

One light burned in the patrol quarters and he knew Stuart wouldn't sleep until he came back. Suddenly, a shadow moved along a wall across the street. Ben kept his eyes straight ahead and continued his path, conscious of someone moving in the alley to his right. All his senses aware, he began to whistle a nameless tune under his breath. When he rounded the corner, he flattened himself against the side of the building and listened.

Low voices droned on in the alley. Ben edged along the wall, stepping carefully to avoid the old, loose boards.

"I need another delivery, Red. I gotta buy food for Christmas." Tommy's changing voice was unmistakable.

"I ain't trustin' nothin' to you, boy. I heard you drank the last delivery and puked up your guts," a rough voice replied.

"It won't happen again. I promise." An edge of desperation in Tommy's voice skittered up Ben's backbone, setting off an alarm deep within him.

"I said no, now git away from me."

"If . . . if you don't let me make this one last delivery, I'll . . . I'll go to the Mounties."

There was the sound of a scuffle and Ben's fingers closed around the cold wood of his gun stock still in its holster. "You sell me out, boy, and I'll put a bullet through your head. You understand me?"

Tommy's response was muffled, then the conversation paused.

"You want to work so bad, boy. I got a job for you. I got me a shipment comin' in over the border in a couple of days. You take my wagon and go out to meet it. Then you deliver it where I say. You do this and we'll talk about you workin' again. Deal?"

Tommy hesitated. "Deal."

Ben stepped back and flattened himself in the recess of a doorway as Tommy hurried past, his head down. When Ben heard the other set of footsteps fade, he stepped out into the street. Overhead, the northern lights arched and swayed to some ancient rhythm. Helplessness tingled through him, his mind replaying Tommy's desperate words. A protectiveness toward Anna and the children rose within Ben, something he hadn't known was there . . . until this moment.

He resumed his path toward headquarters, aware of every shadow, every movement. Were this any other person, he'd intercept the shipment, arrest the participants and be done with Red Ferguson. But this was Anna's Tommy, a young man who'd veered off on the wrong path for the right reason, shedding his childhood much too soon.

Ben glanced overhead again as the northern lights pulsed and snapped like a bullwhip, and wished he were Santa . . . with the power to make time stand still.

* * *

Ben shoved the stack of papers away from him and placed the ink quill in its well. A headache drilled relentlessly between his eyes. He pinched the bridge of his nose and closed his eyes. Her face appeared, just as it had all of last night. She haunted his dreams, his waking hours, even his headaches. Funny how a man's life could be turned upside down in a matter of hours.

"We caught another young'un."

Ben opened his eyes and blinked to focus. Stuart stood in the doorway, a young boy by the collar. "Caught him slipping a bottle to old man White down by the river." Stuart pulled the stoppered bottle from his coat pocket and waved it in the air. "Even though this cub won't talk, at least not right now," he glared ominously at the lad, "I'll bet money it's Ferguson's stuff."

Ben watched the youth glare right back at Stuart, then wither when Stuart's left eye wandered to the right. Disguising an escaped laugh with a cough, Ben rose from the desk and crossed the floor.

"What's your name?" Ben asked the boy dangling from Stuart's grasp like a kitten from its mother's mouth. The boy's expression was hardened, aged far beyond his years. He glanced up at Stuart, then back to Ben.

"Daniel Summers."

"What do you know about this, son?" He took the bottle, unstoppered it and sniffed. True rotgut.

"I ain't gotta say nothin'."

"That's very true. You don't have to say anything now. The judge will be in town in, let's say . . ." he paused to walk over to a wall calendar, allowing their well-practiced theatrics to sink in, "two weeks." He ran a finger over the paper wishing the judge appeared even twice a year. "It will be Judge Wilkins, too. Pity."

He strode slowly back across the floor. The boy couldn't be more than twelve or thirteen.

"What do you mean, 'pity'?" He raised suspicious eyes.

"I mean, Judge Wilkins hates to travel, especially this time of year. He has to come all the way from Winnipeg and he misses his family and Christmas. He's usually in a foul mood by the time he gets here. Isn't he, Constable McGuire?"

"That he is. But, the good thing is, we get to clean out the jail." He gave the lad a slight shake. "Most folks gets hung."

The boy's eyes widened and the tough expression slipped for just an instant as he looked between the men. "Yer both lyin'."

"Maybe we is and maybe we ain't. You want to bet your scrawny life on that, cub?"

The boy's face hardened. "Yeah. I'll bet yer bluffin'."

Ben nodded his head toward the jail. "Throw him in the tank, Constable McGuire."

Stuart pulled the boy toward the jail, shoved him inside and made a great noise slamming and locking the door.

"How long you reckon it'll take?" Stuart said softly as he dropped the keys in Ben's desk drawer.

"Old man Fraser should be here in about an hour. Nasty drunk and loud." He pulled a pocket watch from his pocket. "I'll give the lad an hour after that before he's ready to tell all." He snapped the gold watch shut and returned it to his pocket. "Did you tell his mother what we're about?"

"Yep. She and his pa were embarrassed and scared. I told 'em we'd take good care of the lad, but that he'd get the scare of his life and wouldn't want to never see any whiskey again as long as he lived."

"And he won't. Not after an hour in the same cell

with Fraser. Did the parents know anything about where the boy got the whiskey?"

Stuart shook his head. "Said they couldn't imagine, but that they were beginnin' to think the lad was makin' too much for work at the sawmill."

"Are the ma and pa down on their luck?" Ben asked, turning in his chair to see the boy. He sat on the bench in the cell, clothes tattered and torn, head down. He was almost a mirror image of Tommy, and a chill ran over Ben.

"The pa broke his leg a few weeks ago and ain't been able to work. The lad here's been makin' up fer it at the sawmill."

"Ferguson's preying on others' misfortunes, but how is he finding them? How is he gettin' the boys to go along with it?"

"Promisin' them the moon, probably."

Daniel raised his head and shot Stuart a fearful look.

"What would we have done without your lazy eye, Stuart?" Ben asked softly.

Stuart chuckled. "We'd a had to come up with somethin' not nearly as convincin', I'll vow."

"You gotta let me outta here!"

Ben rocked back in his chair, propped his feet on his desk and opened a newly arrived newspaper from Ottawa. Daniel had only been in the same cell with Fraser for about fifteen minutes. Fraser was banging the steel bars with a tin cup and singing wildly off key.

"I cain't stand this racket."

He turned the page and heard Fraser retching. "Not much longer now," he muttered to himself.

"Damn you, old man. Hey, Mountie. Let me out. I'll tell you what you want. Ferguson be damned."

Ben let the chair slam forward and grabbed his keys.

"You sure you're ready to talk, lad? If not, back in the cell you go and this will get worse before morning, I promise."

"Yeah, I'll talk." His voice was frantic. "Just let me out."

Ben turned the key in the lock and Daniel slipped out. Ben grabbed Daniel's shirt and hastily slammed the door shut.

"Where'd you get the whiskey?" He escorted Daniel to his office and pushed him into a chair.

Daniel dipped his head, then looked up. "A man named Ferguson came to me at the mill. Said he had a business deal for me and wanted me to get some friends. He said it'd be good money and my pa's laid up with a busted leg. He said all I had to do was deliver this bottle to Mr. White down by the river."

"Did you know it was whiskey?"

Daniel stared at the floor. "I sorta suspected it was somethin' bad, but I don't look no gift horse in the mouth."

"Well, you should have looked at this one's teeth, boy, because Ferguson sold you a nag. How many other boys are in this?"

"I ain't snitchin' on nobody. That weren't part of the deal. You said all's I had to do was tell you where I got it and I done that. Can I go?"

"Not quite yet." Ben paced around the chair. "Where does this man you met get the whiskey?"

"I don't know. He brings it to me at the mill."

"Is Mr. White the only man you deliver to?"

Daniel shook his head. "On Wednesdays I always take a load of slats out to the Blackfoot village. There's a case hidden under the lumber and I get the money from the Injuns when I'm out there."

Ben swore under his breath. Was the impending shipment also destined for the Blackfoot village? Even one load of whiskey could decimate the village for months, producing fathers too drunk to hunt, mothers too drunk to care for their children. Whiskey, the white man's gift to the Blackfoot, he thought bitterly.

"Go on home, Daniel. Don't let me see you in this office again and don't deliver any more whiskey."

Daniel shot a glance at the jail cell. "No, sir, I won't."

Well, at least Ferguson would be one delivery boy short for tomorrow anyway. He'd assign a patrol of men to ride through the streets regularly, be more visible, and keep an eye on groups of boys. Maybe that would discourage deliveries for a while, at least until he could get his hands on Red.

"How long did the lad last?" Stuart asked as Daniel squeezed out the door around him.

"About fifteen minutes." Ben straightened the desk, glad to give up his shift to Stuart. "He identified Ferguson and told me how he gets the whiskey to deliver." He quickly filled Stuart in on his plans.

"I'll walk the streets meself tomorrow." Stuart straightened the collar of his shirt and drew himself up to full height.

"Fraser is already well underway with this night's activities." Ben nodded toward the jail.

"I'll handle Fraser in the mornin'. He can yell all he wants tonight." Stuart sat heavily, the chair protesting beneath his weight. "Did you find out anything 'bout that shipment Tommy was talkin' about?"

Ben shook his head and shrugged into his heavy coat. "No, but I intend to do some checking around tomorrow."

Ben strode through the streets of the fort to the small settlement clustered around the front gate. He'd spent the day patrolling the streets to no avail. If anyone knew

Red Ferguson's plans, they weren't talking. Even a short patrol down to the river had yielded nothing but wet feet and fatigue.

A small, neat house sat the end of a rutted and muddy street. Knocking on the door, he stamped his feet to fend off the cold creeping in through the hole in his boot.

Mrs. Fitzgerald swung open her stout door and the aroma of baked bread rushed out. A fat, yellow tabby slipped through the crack and coiled itself around his legs. "Good evening, Constable."

"Is it ready?" Ben asked, leaning forward to peep inside.

Mrs. Fitzgerald smiled, gathering up wrinkles at the corners of her eyes. "Of course it is. Come in. Wipe your feet." She pointed at a burlap sack spread across the porch and stepped back, holding the door. "You must have a piece of bread and some tea before you leave."

The cat slipped in just before she slammed the door shut and pulled the latch. "It's just out of the oven," she said over her shoulder as she waddled toward the kitchen.

An excuse sprang to Ben's lips. He wanted to take care of this bit of business and be on his way, but Mrs. Fitzgerald's cheerful voice triggered his guilt. She loved visitors and detained every one as long as possible.

Ben followed her and glanced around the corner. Her back to the door, she was carefully laying fresh slices of bread on a plate, humming under her breath. With a sigh, he took off his buffalo coat and wandered into the living room.

His boots made footprints in the pile of deep, rich rugs. Dark cherry furniture, brought from back East, gleamed beneath generous coats of oil. Ben lifted a lace curtain and stared out across the snow. December 20.

Four days until Christmas Eve and he still hadn't found out where the whiskey shipment would be delivered.

"Here you are, Constable." Mrs. Fitzgerald set a delicate silver tray and teapot on a low table. "It is so nice to have visitors. Especially at this time of year. Please, sit down." Elegantly, she swept her skirts aside and perched on the settee. The yellow cat jumped up on the arm of the chair and watched him through narrow slits. Ben sat carefully on a delicate love seat.

"Do have some buttered bread." She handed him a small plate, then served a piece of bread covered with butter.

Ben accepted and leaned back, trying not to look as anxious as he felt.

"Your costume turned out just lovely. Mrs. Radford had some wonderful red flannel and Mrs. Scott had just carded some wool that made a delightful beard." She sipped her tea. "I must say that I am very curious as to what you intend to do with the costume. Is this for a Police function? I had heard that Constable McGuire was going to be Santa for the children at the Christmas ball and I know that he has his own costume. Why, I made it myself last year."

"Yes, Stuart is our Santa for this year," Ben answered, feeling an interrogation coming.

"Are we to have two Santas?" She watched him over the rim of her cup.

Ben sipped his tea, carefully measuring his words. Mrs. Fitzgerald's curiosity was exceeded only by her cat's. "No. This is for me personally."

"Indeed." Her eyes glittered with excitement. "I think you will make a wonderful Santa for some lucky boy or girl, Constable."

After considering several vague explanations, he decided the truth would be best. She'd know the real story by morning anyway. "I'm going to play Santa for Anna Snow's children."

Her eyebrows shot up. "Mrs. Snow's children? I didn't know that you were acquainted with that woman."

"Yes, we are."

Mrs. Fitzgerald leaned forward and clattered her china cup back into its saucer. "You do know that her husband was a renowned whiskey trader?"

"So I've heard," Ben replied, controlling the itch of annoyance growing within him.

"Then perhaps you should know that she is still involved in trading whiskey and that her morals are . . . less than pristine." Her voice fell to a conspiratorial whisper and, despite the anger rising in him, Ben sensed a source of information sitting right in front of him.

During his years in the Force, Ben had often found that the elusive information he sought circulated over store counters and in church yards right beneath his nose.

"No, I didn't know that." He frowned and tried to look disturbed.

"Well, I don't hold with gossip, Constable, but I'm sad to say it's true. That oldest boy she took in, Tommy I believe is his name. Well, rumor has it he and a whole gang of boys go out hunting birds on that island in the river, but they don't come back with ducks. No, they come back with their pockets full of bottles of rotgut whiskey."

So, that's how they get it, Ben thought. Fighting a smile, he placed his cup and saucer on the silver tray. "How do you know this, Mrs. Fitzgerald?"

She drew back as if insulted, then her expression softened to patient endurance. "Why, everyone knows that, Constable."

"Have you heard who brings them the whiskey?"

"Yes, as a matter of fact, I heard a man's name mentioned. Someone named 'Red,' I think. LouAnne Holmes heard that from Susie Watkins who heard it from Mrs. Stanton. Her husband owns the general store, I'm sure you know."

"I know Bill Stanton." Wondering if the storekeeper had anything to do with the sale of the whiskey, he waited to see if Mrs. Fitzgerald would offer any more information.

She smiled at him, reminding him of the fat, sly cat at her elbow, and he knew she had saved the gold nugget of information for the last. "Are you sure you have plenty of men on duty for tomorrow night?"

This is like fishing, Ben. You just have to give her enough line, then land her. "No more than usual. Why?"

Her smiled widened. "Well, you should put more men on, Constable. I suspect you will need them."

"And why is that?" He rubbed his hands down his pants legs and made himself look ready to leave. Perhaps his actions would hurry her story to its end.

She leaned forward. "Because there's a shipment of whiskey coming into Fort McLeod tomorrow night. A shipment large enough to create total confusion in our little settlement, Constable."

"Well, I will look into the matter, and thank you for bringing it to my attention." Ben stood. "Could I get that suit from you?"

"Oh, yes." She hurried off to the back of the house and returned with a box. "Everything's in here." She started to hand it to him, then drew back. "I do hope that you have better judgment than to get involved with a woman like Mrs. Snow, Constable. I hope that you are surprising these children out of a sense of civic duty and not out of some romantic involvement."

Ben took the box from her. "All children should have

a surprise on Christmas no matter their circumstances. Don't you think that's only charitable?"

Mrs. Fitzgerald paused. "Yes, of course," she said finally.

"Good night." He swept his coat off the rack and hurried out the door before she could think of something else to berate him for.

A stiff, cold wind had swept aside the few high, wispy clouds, and stars filled the night sky. Drawing his collar up around his ears, Ben walked aimlessly, liking the way the wind made his skin tingle, made him feel alive. He'd spent his entire career in the Northwest Police going where he was sent, doing what he was told. Only until the last few days, until Anna, had he realized that something vital within him slept, waiting to be awakened.

And Anna had awakened it.

Restlessness uncoiled in his stomach as her memory arose again. A faceless memory. He remembered not an image, but rather a touch, a brush of skin against skin, the intimate heat of another body close.

He looked up and found himself outside her door. A feeble light shone through the cracked glass and out onto the snow. He raised his hand to knock, then wondered what excuse he could give for being there. He glanced down at the box tucked beneath his arm and rapped on the door.

The door scraped open and Anna's face appeared in the crack. "Ben." Her face blanched. "Has something happened?"

"No. I was just out walking and wanted to show you something."

She swung the door open and stepped back. An old, faded wrapper wound around her nearly twice and pooled on the floor at her feet. Strands of hair straggled down her cheeks and dark circles shadowed her eyes.

"What's wrong?" Ben asked, his senses suddenly alert.

"Nothing," she answered, turning away. "The children have colds, that's all."

Her words didn't ring true and Ben stepped inside and closed the door behind him. He glanced toward her bed, rumpled and tossed. Tommy's pallet lay by the fire empty.

"Where is Tommy?"

She turned to face him and searched his eyes, trying to decide whether or not to trust him.

Finally, she shook her head. "I don't know. He's been gone since early this morning." A tear slid down her cheek. "He's never out this late."

Above in the loft, Ben heard muffled voices. "Where did he go?" he whispered.

"He said last night Mr. Stanton had a small job for him this morning. Unloading some firewood at a homestead east of here." She turned to pace to the window. "But he said he'd be back early."

Standing at the window, the too-big clothes hanging off her, she looked vulnerable and lost, swathed in a world that was equally too big.

"He's in some kind of trouble, isn't he?" Ben stepped up behind her and cupped her shoulders with his hands.

She nodded, the back of her head rubbing against the serge of his uniform. "I'm afraid so. He takes on too much responsibility for me and the children. He should be a child and he behaves like a man."

He turned her to face him. "I'll go find out from Stanton where he sent him and ride out there. He's probably already on his way back."

Cornered into trusting him, she nodded reluctantly.

Her body tensed as he drew her against his chest. Even through the layers of his uniform, he could feel her heart beat, a steady, slightly fast staccato, joined with his own. She was so small, nestled beneath his chin, her hair soft against his cheek. Yet, he knew in a second she could pull away and defy him. She was granting him a liberty he sensed she had given no one in a long time.

When she tipped her head back to speak, he smothered her words with his lips. Suddenly, the need to kiss her overcame everything else, every practiced restraint, every warning singing in his head. Her response surprised him. She slid her arms around his waist and pulled him against her, firing his blood, washing away the concerns of a moment ago.

"I'd better go," he whispered against her lips and she nodded.

He stepped backward, the very last thing he wanted to do at that moment. "I'll bring Tommy home."

She nodded, fingers pressed against her lips.

He towered over her, tall, confident, his eyes gentle and dark. Everything within her wanted to trust him, to lay this problem at his feet, but doing so might cost her her precious children. He was still the law and still had the power to take them away. Would he do it?

She glanced up into his face and read compassion there, but mingled with something deeper, something not quite controlled. She sensed she held a certain power over him, but a voice warned her not to use the power, else she would set into motion events she could not call back. She'd been fooled before by a man. Badly fooled.

Ben opened the door and stood silhouetted by the light of the waning moon. "I'll be back before morning."

She nodded and he closed the door behind him. Pulling aside the tattered curtain, she watched him stride through the snow, taking her hopes and her heart with him.

4

Two wagons crunched through the snow, tiny silhouettes against the vast night sky. The occasional jingle of harness buckles broke the cold, still silence. A full moon dusted the earth with silver.

Huddled in his buffalo coat, Ben watched from the thicket as steam rose from the back of his lathered horse. One of the wagons hit a bump and rattled loudly. Ben's heart slid down into his boots when Tommy turned his head to glance around.

"Stupid time to move the whiskey," Ben muttered into the muffler wrapped around his neck and mouth. Why would a canny smuggler choose a night as bright as this one to move his shipment? And why would he trust the shipment to two young boys instead of seasoned ruffians. There was certainly no shortage of them around the fort.

The wagons neared a rocky outcropping and slipped behind a group of boulders. Ben followed, keeping his horse just inside the cover of the trees, then crossed the open distance quickly as the wagons disappeared.

He left his horse tied to a young aspen and slid around the rock face until he heard voices.

"I caught you red-handed, cub. There's no need to

make things worse for yourself." McGuire's words echoed against the rocks.

Ben edged closer, confused.

"I don't know nothing, I tell you." Tommy protested.

Could this be some elaborate trap set by Ferguson? But to catch whom?

Weapon drawn, Ben moved to peek around the rock. Stuart held Tommy by the collar and a patrol of Ben's own men held the other youngster in custody. Ben stepped into the circle of light shed by several oil lanterns.

"Ben." Stuart looked up, startled. "You didn't go to Calgary?"

Ben frowned. "Calgary? No. What's going on here?"

Stuart frowned. "You left me the note yerself, Ben."

"What note?" Ben holstered his gun and met Tommy's accusing eyes.

"You left me a note on the desk. 'Whiskey being brought to Keyhole Rock on Thursday night. Take patrol and wait in canyon. Have to ride to Calgary.' Them's your exact words, wrote down in your own hand."

Ben shook his head. "I left you no note." He glanced at Tommy. "I found out about this operation another way."

Stuart looked down at Tommy. "Somebody set a good trap for Ferguson and his brew."

"Or a good decoy."

Ben moved closer and Tommy glared at him. "Damned Mountie. I knew you'd double-cross me."

"Why don't you tell me everything you know about Red Ferguson." Ben knew arguing his intentions to Tommy would be futile at this point. He grabbed Tommy's coat sleeve, but the boy wrenched away, twisting in Stuart's grip.

"I'm not tellin' you anything. You snuggled up close to Miss Anna just to get to me, didn't you?"

"No, Tommy. I didn't. It looks like somebody's used you as a decoy. Now, where's the real shipment headed?"

Tommy pressed his lips together and looked away.

Stuart relinquished his grasp as Ben took Tommy's arm and yanked the boy around to face him. "This is your chance to be out of this, Tommy, done with Red Ferguson once and for all."

"Who says I wanna be out of it?" Tommy raised his chin and boldly met Ben's gaze.

"You're a smart man, Tommy. Surely you can see there's no future in this sort of thing."

Tommy's eyes were old beyond his years. "All I see is you damned Mounties sticking your noses in everybody's business. Who made it right for you to tell a man when and where he can have a drink?"

Ben's anger flared, but he quickly snuffed it, choosing his words cautiously. "Those aren't your words. You're listening to the wrong sort of men."

"And you're the right sort, Constable? Romancin' Miss Anna just to get to me?"

Ben glanced at his patrol, shuffling their feet and staring beyond the light.

"What's between Miss Anna and me is just that. Between us. It has nothing to do with you."

Precious minutes were slipping by. The real shipment was surely en route. If he was going to intercept it, Ben had to move quickly.

"If you don't tell me, Tommy, I'll have to arrest you and you'll stay in jail until the judge comes."

Tommy's gaze never wavered. "A damned Mountie killed my pa. I got no love for the lot of you, and I'll never tell you nothin'."

"Take him in." Ben turned on his heel and walked

away, wondering how he was going to explain this to Anna. Stuart wound ropes around Tommy's wrists. The sound of his struggle ran up Ben's spine and lodged in his stomach.

"I'd like to settle this without compromising the boy," Ben said, peering underneath the tarp that covered empty crates in the bed of the wagon. He glanced up at Tommy, still glaring at him from the grasp of another constable.

Stuart paused. "I thought you knew." His voice was low, ominous.

Ben shifted his gaze to Stuart's face. "Knew what?"

Stuart swallowed and hesitated.

"Spit it out, Stuart."

Stuart kicked at a pile of snow. "McLeod himself knows about this. He assigned the patrol I brought with me. Said he was going to make an example of this one." He nodded toward Tommy.

Ben's heart turned over in his chest. Tommy would be prosecuted, jailed, if not hanged. James McLeod hadn't moved a force of men across a continent to be thwarted by one whiskey trader and his stable of deliverymen. He meant to stamp out the whiskey trade in the area, no matter what measures were involved.

"That's not all." Again, Stuart's face was sad. He reached out a beefy arm and clasped Ben's shoulder. "You've been appointed guardian of all Mrs. Snow's children until representatives can get here from Ottawa."

"How'd you find this out?" The world spun for a second, then righted itself. Someone was manipulating things, someone with the connections and means to do so. Possibilities flashed through Ben's mind. Who would gain from Anna Snow losing her children and Tommy going to jail? No one. At least no one he could think of.

"She should already be served with the order," Stuart said in a small voice. "I sent Tucker out with it just before we left the fort. I thought you knew all about it."

He glanced in the direction of the fort, hidden by night and by distance. He could almost feel Anna's pain, her betrayal. He had done what she feared most. "Did this come down from McLeod, too?"

Stuart shook his head. "Came in by rider from Ottawa this morning."

Ben walked away, then paced back. "How does all this connect?"

Stuart shook his head. "I don't know, but I'm willing to bet Mrs. Fitzgerald's Christmas bread pudding that it does."

Anna stared at the papers in her hand, unmindful of the cold air sweeping in past her feet.

"Ma'am? Could I come in and shut the door?" The young trooper's voice barely broke through the thoughts tumbling around in her head. Betrayal crept through her, numbing her as it worked its way to her brain.

"Yes. Please." She stepped back, wondering briefly how she made her legs work.

"Um. The papers say I have to take the children now." Hat in hand, the young man shuffled his feet and glanced over his shoulder, anxious to be away.

Anna turned, seeing the room pass in a collage. Susie huddled behind Pat, clearly confused, yet knowing something bad was about to happen. Sinopa stood by the fireplace, a worn blanket in her hand, staring straight and unflinchingly at the trooper.

"What about Pat? He's my son."

The young constable stared at his feet. "Him, too."

A sob caught in Anna's throat, threatening to choke off her air. She wouldn't cry in front of the children. She wouldn't. They were frightened enough.

"It's all right, children." She pasted on a smile and turned to face them. "You're going to visit the Mountie office. Would you like that?"

Pat glanced out the window. "It's the middle of the night, Ma. Is something wrong? Are the Injuns comin'?"

"No, nothing like that." Anna tried to think of some reason they'd accept, some words that wouldn't frighten them.

"You see," she began, forcing a smile to her lips. "Sometimes Santa gets behind in his work and then the Mounties have to help him. They're waiting for you to tell them what you want Santa to bring you." The explanation was ludicrous, she knew it even as she said it. But it was the only thing that came to mind . . . that and Ben's last words.

She was stupid. Blind and stupid to allow herself to be taken in by a handsome man in a red suit.

Pat's face lit up at Anna's explanation and Susie slid out from behind him. "Really?" she piped.

"Yes. Now run get your coats and we'll go with the trooper here."

The children scurried away and Anna excused herself to her bedchamber to change clothes. She plucked her dress off the peg in the wall, while tears burned her eyes and sobs welled up in her chest. As she pulled the thin cotton over her head, her breaths came in gulps and she fought for control. *Somehow I'll fight this,* she told herself as she buttoned the last button. Somehow she would convince the authorities that the children belonged with her, not in some institution. Damn Ben Parker. Damn him for coming into her life.

* * *

"These papers all seem to be in order." Ben stared down at the documents in his hand, not reading them, dreading looking up at Anna. "The children must stay here with me." The words stuck in his throat.

Pure hatred burned in her eyes as she met his gaze. She'd never believe he hadn't orchestrated this whole thing.

"Do you have someplace more suitable for the children to stay?" Anna glanced around the office, her voice cold and hard. "I hardly think a jail, even a Mounted Police jail, is an appropriate place for children."

Ben barely noticed Stuart take the papers from his hand.

"I . . . ah, Mrs. Fitzgerald has kindly agreed to allow them to stay with her for the night."

Anna sniffed. "Mrs. Fitzgerald? A spinster? What does she know of children? Can she treat a fever in the night? Can she quiet their nightmares? Can you, for that matter, Constable?" She clutched Pat tight against her legs and Susie hung on to her skirt.

Anna's voice rose and he knew she was fighting the tears. Hell, so was he. And Tommy's stony face staring at him between the bars wasn't helping. Ben stepped forward and took her elbow. "Could I speak with you privately for a moment?"

"Is this another attempt to sully my reputation?" she hissed at him.

"Anna, please. Don't make this any worse."

She nodded curtly, then ran her fingers through Susie's curls. The little girl clutched a ragged doll tighter to her chest.

"Come and sit on Stuart's lap and tell him about that dolly." Stuart sat down in a chair, held out his arms to her, and continued to read the legal papers, glasses perched on the end of his nose.

Susie pulled and yanked on his red jacket to clamber onto his lap and began to jabber. Stuart agreed with occasional grunts, his attention fixed on the papers.

"I didn't know about this, Anna," Ben whispered when he had led her off to a corner of the office. "I swear I didn't."

She glared up at him. "Of course you did. How long had you planned this?"

"I haven't planned anything. This is as much a surprise to me as it is to you." He gripped her elbow, but she wrenched away.

"How much of what has been said between us was a lie, Ben?" Her eyes glistened with tears, and her lips quivered, begging him to still them.

"Nothing between us has been a lie."

She looked into his eyes for a moment, then away. The chill of her anger closed in around him.

"I don't know who contacted Ottawa. It certainly wasn't me. I have no reason to want to remove the children from you. It's obvious you love them and they love you." He wanted to touch her, but drew back his hand.

"Save your stories for the whores in the saloons."

The bluntness of her words stabbed him, but the icy stare she settled on him hurt worse.

"I know what the whole settlement thinks of me," she continued. "They expected me to grovel at their feet, to beg for work or scraps from their tables. Instead, I survived. And I did it on my own and without a man, a sin I'm sure I'll never be forgiven." She narrowed her eyes and leaned in closer, her lips almost brushing his. "I warn you, Constable. You've chosen a formidable opponent in me. You fight for what's deemed right and acceptable, to assure the good citizens that their lives won't be tarnished or affected by those less fortunate. I, on the other hand, fight for survival, for the lives of my babies." She leaned closer and her lips brushed against his. He fought to keep his arms at his sides, to not pull her against him and whisper promises he couldn't keep.

"Which of us do you think will win?" Her warm breath caressed him, then she pulled away, leaving the air charged yet cold.

"What about Tommy?" She nodded to where Tommy sat in the jail cell, his head cradled in his hands.

"The judge will be here after Christmas and he'll decide what's to be done." Ben tried to keep his voice even, to not betray the emotion raging through him.

For the first time, Anna's eyes mirrored her fear. "What will he do?"

Ben had hoped she wouldn't ask that question. "I don't know. He may release him into my custody, or he may decide to prosecute him."

"What I want to know is why? What do you gain by doing this, Constable? A promotion? Accolades for cleaning up Fort McLeod? Or is it your intention to rid the settlement of the 'Infamous Widow Snow'?"

Anger and hurt flashed through her eyes, revealing the distrust rooted deeply in her soul.

"Anna, listen to me." Ben's fingers touched her shoulder. "I swear to you, I had nothing to do with this evening. Someone left a note here in the office telling Constable Stuart where to find Tommy and the shipment of whiskey. I received my information from another source."

"And what would you have done had you been the one to find the note?"

Ben took a deep breath. "I'd have acted exactly as Stuart did."

Anna studied his face for a moment, then looked around him to the children. The anger on her face slipped away into sorrow. "I hope you can live with yourself, Ben Parker."

"Constable." Stuart slipped his glasses off his nose and motioned with his free hand. "Could you come here and take a look at this?" He waved the document in one hand and steadied Susie with the other as he bounced her on his knee. The other children clustered around him, chattering and giggling, wonderfully oblivious to their situation.

Ben left Anna in the corner, her arms wrapped around herself.

"See this passage here." Stuart pointed a finger to a line of script. "It says that the children will be placed in an appropriate home at the discretion of the guardian. That's you." Stuart smiled. "I can't think of a more suitable home than the one they just came from."

Ben shook his head. "That might make matters worse."

Stuart lifted a laughing Susie off his knee, replaced her with Pat, and the make-believe horse ride began again. "Can't say this could get much worse."

Ben nodded, the lead weight on his heart easing a bit. The action might cost him his job. Surely it would cost him a good dressing down from James McLeod. Ben took the papers and Stuart's glasses. He skimmed the document, handed it back to Stuart, then turned to look at Anna.

She looked away, refusing to meet his eyes.

"The papers give me the choice of where to place the children until the authorities arrive from Ottawa."

"And where, with your intimate knowledge of children, have you decided, Constable?"

"With you."

Anna searched his face, eyes narrowed. "What do you have in mind? Do you think to use the children and I as bait? Are you willing to use us to uphold your oath?"

Ben wanted to pull her to him and kiss the biting

words right off her lips. "I want the children to go home with you, because that's what's best for them."

Anna glanced over at Tommy's face, forlorn and frightened. "What about Ferguson?"

"I'll take care of Red Ferguson."

Again, she fixed him with a suspicious stare. "What do you gain by allowing the children to stay with me?"

"Your happiness." He hadn't meant to whisper, but the words came out soft and low.

She stared at him a moment longer, her face unreadable. Then, she swept past and herded the children together like chicks. "Let's go home now."

"I'll hitch up the sleigh and give you a ride home." Ben reached for his coat.

"No, thank you. We prefer to walk." Without a backward look, Anna guided them out of the office and slammed the door.

Stuart whistled beneath his breath. "I'd not be in your shoes, lad."

"Neither would I."

"Especially since I read this passage." Stuart handed over the papers, pointing out another line. " 'The guardian shall have an active role in monitoring the daily progress of the children in their new surroundings.' "

"I wouldn't want to be you the first time you go a-callin'."

"Come in, Constable Ben." Susie opened the door wider and stepped back. She stared down at the floorboards, her face solemn. Her black ringlets were damp and hung down the back of a faded, but clean and ironed dress.

"Why, thank you, Susie." He squatted down to her level, but she looked away from him.

"No smiles for Santa today?"

She stared up at him with huge, liquid eyes. "You're not Santa Claus."

Ben pushed his hat back on his head. "Well, of course I am. Didn't Miss Anna tell you so?" He raised his head at a soft swoosh near his ear.

Susie looked from him to Anna, who had come to stand at his side. "Santa is a nice man. He wouldn't make us leave Miss Anna."

Anna's look challenged him to explain things. "Wouldn't you like a home of your own with a mommy and a daddy?"

"No!" Susie wrapped herself around Anna's legs, hiding her face in the fold of her skirts.

"And where did you learn this diplomacy, Santa?" Anna hissed as she bent to pick up Susie.

Ben sighed and stood. Anna took Susie to the kitchen and sat her on the table. After a few soft words, Susie unwound her arms from around Anna's neck and accepted a bowl of dried beans to unstring.

"This is a great start," Ben muttered beneath his breath as he pulled out a chair and sat down.

With soft words and gentle touches, Anna soothed Susie's fears and finally convinced her to scamper off to play. He gasped when Anna plopped the half finished bowl of beans in his lap.

"How is Tommy?" she asked as she turned back to her supper preparations.

"He's fine. Stuart owes him twenty dollars in poker."

Anna gasped and whirled around. "You're letting him gamble?"

Ben shrank under the scorching look. No, his visit wasn't going well at all. "The boy has to have something to do, Anna."

"I would assume that you, with all your worldly knowledge of children, would encourage him to pursue some other pastime, such as reading." She regarded him with one raised eyebrow.

"Well, Anna, I guess I'm just not as wise as Santa, because I didn't think of that."

"I have books. I'll take him some tomorrow." She turned away, rattling a pan louder than necessary. "If you don't object."

Ben yanked a handful of beans free from their string and winced as the thread sliced into his fingers. "Of course I won't object." He shook his hand and set the bowl of beans on the table with a clatter.

"Have you heard anything from the judge?"

"Judge Wilkins is due here Christmas Eve."

Anna's hands stopped moving, but she didn't turn around. "So soon?"

"His sister lives in Calgary. He's coming here as a favor." Ben regretted his choice of words the second he said them.

"A favor? Is that all the importance you give this? One favor from the judge and Tommy is out of your hair?" She flattened her hands on the counter.

"Damn it, Anna." Ben shoved the chair backward and stalked into the kitchen.

"Don't use profanity in this house." She whirled to face him, bracing her hands on the counter behind her.

"I'm sorry, but Anna Snow, you'd make a saint curse. Why are you so distrusting?"

She paused, pointedly avoiding his gaze. "Trust can cost you your life and your dreams. Distrust only costs you your happiness."

Throughout dinner the children watched him with suspicious eyes, following his every move, making him as jumpy as a cat. When Anna finally shooed them all upstairs to bed, he breathed a sigh of relief. Maybe now he could convince Anna that he didn't have horns growing straight out of his head.

"They're exhausted, poor dears." Anna demurely gathered her skirts around her legs as she descended the ladder from the loft and stepped down into the kitchen. "They've worried themselves sick."

Ben shifted in the creaky chair. "Look, Anna. I have no intention of taking them away from you. As I said before, I didn't file for the order. I don't know who did."

She sat down opposite him, dark circles shadowing her eyes. "I'm too tired tonight to try and outfigure you. If you've seen enough to satisfy your reponsibilities to Ottawa, why don't you just leave?"

"I didn't come here to check up on you."

"Then why did you come?"

"To see the children. And you."

Soft firelight glinted off his hair as he leaned forward, his eyes intent on hers. She'd turned down the lamps to save oil and now she was sorry she had. In fact, she wished they were blazing at their highest. In the soft light, he looked irresistible. *Oh, Anna. Will you ever listen to your common sense?*

"Who do you suppose contacted Ottawa about the children?" he asked, hands folded on the table. He was diligent in his questioning, she'd give him that.

Anna sighed. Perhaps he was telling the truth. "A few months ago, some of the local society dragons approached me and said they were concerned about my reputation. They didn't think the children should be with me."

His lips twitched. "And?"

"And, I said some things I shouldn't have."

"Such as?"

She drummed her fingers on the table. Now, in her mind, her words sounded juvenile and irresponsible, not the kind of things a grown, responsible woman should say.

"I told Mrs. Stanton she was a picky old biddy."

His laugh was warm, inviting, contagious. He briefly touched her hand, then leaned back in his chair. "You do have a way with words, Anna Snow. What was her reaction?"

"She threatened to bring the Mounted Police into the matter and have the children taken away." Anna raised her face. "But I didn't think she'd do it. She's always blustering about something. Ever since I've been sewing for her, she's the most frustrating, infuriating woman . . ."

"You're a seamstress?"

"Yes." He seemed surprised at her answer. "Why?"

He smiled, a slow cat smile that ran over her like warm honey. "You don't seem the type."

"I have children to support. It's an honorable profession."

"Indeed." The crackling of the fire grew louder. "What is Santa bringing tomorrow night?"

Gnawing guilt robbed Anna of the pleasure of the moment. "I have a few things. I found a doll and dressed it for Susie. I made Sapino a new dress and Pat a new shirt. I knitted Tommy new socks." She'd not been able to buy them anything from the store and she'd so wanted this Christmas to be special.

"And what is Santa bringing Miss Anna?" His fingers closed around hers, surprisingly warm and soft for a man who spent his life outdoors.

Her first thought was to snatch them away from him, but she didn't. "I hope he is bringing me my children."

His grip tightened. "Santa Claus is magic. He makes wishes come true. Don't you know that?"

"I only hope that Santa is fair."

He rose and moved around behind her before she

could think or figure his next move. Warm hands slid around her shoulders and urged her to stand.

He turned her to face him. "Go with me to the ball."

Temptation whispered in her ear. How long had it been since she'd been to a dance? How long since she'd whirled around a dance floor, held in a handsome man's arms, oblivious to the world spinning past?

"The Christmas Eve ball? I can't. The children." The momentary flush of excitement faded into suspicion. "What kind of mother would I be if I left my children on Christmas Eve?"

His face gave away nothing—no scheme to undermine her, no hint of trickery.

"We'll take the children with us. Other families will be there. They'll have a wonderful time."

His grip tightened on her arms, reminding her of their kiss in the fragrant evergreen thicket.

She tried to find some anger, tried to kindle the fury she'd felt yesterday, but his eyes were sincere and it was the day before Christmas Eve. The pesky voices in her head urged her to go.

"No, I won't go with you, but I might see you there."

A calico sea of silk spilled over the rough, board floor of Anna's house—red, green, blue—various scraps left over from ball gowns. Seated in the middle, Anna held up first one scrap and then another.

"What about this?"

Susie sat cross-legged, winding strips of material around her doll. She looked up, lips pursed, and shook her head. "No, I don't like that color." She picked up a scrap and rubbed the silky material against her cheek. "This feels good, don't it?" She leaned forward and rubbed the scrap against Anna's cheek.

"Doesn't it," Anna corrrected through a mouthful of pins and nodded in agreement.

"Do you like Constable Parker?" Susie leaned closer. "He told me to call him that so's nobody would know who he really is," she whispered.

Anna paused, sensing a question-and-answer session coming. "Yes, I like him."

"But I thought you were mad with him."

Anna stopped fumbling through the fabric. "I am."

Susie's eyes were large and serious. "Is he going to make us go away?"

"No, baby, he's not."

"Is somebody else going to make us go away?"

Anna pulled Susie onto her lap. "No. They are most definitely not." She wrapped her arms around Susie and reached for a large piece of fabric. "What about this scrap of blue. It's from Mrs. Stanton's dress. Think she'll notice?"

Susie bobbed her head yes. "He smiles funny when he sees you." She shrugged her shoulders and giggled.

"Who?"

"Constable Parker."

"Oh, he does?"

"Uh huh. He gets a funny look on his face, too." Susie scrambled off her lap to sit amidst the scraps.

"What do you think of this?" Anna held up the bright red silk top from a gown whose bodice she'd replaced for Mrs. Stanton's daughter. "And add this." She held up the green skirt from another customer's dress. "Do you think Mrs. Stanton's daughter will recognize the old top to her dress?"

"He'll like it." Susie giggled, then turned her head to the side. "Is he a daddy?"

Anna swept aside the other remnants of fabric and began to pin the two parts together. "No. He's not married. Remember he told you that when we went to gather greenery."

"Then could he be our daddy?"

Anna nearly swallowed the mouthful of pins. "No. He couldn't."

"Why not?"

Anna sighed. "Well, for him to be your daddy, he'd have to be married to your mother."

"But I haven't got a mother. Except for you. What if you were my mother, Miss Anna?" Susie stared up at her expectantly.

"Oh, Susie. This is more complicated than you think."

"What's com-ple-caked?"

"Look, we can make Dolly a dress just like mine." Anna held up scraps of the red-and-green silk and Susie began to wind them around her doll, her questions momentarily forgotten, much to Anna's relief. Her questions struck much too close to some of the daydreams Anna had been having lately—silly, girlish fantasies she should have long since outgrown. When Jasper died, she promised herself she would never again depend upon another person, much less another man. And now, her traitorous heart leapt whenever Ben came into sight and the touch of his fingers made her knees weak.

"Why can't he?"

"Why can't who what?"

"Miss Anna, you're not paying attention." Susie shoved out her bottom lip, the scraps of fabric forgotten. "If you could be our mommy and Constable Parker could be our daddy, would we still have to leave and go live with other people?"

"Well . . . no, I guess not. But, Susie, it's not that easy."

She shrugged and picked up her doll. "I don't see

what's so hard about it. You like him and he likes you." Her face broke into a wide smile. "And it would be so much fun."

Indeed it would, Anna's mutinous little inside voice said.

5

Anna's needle flashed in and out of the smooth fabric. It was nearly noon and she still hadn't finished her dress for the dance. She stopped and clasped her trembling hands together. Why was she so nervous? She hadn't agreed to go to the dance with him, only to be there. She'd felt safe with that arrangement then, maintaining a shaky wall of independence between them.

She picked up her dress and began to sew. "Ouch." She jabbed the needle into her finger, then shook the injured digit and popped it into her mouth.

Insistent rapping nearly made her drop the garment to the floor. Rising from her chair, she hurried to the door.

Ben stood behind a Blackfoot couple, his face gray, his eyes sad. The silk dress slid out of Anna's hand and pooled around her feet.

"This is Sinopa's aunt and uncle," Ben said softly. "They've come to take her home with them."

The man and woman nodded briefly, no readable expression on their face.

"Please, come in." Anna picked up the dress and swung the door open. Ben spoke softly in the Blackfoot tongue, and the couple stepped inside.

Anna indicated two chairs by the fireplace, her heart pounding in her chest. *No, it couldn't be. Not yet.*

"They're from farther north in the territories and just heard about the death of Sinopa's mother and father at a tribal gathering. They came as soon as they could." The roughness of his voice wrapped around her.

"They want to see her?" The question was stupid, Anna knew, but somehow the doubting words helped keep the truth at bay.

"They want to take her to live with them." He moved a step closer, but didn't reach out to touch her.

Anna's world reeled, and Ben's words came back to haunt her. Giving up one of her children would not be easy.

"Where is she?" Ben asked softly.

Anna glanced again at the couple, their faces expressionless. "She's upstairs making paper chains. I'll get her."

With feet of lead, Anna climbed the ladder to the loft. Sinopa sat cross-legged on Pat's bed, flour glue on her face and fingers, smiling across at Susie. Torn strips of old newspaper lay in their laps and an unfinished chain streamed off the bed. Despair gripped Anna's heart, but she knew she couldn't show Sinopa her sorrow, or Ben, either, but for very different reasons.

"Sinopa."

The little girl turned her head. Anna motioned to her, then held out her hand. Obediently, Sinopa followed Anna down the ladder. Ben stepped forward, squatted down, and began to talk to the child. She watched his face intently, then looked up at the couple. Their faces broke into radiant smiles. The man stood, moved toward Sinopa, speaking slowly, softly. He stopped, leaned down and braced his hands on his knees.

"What's he saying?" Anna asked.

"He's reminding her of the time she was visiting their village and fell into the hornets' nest."

Sinopa frowned and glanced at Anna. Then she smiled and threw her arms around the man's knees, chattering freely.

"They came to headquarters yesterday. They'd only just learned that Sinopa was here."

"How wonderful that she has family," Anna said, feeling exactly the opposite.

"She'll be better off with her own family, her own people." Ben's hands clasped her shoulders from behind, his fingers gently kneading.

"I know that." Anna fought to keep the tears out of her eyes and voice. Sinopa's last memory of her must not be a sad one.

The uncle rose from his squatting position and came to stand in front of Anna. He glanced up at Ben, then looked Anna in the eyes and began to speak in Blackfoot.

"He thanks you for caring for her. She tells him that you were very kind to her," Ben translated.

Anna nodded, not trusting her voice.

"He also says that Sinopa will be loved very much in his home."

Anna nodded again and blinked away tears. "Please tell him that he is very welcome and that Sinopa was loved very much here, too."

As Ben translated, the uncle's brown eyes softened and he laid a hesitant hand on Anna's forearm. "You are good woman," he said in broken English. Then he turned and nodded to Sinopa. She clasped her aunt's hand and moved toward the door.

They had reached the threshold, when Sinopa turned back, ran to Anna and hugged her knees. She looked up, smiled broadly and said, "Merry Christmas."

Anna pressed her fingers to her lips. For days, the other children had been trying to teach Sinopa these first English words.

Sinopa scampered out the door and into the weak sunshine of a winter's day. The door swung shut and Ben's arms closed around her. The suppressed sob escaped, and tears dripped onto the red serge of his jacket sleeve.

"You knew this day would come," he whispered.

"This is the way it should be, it's the way I planned it."

"But it's harder than you thought."

Anna nodded.

She turned in his arms, her vows of independence momentarily forgotten, traded for the comfort of an embrace. His arms coiled around her and drew her close.

"Miss Anna? Where's Sinopa going?" Susie asked as she and Pat scrambled down the ladder.

Anna drew out of Ben's arms and quickly wiped her eyes. She turned, pasting a smile on her face. "That was Sinopa's aunt and uncle. They heard about her mother and father dying and came to take her back to live with them. Isn't that a wonderful Christmas present for her?"

The corners of Susie's mouth tipped down. "She didn't say good-bye."

"Well," Anna squatted down, "she told me to tell you so. And guess what?"

Susie narrowed her eyes. "What?"

"She said Merry Christmas."

Susie smiled proudly. "I taught her that."

"Yes, you did. Now why don't the two of you go and finish those chains."

They hurried back up the ladder, their sorrow temporarily replaced by Christmas excitement.

"They don't realize she's not coming back," Anna said, more to herself than to Ben.

"No, they don't. What about you?"

Anna turned, making sure her mask of calm acceptance was in place. "I'm not heartless or stupid. I truly hope that my heart will be broken again and again when Tommy and Susie find a home with loving parents."

A nugget of an idea formed in Ben's mind, a thought so simple and yet so jarring, it shook him to his core. He watched Anna's gaze return to the closed door and the thought suddenly seemed very right.

Strains of "Silent Night" drifted from between the warped boards of the Northwest Mounted Police barn. Cheerful voices intertwined with the music drifting up toward the heavens.

Anna pulled her shawl around her shoulders and felt Susie wedge herself between her knees when the double barn doors opened, spilling a path of light out onto the snow.

"It's all right." Anna pushed her forward with a little nudge. Pat whispered something in Susie's ear and she smiled and took his outstretched hand.

"We're going to find the other children," he said in a solemn voice. Anna stifled a smile and nodded. Christmas parties belong to children, she told herself.

She glanced down at her mix-and-match dress and smoothed the silk, suddenly feeling very obvious. How she wished she'd allowed Ben to bring her and the children. Now, she doubted the wisdom of her independence. There had been an intensity to his gaze, a meaning that bypassed her brain and corresponded to a need deep within her. And it was terrifying, as if all her careful control had suddenly been thwarted.

"Mrs. Snow."

Anna raised her eyes to meet Mrs. Stanton's gaze.

"I certainly didn't expect to see you here tonight."

Deep in thought, Anna had almost walked straight into the woman.

Mrs. Stanton looked her up and down, pausing for a moment on the red bodice of her dress. "Are you alone?"

Anna felt the hair on the back of her neck stand in response to the implication in her words. "No, as a matter of fact, I am here with Constable Parker."

Mrs. Stanton pointedly glanced around. "I don't see him, but he was here earlier, helping the other men bring in wood for the fire." She narrowed her eyes. *Liar.*

"Yes, I knew his services were needed here, so the children and I came on our own."

Mrs. Stanton's eyebrows went up another notch. "Indeed. You arrived alone?"

"Yes, and if you would excuse me, I must see to the children."

"Mrs. Snow."

Anna stopped, her back turned.

"Your dress is quite . . . unusual."

"Yes." Anna turned around. "Ben says I remind him of a Christmas ornament."

"Indeed."

Anna turned back, as a satisfied smile crept across her face.

Scarlet was the color of the evening. Officers and constables alike filled the barn. The floors had been swept and scrubbed until the scarred and gouged boards looked new. The empty stalls were hung with greenery and candles. Overhead, a huge paper star hung high in the hay loft.

A band in the corner was sawing out "Good King Wenceslus" and accompanying voices sang along cheerfully. Anna closed her eyes, breathing in the holiday scents and listening to the swell and ebb of the conversations around her.

She stood there, glowing, the soft light of lamps enriching the green and red of her dress. Small wisps of hair stirred around her face, touching her cheeks as Ben wished he could do. How intimate were those curls that lay on the back of her neck, hugging their tendrils to her soft skin. He was in love. There was no doubt. When it had happened, he couldn't say.

"Enjoying the party?" How inept the words sounded in light of the emotions churning within him.

"Hmmm. Oh, yes." She opened her eyes and his heart slid down into his finely polished boots.

"Where are the children?" *The ones we will take into our hearts and the ones we will make in our bed at night.*

She glanced around the room. "They're over there." She extended an arm and pointed to a distant corner. Ben followed her gesture. Susie's dark, curly head bobbed conspicuously amid the group of children. Little Pat was pressed close to her side, looking very territorial. A chuckle tickled the back of Ben's throat.

"They seem to be having fun." He turned back to her, drinking in the blue of her eyes, the chestnut highlights of her hair, the delicate line of her dress, so carefully hiding soft, feminine flesh underneath.

"Would you like to dance?" Ben took her hand, amazed at the smallness of it, the fragility of the bones, the strength of her grasp.

She gazed up at him a moment. "Yes, I would like to, very much."

She moved easily into his arms, as if she'd been there a thousand times, and placed one hand on his shoulder, burning his skin through the thick serge.

Together they moved into the swaying crowd. She danced lightly, accurately following his lead.

Anna Snow, will you so easily follow me in life?

"I beg your pardon. What did you say?" She leaned closer, her head tilted back to look up at him.

Dear God, had he spoken aloud? "Nothing. I didn't say anything." He felt the flush creep up his neck and she frowned.

"Are you too warm, Constable? Surely in that uniform you would be hot."

She was giving him the perfect opportunity to take her outside, into the chill of the December night, and kiss her until she loved him as much as he loved her.

"No, I'm fine." *Coward.*

Ben pulled her a little closer, and she came willingly. She was so soft in his embrace. The gentle scent of her swirled up between them as they moved in perfect unison. The seed of an idea that had kept Ben's thoughts in a whirl for the last day bloomed into hope, and his thoughts leapt ahead to tomorrow and then to next year.

Then, the music halted and she stepped out of his arms, glancing around for the children. "There they are." She gripped his hand and pulled him toward the corner along with her.

A checkerboard was spread out on the floor and buttons filled several of the black squares. Pat sat on the floor, his withered arm tucked up on his lap, his eyes fastened to the board. Across from him, another boy bent low over the board, studying the buttons.

"It's your move, Billy," Pat said.

Billy frowned. "You got me trapped."

"Then I guess I win." Pat grinned and the surrounding children laughed and clapped.

"Ain't no cripple gonna best Billy Dawson." Buttons scattered and the checkerboard flew to the side.

Billy jumped to his feet. Anna started forward, but

Ben gripped her hand. "Just watch," he whispered into her hair.

"I can't just stand by—" Anna began.

Billy lunged forward, but Pat deftly dodged him. Billy fell to the floor with an "oomph."

"I'll get you," he ground out between clenched teeth.

Billy lunged again. Pat stuck out a foot and sent the bully to the floor once more.

Billy started to rise, but two other boys stepped in. "You was whipped fair and square," said the older of the two.

"Where'd you learn them kind of moves?" Billy asked, dusting off the seat of his pants, a hint of reluctant admiration in his voice.

Pat shrugged. "Just someplace. I'll teach you if you want."

"Sure." The children trooped outside, the argument forgotten.

Anna turned to stare at Ben. "How did you know . . ."

"I saw him do it once before. With another gang of children."

Her eyes widened. "You *let* him fight?"

"He has to learn to stand on his own, Anna. And to do that, he has to gain the respect of these children. This was his way of doing it."

"But he's so small and so young."

"He won't always be either, and you won't always be there."

Ben put his arm around Anna as the band began a spirited reel. "Would you like to dance?"

She shook her head, her lips pressed together, tears brimming in her eyes.

"Something to eat, then?" His fingers ached to brush away the tears. No, to kiss them away, to taste the salt, the essence of her. He wanted to make time stand still and to give her all the children she'd ever want.

She nodded and he guided her through the crowd to the table loaded with holiday food.

"Mrs. Snow."

Anna turned toward the voice at her ear. Mr. Stanton stared down at her, his gaze boldly sweeping her from head to toe. "I think you owe me something."

Ben stiffened at the innuendo in Stanton's voice, adding weight to his growing suspicions about the store owner.

"I beg your pardon?" Anna asked.

"I went back over some of the work that hellion Tommy has done for me, and I believe that I am missing some items. You wouldn't know anything about that, would you, Mrs. Snow?"

Ben could almost feel his hand shoot out and close around Stanton's scrawny neck. He clenched his fist and kept it firmly at his side.

"No, I don't," Anna answered evenly. "What sorts of things?"

"Well, . . ." Stanton juggled his plate laden with food. "A knife is missing, a pair of shoes. A packet of needles."

"Are you saying that Tommy took those things?" Anna asked calmly.

Ben met Stanton's gaze over Anna's head, issuing a silent warning and revealing his interest.

"Why, no. Of course not. Perhaps the lad misplaced the items. You could mention this to him the next time you visit him in jail?" Stanton smiled slowly, his thin, black mustache quivering.

"Would you like to file a theft report, Stanton?" Ben asked, holding the man's gaze.

Stanton looked from one to the other, anger snapping in his eyes. "No."

"I'll mention this to Tommy tomorrow, Mr. Stanton."

He turned to leave, then stopped and looked back.

"Oh, by the way. I believe that my daughter has a dress much like that one. The very same color. Good quality silk."

Anna's cheeks colored a delicate pink. "Why, of course. Her red one. A lovely garment."

"My wife would like the extra material from her alterations returned. At your convenience, of course." Anna met the bastard's gaze evenly, and the origin of her dress became painfully clear. He nodded and swept away, his arrogance trailing behind him.

"Stanton's up to his neck in this whiskey trading," Ben said between clenched teeth. "I just can't prove it." With a hand to the small of her back, Ben guided Anna through the crowd. He handed her her wrap and led her out into the chilly night.

Low voices drifted back to them from dark places. Lovers, Ben thought, closing the door behind him.

Anna leaned against the side of the barn and bit into a piece of pie. "Do you really think Tommy took those things?"

The pie was apple, judging from the smell. Apple with cinnamon. A tiny bit of crust clung to Anna's lips.

"Do you, Ben?"

"What?" He tore his gaze away from her lips. "No, I don't think so. Stanton's trying to divert suspicion from himself."

Her tongue slipped out and captured the bit of pastry. A gnawing restlessness moved into Ben, an urging that pushed its way into the forefront of his thoughts. Never in his life had he wanted to kiss a woman so badly. Every nerve in his body urged him forward, but another tiny voice cautioned him, the same voice that had saved his life innumerable times. Widow Snow's reputation was bad enough, if only created by rumor. Kissing her here, in public for all to see, would only cast further shadows on her. She deserved better. And she would get better. As his wife.

"I should take the children home," Anna said breathlessly at the end of a reel. "It's getting late, and it is Christmas Eve."

"I'll get the sleigh." He stepped away from her quickly, too quickly, she thought.

Anna moved backward a step. Perhaps the tension of being seen with her was too much for him. As the evening went on, he had become more and more withdrawn. Now, all she wanted to do was to get home and tuck the children into bed. "We'll wait for you in front."

He strode away, tall and straight.

"Miss Anna?" Susie tugged at her dress. "Is it time for Santa yet?"

"Almost. We're going home now." Anna bent down to Susie's level.

Susie leaned in closer. "Pat says there's an awful lot of Santas around here." Her whisper was so loud and raspy that several people around them turned and laughed.

"They're just his helpers," Anna whispered back.

"Constable Ben is just one of his helpers, too, isn't he?"

Anna debated her answer. Apparently there'd been some discussion of the topic among the children.

"Can you keep a secret?" Anna whispered.

Susie bobbed her dark curls.

"He is the head helper."

Susie's eyes widened. "And is Santa coming later?"

"Yes, but you have to be home asleep. He can't see you."

"I have to go find Pat." Susie darted off, and Anna straightened with a laugh.

"A charming story, Mrs. Snow." William Stanton stood at her elbow, a glass in his hand. "So Parker is the 'head helper'?" His drunken smile slid into a leer. "In what capacity does the good constable 'help'?" He leaned over until Anna could smell the whiskey—rotgut whiskey.

She recoiled from the stench, remembering Tommy's experience. A scathing retort sprang to her tongue, but at that moment, Susie and Pat caught her hands and began to tug her toward the door. As she hurried after them, she looked back over her shoulder and saw Stanton laughing.

"Do you have your costume?" Anna whispered to Ben as they pulled away in the sleigh.

He nodded, his eyes on the street ahead.

Anna glanced back over her shoulder. The children were staring at the sky, watching for Santa Claus. They passed the Mountie headquarters and her heart lingered for a moment with Tommy.

"He's fine," Ben said, his voice close to her ear. "Stuart stayed with him for Christmas." He turned to face her. "You can see him tomorrow before the hearing."

Her mood plunged. Tomorrow would decide Tommy's fate. How could she have gone to a party when one of her children was in jail? What kind of person was she?

"There's nothing you could have done by staying with him," Ben said, reading her mind for the second time. "He has to face this alone, Anna. You can't save him from himself."

She burrowed deeper into the buffalo robe spread around her shoulders and over her lap. Somehow it was disquieting to have someone reading her mind, anticipating her thoughts. But it was intimate and personal. She stole a glance, but he stared straight ahead.

As soon as they reached the house, the children tumbled out of the sleigh and rushed for the door, eager to be in bed before Santa came.

"I wish they'd go to bed that easily every night," Anna said, reluctant to leave the warmth of her robes.

"I can remember hurrying through chores so Santa wouldn't come and catch me awake." His laughter was a deep rumble in his chest. "I'm sure Santa could smell me a mile away."

"You should get into your costume before they're sound asleep." With one fluid movement, she was out of the sleigh and on the porch. She poked her head inside, listened for a moment, then smiled and closed the door softly. "They're upstairs, but I hear lots of whispering."

Ben climbed out of the sleigh and reached under the seat. "Go inside. I'll make my entrance in a few minutes."

Anna closed the door behind her, leaving Ben standing by the sleigh. He took the bundle and stepped into the shadows between her house and the next building. Shedding his uniform jacket, he stepped into the Santa suit Mrs. Fitzgerald had made and buttoned up the heavy coat. The wool beard itched mightily, but he successfully tied it behind his ears, then donned the Santa cap. He moved to the back of the sleigh and retrieved a large bag. Anna had given him her presents for the children yesterday and today, he'd added a few of his own.

He made a great commotion as he stepped up onto the porch and heard childish titters and whispers. The door opened easily and he stepped inside. Anna was nowhere to be seen. By the fireplace a single candle burned beside a handmade crèche on a table.

He laid out the presents, all carefully wrapped in sewing scraps, then he added two of his own, cheerfully done up in paper and ribbons. The last present, he slipped into his pocket.

Overhead, he heard an intake of breath and looked up. A tiny face . . . no, two . . . peered down through the ladder hole. Summoning up all the air he could, he laughed, sounding the way he supposed Santa would, deep and throaty. The two sets of eyes rounded, then disappeared in a flurry of whispers and giggles. He waited a few minutes, but all was silent.

Holding in the urge to laugh again, he moved toward the door. Anna intercepted him, moving like a shadow from her bedroom.

"I think you were a success," she whispered into his ear, her breath making the wool beard tickle his ear.

He nodded, then motioned her out onto the porch. With the door safely shut behind them and the curtains closed, he dropped the bag and ripped off the beard.

"By my soul, this thing itches." He raked at his face with both hands.

Anna laughed, then sobered. "I can't thank you enough for what you've done. You've given them a Christmas memory they'll always carry with them."

In the dim light, her face was soft, open. He leaned closer. Her breath raked over him, giving him un-Santa-like urges. His lips met hers, tender and searching, seeking a full union. He had expected her to resist, even to back away. Instead, she stepped forward into his embrace.

He pulled her close. Flames flared within him, then spread into a radiant warmth that settled in the pit of his stomach. He pulled her hairpins out one by one until the entire chestnut mass tumbled around her shoulders. Her fingers spider-walked up his neck, tangling in his hair.

"Marry me, Anna," he whispered against her lips. "Please, marry me."

She stepped away from him, her eyes wide. "What?"

He hadn't planned it this way, but his heart had spoken, committing him to things his mind was too stubborn to admit. "Will you be my wife?"

She shook her head as if to clear it. "You want me to marry you? Why?"

"Why?" Her question stopped him cold. How could he put into words why he wanted her at his side?

"Because I love you."

"But . . . but . . ."

Slowly, his heart sank. Of course she wasn't in love with him. She had given him no reason to believe she was. Damn his infernal impetuousness. Somehow, he'd spun himself a fable in which Anna Snow was in love with him, then he'd acted on it. *Damn. Damn.*

"Ben, I'm flattered." She spread her hands helplessly. "But we never . . . we never talked about this. About the children. Tommy. I never knew . . ."

What was she saying? she asked herself. She was babbling, searching for some reason to say no and deny herself the thing she wanted most. Her future was standing in front of her. All she had to do was reach out and take it. But she couldn't. Was it Tommy? No, it was her basic distrust of the entire world. She just couldn't lay her life in someone else's hands. Not now. Not yet.

"I'm sorry." He picked up the bag and started for the sleigh. "Forgive me. Perhaps the holiday season . . ." He let the rest of the words drift off. "Merry Christmas." He plunged a hand into his pocket and came out with a small box wrapped in paper and ribbon.

Anna reached into the pocket of her skirt and produced a box, wrapped in green silk. "Merry Christmas."

"Open yours first." His voice was strained and he avoided her eyes.

She carefully untied the ribbon and the paper fell

away. She opened the tiny box and lifted out a delicate gold necklace. A heart-shaped locket dangled at the end.

"Oh, Ben. It's beautiful." Tears clogged her throat. Why was she so stupid? What was she passing up? "Please put it on me."

She held out the necklace, but he shook his head slowly. "Don't ask me to touch you right now," he whispered.

Anna lowered her hand and knew his heart was broken. "Open yours."

He untied the bit of ribbon and the cloth fell away. Lying in the fabric was a silk scarf, made of bits and pieces of fabric, all carefully trimmed and stitched to fit together.

"I thought you might need something extra out on patrol."

He raised his eyes, dark and filled with pain. "Thank you." He draped the scarf around his neck. "I should be going. The hearing is at ten in the morning."

Anna nodded numbly. *Don't let him ride away,* a voice in the back of her head screamed. "Good night, and Merry Christmas."

He climbed into the sleigh and picked up the reins. "Sleep well."

Anna nodded and felt the tears coming as the sensation of sleeping in his arms inserted itself into her thoughts.

He flicked the reins and the horse trotted forward. In a matter of seconds he was gone.

Anna closed the door and listened for a moment before going into her bedroom. All was quiet upstairs. She turned up her lamp and held the locket underneath the light. Tears clouded her vision, but she blinked them away and saw that the front of the locket was etched with twining vines. She opened the locket. Inside were four tiny locks of hair—one brown, one red, one straight black, and the other a black curl. Tommy and Pat, Sinopa and Susie. She dropped the locket into her lap and clamped a hand over her mouth. Tears spilled down her cheeks as the old clock on her mantel chimed midnight.

6

Ben drew the team to a stop once he was far outside the gates of the fort. A full moon hung white and brilliant in a clear, star-encrusted night sky. Damp cold crept in beneath the Santa suit, but he didn't care. He laid the reins on his knees and pulled the gloves off his trembling hands. How could he have just blurted it out like that?

How long had he loved her? He couldn't remember. Maybe it was the first time she soothed his pain with her cool hands. Maybe it was seeing her silhouetted before the crackling fire, when she'd awakened in him wants long buried and denied. But tonight, the idea had seemed so clear, so simple. He loved her. He wanted her as his wife. Together they would adopt the children, give them the home Anna was so desperate they have. Obviously, she didn't see the simplicity of the solution.

Propping one foot on the side of the wagon, Ben pulled the cap off and laid it on the seat beside him, reveling in the shock of the cold air. Anything to feel something other than the pain slicing neatly through him. He'd acted like one of the young constables he often counseled against taking on the responsibilities of a wife and family *and* service in the Force. And he'd done worse. He'd actually proposed to a woman who wasn't in love with him, who distrusted him down to the heels of his boots.

He stepped down from the wagon, sinking ankle-deep in a snowdrift. He bent and scooped up a handful of snow, then rubbed it across his face, hoping the cold would stop his thoughts from spinning.

The sound of a cocked gun stopped his heart from beating instead.

"Well, hello, Santy."

"Red Ferguson."

Ferguson grinned. "Bet you didn't expect to see me. Any of them boys of yours find their way back yet?"

The cold of the gun barrel was chilling a spot just over Ben's left ear. "Where are my men?" Alarm bells clanged in his head.

"Aw, I didn't hurt 'em none." Ferguson ground the gun barrel into Ben's skin. "I just misled 'em a mite. They'll probably be back for Christmas supper."

"What do you want?" Ben grimaced as Ferguson yanked one of Ben's arms behind his back.

Ferguson chuckled. "You and me are gonna take a little ride whilst I tell you a Christmas story."

Ben saw a bright light, then pain eroded his consciousness and he slipped away into welcome blackness.

Rough boards jabbed at his cheek and something foul held his mouth open. Blinking away the cobwebs of unconsciousness, he realized that his hands were tied behind his back and his feet were bound together. He was lying on a wooden floor in the dark. He heard a groan and wondered if it was his.

"I told you to kill him, not bring him here." A familiar voice came to Ben, muted and low.

"Aw, I just wanted to have a little fun with him first. Me and this Mountie go back aways, Stanton. Don't deny me the pleasure of seeing him suffer first. Him being so all-fired smart and all."

"You've compromised this whole operation with your games."

"Ain't nobody gonna know he's here. I'll kill him later, maybe even leave him in his Santy suit." Ferguson's laugh was dry.

"Well, I'm going home. Mrs. Stanton is expecting me. I'll meet you tomorrow afternoon at the old wash and we'll settle up then."

Somewhere in the dark, a door closed and suffocating silence fell around Ben. He heard another set of footsteps pace aimlessly across uneven boards. Various odors worked their way into Ben's brain. Molasses, sweet and pungent; leather, sharp and comforting; dry goods, starched and clean.

Stanton's store.

Closing his eyes, Ben concentrated on drawing a picture of the shop in his mind. He wasn't in the front room, he reasoned. The floor beneath his cheek was gritty and dirty. Stanton kept a clean store, if nothing else. So, he must be in the storage room out back.

He opened his eyes and waited to become accustomed to the darkness. Deep blackness mellowed into shades of gray. Stacks of feed sacks towered over him. Rolling over onto his back, he could see steel traps dangling from the rafters overhead. Small slits of light filtered in through cracks in the wall.

He'd been here just a few days before. *Think, Ben, think.* Mr. Stevens had brought a scythe in to sharpen, he remembered. He glanced toward the door and could make out the shape of the scythe leaning against the sharpening stone. Rolling over and over, stopping only to adjust his direction, Ben bumped up against the wooden handle. He struggled into a sitting position and sawed loose the rope binding his hands.

He removed the gag and tested his jaw. Then, he crept to the adjoining door. He could hear Ferguson inside the store, sloshing what smelled like whiskey into a tin cup. If he judged the distance correctly, Red was just on the other side of the door, helping himself to what was behind the counter, most likely.

Ben glanced at the cracks between the boards where the pink light of dawn worked its way inside. His hand closed around the scythe. He counted to three and threw open the door.

Anna's hands shook as she pulled on her gloves. She glanced at the clock on the mantel. Nine o'clock. One hour before the hearing.

"Miss Anna? Can I wear my new dress for Mr. McGuire?" Susie bounced into the room, spreading wide the skirt of a blue-sprigged calico dress—her Christmas present from Ben.

Anna smiled and ruffled her curls. "Of course you can, but don't get it dirty." The blue of the print matched Susie's eyes, and Anna wondered if Ben had chosen it for that reason.

"Can I wear my new shoes? Just in the house?" Pat slipped around the curtain, stepping carefully on the rugs in his new leather boots, also a present from Ben.

"Yes. Now, you two have to be good for Mr. McGuire."

Pat smiled widely. "We can play checkers on the board that Santa brought."

"Me, too," Susie insisted.

"Girls don't play checkers.

"Do, too."

"Do not."

Anna had opened her mouth to correct them when someone rapped on the door. Casting them both a displeased look, she hurried to open it, nurturing a tiny hope.

"And was Santa good at this house?" Stuart stood on the porch, his hat in his hand.

Anna smiled, feeling her skin stretch tightly across her face. An hour and several pans of cold water had done little to erase both the tears and the sleeplessness from her face. "He was very good. Please, come in."

She stepped aside, and both children attached themselves to Stuart's knees. He staggered off, the children shrieking as he pretended to stumble and fall.

"Santa brought us a checkerboard," Pat proclaimed.

"He did, did he? Well, why don't we try it out?"

Pat and Susie scampered off, and Stuart turned to Anna. "How are you this morning?" His eyes searched her face.

"I'm fine. A little anxious."

He frowned slightly and glanced quickly around the room. "Is Ben here?"

A chill ran up Anna's spine. "No, of course not."

"I'm sorry. I didn't mean . . ." Stuart paused and scratched his head. "It's just that the lad didn't come back to the jail last night, and I hoped . . ." He stared at the floor, worry furrowing his brow. "Half the patrol has been out chasin' Ferguson all night. I imagine Ben is with them." His voice faltered. Worry settled heavily in Anna's stomach.

He searched her face, calm wisdom in his eyes. "I don't know what happened between the two of you, Mrs. Snow, but Ben is a good man. He'd not harm a soul that didn't cross the line of the law."

"I know that, Mr. McGuire." Anna felt tears stinging again, but she mentally shook herself. She couldn't think about Ben right now. It would take everything she had to get through this hearing with Tommy. Besides, Ben would be there when she arrived. He would.

"I have to be going." She tied on her bonnet and

reached for her purse. "Tommy and I should be back before lunch."

"The children and I will be fine."

Anna turned to leave and Stuart gently caught her wrist. She half-turned to meet the gaze from his kind, brown eyes.

"I knew your husband, Mrs. Snow. Begging you pardon, he was bad from the start. You shouldn't judge us all by his scale."

Anna nodded numbly, feeling tears threatening again. She stepped outside the door and shut it firmly behind her. If God was willing, Tommy would come back with her and they'd have their Christmas dinner all together.

If God was willing.

"Let's get on with this. There's a stuffed goose waiting for me." Judge Wilkins raised his head to peer through gold-rimmed glasses. Small and wiry, the judge was considered stern but fair. Seeing him now, sitting behind the desk in the cramped patrol office, he seemed even more imposing. And impatient.

Anna glanced behind her where a small crowd had gathered despite the fact it was Christmas morning. But Ben wasn't there. She stared down at her fingers, tightly laced together. He had deserted her, probably found some reason to be far away this morning. She closed her eyes and pictured his face again as he heard her fumbled refusal. Only at that moment, after the words were said, had she realized she loved him, loved him enough to say yes.

She opened her eyes and looked around the room again. Young Constable Evans sat beside Tommy and glanced over his shoulder toward the door every few seconds. On the other side of Tommy sat James

McLeod, commander of the fort. Imposing with his dark hair and beard, he had a reputation for broaching no nonsense, neither among his men nor with his prisoners.

"I understand, Commander, that there are actually two matters on hand here? The suspected collaboration in whiskey trading and the matter of the custody of some orphans?" Judge Wilkins peered over the papers. "Are these two cases related?"

McLeod stood, straight and impressive in his uniform. Tommy glanced back at Anna and smiled slightly. It will be all right, his look said.

"Yes, Your Honor. The children in question and this young man are in the care of the same woman, Mrs. Anna Snow."

Whispers washed over the room, quelled by a glance from the judge.

"Is Mrs. Snow here?"

"Yes, I am." Anna stood, praying her legs wouldn't collapse.

The judge watched her for a moment, then grunted softly and returned his attention to the documents in his hand.

"Young man, you are accused of cooperating with a whiskey trader named Red Ferguson. Further, you are accused of delivering his illegal whiskey to his customers. Is all this true?"

Tommy glanced back at Anna, his eyes large and terrified. He searched her face, looking for an answer. Then, he seemed resigned and returned his gaze to the judge.

"Yes, it is," he answered in a shaky voice.

"You admit your guilt?"

Tommy drew in a breath. "Yes, sir, I do."

"No, wait." Anna sprang to her feet, and heads turned toward her. She ignored their disapproving looks, fighting the panic growing within her. Where was Ben? He would straighten all this out, convince the judge it had all been a youthful indiscretion. But Ben was not here and Anna tried to concentrate on her anger instead of her fear.

"Please sit down," the judge warned with an icy stare.

Her heart hammering against her ribs, Anna ignored him and moved toward the front of the room. "Please, Judge Wilkins, there are other circumstances here."

The judge pulled off his glasses and twirled them in one hand. "Mrs. Snow, as guardian of these children, how did all this come about without your knowing?"

"It ain't her fault, Your Honor." Tommy jumped to his feet. "I lied to her, good lies, too. She couldn't have known."

"Are you aware, young man, that this is a serious crime? One for which you could be hung?"

Tommy swallowed. "Yes, sir."

"And did you know when you started all these shenanigans that this was a hanging offense?"

"Yes, sir."

"Since you have admitted your guilt, you leave me no choice except to sentence you." Judge Wilkins narrowed his eyes.

Tommy squared his shoulders and raised his chin.

The judge continued to stare at Tommy, letting his words hang heavy in the air. "But I would like to wait on that until I hear the other case." The judge straightened the set of papers and laid them neatly to the side. He then picked up the next stack and read them closely.

"Mrs. Snow? Would you please approach the bench?"

Somehow, Anna found her legs and managed to walk to the desk. Behind her, she could feel every pair of eyes in the room boring into her, hungry for her demise.

"You have four children in your care, including your own son. Is that correct?"

"I have three now, Your Honor. Sinopa's aunt and uncle came for her once they heard of the death of her parents."

"I see, and you count young Tommy here in that total?"

Anna glanced at Tommy. "Yes, I do."

Judge Wilkins laced his fingers together and rested his chin on their apex. "Why don't you tell me why you think it would be a good idea for these children to stay with you?"

Anna took a breath. Her whole life, her children's lives, would be salvaged or crushed with her next words. "Every child needs love, Your Honor, and I can give them that. Every child needs a home and a family. I can give them that, too."

"You are widowed, are you not, Mrs. Snow?"

"Yes, I am."

"Isn't taking on the feeding and care of three children all alone a rather large responsibility?"

"It's a responsibility that I don't take lightly. I went into this venture with my eyes open."

"Perhaps, but possibly with your eyes too large for your pocketbook." The judge settled back in his chair. "Mrs. Snow, why do you think Tommy became involved with Red Ferguson?"

Judge Wilkins wanted her to admit that the financial responsibility was too much for her alone, a mere woman devoid of the support of a husband, Anna thought, again drawing on anger to force the next words out. "I'm sure, Your Honor, that Mr. Ferguson promised him money and excitement, which proved irresistible to a young man."

"And do you think that your present financial situation had anything to do with his decision?"

Anna felt the stares of the observers rake her back. "We both know that is probably true," she said softly.

The judge leaned forward over the scarred desk. The sternness in his face eased and his eyes gentled.

"Mrs. Snow, surviving on meager money is no crime, nor is it a sin." His voice was low so only the two of them could hear.

"I'm not worried about your ability to love and provide for these children. My mother and I survived on a seamstress's income after my father died. I *am* worried about their lack of a father's influence. My uncle lived near and stepped into the role of father for me. These children have no one to provide that for them and, in these long years as judge, I have seen this lack give rise to problems in young men time and time again. I would not be rendering my best judgment if I left three children with an unmarried woman when there are fine families here in this fort, with two parents, who would accept these children into their homes."

Anna swallowed, feeling the children slip out of her arms. "Then I ask Your Honor why these 'fine families' have not come forward before now? I have made numerous requests for homes for these children. I have contacted the church and even posted notices at Mr. Stanton's store and have not received even one answer."

"Your own son is one matter, but these other children—"

The door burst open and a flurry of snowflakes whirled in on a blanket of cold air. Ben stepped inside, shoving Red Ferguson in front of him. The Santa suit was torn and dirty and his cap perched at a comical angle.

"Constable Evans."

The young officer beside Tommy rose and hurried to the back.

"Put Mr. Ferguson in the jail."

Evans hauled Ferguson to the back of the room and the jail door closed with a satisfying click.

Ben strode to the front, twitters of laughter following him.

"Red Ferguson was the mastermind of this whiskey ring, Your Honor. And I have learned there are more people involved, businessmen here inside the fort. Evans."

Feet scuffled against the wooden floor. Constable Evans nabbed William Stanton as he attempted to dash from the room.

"And I suppose I shall have to deal with these two before I get to my goose. Is that correct, Constable?" The judge drummed his fingers on the desk.

Ben smiled. "Yes, Your Honor."

"Let's say we let Mr. Ferguson and Mr. Stanton stew for a while and I'll see them after Christmas." Judge Wilkins's expression was so hopeful and eager that Anna stifled a smile.

"That will be fine, Your Honor."

"Now, back to this matter at hand. I understand, Constable, that you were the arresting officer here?"

Ben glanced at Anna, the hurt from last night still evident in his eyes. "Yes, I was."

"I was telling Mrs. Snow here that my concern for the children is not her income, or lack of it by some standards." Anna heard Mrs. Stanton's breathless muttering.

"But I am concerned that these children lack a father's guidance. Children should have that whenever possible, even if it is from an uncle or some other close relative. Choosing to raise these children alone, Mrs. Snow is depriving them of the chance at a home with two parents, mother and father. So, with that in mind—"

"Judge Wilkins, Constable Parker and I have already

discussed a solution to that problem." Anna turned toward Ben, quelling the urge to laugh at his dirty face and his hat with the preposterous white ball bobbing on the end. She searched his eyes, hoping for some glimmer of the love she'd seen there last night, hoping his proposal hadn't been the result of too much eggnog and holiday cheer.

"I've asked Mrs. Snow to be my wife." Ben's eyes darkened dangerously and a shiver ran over Anna.

"Well?" The judge propped his chin on one hand and looked back and forth between them. The whispering behind them hushed, and for an instant, the whole room held its breath.

For a moment, Anna teetered high on the cliff of independence. Once she said yes, she would tumble over the precipice and down into the dark unknown, forever placing her life in Ben's hands.

"And I said yes."

The room erupted behind them, a mixture of 'I nevers' and laughter.

Ben pulled her into his arms and kissed her, dusting her with snow and ice. When he drew away, he took her fingers in his and his face sobered. "I have to know," he asked in a hoarse whisper, "is this because of the children?"

A small sharp pain stabbed Anna in her chest, but a voice whispered she deserved that. "No, this is because of you. I was frightened last night, scared to entrust my life to anyone else."

"What changed your mind?"

Anna smiled up at him. "My heart."

The judge, eyes twinkling, looked at Ben. "Is this something I can take care of today?"

Ben slid an arm around Anna and snugged her against his hip. "Judge Wilkins, you can tell your nieces and nephews that you married Mr. and Mrs. Santa Claus."

A thick Christmas snow twirled down, huge flakes suspended in the air for a moment before they plunged to the snow-covered ground. Ben squeezed Anna's fingers through her glove. Her hand was so small, so delicate.

She looked up at him, snowflakes perched on her eyelashes. "You know, before now I always hated to see snow come. But today, it's as if I'm seeing it for the first time."

Ben stopped and pulled her against him. She fit neatly in his arms, her head reaching to just below his chin. Their wedding had been brief, witnessed by dozens. Now, eagerness to be alone with her raged through his veins.

They'd stopped by his room so he could change out of the tortured Santa suit. There, he'd drawn her into his arms, tempted to make her his there on the narrow, hard bunk. But somehow the notion seemed cheap and hurried. He wanted her, but he wanted her in her bed, in the home they would share with the children, with *their* children.

"What are you thinking?" she asked, her eyes innocent, yet seductive.

Ben smiled, again feeling the heat of anticipation coil in him. "I was thinking how cold my feet are."

She smiled slyly. "Liar."

She moved out of his embrace and caught his hand again. As they stepped up on the porch, the door flew open.

Susie stood there, her eyes wide. "Is it true, Miss Anna? Did you really marry Santa?"

Beyond her, deeper into the room Anna could see

Tommy, leaning against the fireplace, smiling. The judge had released him into Ben's custody. Stuart stood by his side, a grin plastered from ear to ear. A dirty apron hung loosely around his generous hips and the aroma of roasting meat swirled around them. Garlands of greenery arched across the room, a sprig of mistletoe dangling from the center.

Anna squatted down to meet Susie's eyes. "I married Constable Parker this morning. Remember we talked about him being the head helper?"

Susie's bottom lip rolled out. "I didn't get to see the wedding."

Anna touched the end of Susie's nose. "Well, it happened very quickly, and besides, you're going to get to see the party, and that's the fun part."

"I can see that I will have to help you define fun, Wife." Ben leaned down, tempted to touch the tangle of curls at the base of her neck, the curls that always tantalized him, invited him to nibble the little ridge her spine made beneath the skin.

Pat sidled closer and yanked on Ben's jacket hem.

"Are you my daddy now? I didn't really know my other daddy. I can't remember what he looked like. Mommy says I was real little when he died."

Ben knew he'd someday have to explain to Pat what happened to Jasper, explain to him what could make a man abandon family and love for monetary gain. But not now, not tonight.

Ben knelt. "Do you want me to be?"

Pat nodded. "Can I call you Daddy?"

Ben gathered the little boy in his arms and struggled with the lump in his throat that threatened to choke off his breath. A warm, soft hand smoothed down his spine, comforting him, warming him even through the thick surge of his uniform. Anna's fingers crept though his hair for a second, scattering their warmth.

"Come, children, we have a Christmas supper to eat," Anna said, slowly disentangling her fingers from his hair.

The children scampered to the table, resuming their good-natured bickering and squabbling as they took their chairs.

Tommy waited by Anna's chair and solemnly pulled it out for her. She paused and looked into his face. "Thank you, Tommy."

He hesitated for a moment, then threw his arms around her. "I won't ever let you down again." His whisper was audible only to Ben as he stood at Anna's side.

Anna wiped away a tear and sat.

"I've arranged to take the children home with me," Stuart whispered as he swept by bearing a stuffed goose.

Ben glanced up and Stuart winked.

Across the table, Susie was wiggling up to the front edge of her chair, jelly already smeared across her right cheek. Spearing a piece of bread on her fork, she swirled it around in a jelly-butter mix on her plate and popped it into her mouth.

"You little rascal, I told you you'd ruin your supper with that jelly," Stuart scolded as he whisked the plate away.

Pink tongue flashing out to catch the last bit of jelly, Susie grinned broadly, showing a newly vacant spot in the front of her teeth. She leaned forward to place a jelly-coated finger on Ben's chest. "See, I told you I'd find you a wife for Christmas."

"Why are we going home with you?" Susie asked as Stuart tried to wrestle her into her coat.

"To give your mommy and daddy time . . . to discuss some things."

"What kinds of things?" She whirled around and her arm dropped out of the coat sleeve.

Stuart straightened with a sigh. "I'm too full to tussle with you, Susie, unless you want to see an old man pop."

Susie giggled and slipped on her coat. "See? I can do it myself."

Ben laughed, trying to keep his attention on the children and away from Anna, who was perched tantalizingly on the arm of his chair.

"You children be good for Mr. McGuire," Anna reminded as they moved toward the door.

Pat and Susie nodded and Tommy reddened.

"Tommy here will help me keep these two imps straight." Stuart put on his torn and mended coat. "I'll have 'em back by sunup," he said beneath his breath. "There's limits even to my patience."

Pat moved to Ben and planted his one good hand on Ben's knee. "We're going to help Mr. McGuire decorate his room. Don't you think he'd a-done that by now? He says he needs our help."

Susie shoved past him, clambered onto Ben's lap, and planted a jelly-sweetened kiss on his cheek. "And you take care of our mommy."

"Oh, I will," Ben said, and Susie tumbled off his lap and skipped out the door.

As soon as the door slammed, Ben yanked Anna into his lap. She turned in his arms, warm and soft, and Ben thought he'd die of wanting her. She wound her arms around his neck, her fingers ruffling his hair.

"Happy?" he asked, and she nodded, her eyes full of love.

Ben slipped an arm under her shoulder and pulled her up to meet his lips. She tasted sweet, of jelly and pie and Anna.

Only her rapid breathing and racing heart betrayed

her emotions as she smiled slyly up at him. "And now that I'm Mrs. Claus, just what does that job involve?"

Ben rose out of the chair, scooping Anna up in his arms. He kicked off one boot and then the other. Padding toward the bedroom, he leaned down and whispered in her ear, "Let me show you just what the job involves, Mrs. Claus, and I guarantee it has nothing to do with elves or reindeer."